RETROVIRUS

T. L. HIGLEY

BARBOUR
PUBLISHING

© 2002 by T. L. Higley

ISBN 1-59310-667-X

Acquisitions & Editorial Director: Mike Nappa
Project Editor: Jeff Gerke
Art Director: Robyn Martins
Cover image © GettyOne, Inc.

Published in association with the literary agency of Janet Kobobel Grant, Books & Such, 4788 Carissa Ave., Santa Rosa, CA 95405.

Published by Barbour Publishing, Inc., P.O. Box 719, Uhrichsville, Ohio 44683, www.barbourbooks.com

Our mission is to publish and distribute inspirational products offering exceptional value and biblical encouragement to the masses.

 Member of the
Evangelical Christian
Publishers Association

Printed in the United States of America
5 4 3 2 1

Acknowledgments

I have been overwhelmed by the help and support of friends while working on this project, and I am so grateful for each of you.

Scott Taylor, your biotech knowledge never ceased to amaze me. Thank you for answering all my stupid questions, late into the night and from distant shores.

Randy Ingermanson, you have been both friend and mentor, and I can't thank you enough for the countless hours you've selflessly given to me.

Bette Jo Smith and Michelle King, my "first readers" and continual cheerleaders, you both are so special to me.

My editor, Jeff Gerke, your constructive guidance was always delivered with sensitivity as well as wisdom, and you worked harder than I ever dreamed an editor would.

My agent, Janet Grant, your expertise and guidance have been so helpful. I look forward to many more projects together.

My fantastic husband, Ron, you have been an encouragement and an asset from start to finish, and I couldn't have done it without you. Rachel and Sarah, my junior cheerleaders, thanks for giving up part of Mom to help make this book happen. A big thank-you to my parents, who have been giving me the confidence to keep writing since the first time I picked up a pencil.

And all the others in my church family who have helped or encouraged or taught me in so many ways, you are all part of this work!

To the One who offers life,
I offer the firstfruits of my writing.

May my very breath and being
rise to You, their Source and Goal.

—TLH

Prologue

Gregory pounded his fist against the hospital corridor wall. He pulled his phone from his pocket and dialed a number for the third time that day.

Pick up. Pick up, you stinking politician.

A male voice cut the ringing short. "Hello?"

Gregory took several steps away from Michael's room. "This is Gregory Brulin."

"Dr. Brulin, I have nothing more to say to—"

"Then listen to me, Chapman. This situation is unacceptable. You have put our entire future in the hands of fanatics!"

"I hardly think they've been given that much power."

"Chapman," Gregory said, "you know who I am, and you know this research is the key to the future of disease treatment!"

"I understand that you—"

"You understand nothing! Unless you move to lift the new restrictions on embryo research, you are sacrificing the future of mankind on the altar of your political popularity!"

"I resent that, Dr. Brulin."

A tap on his shoulder turned Gregory around. Rose, the petite nurse who had lovingly watched over Michael since his newest crisis began, stood behind him.

"He's asking for you," she said.

Gregory nodded and held up one finger. Rose turned toward Michael's room.

"Listen to me, Chapman. My five-year-old son is dying. Dying, do you understand? And every day that research is delayed means more people like my little boy die. We were so close to a cure—before you sold out genetic progress to pacify ignorant extremists like the Hendricks Forum."

"There is nothing I can do, Dr. Brulin."

Gregory swore. "Lift the restrictions! My son may rally. A cure may be found in time!"

"I'm afraid you don't understand the complexities—"

Rose returned. "You'd better come, Dr. Brulin."

Gregory took one look at her face and snapped the phone shut.

The blinds in Michael's room had been closed against the brightness of the afternoon sun, but Gregory hadn't opened them as the day had worn on. He tiptoed into the darkened room as though the sound of his footsteps might loosen Michael's weak hold on the thread of life.

In the twilight, Michael's face almost seemed to glow against the white sheets, his freckles standing out like splatters from the rainy-day mud puddles he loved to stomp. Gregory's throat constricted.

"Hey, sport. How ya doing?"

Michael's eyes were closed, but the corners of his mouth twitched upward at the sound of his father's voice.

Rose came from behind and leaned over Michael. She brushed the hair from his damp forehead, resting her hand there for a moment. She whispered to Gregory, "Is there someone else we should call?"

Gregory shook his head. Who was there to call? Michael had called for his mother a few hours before, had pushed his father away when Gregory tried to comfort him. Gregory had almost wished the boy's mother could be found, even if she had to be dragged back from whatever indecent situation she had last fallen into.

"He's having a hard day," Gregory said to the nurse. "He'll be better tomorrow. He always comes around."

Rose guided Gregory toward the far side of the room.

"I'm so sorry, Dr. Brulin." Her voice was low and compassionate. "I know how difficult this is. But don't miss the chance you have to say good-bye."

Gregory shook his head again and pulled away. "No. There's still time. I can make some more phone calls—"

Rose smiled. "Go hold your son, Dr. Brulin."

And he did. He held Michael as though he could keep the precious life from slipping away. He held him as the stars came out and the room chilled and the boy's breath grew shallow. He whispered his name as Michael's breath finally stilled. Even then he held him, rocking him gently and promising him that everything would be all right.

Sometime later Rose returned. She eased Michael's body from his father's embrace and led Gregory to the corridor. "The doctor needs to see him now."

Gregory leaned his head against the wall. It was then that the tears came, silent at first, and then in heaving sobs that doubled him over at the waist, his hands on his knees.

When the storm passed, he slid down to the floor, his back against the wall.

He spoke, and his voice was harsh and cold, as though the tears had washed something away.

"I swear to you, Michael, I won't let them get away with it. I won't let the world be a place where little boys are allowed to die."

 **Part One**

SHADOW OF DEATH

Death is the destiny of every man;
the living should take this to heart.

ECCLESIASTES 7:2

CHAPTER 1

Monday, January 17

Nick Donovan snapped open the plastic case and lifted the syringe from its sculpted felt cushion as though it held water from the Fountain of Youth.

Pulling a man back from death with the plunge of a syringe was an almighty thing. Nick felt the power of it every time he began a new clinical trial.

Nick stood beside the hospital bed of a man who seemed shriveled in the one-size-fits-all hospital gown the nurse had forced on him. His left hand twisted the sheets between his fingers like an aging toddler with a security blanket.

Nick cradled Leon Weinman's wrist and raised the arm. It trembled in his grasp. Leon's eyes locked onto Nick's, and he seemed to beg for courage. Nick nodded and smiled. He held the needle to Leon's arm and took a deep breath.

"Wait!" Leon jerked his arm away.

Nick exhaled. "What is it, Leon?" He lowered the syringe.

"Explain it to me one more time." Leon's lower lip trembled as though he thought he were asking for too much.

Nick patted Leon's hand. He glanced over his shoulder at the rest of the research team. They had massed behind him in Room 306 of the Franklin University Hospital, hovering like mother hens over one sickly chick.

Nick's petite, redheaded wife, Kate—a member of the research team that had developed this therapy—gave him a tight smile from the corner.

"Dr. Rogan?" Nick said, raising his chin toward the director of the institute. "Would you like to set Leon's mind at ease?"

"You go ahead, Dr. Donovan." Rogan had remained in the background throughout the morning, forcing Nick to take the lead. Nick turned back to Leon, keeping one hand on the man's shaky arm.

"Leon, we've got a clear outline of the genes involved in your cancer. That's why you qualified for this experimental study, remember?"

"So you're going to give me some virus that's going to cure the cancer? You're going to get me sick to heal me?"

Nick smiled. "Almost. We need a way to get the therapeutic genes into your DNA. We call it a gene carrier or a 'vector.' The best vectors we've found so far are viruses. Viruses do well delivering their genes and multiplying. So, yes, we'll be using a virus to deliver your treatment. But don't worry: We've removed its disease-causing genes and replaced them with the therapeutic genes you need, the ones that we hope will produce the needed proteins and go to work on the cancer cells to stop them from reproducing. Is that a little clearer?"

"How long is this going to take?" Leon twisted the sheet again.

"The injection of the retroviral vector will take only a few moments, like any injection. Then we'll monitor you for a few days, to make sure everything's going according to plan. After that, you can go home, and we'll keep a close eye on the cancer to see what's happening."

Leon nodded, and the group behind them seemed to take a collective deep breath. The moment had arrived.

"We're gonna knock this cancer from here to Sunday, Leon, don't worry." Nick squeezed his shoulder and smiled. It seemed to help. He lifted the wrist again.

And plunged the syringe into Leon Weinman's arm.

Leon leaned back on the raised bed, closing his eyes as though giving the vector permission to speed its course to his damaged colon.

The team exchanged smiles all around the room as Nick replaced the syringe in the case. They talked quietly for awhile about the next step but finally filed out to leave Leon alone to rest.

They crowded into the main waiting area, each of them claiming one of the cherry red plastic seats that lined the perimeter of the room. A large television hung from the ceiling, but no one bothered to turn it on. In the corner, a small coffeepot sat on a warmer.

From the acrid smell coming from the pot, Nick assumed it was last night's brew. Better than nothing. He filled a Styrofoam cup and flopped onto the molded plastic seat, exhausted even though it was only ten in the morning. Kate sat next to him and held his hand.

Dr. Rogan balanced on the edge of the seat on Nick's other side. "We should be able to begin with number five soon if this goes well."

"If?" Nick noted the usual trace of pessimism in Rogan's voice.

"No reason to think otherwise, I suppose." Rogan settled back in the chair. "The three before Leon are progressing well."

Nick leaned his head back against the wall and made his hundredth mental note about what he would do differently when Rogan retired in a few months and Nick was named the new director of the Gene Therapy Institute. Kate rested her head on his shoulder.

Seven heads turned as a nurse stepped into the waiting room. Professional concern lined her face. "His temperature is spiking," she said, looking at Nick and Rogan. "They asked me to tell you."

"What?" Nick crushed his cup and jumped to his feet. The hot liquid splashed onto his hand. He tossed the broken cup in a nearby trash can with a muttered curse and shook the coffee from his hand. The rest of the team were on their feet with him.

In this situation, fever probably meant only one thing: Leon's immune system was rejecting the vector.

"What's going on?" Rogan shot an accusing look at Nick.

"It's the same dosage, the same vector as the other three!" Nick's mind raced through possible causes for rejection.

Kate squeezed his arm, but Nick pulled away.

"I've got to get in there." He pushed past her and flung open the double doors that led to the ICU.

A middle-aged nurse intercepted him. She held up a hand as

a barrier, inches from Nick's chest. "I'm sorry, Dr. Donovan. We've been asked to keep your research team in the waiting area. The ICU doctors need unlimited access to Mr. Weinman at this time."

Nick took a step forward, but the nurse blocked his path.

Rogan pulled at him from behind. "Let's go back out, Nick."

Nick glared at the nurse. "Keep us informed."

She nodded with a tight-lipped smile.

The research team swarmed Nick and Rogan as they reentered the waiting area. "What's happening?"

Rogan raised his eyebrows at Nick. "Good question."

"They'll tell us when they know anything." Nick pulled away from the rest and returned to his chair.

Kate sat beside him, bringing her face close to his ear. "Is he going to be okay?"

Nick rubbed his forehead. "I don't know what could have gone wrong! I hate this."

A painful memory rippled at the borders of his consciousness, threatening to overwhelm him. A hospital room. His sister's fingers wrapped around his own. Helplessness. He forced the memory to recede.

Kate draped an arm around him and squeezed till he looked at her. "I love you," she whispered. "We'll get through this."

He leaned his head over till their foreheads touched.

Even though it was more than four years ago, Nick still couldn't believe she'd said yes when he'd proposed. He knew that everyone in grad school had told Kate she would be crazy to marry a workaholic like Nick. When Kate entered a room, even the dust seemed to sparkle. Her curly red hair matched her playful spirit. Every child she met worshipped her, and Nick almost believed his parents favored her over their own son. But she had said yes, and he was more glad about it now than ever.

The day passed in inches. Leon's fever hit 104 degrees before dropping and then climbing again. Most of the team left by late afternoon. Nick, Rogan, and Kate stayed. At four o'clock Kate tried to convince Nick to leave.

Nick shook his head and stretched. "You go home, hon. I'm staying until I know he's stable."

"You've had a long day already," she said. "What time did you leave this morning? You didn't even say good-bye."

Nick shrugged. "You looked so peaceful; I didn't want to disturb you."

"I woke up early, and you were already gone."

Nick heard the annoyance that edged her words. "I had things to do, Kate. Today was a big day."

"I know. But it seems like you always have things to do. You were here last night until eight o'clock. Where does your contract say you have to put in fourteen-hour days?"

"C'mon, Kate," Nick said, stretching an arm around her and tangling his hand in the heaviness of her red hair, "you know what today is."

She pulled away. "It's not about today, Nick. You work like this all the time."

Rogan glanced up from his magazine across the waiting room.

Nick glared at Kate and flicked his eyes in Rogan's direction. "It'll pay off soon, Kate," he said softly. "You know that."

She looked away. "And what happens if Leon doesn't make it?"

"Don't even say that!" He stood and stepped to the coffeemaker. The pot shook in his hand as he poured himself his thousandth cup of the day.

The middle-aged nurse reappeared. "We're having some problems. The doctor will be out in a few moments to speak with you." When the ICU doctor emerged from the double doors, Nick, Kate, and Rogan jumped to their feet. The doctor's white coat bore the name "Dr. Orland" stitched in blue above the chest pocket.

Orland removed wire-rimmed glasses and pinched the bridge of his nose before speaking. "His colon is exhibiting some additional damage," he said. "Our options are limited because of the cancer."

"Additional damage?" Nick said. He shook his head. "That

shouldn't be. What can I do, Doctor?"

Dr. Orland turned a disdainful eye on Nick. "I don't think we need any more of your help right now."

"I've got to at least see him," Nick said, angling around Orland and heading for the ICU.

"Hold on there, Dr. Donovan." Orland backed up, grabbing unsuccessfully at Nick's arm.

Nick pushed through the doors once more. This time there was no nurse to stop him. He jogged through the ICU, searching curtained cubicles for Leon. Finally he spotted the man's face turned toward the opening as though he were expecting Nick.

"Dr. Donovan." Leon's voice cracked as he extended a blue-veined arm from under the hospital-issue blanket.

"Leon." Nick swallowed hard. The man's condition had degenerated markedly in only a few hours.

Orland's fingers tightened around Nick's upper arm. "Look, Dr. Donovan, you can't be in here."

Nick yanked his arm away. "What's the problem?"

"I just thought," Orland said, smiling through clenched teeth, "that maybe you've done enough for Mr. Weinman already."

"I'm not leaving." Nick turned his back on Orland, wedging himself between Leon and the irate doctor.

Orland's steps receded from the cubicle, but Nick heard his lowered voice at the nurse's station.

"Call security."

CHAPTER 2

Tuesday, January 18

Nick finished the last bite of his bagel and dragged himself up the crumbling steps of the Hawthorne Building. Balancing his half-full Starbucks cup and his briefcase, he swiped his keycard through the box on the door. Upstairs, Nick headed for the private door of the Gene Therapy Institute.

The dropped ceiling and overflowing shelves in the Microscopy Lab drove Kate crazy, but Nick's adrenaline always started pumping the moment he stepped through the door. To him the chemical odors smelled of life—life that he was preserving, discovering—even inventing—in this room.

Nick stashed his briefcase and coat at the end of the counter-height lab bench. He never used the private office that was technically assigned to him. He'd rather be in the center of the action. This morning all the action was at the hospital.

Nick pulled a stack of binders from the shelf above the lab bench and lined them up. He'd launch into them as soon as he'd started the coffee.

While coffee percolated in the institute's tiny break room, Nick came back to the Microscopy Lab and went to his computer. The daily JAMA update, the American Medical Association's journal, was waiting in his inbox. He scrolled through the various topics as he did every morning. By the time he finished, he could smell the coffee.

The sound of the institute's door opening sometime later roused Nick from the slide under his microscope. He was surprised to find that an hour had disappeared.

Brett Adams slipped onto the rolling stool beside Nick with the familiarity of a family member.

"Morning," Nick said, looking into the eyepiece, once more delving into the secrets of the genome.

"Hey, old man." Brett grabbed a three-ring binder from the shelf above him.

Nick snorted. "You thought I was gray before. This thing's going to make me look ancient."

"Any news yet?"

"Nothing new. Did you notice if Kate's here yet?"

"She's in the Tissue Culture lab, I think," Brett said. "She doesn't seem too happy with you this morning."

Nick managed a smile. "Nobody's happy with me this morning."

"You'd better not make that girl mad, old man," Brett said. "You know there's about a hundred guys lined up to take your place."

Nick let his smile turn to a scowl.

Brett shrugged. "I'm just saying—"

"Give it a rest, okay?" Nick threw his pen onto the counter. He turned from Brett and mashed the tense muscles in the back of his neck. He walked over and dropped into the office chair in front of the lab's main computer. Maybe his daily motivational nugget from the Success Quotes E-mail list would focus his thinking.

Today's message seemed tailor-made: "You have within you all you need to achieve your dreams. Your success in life is proportional to your acceptance of this truth about yourself." He took a moment to repeat that first line to himself several times.

Brett appeared behind his shoulder. "What's with you and those quotes every day?"

"They're good motivators."

Brett shook his head. "I don't think you need those, Nick. You've got to be the most motivated guy I know."

Nick closed his E-mail program and stood. "Doesn't seem to be helping much today."

"Yeah, well, most people are content to send off a buck to 'save the whales.' It's a little trickier when you decide to save the whole world."

Nick shrugged. "I'm going to the hospital."

Outside the institute's wing, he steered his vision away from the glass trophy case in the hall. Where trophies should have been, five brass urns rested behind the glass, each one preserving the ashes of a pioneer in the field of genetics. Nick avoided the trophy case as though death were contagious.

The rain-slicked cobblestone walkways slowed his step. He navigated through students and their sharp-spoked umbrellas, winding through the courtyard that would take him to the university hospital. Two hundred years of progress had not changed the courtyards and brick buildings of Philadelphia's Franklin University campus. From the exterior, no one would imagine that within these walls a biotechnical revolution raged, a revolution in which Nick Donovan had enlisted: technology's war against disease.

Yesterday, four years of repeated laboratory trials and mind-numbing research had distilled into one syringe. One deadly syringe. Today, the memory that had threatened to surface in Nick's mind nudged at him again. He quickened his pace and skidded into the hospital lobby before his thoughts got away from him.

Nick's colleagues, including Kate, wandered into the hospital throughout the morning. They waited and whispered, huddled in conversation circles.

Kate slipped into the seat beside him after talking with Brett for several minutes. "You doing okay?"

Nick shrugged. "I should probably be getting something done."

She sighed heavily.

He glanced at her and tapped his fingers on the chair. "I know I've been a little hard to live with. I'm sorry. I'm just stressed out over Leon."

She smiled and patted his arm. "It's hard to concentrate on anything else, I know." She gave him a quick kiss. "Can I get you anything?"

Nick smiled and shook his head. "But thanks for checking up on me."

"That's my job."

Strangers—friends and family of surgical patients, mostly—drifted in and out of the hospital as the morning passed. One person spent most of the morning there, a narrow man with a persistent facial twitch. He held a hunting magazine in front of him, but Nick couldn't shake the feeling that the man was reading him instead.

When the hands on the wall clock crawled around to eleven, a white-coated doctor appeared in the waiting room. The entire team looked up.

"Ms. Martinez?" The doctor motioned to a young woman sitting alone in the corner. She stiffened and stood, following the doctor. The rest of them hunkered back into their uncomfortable positions.

Caffeine overdose and worry rankled Nick's nerves. Leon's condition continued to roller coaster. When Kate brought Nick a late lunch, his stomach churned with drawn-out tension. As he unwrapped the lukewarm Big Mac, he noticed that Kate had gotten herself a Happy Meal, complete with a toy from the latest kids' movie. He sensed that she wanted him to say something about it, that it was a ploy to open the door for another discussion about children. Even today, even in the midst of a crisis, she couldn't let it go. He didn't take the bait.

During the afternoon, the rest of the team returned to their homes and families. Nick convinced Kate to go home at five o'clock.

After she left, Nick stared at the wall, his eyelids drooping with the stress of the day. He focused on a stain creeping down the opposite wall from a water leak in the ceiling. A cleaning woman with a tight hair bun came into the waiting room, her metal cart overflowing with supplies, one wheel resisting the direction of the others with a grating protest. She stopped in front of Nick.

"You need to use the rest room?" she asked.

Nick gave her a half-smile. It had been a long time since any woman had asked him that question. "I think I'm fine, thanks."

"I'm just asking 'cause I'm gonna clean it."

Nick lifted his head and grinned. "I hope your boss knows what a thoughtful employee you are."

She puckered her forehead. "Don't know anything about that."

"Well, you get my vote for employee of the month."

She disappeared into the rest room, shaking her head.

Nick dropped his head into his hands, his thoughts returning to Leon. He surrendered to a moment of anger. The study had been successful until yesterday. The Phase 1 clinical study had gone flawlessly, and the other Phase 2 trials were progressing with no indication that this one would be different. However, unless the outlook brightened, Nick could kiss the promotion to director good-bye. Not to mention poor Leon.

Nick must've dozed off in his chair, because a quiet cough roused him. He jumped to his feet in front of Orland, the ICU doctor.

"He's holding his own." Orland's chin jutted forward. "We may have managed to avert your disaster. We can handle things here just fine on our own," he said, turning away. "Why don't you check in with the nurse in the morning?"

Nick nodded, letting Orland's arrogance roll off him. He rubbed his hand across the day's growth on his face. It would be good to get home to Kate. He gathered his coat and briefcase and headed for the parking garage.

His black Ford Expedition huddled in the shadows at the edge of the garage, the only space available when he had pulled in this morning. Tonight empty spaces lined the perimeter. A shuffling noise whispered along the concrete walls, and Nick felt a sudden spark of fear dance along his nerves. Someone else was here.

He pulled his keys out of his pocket as he walked behind the car. On the driver's side the keys slipped from his fingers and clanged to the concrete floor. Nick bent to retrieve them. When he stood, a figure stepped out of the darkness in front of him. Nick jerked his briefcase out in front of his body.

A lean man, still half-hidden in shadows, faced him without expression.

"What do you want?" Nick asked.

The man watched him. The muscles below his left eye twitched, bringing his face to Nick's memory.

"You were here this morning," Nick said. "In the waiting room."

"My name is Chernoff, Dr. Donovan."

The name meant nothing to Nick. The man's eye twitched again. Nick lowered his briefcase and waited.

"I've been anxious to speak with you." Again Chernoff let silence drift like a dead thing between them. "I've been waiting for a good time."

"What do you want?"

"I have a message for you," Chernoff said, "from my employer."

"Who are you?" Nick jingled his keys, locating the remote alarm.

"A messenger." Except for the twitch, Chernoff's facial muscles remained slack when he spoke. "I bring you a job offer, Dr. Donovan. My employer is interested in having someone of your—expertise—on his team."

"What team? What employer?" Nick tried to push past him, to edge toward his car, but the man didn't move.

"Are you interested in a change, Dr. Donovan?" Chernoff asked. "Something with more financial potential than you could find in an educational institution?"

Nick's curiosity needled him. "What kind of a position are we talking about?"

"The particulars are not important now, Dr. Donovan. All you need to know is that my employer is prepared to multiply your income and offer you a position on the cutting edge of technology and business. May I tell him that you are interested?"

Nick's mind dashed through possibilities. He would soon hit the professional ceiling at the university—or the basement, if

Leon had a relapse—but dozens of corporations were jumping into the genome research business, anxious to be among the first to use the lucrative genetic discoveries. The private sector would value his talents and knowledge.

But Nick wasn't really interested in money. He wanted to cure disease. If things improved for Leon Weinman and the rest of Phase 2 succeeded, he would have Rogan's desk in a few months and he could begin to carry out his own vision for the institute. Did it make sense to give up what seemed like a sure thing to start again somewhere else?

"No, thanks." Nick pushed past Chernoff. "Tell your employer I'm satisfied where I am, but thanks for the interest."

Chernoff's eye twitched again, and he scowled. "Perhaps you will change your mind." He reached into his coat pocket.

Nick glanced around the empty garage. Where was everyone tonight? Was he alone with this walking cadaver?

"No, I don't think so," Nick said, his eyes on the hand inside the coat.

Chernoff's gaze bore into him. "Things change. Sometimes unexpectedly." He pulled his hand out and slid it across the empty space between them. "Take my card, Dr. Donovan. Call me if you reconsider."

Nick took the card from the raw-boned hand and shoved it into the pocket of his jacket.

"Thanks." He unlocked the car and jumped in. Chernoff stared at him from beside the car. Nick closed the car door and started the engine. When he turned to look for Chernoff, the man was gone.

CHAPTER 3

Gregory Brulin tapped his cigar over the gold-plated ashtray on the corner of his desk. He puffed on it again, savoring the taste. He stood at the wall of windows in his office at the corporate and research facility of SynTech Labs, watching the sun lose its battle with the gray haze over the artificial lake. A row of cars wound slowly around the lake, the five o'clock mass exodus. They moved toward home and family. Gregory felt a twinge of envy.

He leaned his head against the window and peered down to the ground level. The patterned-brick executive parking lot was half full. He watched as a black Lincoln Town Car swung into the lot and slid to an entrance below him. Gregory took a moment to appreciate the sleek lines of his new car.

The phone on his mahogany desk buzzed. "Yes, Sonya?"

"Your car is ready."

"Thank you."

Gregory snuffed out the cigar, leaving it in the ashtray for the cleaning staff, and strode to the coat tree beside his office door, taking his wool overcoat from the hook. He slipped the coat on, ran a hand over the dark hair his coat had rearranged, and opened the door.

Sonya stood on the other side, waiting to lock it behind him. "Good night, Dr. Brulin." She smiled.

He grunted.

Downstairs, Gregory stepped to the curb as the man opened the back door of the car. "Take me to the center."

The car circled around the artificial lake. Gregory pulled out his phone and dialed the Gene Therapy Center's number, his heavy gold rings glowing red in the dim light. "Get me Edwin Helmsley."

The call transferred, and Helmsley picked up. "Yes, Dr. Brulin?"

"I'm headed over there. I want to meet with you."

"Is there something I can help you with?"

"You know I wasn't happy with the last reports I saw. The numbers weren't good enough. I want to go over the new reports. I plan to make my presence felt by the staff there tonight."

"I'll have the report ready for you, Sir."

Forty-five minutes later, the car edged to the curb in front of the Gene Therapy Center. His driver opened the curbside door.

"Wait for me," Gregory said.

A spacious waiting room welcomed patients to the SynTech Gene Therapy Center like the lobby of a five-star hotel. Live plants, upholstered couches, and classic end tables clustered in intimate groups inviting patients to relax while they waited for an appointment. A symphony by Mozart played in the background tonight, and staff members spoke in near-whispers as visitors approached the front desk.

Gregory stopped inside the door to take in the atmosphere, noting with satisfaction the faint scent of flowers that infused the air. In the center of the lobby, a large, white statue of Aesculapius, the Greek god of healing, beckoned visitors like the gracious host of an ancient party. Gregory walked toward the statue and smiled. Aesculapius, who restored the dead to life. He patted the base. "We'll do great things here," he said.

A young woman, her hair forced into a tight knot behind her head, smiled at Gregory from her station at the front desk. "Good evening, Dr. Brulin. Mr. Helmsley is waiting for you in the conference room."

Gregory nodded and pushed open the double doors that led to the inner recesses of the center. The long hallway before him branched into several others, but he opened the first heavy door on his right and stepped in. The door sealed behind him.

Helmsley sat at the end of a polished black table, his elbows on its surface, fingertips pressed together. His face seemed more pinched than usual tonight and his lips even more taut. He acknowledged Gregory's entrance with a stiff nod.

Gregory dropped into the chair at the far end of the long conference table. He unbuttoned his coat but didn't remove it.

Helmsley slid a bound report across the table toward Gregory's end. It slowed to a stop a few feet short. Neither man moved to retrieve it. It lay there abandoned for several moments. Gregory lifted his eyes to glare at Helmsley. The man finally rose to his feet, stretched across the table, and gave the report the nudge it needed.

Gregory picked it up and glanced through it. The first few pages were worthless. He moved through to the columns of numbers and percentages. "Numbers are down again this month."

Helmsley pressed his fingertips together. "I have observed a recent waning of media attention. Insurance complications have increased. Perhaps you should be giving more attention to marketing."

Gregory dropped the open report onto the table and leaned over it. "I'll decide where my attention goes, Helmsley."

Helmsley studied the ceiling.

Gregory placed his elbows on the table, pressing his eyelids shut with two fingers of each hand. Then he studied the report again. "It's more than marketing. The percentage of people returning for treatment after they've been here for counseling has dropped, as well."

"Yes, I noticed that."

Gregory flicked the report closed. "I want to talk to every counselor in the building. In this room. In ten minutes."

Helmsley nodded, his lips forming a tight seal.

Gregory returned to the lobby and looked through the windowed front wall into the darkness. In the orange glow of the parking lot lights, he could see spindly trees planted like sentinels along the perimeter, bent and swaying. The lobby felt like a haven from the biting January wind.

The idea of installing gas fireplaces in the center drifted into his mind. The evenings were the center's busiest times because people who couldn't miss work for an appointment could come at night. A warm fire in the lobby as they escaped the night air might be welcomed.

At first, patients had poured in to avail themselves of the new technology streaming out of SynTech Labs. But, as Helmsley had said, interest was waning. Gregory could not allow that. The fulfillment of Phase 1 of his plan—no, his destiny—depended on large numbers of people coming for treatment. Not just any people. Certain people.

That was where Nicholas Donovan came in. A gene therapy for cancer had not been perfected yet, but Nick's research was as close as anyone had gotten. And a cancer therapy was the one thing that could draw people to the Gene Therapy Center like mice to a well-baited trap. Gregory needed Nick—and his research—working for SynTech. It would probably take more than money to lure Nick away from the university. Gregory was prepared to do whatever it might take.

The glass double doors beside him swung open, and a gust of cold air propelled a young woman and a small boy into the lobby like dry leaves blown off the street. The woman stopped inside the door to rake strands of brown hair away from her face and straighten her jacket.

The boy at her side was four or five years old. Gregory's stomach twisted when he looked into the boy's adorable face, but he ground his teeth together and kept his expression impassive as the boy looked up at him. One small hand lifted in a small wave. Gregory nodded in response.

"Okay, Ryan," the woman said, "Mommy has to talk to the lady at the desk. Then we'll sit on one of those pretty couches and read your book while we wait for my appointment." She pointed to the side of the lobby. "Why don't you sit on that couch right there? I'll be over in a minute."

The woman hurried over to the front desk, but the boy stood

rooted to his spot, his eyes returning to Gregory. "Hi." The boy's open smile revealed one missing front tooth.

"Hello."

"I'm Ryan."

Gregory's heart tightened, and he tried to look away.

"What's your name?" the boy asked.

"Gregory."

The boy nodded, a serious frown furrowing his forehead. "That starts with a *G*."

"Yes. Yes, it does." Gregory swallowed. The boy's wind-blown hair needed smoothing. He almost reached his hand out.

The mother was back a moment later, an apologetic smile on her face. "Ryan, I told you to sit down, honey." She looked up at Gregory. "I'm sorry. He chats with everyone, I'm afraid."

Gregory forced a smile. "He's a—a beautiful boy."

"Thank you."

Gregory noticed a gold cross on a delicate chain hanging just below the neckline of the woman's sweater. His mood grew cold.

The woman's smile faded. She herded Ryan toward a group of couches and sat down beside him, their backs to the front door.

Gregory felt a moment of remorse over what the future held for the little boy. He shook his head, annoyed with his guilt. It was a mistake to come here, to let it get personal. Better to see simple numbers on reports than the faces of those who must be sacrificed to the greater cause. There had certainly been no remorse for another fair-haired little boy four years ago. He could not allow it to get in the way now.

He stalked across the lobby and shoved open the doors to the conference room, leaving regrets behind.

The meeting with the counselors lasted fifteen minutes. He berated and threatened them like a tyrant until they cowered out of the room, promising to increase their percentages. When people came for genetic counseling, he said, he expected them to make an appointment for treatment on their way out.

It was seven o'clock when Gregory stepped out to the curb where his car idled. The frosty air burrowed under his coat. His driver hopped out and opened the back door. Gregory ducked in, pulling the door closed behind him.

A tiny orange glow inside the car startled him. A dark figure slouched in the backseat, a cigarette smoldering between his lips. Gregory's hand jumped to the door handle.

"I'm sorry to startle you, Dr. Brulin." The monotone voice seemed to drop at his feet with an audible thud.

"What is it, Chernoff?" Gregory motioned to his driver to wait outside. "Don't smoke in my new car," he said. He lowered the window, snatched the cigarette from Chernoff's mouth, and tossed it out the window.

"I've come from the university." Chernoff's vacant eyes rested on Gregory.

"And?"

"Donovan said no."

Gregory twisted the custom-made gold ring on his left hand, studying the SynTech logo. "Anything else?"

Chernoff shook his head. "He's not interested. I watched him. He is too invested in his work at the university to walk away."

Gregory leaned back against the cold upholstery of the car and closed his eyes. At length he spoke. "Then we must destroy his investment."

Chernoff waited.

Gregory sighed. "Do whatever it takes."

Chernoff disappeared into the night, the door slamming behind him.

The interior light blinked out a moment later, leaving Gregory in darkness to contemplate how far he'd come, and yet how far he had to go.

Chapter 4

Porch lights flickered on as Nick cruised through the tree-lined neighborhood of the Oxford Ridge development. On his own street, Chaucer Circle, yellow squares of lighted windows welcomed home the weary. The sun hung low in the sky behind him, reflecting off the buff-colored townhouses in a warm glow and creating silhouettes of the mature maple trees that anchored each driveway along the street. A neighbor, just arriving home, slammed his car door and lifted a hand in greeting to Nick as he passed.

Chaucer Circle ended in a cul-de-sac, with Nick and Kate's townhouse in the center of the circle. Nick slowed, as another neighbor's dog ran to the curb to inspect the new arrival, and then continued into his driveway. The green digits on the dashboard glowed 5:37. He'd shaved two minutes from his usual commute time.

He could see Kate inside, framed by the living-room window. A match blazed at her fingertips. She lit a candle on the glass table beside his Steinway baby grand piano. He took a deep breath and watched her for a moment. Even from the soundproof interior of his car, he knew music played inside the house. Probably one of her tenors, crooning an aria from a favorite opera.

Perhaps it was the cocoon of the car, but the distant memory at the shore of his mind for the past two days threatened again to flood through him. Natalie.

He took the keys from the ignition and opened the car door.

He was right about the music. She had lit a fire, too, and Nick smelled tomatoes and onions. On nights like this, Kate always remembered that Nick's mother was Italian. Nothing soothed the soul like a good marinara, his mother would say. He dropped his things and himself onto the couch.

"Nick? Is that you?" Kate called from the kitchen.

"What's left of me."

Kate wiped her hands on her apron as she came out and sank down beside him on the couch. "I didn't think you'd be home this early. Any change?"

"Leon's stabilized," Nick said.

"Oh, that's wonderful, honey! See, I knew it would all work out."

"It's a good sign." He closed his eyes and leaned back against the upholstery. His head felt like it weighed a hundred pounds.

Kate leaned her cheek against his shoulder. "Are you up for pigging out on pasta?"

Nick laughed and nodded, his eyes still closed.

"It'll be ready in a few minutes." She kissed his cheek and returned to the kitchen.

Nick loosened his tie and unbuttoned the top button of his shirt. *I should head upstairs to the treadmill.* Instead, he propped his feet on the coffee table and stared out the front window, watching the orange ball of the sun dip below the trees. The mantel clock above the fireplace ticked a hypnotizing rhythm, and his eyelids grew heavy.

Kate called him to the table before he had time for a nap.

"I talked to Melanie today," she said.

Nick forked angel-hair pasta onto his plate and smothered it with red sauce. "Hmm."

"She says little Anna is already the most popular girl in first grade."

"Takes after her aunt." Nick smiled.

Kate covered his hand with hers. "She's adorable, isn't she, Nick?"

Nick coiled pasta around his fork.

"I mean it, Nick," Kate said, laughing. "When I'm around her, I feel different. Like that's what life is about, you know?"

Nick's smile faded.

Kate pushed her pasta around her plate with her fork. "Never mind," she said. "I didn't mean to bring it up tonight. It's been a long day."

Nick took a drink of iced tea. "Kate, you don't have to tell me that you want kids, okay?"

"I didn't."

"Because I know you do. You've wanted kids ever since we got married. But we're having fun just you and me, aren't we? Why all of a sudden do you have to take every opportunity to harass me about it?"

"Every opportunity? I haven't said anything in days!"

"What about the Happy Meal today?"

She shook her head. "Now you're getting paranoid! I wasn't very hungry, so I got a kid's meal. So what?"

"Fine. Sorry. I just don't understand why you're so obsessed with having children."

She sighed. "I'm twenty-nine. I don't have forever. And you're thirty-four. Do you want to be an old man when your children are still young?"

"I'm not an old man yet, Kate. We've got plenty of time."

Kate picked at her food.

"It's not that I don't want children, Kate. I like Melanie's kids. One day I know I want to have a family. But the long hours are just beginning to pay off. In a few more years I will have gotten so much further."

"I don't care about any of that, Nick. It doesn't take a successful career to raise happy kids."

Nick sighed. "I'll be ready someday, Kate. But not today, with Leon Weinman hanging between life and death."

They finished the meal in silence.

* * *

Hours later, Nick's mind tunneled through the heavy weight of sleep, grasping at the sound that called to him. The phone jangled beside him on the nightstand. He clawed at the receiver in the dark, rising on an elbow as he did.

"Hello?"

"Nick, it's Rogan."

Nick squinted at the red digits blurred beside the phone. Why was his boss calling at 3:37 in the morning?

"Nick, are you there?"

"Yeah, I'm here. What's happening?"

"I need you down here, Nick. At the hospital. Now. We've got to figure something out to reverse this."

Nick sat up, fully awake. Kate moaned beside him.

"Reverse what?"

"We're losing him, Nick. Losing him fast."

"I'll be there in thirty minutes."

He was on his feet before Rogan disconnected. He grabbed jeans and a shirt from a nearby chair.

Kate woke up. "What's going on?"

Nick flicked on the light. "Weinman. Going downhill."

"I'm going with you." She tossed the covers back, stood, and started throwing drawers open.

"Then make it quick."

Five minutes later the Ford Expedition raced out of the driveway. Kate brushed her red curls and checked her face in the mirror behind the visor.

"I don't know how I'll live with myself if he doesn't make it, Kate. I got into this to save lives, not take them."

Kate nodded.

"We lost hardly any animals in our preclinical phase," Nick said, "and Phase 1 of clinical went great. But if Leon Weinman dies, it could be the end of my career."

Kate shook her head. "They wouldn't blame you."

"No one's supposed to die, Kate! You know the precedents as well as I do. Even in experimental medicine, no one's supposed to die. Dr. Nicholas Donovan—he'll heal you or kill you. Which it will be is anyone's guess."

Nick entered the parking garage and jerked the SUV into the first available slot, ignoring the way it spilled into the next parking space. They jumped out and jogged to the garage elevator. Nick jabbed the "up" button. He surveyed the dark lot nervously, expecting shadowy figures to leap out at any moment.

Upstairs they ran toward the ICU.

Rogan stood outside the double doors. "They're not telling me anything. They're in there working on him. All I know is that something went wrong."

Nick flopped into a chair near the doors, and Kate found another.

"This is not good." Rogan shook his head at the floor. "Not good at all."

Nick sat for only a minute before he began to pace the tiny ICU waiting room—a blue-carpeted square with four chairs and a table littered with magazines. The three of them were the only ones in the silent room. As the minutes passed, Nick finally picked up a magazine from the table. Reading seemed to be working for Rogan and Kate. He flipped through a few pages of *Sports Illustrated* and tried to focus on the cover story but finally tossed it back to the messy table.

Thirty minutes later, the doors swung open, and Dr. Orland strode out. He took in the lounge area in a glance. Nick, Kate, and Rogan stood.

Orland met each of their eyes in turn, pausing for one unending moment.

"We lost him."

CHAPTER 5

Wednesday, January 19

Nick switched on the lights in the institute's wing. It was only 6 A.M. After he'd returned home from the hospital, sleep had eluded him. He'd felt he should be here, beginning the task of learning what had gone wrong.

This morning the chemicals in the room smelled to him like death. His stomach churned as he swiped at the clutter on his lab bench to clear a space.

Dr. Orland had no satisfactory explanation for Leon's sudden decline. Leon had been doing well, he said. Then an unexpected reaction to medication plunged him into respiratory distress. He was gone almost before they had a chance to react.

Nick reached for his notebook. The answer had to be there. He read until the words began to blur.

He heard his name. He lifted his head and looked at his watch. Eight o'clock. He must've fallen asleep. He ran a hand through his hair and shook his head.

"Nick," the voice said again.

Nick looked up. "Dr. Rogan. I'm sorry. I guess I must've—"

"Any answers yet?" Rogan asked, his arms tightly crossed.

"No, sir. No answers yet."

Rogan nodded. "Find some."

Nick tried to concentrate through the morning, but fatigue and frustration left him feeling scattered.

Kate poked her head into the lab at twelve-thirty. "Hey, are you going to get some lunch?"

Nick shook his head without looking up.

She came in and stood behind him, squeezing his shoulders. "Come on, Nick. I can see your blood sugar dropping before my eyes."

He gave her a half smile. "I have to find some answers, Kate."

"Just be sure to take a break, okay? You don't have to solve it today."

He nodded and went back to his scribbled notes.

Nick didn't see Dr. Rogan again all day until the director entered the lab at five o'clock. Kate had left an hour earlier.

"Why don't you call it a day, Nick?" Rogan said, leaning a hand against the door frame.

"That's okay, sir. There's an answer here somewhere." He continued to scratch notes.

"It doesn't look like it's going to be up to us to find the answer," Rogan said.

Nick looked up through narrowed eyes. "What do you mean?"

"I just got off the phone with Price."

Harnetta Price, the university president, rarely spoke with any of them. It wasn't a good sign.

"The FDA is putting together an investigative team," Rogan continued. "They'll be here before the week's out to inspect the facility and recommend action."

Nick's stomach dropped. FDA intervention would mean weeks, maybe months of delay in any clinical trials. Nick's career had just been shelved. And the FDA—not to mention the institute and the university—would want to place blame for Leon's death. Would he be the target?

∼   ∼   ∼

The official press release issued by the Gene Therapy Institute of Franklin University within days of Leon Weinman's death asserted that the institute staff had committed no serious mistakes or violations in running the experiment. Nevertheless, the team from the FDA's Center for Biologics Evaluation and Research moved in to search the institute's records and labs like a brood of vultures picking through a pile of meaty bones.

On Friday afternoon, ten days after Leon's death, Nick sat

with the rest of the research team in the small conference room at the institute. He tried to stretch away two hours of tension, two hours of answering questions from Stella Ruhn, the director of the FDA's investigative team.

"Do you need anything else from us?" Nick asked her. He said "us," though he'd been the only one answering questions. Dr. Rogan had been silent at the end of the table.

Stella Ruhn tapped her pen against a clipboard and peered over her black-rimmed glasses. "So, Dr. Donovan, once again, you're stating that the colon damage in study subjects prior to Mr. Weinman did not give you pause in moving on to the next subject?"

Nick closed his eyes. *She's more FBI than FDA.* Ruhn's serious navy blue suit and sturdy shoes made him feel like he was sitting in a police interrogation room. Did she expect to wear him down until he changed his story?

"Ms. Ruhn, we have been over this several times now. The colon damage in the prior subjects was due to the cancer, not the therapy. If they didn't have colon cancer, they never would've qualified for the study in the first place. But the therapy doesn't cause further damage to the colon. How much clearer can I be?"

Stella Ruhn's eyes narrowed, and Nick knew he'd made an error. He looked over at Kate, who shook her head minutely. Nick sat back.

"And your monkeys, Dr. Donovan?" Ruhn said.

Nick sighed. "As I mentioned before, the death of the one monkey in our animal-testing phase was irrelevant. It developed an animal side effect that had nothing to do with our human studies. And the retroviral vector given that monkey was a dose eleven times higher than that used for Leon Weinman."

Nick turned toward Rogan at the other end of the table. Why wasn't the director stepping in here? Nick knew the bulk of questions would fall on him as the head of the research team, but Rogan could at least back him up.

Rogan nodded in Nick's direction.

Stella Ruhn cleared her throat. "We have found several paperwork irregularities here, as well. Copies of consent forms that were not filled out correctly, materials transfer forms that were not filled out at all." She shook her head sadly. "As the person in charge of the study, Dr. Donovan, I would think you would have taken every measure to ensure—"

Nick's patience snapped. "We are busy trying to save lives here, Ms. Ruhn, and you are talking about paperwork? Look, if there was an oversight in our form submission, we certainly apologize, but don't you think that's a little weak? Is it that you just can't find that we did anything wrong so you have to come up with these stupid—"

Stella Ruhn stood and took off her glasses. "We're finished for today." She gathered her things and marched out of the room.

When the door closed behind her, Nick exhaled and dropped his forehead onto the table. Nervous laughter from a few team members did little to ease the tension.

Nick lifted his head toward Dr. Rogan. "What do you think they're going to do?"

Rogan shook his head. "I have no idea. But it seems obvious that they're intent on finding a concrete reason to blame us."

And when he says "us," he means me.

Nick slapped the table with an open palm. "It makes me crazy, the way that woman keeps implying that we didn't even care about Leon. That we were careless with his life. What does she think we're doing here if we don't care about people?"

Several silent minutes passed. Rogan stood and made some comment, but Nick wasn't listening. When Rogan left the room, the team filed out with him.

Kate stayed behind and moved to the seat beside Nick. "What are you thinking, honey?"

Nick breathed deeply. "How could we have lost him, Kate? I don't believe we did anything wrong. I've always followed regulations to the letter. I've had many opportunities for shortcuts over the years, and I've never compromised the safety of a patient. But still—Leon died."

"We can't save everyone, Nick."

Nick pounded his fist on the table. "Why? Why can't we save them all, Kate? It's not fair!" He lowered his head to his hands.

At this rate, he wasn't going to make it through the month as a researcher—much less ever make any significant strides against disease. Everything in educational research took forever. It wasn't like the private sector where corporate funding got things done quickly. Finished and out to the public, where the research could save lives.

Kate's hand on his arm brought him back. "Nick, sometimes death is inevitable. Leon was terminal. He would've died in a few months without our involvement anyway."

Nick lifted his head and looked into Kate's eyes. "But why does death have to be inevitable, Kate?"

She smiled sadly. "I don't know."

ᕧ   ᕧ   ᕧ

Just before noon, Nick heard shouting outside the Hawthorne Building. He stepped to the window and looked down into the courtyard.

A dozen people milled around the steps to the building. Nick wondered if someone had gotten hurt. Roller bladers were always hitting cracks in the sidewalks down there.

One of the bystanders raised a placard, and Nick's stomach tightened. "STOP PLAYING GOD!" blazed from the white poster-board in bloodred paint. Several other banners were raised, and the group began a steady loop at the base of the steps, chanting as they marched.

Nick leaned closer to the window, trying to catch the phrase.

"Stop deadly research! Stop deadly research!"

Nick turned away and headed for the lab door. He needed to get some air.

Two steps from the hallway, Brett Adams slid around the corner and slammed into him.

"Hey!" Nick said. "What's the rush, Brett? You headed over for a look at the demonstrators? College students: always got to have something to protest."

Brett bit his lip and glanced back over his shoulder. He pushed a folder into Nick's hand and hurried by. "Take a look at that, buddy."

Nick looked at him as he took his place in the lab, but something about the set of Brett's shoulders told him to keep moving and leave the questions for later. He walked out the back door of the building, avoiding the protestors in front.

The Student Study Center across the courtyard housed a small lunch counter. He bought a yogurt and a bagel with cream cheese and took them back outside to a bench.

Pigeons pecked at the bricks around the little garden outside the Hawthorne Building. Nick laid his bagel on a napkin on the bench alongside the folder and watched the activity around him for a few moments while he ate his yogurt. The day sparkled, the sun smiling on the old stone buildings. Little ever changed around here, Nick thought. In spite of the twenty-first-century research being done a few yards away, it still looked like the eighteenth century around campus. Nick pictured one of America's founding fathers striding through the courtyard, brass buttons and silver buckles gleaming.

Curiosity roused him, and he picked up the folder Brett had shoved at him. Inside lay two sheets of paper on institute letterhead. It was a photocopy of a statement from Dr. Rogan, on institute letterhead, addressed to Stella Ruhn at the FDA. Where had Brett gotten it? Probably Marianne, Rogan's secretary who had big plans for herself and Brett.

The letter had scapegoat written all over it. Someone had to bear the responsibility of what had happened. Only two people were in a position to be the sacrificial lamb. Rogan must have decided that he could either assume the blame for the institute as a whole, or place the blame on the head of the research team and hope to maintain the institute's good name—and his job.

A pair of sneakers walked over the cobblestones near his feet, stopping in front of him. Nick looked up.

"Hey," a young man nodded in greeting. A bike leaned against his body as he unstrapped a helmet. He swung a bulging backpack off his shoulders and plunked it onto the ground, throwing himself onto the bench beside Nick.

"Hi," Nick said.

"Awesome day, isn't it?" he asked, his eyes roving around the courtyard as if to drink it all in at once.

"Yeah, great."

"Makes you anxious to see what the future holds."

Nick snorted. "For people who have a future." Nick went back to the statement. His eyes fixed on one paragraph.

We have moved aggressively in certain areas and recognize that we have considerable work to do to ensure the best possible conditions for clinical trials. We regret that Dr. Donovan's haste to bring his research to Phase 2 human clinical trials may have resulted in Leon Weinman's untimely death.

So this was how they were going to play it. Nick could picture Rogan and Harnetta Price sitting in her plush office, planning how to put the best face on the disaster. The institute would still be suspended from performing human trials, Nick was sure. By offering up Nick, the bulk of their projects might be spared, and they could preserve the possibility of beginning trials again in the future.

Would he be asked to resign? Probably not. They needed him. But he would not be director next year. It was back to working with monkeys and rats and more testing, testing, testing. Four years, wasted. Nick buried his head in his hands, the bagel forgotten beside him.

Several minutes passed before Nick stood to leave, suddenly embarrassed that a student had seen him so miserable. He glanced at the young man, but he was still studying the courtyard. Nick gathered his bagel and the folder. He shoved the napkin into his jacket pocket.

Nick stood. The young man beside him glanced at him. "Have a great day!"

"Yeah. You, too." Nick headed toward the entrance to his building.

"Excuse me," the voice behind him called.

What now? Nick turned.

"Yeah, you dropped this," the young man said, extending a white card to Nick.

"Thanks."

On the way up the steps, Nick glanced at the card. It was Chernoff's, the morose man who had approached him in the parking garage. It must have fallen out of his coat pocket. He had forgotten all about it.

CHAPTER 6

Tuesday, February 1

Nick found Kate in the kitchen when he arrived home at 5:30. "I need to tell you something," he said.

She pulled a bag of frozen pasta and vegetables from the freezer. "That's good, since we haven't spoken all day."

Nick pursed his lips. "Brett showed me a statement today. I don't know how he got it. Marianne probably gave it to him."

Kate ripped open the bag and dumped it into a large skillet. "And?"

"Rogan's throwing the blame on me."

"What?" Kate turned, her spatula held in midair. "How?"

"Something about my haste to begin trials."

"He can't do that!" Kate said. She slapped the spatula against her hand.

"Yes, he can, Kate."

"You weren't quick to trials, Nick! Phase 1 went perfectly. These tests were right on schedule. Rogan was the one who wanted to hurry."

Nick shrugged. "Still, the letter's going out. I think the FDA's going to go for it. I think they're in on it, actually."

She touched his hand. "What are you going to do?"

Nick smirked. "Go back to working with monkeys, I guess."

"Oh, Nick, I'm so sorry." Kate jabbed the vegetables a few times as though punishing them for Rogan's actions.

Nick smiled sadly. *Even when your career's going down the drain, dinner still has to be cooked.* He pulled a package of chicken from the refrigerator, opened it, and began chopping.

"Well," Kate said, not looking at him, "maybe there's a bright side. At least now maybe you won't have to work so hard."

Nick closed his eyes. After all these years, she still didn't have any idea what his career meant to him. He worked hard because he loved it, because he intended to make something out of his life, because there were people out there who needed what he could give them.

"You'll have more free time," she added.

Nick wanted to stop her, to shout at her that she was being selfish. Instead, he stirred the vegetables.

"Maybe you'll even feel like you have time for children," she said, loading the cutting board into the dishwasher as if she'd asked him to stop for a gallon of milk.

Nick tossed the spatula into the skillet. It bounced once and flew over the side, flinging pieces of red bell pepper with it. "Don't you ever stop, Kate? I'm taking the fall for a man's death! Haven't you been paying attention? My career is destroyed, and all you can see is how it will help you have children!"

Nick headed for the treadmill, leaving Kate to pick up the scattered vegetables.

↗ ↗ ↗

"Mr. Chernoff?" Nick said into the phone.

"Yes."

"This is Nicholas Donovan. We met two weeks ago. . . ."

"Yes, I know who you are, Dr. Donovan."

Nick swallowed at the superior tone of voice. "I've—re-considered—the offer you spoke of that day. I'd be interested in more information about your employer."

"SynTech Labs, Dr. Donovan."

"SynTech?" Nick's jaw dropped. "Is Gregory Brulin still there?"

"He is the one who asked that I contact you."

Nick frowned, his whole history with Gregory flashing before his eyes in a moment. He heard again Gregory's scathing words at the last Genome team meeting Nick had been allowed to attend. Could Gregory really be recruiting him after all these years?

Chernoff cleared his throat. "Come tomorrow morning, Dr. Donovan. Ten o'clock. You know the address?"

"Yes, I'll find it."

"Use the main entrance," Chernoff said. "Ask for me at the front desk. I'll come down to meet you."

Nick hung up the phone and glanced into the hallway from his bedroom. Kate was still downstairs. He hadn't yet figured out a way to tell her about SynTech. There was no reason to tell her tonight, he reasoned. After tomorrow, he'd have a better idea whether or not the deal would actually go through.

Downstairs, he bumped into Kate in the hall. She was wearing her coat.

"I'm going shopping," she said, stepping around him.

"What about dinner?"

"I'm not hungry. Finish it yourself if you are."

Nick frowned. "What are you shopping for?"

Kate shrugged. "I don't know yet."

When the door closed behind her, Nick drifted to the living room and found himself at his piano. Besides exercise, his music was the best way he knew to unwind after a stressful day.

He let his fingers flow over the keys unhindered until he found the right piece. Tension eased in his neck and shoulders with the opening bars of Beethoven's *Moonlight Sonata*. He played quietly, wanting to forget the past two weeks, but the mournful melody was like a haunting echo of the death and failure he was trying to forget.

SynTech Labs. The name intruded into his solo concert.

He needed to call Stanford.

Stanford Carlton, Nick's former professor and longtime mentor, was more of an expert on Gregory Brulin than anyone else Nick knew. Though Nick figured he would probably accept the position—what other options were before him at the moment?—he wanted to call Stanford and get his take on the deal.

Could he give up the comfortable security of his job at the institute? Did he want his time and talent poured into a career that centered around profit? Would this help him help more people?

Behind all his thoughts ran another current: What would Kate say?

He went to the kitchen and dialed Stanford's number. Julia Carlton answered on the first ring.

"Hello, Julia. It's Nick Donovan. Is Stanford at home yet?"

"Stanford is resting, Nick," Julia said.

Nick checked his watch. "Resting at 6 P.M.? Is he getting old?" Nick laughed.

"Stanford is—he's not feeling well, I'm afraid."

Nick sobered. "I'm sorry to hear that, Julia. Nothing serious, I hope."

A lingering silence on the other end brought a pang to his chest.

"Julia?"

"It's cancer, Nick," she said. "He was diagnosed with pancreatic cancer several months ago. He hasn't wanted anyone to know. But the treatment is starting to take its toll."

"Cancer?" Nick said. "How serious?"

"It's not good."

Nick expressed condolences, promised to visit, and disconnected. He replaced the phone and returned to the piano, but the desire to play had left him.

Why does death have to be inevitable?

CHAPTER 7

Stanford Carlton awoke in his study just after six o'clock in the recliner Julia had turned to face the picture window. Had he heard the phone ring? Grogginess caused by the pain medication faded gradually, and he returned to his presleep thoughts. He studied the maple tree outside his window, illuminated by the porch light. One yellow leaf still clung to a branch, trembling in the night air, fighting to endure for one more day before it lost its fragile hold on life.

Stanford went to his desk, picked up the phone, and dialed. The plaque on his desk caught his eye, its "Man of the Year" caption glinting in gold letters. One more reminder of the past.

The private number he had kept all these years was still in service. A voice Stanford would recognize anywhere answered on the second ring. "Hello, Gregory."

"Stanford? This is a surprise."

Stanford leaned back in his leather chair and rested his head. "It's been awhile."

"I heard about the cancer, Stan. Heard you're putting up a good fight, though."

"Yeah, when are you going to find a cure over there?" Stanford asked.

Gregory chuckled. "We're working on it. What can I do for you?"

Stanford picked up a fountain pen and twirled it between his fingers. "I've been thinking, Gregory. About where we left off four years ago."

"Things change, Stanford. Move forward."

"It's the 'moving forward' that concerns me." Stanford took a deep breath. "I've seen the ads for this Genetic Awareness Day you're offering."

"You like that? Marketing promises me it'll pay off."

"You're targeting patients by checking their DNA profiles."

A pause. "How did you know?"

Stanford smiled. "I've known you a long time, Greg, remember? You were talking about that ploy when I was still there. I'm surprised it took you this long to actually go through with it."

"Most of them are grateful to be informed," Gregory said.

"Hmm." Stanford tossed the pen onto his desk and leaned forward. "Do they know you've targeted them for other reasons, as well?"

Seconds ticked past. Finally Gregory spoke. "You've accomplished great things in the past four years, Stanford. I hear about your foundation at every turn. The press loves all those smiling kids you're helping. You've made quite a name for yourself."

"I've spent my time finding ways to better society, Gregory."

"And you think I haven't?"

"I'm wondering, that's all. Wondering if all this genetic awareness stuff is the beginning of what you started planning years ago."

Another pause. "Stanford, when you left SynTech, I didn't argue, did I? Even though you and I had built that company from the ground up, I understood that we didn't see eye to eye any longer." His voice took on a harder edge. "You're not my partner anymore, Stan. What makes you think you have the right to question me now?"

Stanford propped his elbow on the desk and braced his forehead on his hand. The nausea and dizziness hit him at unexpected times. "Has Michael's death poisoned your mind this much, Gregory? I knew you were devastated—anyone would be. But I didn't think you would ever go this far."

"You have no idea what I've built in the past four years, Stanford. Stay out of it."

"I will not stay out of it! Do you expect me to remain silent? I'm telling you that you must stop!"

Gregory laughed. "I've come too far, Stanford. My destiny is laid out for me. Why are you suddenly so interested, anyway? Just go take a pill, old man, and you'll feel much better."

"Listen to me." Stanford lowered his voice, not wanting Julia to hear. "I will not allow you to destroy people just to gain revenge for your own pain."

"Revenge? Is that what you think this is? You're a fool, Stanford. You can't even see what's right in front of you. I'm doing this for all of us, to change the future."

"I can't let you do it."

"You can't stop me."

"I'll call the FDA. I'll tell them this Genetic Awareness Day is just a front for a—for a—"

"For a cleansing?"

Stanford leaned his head back again. "Meet with me, Gregory. Let's talk about this."

"There's no need. Stanford, I've spent four years perfecting my plan. I will carry it out. Don't forget that you've known about it all this time. What will happen to your reputation—to your foundation or to Julia—if all this comes out?"

"I was never involved in that!"

"But you've known. And if it comes to that, I have several convincing documents that would lead the authorities to believe you were an integral part of the plan."

"But that's completely false, Gregory, and you know it! No one would believe you."

"No? Are you willing to take that chance? Willing to throw away everything you've accomplished? I'll ruin you, Stanford."

"You're blackmailing me, then? Is that what you've come to?"

Gregory's laughter was chilling. "Stanford, I decided a long time ago that I would do whatever was necessary to rid the world of the one disease that threatens its existence."

"You need help, Gregory. I know Michael's death was—"

Click. Stanford winced at the abrupt end to the call. He set the phone down and sank back into the chair, eyes closed.

When Stanford opened his eyes, he focused on the plaque. "Man of the Year." He had given the best part of his life to the fight toward his goals and found that what he had believed from the beginning—that he had the potential to achieve great things—had been true. Could he throw it all away now to stop Gregory?

Julia leaned into the study. "Can I get you anything, Stanford?"

He looked up. After thirty years, she was still so beautiful. Still willowy tall and thin, with stylishly short-cropped, graying hair. Julia still took the time every morning to dress perfectly and add just the right amount of jewelry and makeup. She told him once that she did it for him. Stanford blinked away the unexpected tears that clouded his vision. "No thanks, dear."

Julia slipped in and walked around his desk till she stood just inches behind him. She leaned over to rub his temples.

Stanford sighed. "The chemo and radiation don't just rob a man of his strength; they rob him of his dignity."

Julia smiled. "The man who's always controlled everything in his life has found something he can't control."

If she only knew. "But I've done some good things in my life, haven't I, Julia?"

"Oh, sweetheart! Your life is amazing."

"What if I hadn't? What if something happened now to wipe the slate clean? It's too late to start over."

Julia straightened and compressed her lips. "Nothing can take away what you've accomplished, Stanford. You've met more goals in fifty-three years than most men could achieve in three lifetimes."

Stanford smiled.

"Are you sure I can't get you some coffee?" Julia asked.

"Coffee would be good." He squeezed her hand before she left.

It was too soon to die. Despite the awards and Julia's encouraging words, Stanford knew he had not accomplished nearly enough yet. So many things left on life's "to do" list.

And now, a decision to make. One that would affect those he left behind. Should he do whatever it took to stop Gregory, even if it meant destroying the legacy he had worked so hard to build? Or should he remain silent, assured that his achievements would live on after him?

‿ ‿ ‿

Gregory Brulin stood at his office window, staring through the well-lit grounds of SynTech Labs at the black oval of the artificial lake. Stanford's call had been unexpected, but it didn't change anything. Phase 1 of his own plan would go forward as scheduled.

He glanced at his watch. 6:15. Lenny was late with the lists. Probably hacking his way into the Federal Reserve or whatever he did for fun.

He swung his desk chair around at a lazy knock at his office door. Sonya had gone an hour earlier. "Come in."

Lenny entered, a sheaf of paper shuffling through his fingers as he kicked the door closed. "Sorry I'm late, man." He sounded as though he spoke through marbles in his mouth.

Gregory eyed the young man, in his early twenties at most. His spiked black hair competed for attention with a gold nose-ring, and his black T-shirt was emblazoned with the name of some rock group Gregory had never heard of. Gregory wondered if Lenny would be holding up a convenience store somewhere if he didn't work for SynTech. However, the kid was a genius on the computer and essential to the plan.

Gregory sat behind his desk. "Come on, let's get to it," he said. "Give me the numbers."

"Looking good," Lenny said. He dropped one sheet after another onto Gregory's desk. "Here's the new target list. Here's last week's mailing. And responses."

Gregory scanned the numbers, a smile playing across his lips.

Lenny dropped into the chair in front of Gregory's desk and

shuffled through his papers. "I need to know what lists you want me to hack next."

Gregory nodded. "I'll get that to you."

"How do you choose, man?"

Gregory raised his eyebrows at the young man's question.

"I mean, like, what's the deal with the people you're targeting?"

Gregory folded his arms. "Do you know what a retrovirus is, Lenny?"

"Whoa, sounds like some nasty computer worm. Don't worry, though. We're protected."

"Not computers, Lenny. The human body. We use retroviruses to carry healthy genes into people's bodies. But first we have to remove the disease-causing genes from the retrovirus before we can let it replicate."

"What's this got to do with the mailing lists?"

"The people you find for me, Lenny. They are the disease-causing genes of society. We can't let society go forward with the disease-causing genes intact, now can we?"

"People are the disease? Dude, have you been listening to some of my music?" Lenny shrugged. "Yeah, well, whatever. Just let me know where to go next, man. I think we're on track to make next month's Genetic Awareness Day really huge."

Gregory nodded. "I'll contact you in the morning."

"Oh, yeah. One more thing," Lenny said. "I tracked that guy Milburn's entrance into the network."

Gregory sat forward.

"He's not bad, for an old guy. Got into some areas I thought I had locked up tight."

"What areas?"

"The databases. Looks like he's been checking into our strategy for targeting patients. I mean, the disease."

Gregory studied his folded hands. "You may go, Lenny. Thank you."

When Lenny had left, Gregory stretched and turned toward the darkening windows again. His wandering gaze fell on the gold five-by-seven picture frame on the corner of his desk. The five-year-old boy in the picture smiled out to him, his forever-toothless grin bringing a painful smile. Gregory lifted the frame in his left hand and traced the outline of the boy's face with his right forefinger.

A treatment that would have given Michael a normal lifespan was discovered within two years after his death. Embryonic research had been the key. If not for the incessant outcry of embryo-research opponents, the treatment could have been developed much earlier. Michael would not have died.

It was Brian Milburn's chance comment about Michael the day before that had prompted him to put Lenny on Milburn's trail. No one in the company knew about Michael's death— except Sonya, and Gregory was quite confident of her loyalty. The only way Milburn could've known about Michael was if he'd been checking into Gregory for some reason. Now Milburn's curiosity had gotten him in trouble, and he would have to be dealt with.

Gregory set the frame back on the desk. The anger had distilled over the years into hatred for the one disease that threatened all of mankind—those who pressured the government to ban federal funding for embryo research, spreading their poisonous "ethics" into society. They claimed that working with embryos left over from *in vitro* procedures and destined for destruction amounted to taking a life. They shrugged their shoulders when asked about the millions who died from diseases that might be cured by the research from those embryos.

They were the ailment holding back the betterment of mankind, and Gregory knew of only one way to get rid of disease: Eradicate it. So he had begun the cleansing phase of his plan. Once society's disease had been eliminated, Phase 2 of his plan, cloning, could be brought to light. The baby expected six months from now would lead the way. When the time came for Phase 3 to begin, those seven embryos in cryopreserved suspension on Sublevel 3 would finally be implanted in host mothers.

Gregory thought back to Stanford's phone call, Stanford's outrage. He had never understood, and he still didn't. A new era of genetic superiority was about to dawn. Gregory Brulin would lead the charge, and humankind would remember him as a savior.

It would all begin next month with SynTech's first public event: Genetic Awareness Day.

CHAPTER 8

"Kate? Is that you? Hey, Kate!"

Kate swiveled to find the voice in the sea of evening shoppers moving through the crowded mall. A slightly plump blond waved from the other side of the benches and potted trees. She maneuvered a stroller with one hand and reached down to grab a little boy's fist with her other.

"Hi, Lisa!" Kate said, waving.

"Stay there!" Lisa said.

"That's okay," Kate said as Lisa struggled to steer the stroller. "I'll come over."

On depressing nights like tonight, Kate only wanted to eat or shop. She had learned long ago it was easier to return a new pair of shoes than to sweat off a half gallon of Rocky Road. So here she was at the mall.

She and Lisa met in the middle, and Lisa plopped onto a bench with a loud sigh.

"This is a crazy place to bring kids!" She shook her head. "How are you, Kate? I haven't seen you in ages!"

In reality, "ages" amounted to about four years. Lisa and Kate had done graduate work together. They had finished at the same time, but by then Lisa was married and pregnant.

"I'm good. How about you?" Kate's eyes strayed to the baby swaddled in a pink rosebud sleeper in the stroller. If only Nick could picture Kate as a mother of these two precious little ones, even for a moment, she knew he would change his mind.

"Oh, you know," Lisa answered. "Kids driving me crazy." She seemed to remember the little boy at that moment and wrenched her head around to look for him. "Where is he? Randall! Ran—dall!"

Kate felt a moment of panic. Kids could disappear in a flash in a shopping mall. She stood, searching the crowds that flowed by. Lisa remained on the bench.

"There he is," Lisa pointed. The boy had entered the Hallmark store behind them and was lining up stuffed bears on the floor in front of a display.

"Randall Jonathan, you come here this instant!" Lisa yelled across the concourse. The boy ignored her. "Randall!" Lisa stood, hands on her hips.

Kate looked away, embarrassed for her.

His mother's posture must have alerted Randall that she meant business. He meandered over to their bench.

"You stay here near Mommy," Lisa scolded. "Mommy is going to talk to Miss Kate for a few minutes."

Kate smiled down at the boy, but he remained solemn.

"So how about you?" Lisa was asking. "Kids?"

"No, no kids."

"You and Nick didn't split up or anything. . ."

"Oh, no. Nick and I are great." *Sort of.*

"I know, you've still got that great career going."

Kate shrugged. "It loses its glow as a reason to get up in the morning after awhile."

"No way! I never thought I'd hear that from you! You're not going to give it all up to bake cookies and wipe runny noses?"

Kate laughed and pointed to the stroller. "Look at your beautiful girl. How can work compete with that?"

"I thought you wanted to be Marie Curie, Kate."

"Yeah, well. Maybe I want to be June Cleaver." She laughed again. "How did that happen?"

"So what's stopping you?" Lisa asked.

Kate studied the passing shoppers. "Nick's really focused on his career."

"Oh," Lisa said, nodding knowingly. "He doesn't want kids."

"No, he does. He likes my sister's kids. He's just not there yet for us to have any."

Lisa sighed. "Don't rush it, Kate. Trust me." The little one in the stroller let out a wail, as if on cue. Lisa rolled her eyes and reached for a bottle wedged in the bottom of the stroller. "Trust me," she said again. "But then, you're the kind who would wait, aren't you?" she said. "Nick and Kate Donovan, the perfect couple." She shook her head. "You two practically stepped out of a Hollywood movie. Nick, with that premature gray, Richard Gere thing, and you with your perky hair and personality." She sighed. "You guys are living the good life."

Kate forced a smile. Then she pointed past Lisa. Randall had scaled a three-foot-high concrete planter and was swinging from the lowest branch of a dwarf fig tree.

"Be careful, sweetie. That branch could break," Lisa said.

Kate lifted her eyebrows.

"Don't laugh at my jealousy," Lisa said. "I keep up with what's going on. I know you two are down at the Gene Therapy Institute doing all sorts of fabulous stuff. That could've been me, you know!"

"I know," Kate said. "But you have the kids. . ."

A loud crack drew Lisa's attention back to the tree. She had been right. That branch could break. Randall screamed as he tumbled from the concrete planter to the tiled floor.

"Randall! Are you all right, honey?" Lisa jumped to pick him up, and the baby tossed the bottle onto the floor and started screaming again.

Lisa held Randall against her in a crouch and rolled the stroller back and forth with the other hand.

"I guess we'd better get going," she said to Kate. "It was good to see you."

Kate could read the envy in Lisa's expression like it was stamped on her forehead.

"Call me sometime," Lisa said as they disappeared into the crowd. Kate nodded and waved.

Maybe some Rocky Road was what she really needed.

~ ~ ~

Nick was lying on the couch considering another round on the treadmill to work off tension, when the phone rang. Kate still hadn't returned from her shopping spree, but it was only eight o'clock. Nick crossed the living room for the phone.

"Nicholas?"

"Oh, hi, Mom," Nick said. "How are you?"

"How are you, dear?"

"I'm—"

His father's gruff voice cut in. "We heard about the clinical trial, Nick."

"Hi, Dad." Nick dropped to the piano bench and closed his eyes. Of course Dad would have heard by now. He kept up with the latest news in research as though he had never retired. Nick had hoped to keep the news from them until the whole thing had smoothed out.

"What went wrong down there, son?"

Nick knew his dad was really saying, "How did you mess this one up?"

"We're not certain yet," Nick said. "We're trying to determine—"

"You've got to do more than try, Nick! You can't be playing around with people's lives if you're not sure what you're doing! Didn't they teach you that in medical school?"

"Yes, Dad." Nick exhaled heavily.

His mother cut in. "Dear, you know we're proud of the work you do."

"He's killing people, Leona!"

"Don't say that, Patrick. Nick is doing his best, I'm sure. We can't expect everything he does to be perfect."

"Of course not, but we can expect him to keep people from dying in the effort, can't we?"

Nick wondered how long it would take them to remember he was still on the phone.

"Anyway, darling," his mother finally said, "we wanted to be sure you were all right."

"I'm okay, Mom. In fact, I've been offered an interesting position elsewhere."

Why did he say that? He hadn't even told Kate about his call to SynTech yet, and now he was spilling it to his parents.

"Oh?" his father asked. Nick could almost see his eyebrows raised in surprise.

The front door opened. Kate walked in and gave him a weak smile.

"It's too soon to talk about it yet," Nick said. "I'll let you know if anything comes of it."

"Your big sister's changing jobs, too," Dad said. "They're moving her up in the company again."

Of course they are. "That's great, Dad. Give Lizzy my congratulations."

Kate walked past him and headed for the kitchen.

"Watch your back down there at the institute, Nick," his father said. "You've got a career to think of. Haven't made your indelible mark on the world yet, right?"

Nick drummed his fingers on the piano bench.

"Don't let them blame all this on you down there."

No, I'll leave that to you.

"Tell Kate we love her," Mom said.

Nick set the phone on the polished black piano. His mind took him back to childhood, back to the days when anything less than perfection on his report card was pointed out by his father.

"You'll have to try harder," Dad would say. "You need to work up to your potential, Nicholas. I'm not paying for private school so you can make the right friends. Education is the key to your future."

He'd graduated with honors. At every level of his education, he'd graduated in the top five percent of his class. So why did it take one short phone conversation with his father to make him feel like a total loser?

Nick found Kate at the kitchen table, a bowl of ice cream and a book in front of her.

He sat beside her, waiting until she looked at him. "I'm sorry about earlier," he said. "It's just this thing with Rogan, throwing the blame on me. I don't know how I can work with him after this."

Kate nodded, frowning. "I'm sorry for you, Nick. It's not fair."

"Well, you know what they say: Don't get mad, get even."

She laid her book face down, creasing the binding in the way that annoyed him. "What do you mean?"

Nick pulled out the business card he'd been carrying in his pocket. "I was—contacted—by a biotech company. They're interested in hiring me in their research facility."

Kate's brow furrowed, and she brushed the curls from her face. "To do what?"

"That hasn't been spelled out yet, exactly. But I do know it would be a substantial pay increase."

"Where is this facility?" Kate asked.

Nick couldn't read her. He was watching for signs of interest or of disapproval but detected neither. "It's SynTech Labs."

Kate's eyes widened. "Is Gregory Brulin still there?"

"Apparently."

Kate studied her ice cream. "I thought you had nothing but animosity toward him. You're thinking seriously about working for him?"

Nick shrugged. "I don't have many details yet," he said. "I wasn't really considering it at the time. But now. . .I'd at least like to find out what they're offering."

She leaned back against her seat.

"Well?" Nick asked. "What do you think?"

"I guess I don't know what to think, Nick. You've always seemed more drawn to helping people directly or to research in its purest form. This," she said, holding the business card at arm's length, "feels like it's all for the sake of profit. And I wouldn't expect you to want to work for G—for Dr. Brulin."

"We can't kid ourselves, Kate. Even now every bit of the research we do at the institute is about money. It's just a little further removed from us. And a job at SynTech would mean developing cures for thousands of people."

She shrugged. "I guess you're right. . . ." Her voice trailed off.

"What?" he asked.

Her green eyes flashed for a moment. "I feel like I can't tell you what I really think, or you'll go crazy again, like you did earlier!"

"I said I was sorry."

"I know. It's just that I'm not sure what I want. I thought I was ready to have a baby, but after tonight at the mall. . .now I don't know. I need to figure it out. But I'm afraid that if I am ready, and you take this job, it will give you one more excuse."

"I don't know, Kate," he said. "A new job usually means lots of overtime hours, trying to learn everything that needs to be learned."

Kate sighed. "You see what I mean? Nick, you've always said that once you felt you were really getting somewhere with curing disease you'd feel the time was better for children. Well, you've just told me that this job would allow you to help thousands of people. By your own words, that would mean we're ready to start a family, right?"

Nick nodded. It was a fair question, and he couldn't just brush her off. "I guess a baby doesn't happen all at once, right?" Nick swallowed. "Yeah, I guess if you decide you're ready, the new job would make the difference for me."

Kate shrieked and gave him a huge hug and passionate kiss.

Nick should've felt warmed by Kate's affections, but instead, something inside him had grown cold.

That's what happens when you lie to someone you love.

CHAPTER 9

Wednesday, February 2

It took almost an hour to reach West Chester, the suburb of Philadelphia where SynTech Labs had its main facility. The quaint town had preserved its historical heritage with brick streets bordered by black lampposts and mature trees. Corporate America had only quietly intruded with a handful of office buildings throughout the town. Nick noted the names of SynTech's corporate neighbors as he traveled to the other side of the town. He was in good company.

He passed the last of the maple trees and the horizon opened up on his left as though he had emerged from a tunnel. Hundreds of acres had been cleared to make room for the monstrous facility set back at least a half mile from the road. He turned into the tree-lined drive, cruising through the center of a field as well-groomed as a golf course.

The road sloped downward to a massive ice blue lake in front of the building, a perfect oval surrounded with pearly white stones. He turned left to drive around the lake and noticed several people walking around it, following an asphalt path. Halfway around the lake he passed a small yellow sign bearing the silhouette of a turtle with the words "Wildlife X-ing" under it. Nick chuckled. The place was about as wild as a mausoleum.

The building was as perfect as the lake, three wings running parallel to each other with a wing adjoining them on one side, like a giant *E*. Each wing stood three stories high, with dozens of windows running the length of it. Darkened glass windows stared down at Nick like unseeing eyes. Six parking lots spanned the length of the facility, joined by brick walkways and surrounded by symmetrically pruned trees.

Nick parked and headed toward the right side of the building, where three flags signaled the main entrance. Near the door, two rows of towering holly bushes lined the brick courtyard, their shapes carefully sheared into cones. All in all, the facility seemed designed to appear natural, but was far too perfect to pull it off. Like a cemetery, he thought.

Just through the main doors, he descended to the lobby and faced the front desk.

A young woman looked up after he had stood there a moment. "Yes?" she asked, her face a flawless, plastic smile.

"I'm here to see Mr. Chernoff."

"Yes, sir." She punched a few numbers into a phone and picked up the receiver. "What's your name?"

"Nicholas Donovan."

"I have Mr. Donovan here for you," she said into the phone and then hung up. "Could you spell your last name, please?"

He did.

"Make and model of your car?"

"Ford Expedition."

A moment later she handed him a plastic name badge with a yellow card inserted into it. "Here you are. Please wear that as long as you're on SynTech grounds. You can return it to me when you leave or just give it to Mr. Chernoff."

Nick took the yellow badge, clearly marked "Visitor." His name and Chernoff's name appeared below the title. He glanced around as he clipped it to his jacket. The lobby held a small reception area, a dozen or so chairs arranged into two groups. He wandered over to one and sat down, but Chernoff showed up a moment later.

"Dr. Donovan." Chernoff nodded, unsmiling. "Come with me."

Nick followed him down the main hall of the facility. They took the elevator to the third floor. When the doors opened, a spacious reception area greeted them. An attractive, thirty-something woman worked at a large desk in the center.

"Dr. Donovan," Chernoff informed the woman.

"Hello," she said, smiling and holding up a manicured finger as she pressed a button on her phone. "Dr. Donovan is here, Dr. Brulin."

She nodded. "Go right in."

Gregory Brulin did not appear to have aged. As he smiled and rounded his desk, Nick remembered how well the man handled people.

"Dr. Donovan," Gregory said, extending heavily ringed fingers.

Nick shook his hand, taking in the designer cologne, the Italian suit, and the lavish office décor all at once. His gaze came to rest on a collection of small statues perched at the front edge of Gregory's desk.

"Sit down," Gregory said, extending his hand toward a chair in front of his desk and returning to his own chair behind it. "I've heard good things about you over the years, Nick."

Nick smiled. "Not lately, I'm sure."

Dr. Brulin waved the comment away as if the disaster at the institute were of no consequence. "I keep a close eye on the research going on outside SynTech Labs. Your name surfaces often. You're doing good work."

"Thank you, Dr. Brulin."

"We're not professor and student any longer. Please, call me Gregory."

Nick smiled. "All right. And I've been following SynTech's explosive growth since you and Stanford Carlton began it."

Gregory nodded. "There are days I wish Stanford were still here. Have you heard that he has terminal cancer?"

"Yes. He's a good man. It's a shame."

Gregory shifted in his seat. "I wanted to meet with you myself, Nick, instead of handing you over to Human Resources, since we're—friends—from the past."

Nick heard him hesitate over the word. He was surprised he'd used it at all. He relaxed into his chair.

"I'll get straight to the bottom line, Nick. SynTech Labs is the fastest-growing biotech company in the country. Our stocks are climbing and industry experts are watching."

"I'm impressed," Nick said.

"SynTech's main focus at this time is on gene therapy. The SynTech Gene Therapy Center—over in the city—is profitable. People are pouring in, seeking our patented therapies for everything from baldness to heart disease. Many of these therapies are aimed at people who have not yet been diagnosed but who have a predisposition to the condition. We notify them that a genetic red flag has surfaced in their records in the GenWorld database. They come in to have recombinant DNA inserted into their own DNA, ensuring that they will remain healthy."

Nick nodded again.

"We need scientists, Nick, investigators of your caliber to develop new therapies. The more therapies we develop, the more centers we can open, and the more money we'll make. I plan to open fourteen more centers across the country in the next two years."

"I'm impressed," Nick said again, meaning it this time. He remembered Kate's objections to research for profit as opposed to education. However, Gregory didn't seem to be embarrassed at all by his drugs-for-dollars approach.

"I'd like to bring you in as soon as possible, Nick, to start on some new cancer research."

Nick nodded quickly. "Sounds great."

"Actually, to clarify, I'd like you to head up the block of teams we'll eventually have working on cancer research. Right away you'd just be a regular researcher, like you were at the institute. You'd have a lab and assistants of your own. I'd want you working to get a certain cancer treatment to human trials. But that would just be for the immediate future." Gregory paused, leaning forward in his chair. "Ultimately I need someone to provide the vision for all the teams, someone who understands gene therapy. I want you."

"Me?" Nick said. "What do you mean 'provide the vision'? I'm most comfortable in a lab, like you said. I don't know if I can do more than that. Maybe I could advise. . ."

Gregory sat back. "When we get to that point, Nick, you'll be Senior Vice President of Cancer Research."

Nick breathed deeply. "Whoa. I'm not sure what to say. An administrative position? I'm not really looking for a corner office—I'm more interested in research."

"I realize that, Nick. That's why I want you. I'm certain that cancer therapies are going to be SynTech's major source of profit for the foreseeable future. I need someone to head up the department who really cares about what the teams are doing. I'll give you whatever assistance you need with administrative duties so that if you want to stay involved in the trenches, you can. But as vice president, you could create the vision to reach even more people with cures."

Nick's heart was pounding. "Well, Dr.—Gregory, I have to say this is a little surprising." He tried to read the man's face. "Can I ask why you've sought me out, after our. . .past experience together?"

Gregory shrugged. "I remember you as a smart kid, Nick. A little too full of yourself, perhaps, but eager to take on the world and solve its problems."

"You had me kicked off the Human Genome Project research team."

"You were young and inexperienced, Nick. The team only had so many posts, and the work was competitive. But you've distinguished yourself since then."

"You said I wasn't able to 'see the big picture,' if I remember correctly."

Gregory smiled. "It was years ago, Nick. I want you here as a researcher now. And as a VP in a year or two."

Nick's mind raced with the possibility being offered to him. A mental picture of his father visiting his executive office almost brought a smile. More importantly, he'd be instrumental in delivering lifesaving therapies to thousands, maybe millions of people.

The two talked about salary and benefits. Nick said he'd need at least three weeks to tie things up at the institute so he wouldn't be leaving projects and people high and dry. Gregory told him to take his time. When Nick could think of no more questions, Gregory leaned forward in his chair.

"What do you say, Nick?"

Nick nodded. "Gregory, I'd love to join your team."

Gregory stood and shook Nick's hand. "I'm certain we'll both be glad you did."

~ ~ ~

Nick's thoughts collided during the drive home, one side troubled at Gregory's obvious profit-margin outlook, and the other side excited about all the people he would be helping with the disease treatments he developed there. A job with this company could translate into many more people helped than years of uncertain research at the university could. His life could have significant impact here.

When Nick arrived at home, Kate met him at the door.

"Well?" she asked. "What happened at SynTech today?"

Nick maneuvered around her and hung his jacket in the closet. "They offered me a position."

Kate grabbed his arm, smiling. "Really?"

They sat on the couch, and Nick gave her the rest of the details about the job, the salary, and the senior vice president position.

"So," she said, looking at the carpet, "how was he?"

"Who?"

"Dr. Brulin."

"I didn't realize you knew him that well."

Kate swallowed. "No, I, uh, I was just wondering if he'd changed much."

"No, actually, he looks exactly as he did when I had him in school. He's done quite well for himself, I think." He put his arm around her. "So what do you think?"

She looked suddenly worried. "Um, about what?"

"About the job, Kate. Should I take it?"

"Oh, that! Hmm. Well, given the situation at the institute, I think you'd be crazy not to take it."

"I agree," Nick said.

"So this is the next step for us, then?" She smiled brightly.

"Yeah, the new job will change things."

Kate's smile hadn't dimmed. "Like the number of people in our family?"

Nick studied his hands, folded in his lap. "I thought you weren't sure about the baby thing anymore."

"I've been thinking about it all day. It was just cold feet. I don't have to be like. . .other women who have children. I know I'm ready to be a parent."

The silence lengthened.

Her smile drooped. "What's the problem, Nick?"

"I don't know what to say, Kate. It's hard to explain how I feel. There's just something in me that isn't ready for kids yet."

"But you said—"

"I know. But for right now, I feel like I need to concentrate on my career. No distractions. I just haven't made my indelible mark on the world yet. Once that happens, or at least gets started, then I could let up on the focus a bit."

Kate jumped to her feet and looked down at him, her mouth open. "No way, Nick! That's not fair. You told me if you took this job we could start a family! Now you're telling me no? Do you seriously expect me to just say, 'Okay, whatever Nick wants'?" She looked at him narrowly, as if he'd suddenly turned into a beady-eyed mouse. "Did you just say we could start a family so I'd tell you to go to the interview?"

"Kate, I—"

"And now that you've had your interview, you're changing your story?"

"Kate, I'm sorry. I thought I'd feel different, but—"

"I can't believe you would be that manipulative!"

"Please, calm down, honey. Let's talk about this."

Kate closed her eyes and raked her hands through her hair. "What's talking going to accomplish? You've already made your decision. And it has nothing to do with me!"

Nick allowed a note of defensiveness to creep into his voice. "No, I told you before, it has everything to do with being a good father."

"That's just an excuse."

"No, Kate," he said. "It's a choice. I am choosing to focus on one thing right now. I would think you would appreciate that. I don't want to have children until I can give them a significant amount of my time."

"When's that going to be, huh, Nick? When you're retired? Everybody has children when they're still in their careers, Nick. That's just a lame excuse to get what you want."

"No, Kate, I just don't want to be one of those dads who never spends any time with his kids. Can't you respect that?"

"I could respect it," Kate said, her fists balled at her sides, "if I thought you would ever have the time. But I don't. And Nick, I'm afraid of what it might take for you to figure that out!"

❧ ❧ ❧

Gregory turned out the light in his office just before five o'clock. He was pleased with the interview he'd had with Nick Donovan. Nick's research at SynTech could prove to be the most lucrative they'd generated yet.

Still, there was a heaviness in Gregory's chest. He left his office and headed for the elevator.

Chernoff waited, as instructed, in the reception area. He nodded once at Gregory and stepped into the empty elevator beside him. "You got a job for me?"

Gregory sighed, thinking again about Lenny's report about database hacking. "Brian Milburn. Investigator down on Sublevel 2. I need him taken care of."

Chernoff pulled out a cigarette and a gold lighter. "Taken care of?"

"Dead. An accident. That's important. Make it look accidental."

Chernoff nodded, flicking the lighter. "Accidents cost more."

Gregory shut his eyes and nodded.

CHAPTER 10

February in Pennsylvania is an unpleasant month to drown. Somehow Brian Milburn feared the iciness of the water more than he feared the frozen grip of the man who led him there.

Darkness covered them. His captor had waited till night crept across the picnic grounds before pushing the small pistol against the side of his body and escorting him from the car. As the black expanse of water grew closer, Milburn plucked ideas of escape out of the night air and discarded them one by one. No more Frisbee-throwing yuppies, no buildings for hundreds of yards, no one at the boat launch. Nothing to shelter him from a well-aimed bullet. Even the ducks had gone home.

The man who held him was roughly his own height, though so gaunt it seemed that death crept into him by degrees. A wrestling match for the gun would be Milburn's only chance.

The lake's waves tickled the sandy beach, making splashing sounds that skipped his mind back to summer evenings at the lake with his parents. Was life so short as this?

"I'm not ready." He pulled back as the water licked at his shoes, tasting to see if it wanted the rest of him.

The man beside him barked out a short laugh. "Is anyone ever ready?"

"Please." Milburn turned to face his captor. "Tell him I don't care anymore. Tell him I'll walk away." He thought of the yellow notebook, hidden at home, where he had journaled his discoveries. No one had to know about it. In fact, no one did.

"Too late, Dr. Milburn." The bony fingers around his arm released, the pistol anchoring him in place instead.

"You can't just shoot me."

"No. I can't."

This moment was the only chance there would ever be, this

instant under the moonlit sky with the water waiting to swallow him. He lunged for the hand that held the gun.

The gun disappeared. His full weight fell against his tormentor's chest. The cadaverous man pulled him into a stony embrace. Milburn scrabbled for the gun-holding hand. His fingers closed around a narrow wrist, and he pushed. They strained against each other, neither giving ground in a to-the-death arm wrestling match.

The captor broke away. His arm shot upward as though declared the victor. Then he smashed the gun against the back of Milburn's neck.

The black sky, the black water, the fading blackness before his eyes were all Milburn knew as his consciousness slipped away into a watery place.

Part Two

THE PRESENCE OF MY ENEMIES

*Death and Destruction lie open before the Lord—
how much more the hearts of men!*
PROVERBS 15:11

CHAPTER 11

Friday, February 18

Nick tucked the last of his AMA journals into the plastic crate he'd brought to haul his things out of the Gene Therapy Institute.

Brett Adams leaned against the door frame of the Microscopy Lab, watching Nick. His arms were folded and his expression grim. "I can't believe you're really leaving, man. I've been thinking you'd reconsidered, since you had that interview a couple of weeks ago."

Nick shrugged. "Things change." He kept his head down and turned his back to Brett, sorting through the journals and notebooks in the crate.

"Yeah, but—"

"It's just better this way, okay, Brett? Rogan and I can't work together any longer. Not after the way he hung me out to dry with the FDA."

Kate slipped past Brett and came to stand beside him. "Do you need any help?"

Nick didn't miss the tone of obligation in her voice. He shook his head. "No, thanks. I guess this is it." He looked into the crate. "Four years' worth. Doesn't seem like much."

"You were building a career here," Kate said, "not a library."

Nick smiled at her and took a deep breath. "I guess if I've forgotten anything, you can always get it for me."

Kate glanced at Brett and lowered her voice. "I still think it's weird, my continuing here while you head out into big business."

"It's not weird," Nick said. "Our careers are unrelated."

Kate raised her eyebrows. "Yeah, I've noticed that."

"I mean, not unrelated, but I don't see why my leaving should affect your work here."

She nodded and turned away. "Are you going to say good-bye to Dr. Rogan?"

Nick laughed. "Yeah. Good-bye and a few other things."

"Nick, it's not worth it."

"I know."

Nick left the crate on the lab chair and took his final walk to Rogan's office at the end of the long institute hallway. He waved a hand at Marianne, knocked once on Rogan's door, and entered without waiting for an invitation.

Rogan stood and tossed a pen onto his desk. "Leaving, Nick?"

"Yes." Nick started to say more but stopped. Kate was right. It wasn't worth it.

Dr. Rogan circled his desk, smiled, and extended a hand. "It's been a good four years. I think we've done good work together."

Nick raised his hand slowly to accept Rogan's handshake. "Yeah."

"I'm sorry to see you go, of course."

"Yeah, I guess you'll have to find someone else to point the finger at when things go wrong."

Rogan's smile faded. "Nick—"

"Sorry. That wasn't necessary. I know you were just doing whatever it took to salvage your own career—I mean, the institute's reputation. I might have done the same in your position."

Rogan turned his back and returned to his chair behind the desk. "I'm sorry you feel that way, Nick. Dr. Price and I did what we thought best for the university and for the future of gene therapy research. It had nothing to do with my career."

Nick shook his head. "Unbelievable. So you really think that research and the university would have been damaged further if it had been your name on the FDA's hit list instead of mine?"

"We were trying—"

Nick leaned on the desk and bent forward, his gaze boring into his boss's. "You offered me up like a sacrificial lamb, and you know it, Rogan. At least let's be honest here."

Rogan sat back, returning Nick's stare.

Nick didn't move.

"Fine," Rogan said. "If that's what you want to think, if you want to be bitter, I can't stop you. Maybe someday, when you're more experienced, you'll understand better."

"More experienced!" Nick straightened.

Rogan stood. "I think we'd better end this conversation now, Nick. I'm sorry we couldn't have parted on better terms. But it's time for you to leave."

They stared each other down for several tense moments.

Finally, Nick nodded. "Thanks for nothing." He turned and left the office, letting the door slam behind him. "I'll see ya, Marianne," he said to Rogan's secretary. "Thanks for everything."

The young girl raised tearful eyes. "We'll miss you, Dr. Donovan."

"You'll see me once in awhile, I'm sure. And you've still got Kate!"

Nick retrieved his plastic crate from the Microscopy Lab and said a few quick good-byes to the rest of the staff.

He found Kate in the Tissue Culture Lab. "I'm heading out."

She gave him a weary half smile. "You okay?"

"Yeah. I will be."

"How'd it go with Rogan?"

"Um, well, pretty good, I guess. I didn't say everything I wanted to and said more than I should have. So I guess that's a pretty good medium, right?"

She kissed his cheek.

He moved to the door. "See you at home."

CHAPTER 12

Monday, February 21

Nick zipped his jacket and grabbed his briefcase, ignoring Kate's silent protest from the couch.

"I have to go, or I'll be late," he said.

"Fine."

Nick sighed. "C'mon, Kate. I don't want to leave like this."

"Then don't leave at all."

Nick propped his briefcase on the edge of the upholstered chair. "We've been over this."

"You've been over it. And I'm supposed to 'get over it,' right?"

He set the briefcase on the floor and sat in the chair. "Kate, it's my first day at work. Do you really want me to be late?"

"What's stopping you? Go."

Nick sighed. "Kate, do you want me to quit this job before I've even started? Do you want me to sit at home and watch talk shows while you support me? I'm starting a good job today, honey; at least say you're happy for me."

Kate stared at a pillow on the couch. "I am happy for you, Nick. I'm proud of you. I guess I'm still hurting over how you tricked me to land this job. But I guess I'll get over it, right? That's Kate, she always goes with whatever Nick wants."

"Kate, can we—"

"And I guess it would be wrong of me to say you're choosing between this job and me, wouldn't it?" She met his eyes. "But what would you say, Nick, if I did say that? What if right now, at this moment, you were choosing between this job and me? What would you choose?"

Nick rolled his eyes. "Kate! I've got to go. We can talk more about this tonight." He stood and leaned over to kiss her cheek.

She didn't respond.

∽ ∽ ∽

Nick followed a line of cars circling the artificial lake at SynTech Labs. The morning was gray with the threat of snow, and the water churned on the surface of the lake. Nick felt the flutter of excitement he always got at the start of a new project. His first day on the job.

His plan was to dive into the cancer research project Gregory had mentioned and push through to trials in record time. If everything went well, he'd have "Senior VP" below his name on company letterhead long before Gregory predicted—and he'd be a big part of making the world disease free.

Nick took note of his parking space in Lot #3 before heading toward the main entrance of SynTech. By tomorrow he would probably have an ID and could park in the executive lot.

The wind gusted across the lake and wormed its way between his jacket and his body. He quickened his pace to reach the warmth of indoors, outpacing the others who hurried from their cars toward the building.

The building felt nearly as cold as the outdoors, and the gray-and-black color scheme of the lobby did little to warm him. He nodded at the receptionist, not expecting her to recognize him. "Nicholas Donovan," he announced. "I'm a new investigator. Dr. Brulin said I would get everything I need here."

The woman typed something into her computer. A moment later she placed a form onto the counter between them. "Fill that out, please. Someone will call you today to get your picture ID taken care of. You'll use your ID to access any restricted areas you're permitted to enter."

Nick filled out the form as he stood at the counter. The receptionist watched him above the dark rims of her glasses, and he wondered if he should have found a seat before filling it out. He finished the absurdly detailed form and handed it to her.

"Sure you don't need anything else?" he asked, smiling.

"Cholesterol level? Kindergarten teacher's name?"

Her synthetic smile didn't waver. "No, this will be fine for now. Who is your contact, please?"

"Mr. Chernoff, I suppose."

She punched numbers into a phone and spoke into the receiver. "You may have a seat while you wait," she said as she disconnected.

Nick raised his eyebrows but said nothing. Entering SynTech every day was going to be a little different from his usual early-morning banter with Brett at the institute.

In the three weeks since Nick had met with Gregory, he had never wavered from his intention to pursue a career there. Things at the institute were over for him. The scene in Rogan's office Friday still burned when he thought about it. He had half a mind to follow up with a letter, to make certain Rogan understood what a big mistake he'd made.

Chernoff appeared and led Nick through the double doors and into the main hallway of the north wing. Chernoff pressed the "down" button.

"Is my office downstairs then?"

"You'll have an office in your lab."

They took the elevator down to Sublevel 2. Nick noted that there was one more level below them.

"What's on Sublevel 3?"

Chernoff met his question with several silent moments. "Restricted."

The hallway on Sublevel 2 glowed antiseptic white, except for the maroon doors leading into each lab. Three showerheads hung from the ceiling along the hall in case of a fire or a chemical burn. Chernoff led him to the second door down the hall and stopped in front of one of the maroon doors.

A man in light blue coveralls stood outside the door, prying the nameplate from the wall beside it. "Be out of your way in a second, Mr. Chernoff."

Nick glanced down at the maintenance man's toolbox and saw another nameplate lying on it: "Gene Therapy Lab, Nicholas Donovan, M.D., Ph.D." No other investigators were listed. The old plate popped off into the man's hands.

"Out with the old and in with the new, eh, Mr. Chernoff?" The man chuckled. Chernoff didn't respond.

Nick followed the old nameplate with his eyes and caught only the last few letters of the former occupant's name—"burn."

"What happened to the last investigator?" Nick asked. "Did he or she move up or move out of SynTech?"

Chernoff stepped around the worker. "Personnel changes are sometimes unexpected. This way, Dr. Donovan."

Inside the lab, Nick found a setup similar to his old lab at the institute. The perimeter of the room was lined with workstations, cabinets, and steel supports for mounted lights and toolbars above the lab benches. One large lab-bench island stood in the center of the room. Several lab chairs were scattered throughout the room.

"Private office back there," Chernoff said, pointing to a door on the back wall.

Nick nodded. "What now?"

"Dr. Brulin will call you up to his office."

Nick glanced at the closed door at the back of the lab. "Will I—" he began, but Chernoff was already on his way out.

Why was the place so chilly? It felt as if they had turned the entire building into one of the cold rooms where samples were kept inert.

He ran his hand along the polished black lab bench and swung a magnifier light on an adjustable steel arm. He'd oversee the proposal completion from here, checking and rechecking the research in his usual thorough way.

He headed back to the small, windowless office adjoining the lab. It felt like a coffin buried two levels down, in spite of the bright fluorescent lights. Several potted plants hung from the ceiling. Nick noted the clusters of tiny fiber-optic cables that brought sunlight down to his underground office. A computer desk and a couple of chairs sat crammed against each other in the tiny space. The computer was already turned on. The screen saver, an animated double helix strand of DNA, tumbled across the monitor.

So, this is it. I've made the switch into research for profit. He sat at the computer wondering what kind of software he would find on it and how long it would be before Gregory called him up.

It took only half an hour to make the office his—setting up his E-mail account, customizing his software settings, his task lists, and his goal review schedule. He pulled a few pictures from his briefcase and propped them up on the back edge of the desk. A framed shot of Kate and himself, taken at the beach last summer.

You're choosing between this job and me.

Nick shook his head at the memory. He'd find a way to make her understand later. He set another picture out, one of himself with Stanford Carlton, taken the night of Stanford's award ceremony last year. Nick studied the confident, easy way Stanford held the plaque. *That'll be me someday.*

The phone rang. "Dr. Donovan, this is Sonya Galasso, Dr. Brulin's assistant. He would like to see you now."

↶ ↶ ↶

Gregory stood and circled his desk when Nick entered the office. "Nick! I'm so happy to have you here," he said, shaking Nick's hand. "I hope your lab was satisfactory?"

"Sure, sure. It looks fine. The office, too."

"That's great," Gregory said. "Please, sit down."

Gregory's manner reminded Nick of the solicitous mortician at his uncle Colin's funeral.

Nick dropped into the leather chair in front of Gregory's massive desk. His gaze traveled around the corner office, appreciating the spaciousness and the two walls of windows, even if the sky outside was a dull gray. Unlike Sublevel 2, this office had plenty of natural light for the countless plants that hung from the ceiling. Nick smiled to himself. Probably needs the plants for oxygen. The sharp odor of cigar smoke hung in the room.

Gregory returned to his chair. "How is Kate these days?"

Nick raised his eyebrows. "She's great, thanks. I didn't know you knew we'd gotten married."

"Oh, yes, I knew," Gregory said, nodding rapidly. "Nick, I'm glad you've decided to join us. We've accomplished many things at SynTech, but we're just not doing enough yet. The world is being destroyed by disease. I mean to save the world through brilliant investigators like yourself. Together we will find a genetic cure for every disease that would attack humankind. What do you think of that?"

"Well, I think it's a—"

Gregory slapped his desk with an open palm, and the collection of figurines jumped. He leaned forward. "We will not be driven to extinction like other species before us. We will be the first species to take a guiding role in our own evolution. Hence, we will live forever."

Nick kept his face emotionless at this speech, fighting the urge to look around for the rest of the audience. Gregory Brulin was certainly passionate about his work. But passion was fine with Nick. He could get excited about working for a man who was so committed to the progress of the human race.

"Let me outline where we are at present, Nick," Gregory said. "We have a big promotional push going on at the center. This Saturday, we're offering what we're calling Genetic Awareness Day. We've invited certain people who cannot afford gene therapy to come in and receive their treatment for free."

Nick raised his eyebrows. "You're giving away your therapies? Isn't that a little hard on the profit margin?"

"SynTech is not just about profit, Nick. We want to see a healthier population out there."

Nick smiled. "I'm glad to hear it. That's certainly not what I've always thought biotech companies were like."

Gregory relaxed against the back of his chair. "I hope you'll continue to learn how much we care about the health of society."

"So you're giving your therapies away Saturday," Nick said. "Do I need to get involved there?"

"No. I'd like you to understand the process, but most of the work has been done already, and I have a competent director at the center. We're hoping to boost public awareness of gene therapy, take it to the next level of acceptance."

Nick nodded. "It's good marketing strategy."

"I've decided to have you finish the prep work for the next gene transfer proposal we plan to submit to the NIH and FDA."

"What therapy?"

"Fabry's disease."

Nick frowned. "I thought I was going to be put on cancer research."

"I know, and I'm sorry. But we've had—a problem. One of our key researchers, the one who had been working on the Fabry's proposal, is no longer with us. As you can imagine, that has put us in a bind on the Fabry's trial. I'd like you around to bring it through the clinical trials. But once we get FDA approval and put it on the market, we'll shift you into cancer research, okay? The proposal is scheduled for submission to the FDA in three weeks."

"Three weeks? Is it ready?"

"There have been some—complications. Most of the secondary portions are complete, the Informed Consent Document, the scientific and non-technical abstracts. The protocol description needs work."

Nick's mind whirled. "Dr. Brulin, three weeks—"

"Gregory, please. Call me Gregory. The lab you've moved into belonged to that investigator. His team will help you finish the protocol."

"Gregory, I'm not sure I can put the proposal together in

three weeks, no matter what progress has been made. It will take time just to understand the protocol."

Gregory closed his eyes, pressing two fingertips of each hand against his eyelids.

Nick waited in silence, noticing for the first time the imposing grandfather clock in the corner of the room, its pendulum swinging a hypnotic rhythm.

"Nicholas," Gregory finally said, his eyes still covered. "I have watched your career over the past few years and have grown confident that you are the right man for senior vice president of Cancer Research—in spite of our problems in the past."

He looked up. "But my confidence in you will be severely shaken if I find you are not willing to step up to a challenge. Perhaps I was mistaken in believing you capable of the senior vice president position? Perhaps your abilities are better suited to remaining in the Sublevel research labs?" His dark eyebrows lifted, nearly meeting in the center.

Nick smiled and shook his head. "It will be ready in three weeks."

CHAPTER 13

At noon Nick headed for the SynTech cafeteria, his thoughts on the Fabry's proposal. Gregory had outlined his responsibilities, and the deadline loomed large. He would meet Gregory again at the end of the day. In the meantime, he had some time to get familiar with the therapy that the team in his lab would be working on. Other teams had already submitted their various contributions to the project. It remained for Nick to put all the pieces together.

The huge cafeteria bustled with SynTech employees crowding around each of the different stations serving food. Nick stopped inside the door, remembering the tiny lunch counter at the university's Student Center. Here chefs prepared sandwiches to order; stir-fried Chinese food for customers; grilled burgers; and frequently refilled the salad, fruit, and dessert bars. There were iced sodas, hot coffees, and bottled water. The food court narrowed to a cashier's counter, and then the room opened into a high-ceilinged, multiwindowed dining room, filled with round tables.

Nick grabbed a tray, ordered a chicken sandwich, and got an iced tea. After paying, he surveyed the dining room. The noise level was high, with clusters of employees at most of the tables. Nick found an empty table.

The sandwich was just the right amount of spicy, but Nick didn't want to linger. Anxiety over being ready for FDA trials in three weeks had already set in. Gregory had arranged meetings for him with the different teams working on the protocol, but it still seemed impossible. Gregory had to know what he was asking. Was this some kind of test to see if Nick was more capable than he had been as a student? It didn't matter: Nick planned to pass the test. He had every intention of becoming senior vice president in record time.

Twenty minutes later, Nick opened the door to his lab. He saw a figure in a white coat bending over one of the lab benches. "Can I help you?" Nick asked, already sounding territorial about his lab.

The man straightened and looked up at Nick. Stringy, dark hair fell to his shoulders, and his skin had a slightly yellow cast. If not for the lab coat, Nick would have assumed he was a patient in a clinical trial. "I guess that's supposed to be the other way around."

The door closed behind Nick with a hiss and a click that sounded like they had been vacuum-packed into the room.

"Excuse me?" Nick said.

"I guess they're expecting me to help you," the young man said. "I'm Jeremy Butler. One of your investigators."

Nick crossed the distance and offered his hand. Jeremy eyed it for a moment before offering his own, without enthusiasm.

"You been here long, Jeremy?" Nick asked, crossing over to his office.

"About twenty minutes."

Nick laughed, but Jeremy wasn't smiling. "No, I mean at SynTech."

"About three years."

"Three years? You don't look more than twenty. How old are you?"

"How old are you?"

"Look," Nick said, "this isn't going the way I wanted. Sorry I had an attitude when I saw you here."

Jeremy shrugged.

"Tell you what," Nick said, "why don't you come into the office, and we can sit down and talk?"

Jeremy followed him in. "I'm supposed to fill you in on the project." His voice had a strange monotone quality, as though he were talking in his sleep.

"Great." Nick pointed to a chair. "Have a seat."

Jeremy slipped into the chair. "We're working on a therapy for Fabry's disease."

Nick expected him to yawn at any moment. "Right."

"Fabry's disease is a lysosomal storage disease—"

"I'm familiar with the disease, Jeremy. Is the Objectives and Rationale section of the proposal finished?"

Jeremy looked annoyed at the interruption. "Fabry's disease is a good candidate for gene therapy because—"

"Have you been involved in this research, Jeremy?" Nick asked.

"Yes."

"What was the name of the principal investigator on this project?"

"Um, it was Dr. Brian Milburn."

"What can you tell me about him?"

"He was a good guy." Jeremy looked at his shoes. "There's another research assistant, too. But she's out sick today."

"Okay. We've got a lot of work to do, Jeremy. Did you know that Dr. Brulin wants us to submit the proposal in three weeks?"

This time Jeremy did yawn.

"Are all of Dr. Milburn's files on the computer?" Nick asked.

"I guess."

Nick turned toward the computer. "All right. Then I suppose I'll spend some time getting acquainted with the project." He looked at Jeremy. "Why don't you. . .work on the preclinical study descriptions, please?"

Jeremy left the office.

Nick shook his head and concentrated on surfing his computer. The first thing to do would be to find the files. He clicked his way into the hard drive's contents and scanned the list of folders. Whoever had come before Nick had been compulsively systematic. Folders, subfolders, and subfolders within them contained hundreds of files spreading out from the root like a planned community.

He checked for a personal journal folder, but if there had been one, it had been cleaned out. Since Nick's first day as a researcher, he had kept a journal of his work. Every researcher he knew did the same. There were always official research reports to keep, but his journal was a place to jot down any insights he had during the course of a day, hunches he wanted to follow up, even daydreams about where the research could take them. Several years ago he had started creating his daily entries on his computer rather than by hand.

He accessed the Recycle Bin to see if any deleted files from a journal might be in there. It was also empty. Either Milburn had been extremely fastidious or someone had cleaned house before Nick's arrival.

He spent the rest of the day scrolling through hundreds of pages of research. Occasionally he'd send a few pages to the printer, letting them form a neat stack. Jeremy stayed busy in the lab, and for today Nick didn't really care what the kid was doing.

One paragraph caught Nick's attention because it didn't make sense. It was in a file on the retrovirus Milburn had planned to use for his treatment: "I've just come from the speech tonight. The tainted therapies are already arriving."

He heard a step outside the office door. Jeremy poked his head through the door. "I'm leaving."

Nick rubbed his eyes and looked at his watch. It was already five. His eyes were burning from the on-screen reading, and his mind was drowning in two years' worth of research. "Well, could you stick around for a few minutes? I have some questions."

"Whatever."

"I'll be right out."

Jeremy shut the door, and Nick focused again on the computer. He read the strange paragraph in full: "I've just come from the speech tonight. The tainted therapies are already arriving. This has gone on long enough. I am going to the FDA."

There was nothing more like that in the file. Nick checked

dates on other files. The note he'd read had been the last entry created.

What in the world was all that about? It was the kind of entry that belonged in a personal journal, not in a research file. Why had Milburn put it here? What did he mean by "tainted therapies"? And what could have made him so upset that he was going to go to the FDA? Nick suddenly needed to know more about Brian Milburn.

He closed the file and reentered the lab. He gave a casual yawn and leaned an elbow on the waist-high lab bench. Jeremy was working at the centrifuge unit, a three-foot-high metal box that was used to spin vials of substances to purify them.

"I think I've gotten the big picture," he said. "Those files were hefty, though."

Jeremy grunted, not lifting his eyes from the centrifuge.

"What can you tell me about Dr. Milburn?" Nick asked.

Jeremy began closing up the unit. "He was the investigator who was here before you."

"Right. Well, what kind of guy was he?"

"Why do you want to know?" Jeremy asked.

"Just curious."

Finally, Jeremy shrugged. "He was okay."

"Did he, I don't know, ever mention anything about him being suspicious about anything here?"

"Suspicious?"

"Yeah, you know, like something that he might go to the FDA about? Unsafe lab procedures or overspending or tainted therapies, or anything?"

Jeremy's forehead wrinkled. "No. Why would he?"

"Oh, no reason. Just wondering."

Jeremy finished cleaning up. "You need me for anything more?"

The phone rang in Nick's office.

"I guess not," he said. "See you tomorrow."

It was Sonya, Gregory's secretary, on the phone. "Dr. Donovan, Dr. Brulin will be ready to see you in about twenty minutes. Will that work for you?"

"I'll be there, Sonya. Thank you."

Nick returned to the lab. Jeremy was gone.

He returned to the computer and checked his E-mail. He finally took a moment to read the day's Success Quote: "Being successful takes massive, determined action. You can achieve anything if you work hard enough to get it."

A sharp knock out in the lab surprised him. The door buzzed and swung open before he could react. He stood and went out into the lab. A tiny elderly woman backed into the lab, pulling a cart behind her. Nick watched in silence, amused.

"Can I help you?" he finally asked when the door threatened to squash her.

She responded with a muttered curse and a brisk kick at the backswinging door.

Nick crossed the lab and reached the door just as the cart broke loose and made its entry into the room.

"Yeah, sure, now you get the door," the old woman said, pulling the cart beside him.

She wore a green-and-white apron over her clothes and antiseptic white shoes. At her waist, a ring of keycards swung like the iron keys of a jailer. Several containers of water rested on her cart. A pressurized watering can was tucked in beside them, with a hose leading to one of the containers.

"Well, are you going to let me get to it or aren't you?" She waved a hand toward the potted ficus tree behind Nick.

He stepped aside, smothering a smile with a discreet cough. She was like an aging hospital candy striper gone bad. He leaned against the door frame of his private office. "Do you water the plants every night?"

"You don't see them dying, do you?" She swiped at a browning leaf and tucked it into her apron pocket.

Nick shook his head. "I'm Nick Donovan, by the way. I'm new here."

She turned from the plant as though confused. "Yeah? So?"

Nick studied her worn face. She was probably close to sixty-five or seventy, but the years had not been kind.

"So, what's your name?"

A line or two softened around her mouth for a moment. "Nobody ever asks my name. It's Frieda." The hard edge returned to her voice. "Why? You gonna complain about me? You think I want to be pulling this thing around at my age?"

"No, Frieda, I'm not going to complain. It looks like you're doing a great job. I just wanted to get to know the woman taking such good care of my plants."

Frieda's shoulders set against his flattery. She pulled the cart to a hanging plant and squirted water into the pot. "I just do my job," she said. "No more. No less. Don't you have better things to do than harass an old woman?"

"Nah, I've just got some time to kill and a weakness for grouchy old ladies."

"Hmph."

Nick watched her for another moment, until she caught him staring. What kind of life must a person lead to turn old-age sour like that? He smiled at her suspicious frown, but she turned away.

A moment later she tugged at the cart, attempting a U-turn back toward the door. A soft moan escaped as the cart resisted. "Blasted arthritis."

"Let me get that for you, Frieda," Nick said. Before she could object, he pulled the cart across the lab and through the door.

She shook her head on the way out, mumbling to herself. "Next thing you know, they'll be complaining to the boss I'm bothering them. And wouldn't 'Dr. Brutal' just love that." She pushed the cart out of Nick's hands and moved on.

"Thank you, Frieda," Nick said to her back. She waved him off without turning around.

Nick let the door close and laughed out loud. *At least she's a little more real than most of the people here.* Maybe a daily dose of kindness would break down a few heavily fortified barriers. After collecting his things, he turned out the lights, locked his office door, and headed for the elevator.

Sonya was pouring coffee as he stepped out onto the third floor. She smiled and nodded to him.

"Can I get you some fresh coffee, Dr. Donovan?"

He shook his head.

Sonya returned to her desk and announced him to Gregory. They entered the spacious office together, and Sonya handed Gregory a gold-rimmed mug.

Gregory gave her a quick smile and nod. "Thank you, Sonya. Have a seat, Nick."

When Sonya was gone, Gregory lowered the mug and folded his hands on the desk in front of him. "So how'd your first day go, Nick?"

Nick sat down, noticing that the little figurines on the desk had been rearranged since he was last in the office. "Went fine, sir," Nick answered. "The research has been thorough."

"Good. So you think our deadline is attainable?"

"Absolutely," Nick said, sounding more confident than he was.

"Excellent. I knew you were the right man for the job." Gregory was silent for a moment, his long fingers stroking a small figurine on his desk. "Do you know who Osiris was, Nick?"

"A Greek god, wasn't he?"

"Egyptian. The patron of the underworld. He was resurrected by his wife, Isis, with the Ritual of Life." Gregory held up the figurine.

Nick examined it politely. It looked like a greenish mummified pharaoh to him.

"Do you believe in the old gods, Nick?" Gregory asked.

"I'm not sure what you mean."

"Do you believe they were real, that they really existed?"

Nick cleared his throat. The faraway look in Gregory's eyes troubled him. He moved his gaze to a hanging plant in the corner. "Uh, no, I guess I don't. Not really."

Gregory set the figure down with a thud. "That's a shame," he said. "You could learn much from them."

Nick nodded slowly, shifting in the black leather chair.

"I won't keep you, Nick," Gregory said. "I'm sure you're eager to get home to your beautiful wife."

"Thank you, Gregory."

When Nick closed the door behind him, Sonya was typing at her computer. She looked up to give him a quick smile. On a hunch, he strolled over to her desk. "He's intimidating, isn't he?"

Sonya swiveled in her chair. "He can be, yes." She smiled. "But he has a kinder side, too. He has helped me so much."

"Perhaps I will take some of that coffee you offered earlier."

"Of course!" Sonya rose.

Nick held up a hand. "I can get it. Don't let me interrupt."

"Aren't you sweet."

He poured the coffee. "I suppose I should be rushing back to the lab instead of going home. I have more work than I can possibly finish by the time he'd like it done." Nick inclined his head toward Gregory's office, as though he and Sonya were co-conspirators.

"I'm sure you'll do fine," she said.

Nick sighed. "It would help so much if I could talk to Dr. Milburn, though."

Sonya shook her head. "I'm sure it would. It's such a shame, isn't it? His poor wife and children. Did you know he had four children?"

Nick made himself appear nonchalant. He sipped his coffee. "No, I didn't. How long has it been now since he died?"

"Oh, nearly three weeks already, I suppose."

Nick shook his head. "You just never know, do you?"

Sonya nodded, lost in thought.

"I'd better be going, Sonya," Nick said. "Thanks for the java."

"Anytime, Dr. Donovan."

‿ ‿ ‿

Nick leaned forward on the public library's wooden chair, searching the news wires for articles related to Dr. Brian Milburn. An Internet search had yielded the date of his death, but no details. Now a headline caught his attention.

"Geneticist dies in auto crash. Dr. Brian Milburn, 39, of Paoli, died yesterday when he apparently lost control of his car and drove into Silver Lake off Quarry Road. Police say the exact cause of the accident will be investigated. Milburn, a genetic researcher at SynTech Labs, is survived by his wife, Andrea, and four children. Milburn had been recognized in his field. . ."

Nick finished the article and then sat back in his chair.

The library was noisy with chatter from teenagers who were supposed to be studying. A white-haired lady behind the circulation desk shushed them. Nick blocked out the noise and focused on the newspaper, trying to wring out more information than it contained.

A car accident. That was all it was. Nothing unusual. The combination of the mysterious "tainted therapies" note, his vow to go to the FDA, and his sudden demise had made Nick instantly suspicious. Now it just seemed coincidental.

He searched the following few days' worth of news wire reports. Certainly if the investigation had turned up dubious circumstances, that would've been news. However, he found nothing more.

He didn't have time for chasing the wind. Already he regretted leaving the lab with so much work to be done on the proposal. If he pursued whatever it was that had made Milburn want to go to the FDA, he might miss Gregory's deadline and never see "Senior Vice President" after his name.

Snow was falling as Nick left the library, and cold fingers of dread wrapped around him. Checking into Milburn's death had unsettled him. He feared only one thing more than failure. An unreasoning panic he had fought against all his life rose once again to choke him. Nick Donovan was not prepared to die.

Brian Milburn Journal Entry #1
January 26

Writing in diaries is for little girls and sentimental women. This isn't a diary. It's an investigative journal. At least that's what I'm telling myself to keep from falling into melodrama.

Detective Sam Spade here, ready to take on the seamy underside of SynTech Labs and wrestle its secrets into the light.

(So much for escaping melodrama. And something tells me Sam Spade wouldn't chronicle his investigation in a bright yellow, spiral-bound notebook pinched from his teenage son's bookbag.)

Certainly, I'm making far too much of all of this, and before many days pass, I'll be burning this notebook in embarrassment. In the meantime, though, I plan to record my actions here, to journal my findings each night when I come home.

So how did I find myself in the unenviable role of detective? Quite innocently, while searching through the cold storage lab on Sublevel 2. I almost wish I had merely found what I was looking for and headed back to my lab. Instead, I opened a container on the back of the shelves and happened upon something I couldn't ignore.

Why would the cold storage lab have a container of therapies labeled "Version 2"? When did any of our therapies get approved for different versions—much less all of them? What's different about the second versions?

I grabbed the first one I was familiar with, the therapy for Gaucher's disease, and slipped it into my pocket like a shoplifter. Just in time, too. That uptight, little lab rat, Louis Ward, tiptoed into cold storage and nearly gave me a stroke.

Taking advantage of his presence, I asked about the Version 2 vectors. If anyone would know anything about it, he would.

"These particular therapies," he says in that nervous

whine of his, "are not to be delivered until next month, when certain patients will begin receiving therapies better suited for their particular condition." I wonder how many times per day the man uses the word "particular."

"Thanks, Lou," I say, slapping him on the back and nearly knocking off his spectacles. And then I escape.

I would have liked to sequence some of those vectors right then, but it was quitting time, and Andrea needed me home on time tonight. So it sits in cold storage in my lab, waiting for Sam Spade to arrive tomorrow morning.

But I can say one thing for sure: Whatever's different about those vectors, it's not approved by the FDA. And that can't be good.

CHAPTER 14

Tears dripped from Kate's chin as she threw the last few pairs of pants on top of the jumble of clothes in her suitcase. She glanced around the room a final time. On impulse she grabbed a framed picture from her nightstand: her and Nick on their honeymoon in St. Thomas.

A wave of sadness lapped over her, and she flopped onto the bed, the frame in her hand. "Oh, Nick," she said into the air. "What am I doing? Is it worth it?"

She glanced at his nightstand. Only a stack of medical journals, a notepad, and a pen lay there.

It's your own fault, Nick. If you hadn't tricked me to get me to agree to this job, I wouldn't be doing this.

She laid the picture between the clothes in her suitcase and zipped it, standing it next to the other two suitcases she'd already packed. A muffled sob escaped her lips, but she determined not to give in to the crying until she had left.

Kate drove across Philadelphia, through the snow, to her sister's colonial-style home. The sprawling, two-hundred-year-old farmhouse, complete with a roofed porch, had an enormous yard bordered on three sides by woods. A small barn behind the house was home to two goats, a pony, three chickens, and a rooster, which her brother-in-law kept more as pets than for any practical purpose.

Melanie threw the door open as soon as Kate pulled up the winding driveway. Her sister's long blond hair was as straight as Kate's red hair was curly.

"Kate!" Melanie let the screen door bang behind her as she rushed through the snow to her sister's car. She nearly lifted Kate off the ground in her hug. "It's so great to see you. You should have called—I would have made a special dinner!"

Kate tried to smile. "I didn't want to talk about it over the phone." She glanced into the backseat at her suitcases.

Melanie followed her eyes. "What are you doing, Kate? Are you leaving Nick?" Panic edged her voice. She grabbed Kate's hand and nearly dragged her out of the falling snow and into the house.

Inside, Kate took a moment to close her eyes and take in the scents and sounds of her sister's home. How could this place feel more like home than her own home did? Here in the vestibule of Melanie's house, with the smell of a wood fire burning, the pleasant aroma of cookies baking, and the sounds of children's laughter drifting down the stairs, she knew that this was all she had ever wanted.

Melanie pulled her into the den. A fire was blazing in the big stone fireplace. Kate settled into an overstuffed chair beside it, hoping to shake off the chill of the weather.

Melanie laid a quilt on Kate's lap and then sat down across from her. "What's going on?"

Kate shivered. "I don't know, Mel. It's Nick's first day at his new job. We—"

"Wait. This is the new job you told me about on the phone, right? At Synthetic-something or another?"

"SynTech. Right, it's the one I told you about."

Melanie's look was still anxious. "So you can't be here because he's gone to his first day of work. I thought you wanted him to take the new job."

"I did. Until I found out his promise to start a family was just a trick to convince me this job change would be a good thing."

Melanie's mouth fell open. "What? No."

"Yes, Mel, I'm serious. It was just a trick. He told me we could start a family if he took this job, so I encouraged him to take it. Then when he'd gotten the job, he said he'd changed his mind."

"No," Melanie said again. "That doesn't sound like Nick. There must be some other reason for what he said."

"I'm telling you, Mel, he never meant it in the first place. He just told me what he knew I wanted to hear so he could get his way."

Melanie put her hand over Kate's. "So you've left him?"

Kate moaned and let her head fall back against the chair. "I know, I know. I should be happy for him, right? A new job. Lots more money. We should be celebrating. Instead, I left him a note on the kitchen counter and nothing but frostbitten pizza in the freezer." She lifted her head. "Mel, I've got to wake him up somehow!"

Melanie shook her head and gave Kate's hand a squeeze before letting go. "I'm so sorry, Kate. I know how important it is to you. I just can't believe it." She bit her lip. "But even if it's true, do you really think leaving Nick will have the effect you're wanting? How do you know it's going to make him suddenly want to have children if he doesn't want to already?"

Kate felt her eyes fill up. "I don't know what else to do. Now he's making it sound like it's the new job that's preventing him. But he could have stayed at the university, cut back his hours to a normal schedule. When he left for his new job today, it was like a slap in my face. I told him he was choosing between his career and me." Kate wiped the tears from her face with the back of her hand and looked up at Melanie.

"Kate," Melanie said, "I'm not sure this is a good idea."

"I am." Kate shook her head. "I think. Maybe. I don't know."

"Oh, Kate," Melanie said, pulling her sister into a hug. "What a mess."

"I've thought about, you know, just letting it happen. Getting pregnant, I mean. But then I think about Dad." Kate looked at her hands. "About all those weekends when it was his turn to take us, but he was too busy. I would never want my child to feel her daddy was too busy for her, like we did. I just don't know what to do."

Mel shifted in her chair. "Kate, honey, I want to talk to you about God right now." She lifted her hand to prevent Kate's reply. "I know you and I don't always come from the same place when it comes to spiritual things, but I have to tell you that for me, Jesus holds all the answers. And I know He has answers for you, too. Will you let me talk with you about God, Katie?"

Kate felt her jaw tighten. "Oh, Mel, I don't know. At this point, I'm willing to try almost anything. But I don't know if I'm ready to see God around every corner like you do. Because I don't think He's watching every step I take. To be honest, I don't know if God really cares about my marriage at all."

Melanie shook her head. "Of course He does, Kate. Because He cares about you. He loves you more than anyone else in the world does."

Kate smiled weakly. "That sounds nice. Still, I'm not like you, Melanie. I don't think bringing God into everything solves the problem."

"It doesn't solve every problem, not automatically. But He gives you the ability to make it through your problems. Oh, Kate," Melanie said, looking at the floor. "If only you knew how much He wants you to come to Him."

"Mel. . ."

"Okay, okay," Mel said, shaking her head. "Well, can I say that I believe the vows you and Nick made to each other before God were sacred? My thought is that God would probably not want you to threaten to break those vows just so you can, you know, get what you want."

Kate sat up straight. "You think I'm here because I'm trying to manipulate Nick into doing what I want? You think I'm trying to punish him for his manipulation by manipulating him back?"

"Well, aren't you?"

Kate winced. "Well. . .wow, it sounds selfish when you put it that way."

"You picked the words, sis, not me."

"It isn't like that, though. I don't think."

Melanie looked at the fire. "I'm sure everything will work out fine."

"Oh, no, you don't, Mel. Don't start sugarcoating it now. I

may not always like what you have to say, but you know I count on you to tell me the truth."

Melanie smiled. "I think you already know the truth, Kate, but I'll spell it out for you, anyway. I think that you coming here is just a selfish, manipulative way to get what you want."

Kate had to laugh. "Ouch. Can I have the sugarcoating back, please?"

"Hey, you asked! Besides, I care too much to stand by and say nothing. Yes, if what you say is true, Nick did a stupid, selfish thing. It makes me want to give him a piece of my mind, that's for sure. But I can't believe that your leaving him is the right answer." She squeezed Kate's hand. "I'm afraid you might be making the biggest mistake of your life."

༞ ༞ ༞

Nick couldn't make himself pay attention to the medical seminar CD he was listening to, so he turned it off. He exited the highway, headed home from the library. His mind wouldn't turn off about Brian Milburn's death. *Something doesn't add up. What had made Milburn want to go to the FDA?*

When he pulled into his driveway, he saw that their townhouse was dark inside. Kate was usually home by now. Had she gotten held up at the institute?

He dropped his coat on the couch inside the door and went to the steps. "Kate?" He could see their bedroom from the bottom of the steps. It was dark. Nick walked past the piano, through the dining room, and around the corner into the empty kitchen. He checked the machine in the kitchen for messages, glancing out the sliding glass door at the back of the townhouse. No messages and no Kate.

He wondered if he should start dinner. He knew how to cook a few things. Pasta, mainly. He forced aside a little annoyance that Kate hadn't been here to welcome him home after his first day at a new job. The morning hadn't gone well, but she usually came around after a few hours. He'd hoped she would at least try to be supportive.

He flipped the light on and saw the note on the counter. It was in an envelope, propped up against a vase of artificial flowers. He stood across from it, his eyes fixed on the envelope for several moments. Kate often left him notes if she had a change of plans, but always on little scraps of paper they kept beside the phone. An envelope must mean it was something important.

He tore at the sealed flap with shaking fingers. He slid the flowered stationery out of the envelope.

> *Dear Nick,*
>
> *You can't imagine how painful this is for me. I never dreamed I'd be writing a note like this. You know I love you, but I can't keep going like this, in two different directions. And you hurt me so deeply with your trick about SynTech.*
>
> *Something has to change between us. But until it does I feel like we need to be apart. I'm not saying this is permanent, only that we both need time and space to think about our priorities. I hope that we can come to an agreement. Until then I'm going to stay at Melanie's. I love you. I don't know what else to do.*
>
> *Kate*

Nick dropped the letter and collapsed into a kitchen chair. She always had to make a dramatic statement, didn't she? He shook his head and sighed. After the scene this morning, it might take some talking to convince her to come home. However, she'd come home.

Wouldn't she? What if she were serious? *I should have been honest with her from the start.* Stupid. Nick dropped his head into his hands. The room grew fuzzy and disappeared. He loved her more than he'd ever loved anyone. Was she really willing to throw that away over a little disagreement?

What was he supposed to do? Give in to whatever she wanted so that she would come back? He couldn't. He had principles, too, and what he had told her this morning was still true: Right now he had to focus on his career if he wanted to be successful at SynTech. He didn't want to give his children second best. A family would have to wait until he could give them more.

Yet he couldn't live without Kate. He couldn't go through every day knowing the house would be empty when he came home. He couldn't live without her laugh, without the way she teased him and made him smile when he was frustrated, without the way she made him feel when she wrapped her arms around him and whispered into his ear.

He lifted his head and swiped at a tear. What could he do? He picked up her note again. "Two different directions," it said. That much was true. How could he convince her to wait a little longer?

Senior vice president. However, he had to make sure the job was going to work out, that he could meet Gregory's impossible deadline. Could he convince her to wait a little longer—till he was more established at SynTech?

He grabbed his jacket and headed for the Expedition. He would make any promise he needed to, and he would bring her home.

The drive to Melanie's should have taken forty minutes, but traffic was bad at this time of evening, and the snow had made the roads slippery. He tapped his thumbs against the steering wheel as a line of cars in front of him crawled through an intersection, too slowly for him to make it through the green light.

When he finally reached Melanie's neighborhood, he slid into the driveway and jumped from the car without even removing the keys. Melanie's husband, Scott, answered the front door after a few seconds of banging.

"Nick!" Scott stood in the doorway, blocking Nick's view. Nick hoped he wouldn't have to push past his brother-in-law, though he knew he could take on the slightly built guy without a problem.

"Is she here?"

"Yeah, but—"

"Let me in, Scott." Scott stepped aside, and Nick strode into the living room. Kate and Melanie were curled up in chairs in front of the stone fireplace. Kate jumped up, dropping a quilt to the floor.

"Nick!"

"What are you doing here, Kate?" Nick asked. He had meant to sound distraught, but he knew he just sounded angry.

"You read my note. You know why I'm here."

Nick stood his ground near the doorway. "This is crazy. We can work this out. Just come home."

"Uncle Nick!" A flash of pink with dark braids flew around him and then up into his arms.

"Hello, Anna." He smiled, catching her.

"Uncle Nick, you have to come out to the barn so I can show you the new baby bunnies that were just born 'cause they are so cute and—"

Melanie left her chair by the fire and came to the door. She pried the six year old's fingers from Nick's arms. "It's snowing outside, remember, sweetie? Come into the kitchen with Mommy for awhile. Uncle Nick and Aunt Kate want to talk. I'll get you some cookies."

Nick smiled in gratitude as Melanie and Scott left them in privacy.

Kate sat in her chair again. "We can't keep going like we have been, Nick. I can't live that way."

Nick stood behind the couch. He gripped the edge of it till his knuckles whitened. The room seemed to close in on him, with all its antique clutter hanging on the walls and scattered on every horizontal surface.

"Listen, Kate. Things went well today at SynTech. There's a

big project I have to concentrate on right away. But then I'll cut back and. . .we can talk about kids again."

Kate laughed coldly. "Give me a break, Nick. I've heard that before, remember?"

"It's only a few weeks, Kate."

"A few weeks, a few years!" Kate folded her arms. "I'm not falling for it anymore, Nick! Don't you get it? I'm not going to set all my hopes on your finishing one more project. I'm tired of putting my dreams on hold for you, get it? This time you have to change your priorities!"

Nick circled the couch. "Kate, listen—"

"I'm sick of listening! The only thing I want to hear is that you're ready to have a family no matter how much or how little you think you've accomplished in your career."

Nick was beside her, on his knees beside her chair. She pulled her legs up, wrapped her arms around them, and stared into the fire. Nick touched her hair where the firelight made it look like it was aflame, as well.

"Kate, come home," he whispered, suddenly overcome by the thought of going home alone.

She turned her gaze from the fire and looked down at him. "No."

CHAPTER 15

Tuesday, February 22

Gregory Brulin's Town Car pulled up to the curb of the New York City television studio. Gregory gathered his notes and stepped from the car into the slush of yesterday's snowfall.

The drive from Philadelphia to New York had given him enough time to prepare for the nationally televised interview, but not so much time that he'd gotten nervous.

One hour later, after the makeup people finished with him and his microphone was clipped to his suit jacket, the staff deposited Gregory onto the set beside Justin Hardegan of the Hendricks Forum.

Hardegan was an overweight, blustering figurehead, past his prime but still the public face of right-wing fanaticism for the press. Gregory had taken care not to speak to Hardegan since he'd entered the studio. Now he focused on a spot on the beige wing chair where he sat, angled toward the fireplace, with its gas fire and fake mantel. Hardegan sat opposite him in another wing chair. Cameras rolled into place, and lights were switched on. Gregory felt the heat of the lights pulsing onto the top of his head, threatening to melt the makeup they'd insisted he wear. The studio's crew faded into the dusky background behind the lights.

Laura Daniels, the polished, blond anchor of *The Morning Show*, dropped to the couch across from them. "Are you both comfortable with the outline we went over?" She smoothed her tailored suit.

Hardegan beamed at Laura. "Let's have at it."

The floor director counted down and pointed, and Laura studied the camera with a concerned, yet sincere expression.

"Gene therapy," she said. "It's become as much a routine in some parts of the country as childhood immunizations. But concerns and arguments continue to swirl around this controversial issue, and as technology opens new vistas before us, we find ourselves still challenged by the question, 'What makes us human?' "

Laura adjusted her position and nodded across the set toward them. "We have visiting with us today two of the leading voices on both sides of the issue. Dr. Gregory Brulin, Chairman and CEO of SynTech Labs, and Dr. Justin Hardegan, Dean of the Hendricks Forum, a Christian think tank. Gentlemen, welcome."

"Glad to be here, Ms. Daniels," Hardegan said.

"Thank you," Gregory said.

"So, doctors," Laura said, "it seems we have a preview this morning of tomorrow night's formal face-off at the BioEthics Symposium's annual banquet. I understand they've scheduled the two of you for a debate?"

Hardegan nodded. "That's right. Guess they're not afraid of a few fireworks over there, are they?"

Laura turned to Gregory. "Dr. Brulin, let's start with you. SynTech Labs has proved itself a company to watch over the past few years, bringing out several groundbreaking new gene therapies and being hailed as the fastest-growing biotech company in the country. To what do you attribute the success of your efforts?"

Gregory saw the red light go on atop one of the cameras. He spoke right into that camera. "Laura, we live in an exciting time in history. Never before have we understood disease so well or had the tools within our grasp to eliminate it. SynTech has succeeded because we firmly believe in the power of humans to shape their destiny. As early intervention into disease continues, we will see a healthier population emerge over the next few decades." He leaned back into the couch for emphasis. "Who knows what that healthier society will be able to accomplish without the encumbrance of disease holding us back."

Laura turned to his opponent. "Dr. Hardegan?"

Hardegan clasped his hands in front of him, studying them as if giving serious consideration to his words. Gregory resisted the urge to roll his eyes. Hardegan nodded finally, as though ready to deliver his vital message.

"I must agree with Dr. Brulin on one point. This is a new age, a different world. But it is a world that has drifted from its foundations, that has forgotten its roots. Dr. Brulin must focus our attention on the fantastic cures being offered, because only then are we diverted from the fundamental questions we should be asking. Where will all this tampering end? What kind of world will we create?"

"Dr. Hardegan, what specific concerns do you have?" Laura asked, her voice carefully neutral.

"I'm glad you asked that, Laura. Very glad you asked. We've taken what little knowledge we have in this area, and we've run with it, with no knowledge of the outcome. In gene therapy specifically, Dr. Brulin and those like him are claiming to 'fix' a faulty genetic sequence. But how can we know that at the same time they are not disturbing another sequence that relates to a different gene? I'm sure Dr. Brulin would point out that research has overwhelmingly shown that genes are not independent, separate units. The body is interdependent. We don't know what kind of damage we may be doing. By our meddling we might accidentally—"

"Dr. Hardegan's argument is not a new one," Gregory said. "In fact, people were saying the same thing years ago about every new pharmaceutical product put on the market. What about the side effects? And just as with conventional drug therapy, we do our best to test and make safe decisions. Will there be problematic side effects? Will mistakes be made? Quite possibly, as there have been with all medical research. But we learn from our mistakes, and overall, we move forward to create something better. To solve problems. To give people more normal lives."

Laura nodded. Gregory crossed one leg over another. He had the sense that he'd won the first round.

"Normal?" Hardegan asked. "More normal lives, Dr. Brulin? That raises some very serious questions, doesn't it, Laura? What is normal? Who decides? There are many people out there watching us at this moment whom society has termed 'abnormal,' but who take great exception to the label. How are we to distinguish what 'norm' everyone should be held to? Is there, indeed, any such norm at all?"

"Dr. Hardegan," Gregory said, shifting in his seat. "Perhaps you should meet with the parents of a child suffering from a chronic or terminal disease and tell them they shouldn't be 'meddling' with their child's situation. I see this situation every day at SynTech's Gene Therapy Center. I promise you, Dr. Hardegan, they would tell you that no one has the right to impose some arbitrary idea of 'normal' on anyone."

"My point exactly, Dr. Brulin, thank you." Hardegan looked at the show's host. "Dr. Brulin would have us move forward with genetic interfering with no regard to the ethical issues at all."

Laura discreetly consulted her notes. "But, Dr. Hardegan, doesn't the federal government have committees in place to prevent abuses? For instance, the Recombinant DNA Activities Committee—wasn't it established to spell out guidelines on all these issues?"

Hardegan sat forward. "That's what so many people don't understand, Laura. They think the government's keeping a watchful eye on all this, regulating all these scientists so that they don't do anything that would destroy society. That is simply not so! These committees oversee how federal funds are spent on research. Federal funds. That's all." Hardegan waved a hand at Gregory. "Meanwhile, Dr. Brulin and others in industry are funding their horrific experiments with society's money."

Gregory chuckled. "Dr. Hardegan, we are not a mob of Dr. Frankensteins, creating genetic monsters in our laboratories!"

"Perhaps," Hardegan said, turning slowly to Gregory. "But how do we know that?"

"Dr. Hardegan," Laura said, "I believe that even you would agree that gene therapy is here to stay, wouldn't you? If there's no getting away from it, where do we go from here?"

"I'll tell you where we'll go if tight controls aren't placed on researchers," Hardegan said. "We'll move into an era in which our genetic makeup will become public property. Health care coverage will be denied certain people based on predispositions to disease. Predispositions, mind you. You might never contract the disease, but you wouldn't be able to get health insurance because one day you might contract it. Employers will discriminate based on DNA information about intelligence or social behavior. Marriage partners will be chosen based on genetic compatibility."

Gregory shook his head. "This scenario—"

"The psychological impact of knowing one's likely time and cause of death will cripple us," Hardegan said. "Children will be stigmatized, segregated, according to their DNA profiles. And as the richest of us are able to afford to create 'perfect' babies, and the poorest are left with what God gives, a class system such as this planet has never seen will develop, with two almost entirely distinct races—the natural and the genetically enhanced. Guess which one will rule, Laura."

Laura sat back and turned to Gregory, eyebrows raised. "How do you respond to that, Dr. Brulin?"

Gregory sighed. "No human being has any wish to see the world become what Dr. Hardegan has described. But his bleak, science-fiction portrayal of the future ignores one important factor: Genetic progress is not being forced upon us. We, as human beings, finally have the tools at our disposal to create our own future. It is an opportunity to be embraced, not a future to be avoided."

He smiled into the camera. "As we perfect this technology and determine how to use it, I have faith in our strength as humans to firmly hold to the values and, yes, characteristics, that we as a world society deem worth perpetuating. I'm afraid Dr. Hardegan has little faith in us as human beings. I choose to believe we will triumph."

"Oh, I have faith, Dr. Brulin," Hardegan said, "but it's not in—"

"I'm sorry to interrupt, Dr. Hardegan," Laura said, "but we're out of time. I thank both of you for your candid thoughts this morning."

﹏ ﹏ ﹏

As Nick circled the artificial lake on his way into SynTech Tuesday morning, he tried to push from his mind thoughts of the lonely townhouse and the silent morning. He refused to let Brian Milburn's suspicions distract him either.

He bypassed the executive parking lot and parked in Lot #3, where he could enter the building through the revolving doors closer to his lab. Nick let his forehead drop to the steering wheel.

Kate's absence was only a temporary setback, he tried to convince himself. If he could stay focused on the task for the next few weeks, he could prove himself to her and everything would go back to the way it was. Still, there was an unstable feeling in his heart where he had always felt secure. It had almost been enough to send him crawling back to bed this morning. A chilling thought struck him: Was he sacrificing a treasure to gain something worthless?

The gray stone of the building had absorbed the overnight dampness and somehow looked even darker than usual against the inch of new snow. Nick tried to shake the chill as he entered the building. The uniformed security guard stood as usual behind his tall desk, like a nameless concierge. His lips widened in an imitation of a smile as Nick approached the receptionist's desk to receive another badge for the day. Instead of the visitor's badge, she handed him his new photo ID keycard.

When Nick arrived in his lab, neither Jeremy nor the assistant he hadn't met were there. Nick felt the usual satisfaction at having arrived earlier than anyone else, but the thought brought a painful reminder of Kate. He flopped in front of the computer in his little office, accessing his E-mail account. He scrolled through messages, his mind elsewhere.

For the first time, he considered the idea that she could be right. Perhaps he was too focused on his career. Would this new job make him feel any more complete than his work at the institute had? This drive to achieve felt like it was built into him, part of his genetic makeup. Could it be a flaw in his personality? Did he need to relax and enjoy life more? He tried to recreate himself in his mind as a more relaxed "family man." Average house, average car. Middle income, middle aged. Meetings with the PTA instead of the FDA.

He couldn't do it. He didn't have it in him to be mediocre. Someday Kate would thank him. His Success Quote for the day confirmed his thoughts: "Create great expectations and the highest vision possible of yourself and your world. When you believe in yourself and your ability to succeed, nothing will stop you."

There was a message from Gregory on his voice mail.

"Nick, I'd like you to head over to the Gene Therapy Center this morning. Check the place out. A group of prospective clients will be there at eleven. I told Rich Nowinski, the center director, you'd give them the usual speech. Explain the basics of gene therapy, that sort of thing. Then take questions. Shouldn't take more than an hour. Thanks!"

Nick made a quick note to himself, irritated that the errand would interfere with his second day. How was he supposed to get this proposal done if Gregory had him running around giving lectures?

Through his open office door, Nick saw Jeremy slouch into the lab and don a lab coat. The young man waved and got to work. Several minutes later Nick heard the door swoosh open again. He saw Jeremy jerk his head up and push the long strands of hair away from his face—and actually smile at the newcomer.

"Morning, Bernice," Jeremy said.

Nick exited his office. Bernice looked like she was in her early twenties. Her brown hair was cropped close to her head, and she wore little makeup. She hung a waist-length wool coat on a hook beside the door and lifted a hand shyly in Jeremy's general direction. Her attention turned to Nick, and she squinted at him through thick, brown-rimmed glasses.

"Good morning," he said, crossing the lab. "I'm Nick Donovan."

"Oh, hi." She shook his hand nervously.

Nick noticed crooked teeth through her tentative smile. His glance returned to Jeremy, and he saw the unusual triangle they made: Jeremy grinning at Bernice, Bernice smiling shyly at Nick, and himself holding back laughter at the look on Jeremy's face. "Is this our assistant, Jeremy?"

"Huh? Oh, yeah, this is Bernice. Bernice, this is Dr. Donovan. He's our new researcher."

"Call me Nick, please."

Bernice giggled. "Okay." She hung a beat-up purse over the coat hook and took a lab coat from another hook.

"Jeremy and I were about to begin a strategy meeting. Please join us."

Bernice's eyes widened, as did Jeremy's, but Nick ignored the looks. Perhaps SynTech was a lifeless place to work, but inside this lab he could create something different.

CHAPTER 16

The smoky aroma of sizzling bacon greeted Kate when she descended Melanie's stairs into the Early American country kitchen.

Melanie stood with her back to Kate in front of the flat-topped stove, one of the few evidences that this wasn't an eighteenth-century farmhouse. She tonged strips of bacon into a deep skillet and then turned to give Kate a smile.

Kate watched Melanie in her element and felt the familiar twinge of jealousy. The kitchen was a showplace of Melanie's antiquing hobby. Polished copper-bottomed pots hung from iron hooks screwed into age-blackened ceiling beams, and every cranny overflowed with wicker baskets and homespun collectibles in faded reds and blues. A golden-white wooden swan graced the mantel above the stone fireplace that connected the kitchen and dining areas. Kate pulled out a high wooden stool from the island counter and settled in to watch Melanie cook.

"Orange juice?" Melanie asked.

"Sure. But I can get it." Kate slid off the stool.

"No, stay where you are," Melanie said. "You're the guest."

Kate smiled. "That's gracious of you, considering I'm not exactly an invited guest."

Melanie set the glass pitcher of juice down. "You know you never need an invitation, Kate."

Kate saw her sister's eyes glistening. "Mel, are you crying?"

"Oh, I'm sorry," Melanie said, wiping her eyes irritably. "It's just that it's killing me to see you and Nick like this. You should go home, Kate. I could see how he felt when he was here last night."

Kate picked up a small blue-and-white crock. "That's the problem, Mel. I know how he feels. His goals are always the most important thing to him. I can't live with that anymore."

"Can't? Or won't?"

Kate frowned.

Squeals of laughter flooded down the stairs. "Mommy, he's trying to get me!" Anna screamed and ran into the kitchen, her brother trailing by only a few feet. Eight-year-old Benjamin was fair like his mother, while Anna had inherited her father's dark hair. Anna buried her face in Melanie's back. Benjamin slid to a stop.

"It doesn't sound like you minded too much, Anna," her mother teased.

Anna suddenly faced her brother with the expression of a gladiator. "That's because I'm going to get him!" she yelled, leaping away from the protection of Melanie. Benjamin gave a yelp and fled the kitchen.

"Breakfast is almost ready!" Melanie called after them, laughing.

"Don't they have to be at school soon?" Kate said.

"The bus will be here in about a half hour." Melanie brought a plate of scrambled eggs to the pine dining table.

Kate jumped up again and began to set the table, pulling plates and mugs from a cabinet. Even Melanie's dishes made Kate feel as though she had stepped back in time. The blue-speckled crockery felt so much heavier than her flimsy department store dishes at home.

Scott turned up at the right moment and herded the kids into the kitchen. The group claimed chairs. Kate was serving herself eggs when she realized everyone had gotten quiet. Scott looked around the table at all of them, including Kate in his warm smile. Kate felt a surge of gratitude for the quiet, slightly built man who made her sister so happy.

"Dear God," Scott said.

Kate quickly screwed her eyes shut, only a moment after seeing Anna's big blue eyes staring up at her.

"Thank You for the blessings of the day," Scott said. "For family and for the food. We pray that we would bring honor to You in all we do today. Amen."

Scott's prayer was simple and heartfelt, and yet it felt so alien to Kate, as though she had stumbled into a different culture right here in her own sister's home.

Scott grabbed the bacon. "This looks great, Melanie. Thanks."

"Yeah, Mommy, why did you make such a fancy breakfast?" Benjamin asked.

Melanie shushed him, laughing. "Aunt Kate is supposed to think I cook like this every morning!"

"You didn't have to go to any trouble for me, Melanie," Kate said, smiling.

Melanie's eyes caught Kate's in a moment of seriousness. "You're never any trouble."

The meal was noisy, joyful, and delicious. Scott and the kids left in a flurry of kisses and brown-bag lunches, leaving Kate and Melanie alone again, sipping coffee and listening to the silence.

"I don't know how you do it, Mel," Kate said.

"Do what?"

"Keep it all together. The house, the kids, breakfast. Everything."

Melanie laughed. "I really don't make breakfast like this every morning, Kate. Most days it's Cheerios on the run. And you know the house usually looks like an earthquake just hit."

"Doesn't it wear you out, though?" Kate poured herself more coffee.

"Sometimes. There are days when I want to run away by myself for awhile. But. . .you'll excuse me for saying it, but I believe marriage isn't just about getting your own needs met. It's more about finding ways to serve."

"Hmm," Kate said, testing the temperature of her coffee. "That's a lovely thought. But I think it seems a bit unrealistic."

Melanie laughed and began clearing the dishes. "There are plenty of days when it feels unrealistic. I'm no saint, Kate. But God's teaching me that marriage is one of the ways He can make me into the person I was meant to be, if I'm willing to give up my own selfishness."

Kate exhaled. "You still think I'm being selfish by leaving Nick?"

Melanie faced her from the sink, the bacon platter still in her hand. "Go home, Kate. Manipulating Nick to get your way is not the answer. It wasn't the answer when he did it to you, so why do you think it's a good idea for you to do it back to him? Trust me when I tell you that forcing your partner to serve you rather than finding ways to serve him is a sure way to break a marriage apart."

"I don't know how to do that, Mel. I don't think I have it in me to give up what I want."

Melanie turned back to the sink in silence.

"What?" Kate said, worried. "What'd I say?"

Melanie shook her head. "You don't want to hear the only response I have to that, Kate," she said.

"It keeps coming back to God with you, doesn't it?"

Melanie shrugged. "Yeah, I guess it does."

Kate grabbed a few more of the breakfast dishes and brought them to the sink, leaning in to see Melanie's face. The early morning sun streamed through the window above the sink, surprising Kate as it struck new tears on her sister's face.

"What is it, Melanie?"

Melanie dropped her soapy dishcloth and grabbed a blue gingham towel to dry her hands and cheeks.

"It's just that you're right, Kate. You really don't have what it takes to love and serve Nick unselfishly. Because you don't have a relationship with Jesus Christ. I'm sorry; I know you don't like to hear it, but the only way you can do the impossible things is through His power working in you."

Kate picked up the dishtowel and dried the dishes that Melanie washed. They worked in silence for several minutes.

It had seemed like a good idea, leaving Nick to shake him into realizing his mixed-up priorities. Standing here, though, beside Melanie who always seemed to have clearer insight into situations, the whole thing did appear selfish and manipulative. Part of her wished she could turn the clock back twenty-four hours and forget the whole idea.

As Kate placed a large serving bowl into the cabinet below the island, her glance fell on a stack of mail at the corner. The name "SynTech Labs" jumped out at her from a glossy brochure. "What's this?" she asked, picking up the leaflet.

Melanie glanced over and then shrugged. "Oh, that's something that came in the mail. Some drug company or something."

"This is SynTech Labs, Mel. Where Nick started working."

"Really?" Melanie joined her at the island, pulling the brochure from her hands. "I didn't pay much attention to it. I think they're trying to get people to come in for genetic counseling."

Kate leaned in as Melanie opened it. Although it was obviously a mass-mailing, the brochure was lavishly scattered with full-color photos of the Gene Therapy Center and its happy, healthy patients. A small headshot in the corner bore the caption "Gregory Brulin, Chairman/CEO, SynTech Labs."

"Gregory Brulin," Melanie read, turning her puzzled expression toward Kate. "Isn't that the instructor that you—"

"Yeah." Kate nodded.

"Does Nick know about the two of you?"

"I never told him."

Melanie raised her eyebrows.

"When Nick and I met, Nick was still so angry at Gregory for having him removed from the Human Genome Project team that I just never told him."

"Kate, I think you should consider—"

Kate waved the subject away. "Just read what the letter says." She pointed to the inside page which had been personalized with Melanie's name.

Dear Melanie Lange,

SynTech Labs is pleased to announce breakthrough gene therapy technology that has been approved to treat the pre-disposition to Acid Maltase Deficiency.

Your DNA profile has recently come to the attention of the caring group of counselors at SynTech's Gene Therapy Center. DNA patterns indicate that you are at risk for this genetic disease.

SynTech is successfully treating and preventing this debil-itating disease at our center. We would welcome the opportu-nity to meet with you and explain your health options. Please call our toll-free number to set up an appointment with a counselor at your earliest convenience.

"Melanie," Kate said when they'd finished reading the letter, "did you know you were predisposed?"

Melanie shook her head, tossing the brochure back on the island. "I've never gotten tested."

Kate put her hands on her hips. "I can't believe you! It's AMD, Melanie! We've both seen what that disease can do. I took the test years ago. I thought you had, too."

Melanie turned back to the sink. "I can't believe I'm getting junk mail about my personal health issues. This whole GenWorld thing is completely out of control."

"How can you say that? GenWorld is putting together the most complete DNA database in the world. When they're done, the DNA of every person in developed countries will be on file. Do you know how easy it will be to prosecute criminals?"

"But just because I donated blood to the Red Cross doesn't mean I want my genetic code added to their database."

"It's not just blood donors, Melanie. It's employee drug tests, FBI checks, everything. They get their information from nearly every lab in the country."

"That's exactly my point! What happened to privacy?"

"What good does privacy do you if you develop AMD without ever knowing you were predisposed?"

Melanie groaned. "Kate, sometimes I think you keep yourself so buried in the research end of all this technology you don't see any of the other issues."

"What other issues?"

"Insurance, for one. Gene therapy for some diseases isn't covered by insurance yet. But once you're identified as a high-risk candidate for a certain disease, some companies are calling that a 'preexisting condition' if you do get the disease. Preexisting because you were born predisposed to it. They won't cover your expenses."

Kate bit her lip. "Melanie, if it's money, Nick and I can help."

"That's only one part of it, Kate. Don't you see the larger ethical—"

Kate grabbed Melanie's arms and faced her. "Listen to me. I cannot watch you go through what Mom went through. When she—" She swallowed. "I never would have made it through that without you. I can't lose you, too. I can't. Gene therapy can prevent you from getting AMD. You have to do it." She squeezed Melanie's arm until her sister's face softened.

"I'll tell you what, Kate," Melanie said. "I'll make you a deal."

"What do I have to do?" Kate asked warily.

"You go home to Nick, and I'll make the appointment."

⌐ ⌐ ⌐

Nick punched the "power" button on his stereo as he turned the Expedition toward the Gene Therapy Center. It was a forty-five-minute drive from his office and lab at SynTech, just enough time to listen to one of his seminar CDs. He had to keep up with the latest developments in medicine if he wanted to keep his edge.

The trip to the center flew by as he listened, and he was soon parking in the huge lot. He took a moment to appreciate the building as he walked down the sidewalk. Gregory had poured money into making this facility the best in the country, and it showed. Perfectly maintained evergreen shrubs lined the building, in sharply edged, weed-free beds of mulch. The parking lot and sidewalks looked like they'd never seen harsh weather, despite the snow on the ground, and the building's paint was fresh.

Inside, Nick was even more impressed. The atmosphere exuded elegance and tranquility, with its floral-patterned couches and stately cherry tables. Nick studied a small fountain on the side of the huge waiting room. The soothing sounds of splashing water traveled all the way across the room. Nick walked past the large white statue of Aesculapius sculpture, noting it with interest. No doubt one of Gregory's personal additions.

He gave his name at the front desk, and a receptionist escorted him to a small conference room. She left him at the door. He entered the room, and dozens of people turned to watch him with curiosity. Every chair in the ten or so rows across the room was filled. Nick maneuvered past the first few rows to reach the front of the room and stand behind the lectern. The morning sun filtered through the blinds, slanting across the tops of the heads in front of him.

"Good morning," he said, nodding to the prospective clients. "And thank you for making the time to hear more about gene therapy today." He cleared his throat and pulled a few notes he had made earlier out of the inner pocket of his suit jacket. "Gene therapy is breaking new ground in the area of disease treatment. But its basic premise is quite simple. Can anyone tell me what they know about gene therapy?"

A tall man called from the back, "They use viruses."

Nick nodded. "Gene therapy starts with a virus. All viruses, including retroviruses, lack the ability to reproduce themselves. To survive, they must infect a living cell and insert their own genes, which then instruct the cell to make copies of the virus. For gene therapy, we take advantage of this ability for 'breaking and entering.'" He paused as the crowd chuckled.

"First, we remove the disease-causing genes from the virus and substitute the therapeutic gene. The bioengineered virus is called a 'vector.' It has things in common with a virus, but its DNA is curative instead of deadly. It's like the perfect combination of the human and the divine."

A few women in the front row smiled. Nick continued. "This vector is injected into the target tissue. The cell begins sucking the virus inside itself, and the genetic material inside the virus enters the cell nucleus. With the therapeutic genes in place, the cell begins producing a working copy of the protein that had been defective or lacking. The biochemical machinery of the cell has been fixed." Nick glanced around the room, making eye contact with a few. "Any questions?"

One hand shot up. Nick pointed to a man in the back. "I'm confused about the difference between a virus and a retrovirus."

Nick nodded. "A retrovirus is just a specific type of virus. It has RNA as its genetic material, instead of DNA, and it gets its name because of the way it copies its RNA into the DNA of the host cell, sort of in reverse."

"Oh."

The audience laughed, and Nick fielded a few more questions, but overall the crowd seemed to accept the idea easily. Rich Nowinski, the center's executive director, stepped up behind Nick to direct people to counselors for appointments. When the crowd dispersed, Nowinski turned to Nick.

"Rich Nowinski," he said, extending a hand. He was at least six inches shorter than Nick, with thinning hair combed across the top of his head.

"I've heard good things about you," Nick said. He nodded toward the door. "And it looks like you're bringing them in."

Rich nodded, smiled, and nudged his glasses against the bridge of his nose. "The response to the company's last marketing push has been amazing. This Genetic Awareness Day has them flocking in from everywhere." He led the way out of the conference room, into the long hallway leading back to the waiting room. The hallway was silent and empty.

Nick walked alongside him. "Let's just hope they keep coming back when it's not free," Nick said.

"Exactly," Nowinski said, nodding. "Thanks for giving the speech. Although I don't know why Brulin keeps sending investigators down to do it."

"Oh, he's sent others?"

Nowinski nodded. "What's your project?"

"Fabry's disease for now. Then cancer research."

"So you've taken over for Milburn?"

Nick stopped. "Did you know him?"

Nowinski continued walking. "Not too well. We worked together for a short time, years ago. And I talked to him not long before he was killed in the accident." Nowinski paused beside an office door, and Nick noted Nowinski's name painted in black letters on the glass. "Milburn called me after picking something up at the center. Asked a lot of strange questions I couldn't answer. I never did figure out what he was after."

A secretary approached and spoke softly to Nowinski.

"What kind of questions?" Nick asked.

"I'm sorry, Nick. I've got to see to something. It was good to meet you. I guess I'll see you around."

Nick nodded and headed for the waiting room. *I hope so.*

BRIAN MILBURN JOURNAL ENTRY #2
JANUARY 27

Now I know how Sam Spade felt when his partner got knocked off. No more fun and games.

I've kept it all from Jeremy and Bernice. No need to involve either of them. Of course, I'm assuming they're innocent. But I don't know the real deal on anybody, do I?

Everyone at SynTech seems harmless enough. Except for that bizarre security guy, Chernoff. That guy could give a snake the creeps, and I don't mind saying (okay, writing) that wherever he is, I prefer to be somewhere else. But other than Chernoff, I can't imagine anyone at SynTech sick enough to engineer what I found today.

Of course, I'm talking all around it and not actually saying it, aren't I? It's almost too unbelievable to record, but then what's the point of my little yellow notebook?

I sequenced that Version 2 therapy today, and it is most definitely not the version approved by the FDA. I nearly fell off my stool when I read the electropherogram. This is no slight alteration. This is serious, nasty business. This therapy is supposed to treat Gaucher's disease, but instead Version 2 codes for a liver enzyme, and the therapy directs the cells to stop producing it. We're talking cancer. Version 2 causes cancer.

I'd have gone to the FDA today, if it weren't for the fact that Louis Ward told me the second versions won't be used for a few more weeks. I've got some time to play with, a chance to figure out who's doing this. What kind of sicko would change these therapies? I really can't imagine.

But I plan to find out.

CHAPTER 17

The Gene Therapy Institute intercom buzzed in the Tissue Culture Lab where Kate was working under a glass hood.

"Kate, call for you, line 2."

"Thanks, Marianne." Kate put down the pipet she was using and went to the phone. "Kate Donovan."

"Hi, hon."

Kate took a deep breath. "Hi, Nick."

"How are you?"

"Fine. How are you?"

"Fine."

Kate closed her eyes at the inane conversation. "How's the new job?"

"Good. Different than I expected, but it's okay."

"Good."

"Kate, come home."

Kate pulled out a chair and sat. She used her shoulder to hold the phone against her ear while she stripped off her latex gloves. "Nick, I told you—"

"I know we can't seem to agree on this, but can't we be together while we work it out? I can't stand it, not having you at home."

"Nick, you're basically only home when we're sleeping anyway, so what's the difference?"

"Kate, that's not fair."

"Oh, Nick, I just need some space to work things out in my own mind." She listened to his breathing on the other end.

"When, then? When will you come home?"

"I don't know. You're the one who's always complaining about my pressuring you for a date when you'll be ready. Can't you give me some space? I feel like I need to get away somewhere so I can really think, you know?"

"Just don't stay away too long. I miss you."

She reached for gloves again. "Yeah. Okay."

⁓ ⁓ ⁓

Snow fell like frozen cotton balls as Kate pulled her Volvo off Interstate 80 at the Marshall's Creek exit, two hours from home. She'd come this way to Melanie and Scott's vacation house in the Pocono Mountains a dozen times, but she still felt a little thrill every time she launched away from the highway and started into the rural part of the trip.

Her impromptu vacation had only raised a few eyebrows at the institute. Since Nick had left, her relationships there had been awkward. However, she wouldn't be missed for the next two days. Getting away would be great for her. The smooth jazz flowing out of the radio and the dark warmth of the car had already settled her spirit.

Melanie had accepted Kate's counteroffer on her "deal." Melanie would make an appointment for genetic counseling at the SynTech Gene Therapy Center if Kate promised to go back to Nick after she finished her little retreat up there in the woods.

Nick's call today, begging her to come home, had gotten to her. Melanie and Scott were both telling her that she and Nick needed to work things out together, not apart. But she wasn't ready. She'd given Melanie instructions to tell Nick that she was taking some time away if he called. She hadn't even brought her phone. The phone at the mountain house could be used for emergencies, but only Melanie and Scott knew she would be there, and they wouldn't call unless it was important.

She turned the music up as a soft piano joined a smoky voice crooning Gershwin's "Someone to Watch over Me." Nick loved to play Gershwin.

Should she go back to Nick? Was she being selfish and manipulative? She wanted children every bit as much as he wanted to save the world. How could she make him see that? She felt like she was drifting without purpose. She needed an anchor, a reason.

The road began to climb. She peered out into the darkness, gripping the steering wheel with both hands. Tiny, white pyramids had already formed on the fence posts at the edge of the woods. Snowplows wouldn't come through until there was a more significant load to push aside, but the road was only bare in two narrowing black tracks where other tires had recently blown past.

The temperature dropped as she climbed higher up the mountain. She shivered and pushed the heat up to high. The steering wheel felt cold in her hands. As much as she loved the snow, she had never been comfortable driving in it.

A yellow light ahead flickered through the thickening deluge of snowflakes. Kate slowed and saw a small log cabin. A sign swung from a pole: "Bert's Bait and Tackle." She pulled into the four-car parking area. Maybe Bert would have some snacks next to the night crawlers.

Her feet sunk ankle-deep in the powdery snow outside the car. Scolding herself for not wearing her boots, she high-stepped over to Bert's porch, crunching down the wet snow with her sneakers. The inside of the store was warm and well lit.

"Hello!" A deep voice called out from a back room somewhere. Kate glanced around the combination hardware/bait shop/convenience store. A rack of candy called her name.

"How 'bout this storm?" a fifty-something, balding man said as he emerged from a darkened doorway, a pile of ice scrapers in his hands.

She smiled. "Good for business?"

"Always like to keep those snow shovels selling, even this deep into the season. What can I help you with?"

She tossed a Snickers bar on the counter and plopped her purse beside it. "Just this."

"Sure you wouldn't like a shovel?" He laughed, the smile widening his face. "Or an ice scraper?"

"No, thanks." Kate fished out some money, returning the warm smile.

"You headed up farther?"

"Just a few more miles, to Birch Hill."

He nodded. "You got studded tires on that car? Or chains?"

"No. Do you think I need to?"

"It's best. I got some chains back here. I could put 'em on for you."

"Oh, I think I'll be all right," Kate said. "Thanks, though."

"All right. Just you be careful on them roads. There's not much between here and there."

A couple of miles later, the chocolate bar made her wish she'd bought bottled water back at Bert's. There was no way she'd turn back, though. Those two miles had taken her about fifteen minutes to navigate. The snow was falling harder. She could always eat some of that if she got desperate. The swish of the wipers against the windshield pushed the snow aside but made a noisy scrape that jangled her taut nerves. The steering wheel grew clammy under her hands. She wiped them on her jeans.

Her eyes watered from the tense concentration on the white road in front of her. The back end of the car kept wanting to slide sideways. Only fools were out in weather like this—and most of them were smart enough to put chains on their tires. The radio station had been playing nothing but static for ten minutes. She turned it off.

Some time later she decided something wasn't right with the road. She'd seen the county preserve sign a few minutes ago, and the pine trees that crowded up close to the side of the winding road all looked familiar, but she was certain she should have been there by now. Could it really be taking this long? She glanced at the speedometer, trying to do the math in her head. She couldn't be sure.

Another ten minutes of concentrated driving brought her to an intersection. One she'd never seen before. She must have taken the wrong direction at a fork in the road.

She did a slow circle in the deserted intersection to turn around. The car resisted her, like a willful child pulling against his mother's hand. The back end fishtailed as she swung out of the turn, and the car broke free from her control. Fear twisted her stomach. She tried to ease up on the steering wheel.

The tires grabbed again. The car righted itself. She exhaled the breath she'd been holding. How far back had she missed the turn?

She rolled along, intent on the road in front of her and checking for hidden turnoffs. She hadn't seen another car since she'd left Bert's. The woods closed up tight around the road here. The only light came from her high beams. Huge flakes shimmered through the bright light.

She was blinking about a hundred times a minute, her eyelids weighted from the car's warmth, the fatigue, and from staring at the road. At least if she saw Bert's Bait and Tackle, she'd know she'd gone too far again.

The dark form of a deer shot into the road about twenty feet in front of her. She smashed her foot onto the brake pedal at the flash of tan and white.

The car slid out of control. Headlights careened across road, trees, road, trees. Was she moving forward? Sideways? The front corner of the car bounced off something, and then the back walloped into an immovable object. There was a sudden white explosion and then darkness.

CHAPTER 18

A foggy whiteness pressed against Kate's face. She opened her eyes. Was she facedown in the snow? She tilted her head. Heat, not cold, spread across her face. She leaned back.

The airbag had deployed. Her hands still gripped the wheel, but a deflated white balloon buried them. She pulled one hand out and touched the fiery skin on her face. The airbag must have burned her. Strands of her hair had twisted into her mouth. She spit them out and tasted blood at the same time. A gash on the inside of her cheek throbbed.

She paced her breathing, regaining her perception. The left side of her neck stung. She touched it with gentle fingertips. Blood greeted her touch. The seat belt had cut into her neck as it had helped stop her progress through the windshield. Kate tasted salt and realized that tears were on her face. She let them flow, releasing some of the tension.

When she had cried it out, she reached under the airbag again and turned the ignition key. A grinding sound filtered through and then nothing. She tried again. The car was dead.

Now there was something to cry about. She leaned back against the seat, but she was all out of tears. The wind blew snow against her window, piling it up like rising water threatening to drown her.

She leaned her forehead against the side window, searching the snowy darkness for anyone who could help. She could see now that the car faced the road, its back end embedded in a pine tree and its headlights shining up at an angle, attempting to illuminate the night sky.

Kate spotted her purse on the floorboard. She reached across the seat for it. She hated to call anyone to come get her, but it didn't look like she had a choice.

Call? There was no phone in her purse! She had wanted to be completely alone, and it seemed she had gotten her wish.

Thirty minutes later she had not seen a person or a car. The cold seeped into her coat and gloves, warning her that she could not stay in the car forever. There was nothing to do but walk back the way she had come, hoping to reach Bert's store before she froze. Or maybe someone would come along and pick her up.

She pushed the deflated airbag away, slid out of her coat, and yanked her overnight bag over the back of the seat. She pulled out every article of clothing she had brought, piling most of them on before adding her coat. Berating herself again for leaving her boots at home, she opened the car and stepped out. Her neck and right knee were sore. She reached in and grabbed her purse before closing the door. Better to have some identification on her when they found her frozen body beside the road.

One glance at the back of the car told her she wouldn't be driving it again. The trunk had crumpled into the backseat. She looked around again, fantasizing that she would see a cozy log cabin a few feet away. There was nothing. Nothing.

Pure silence fell heavily from the sky, slid down against her skin, and weighed her to the ground. Tears blurred her sight and froze into tiny hailstones on her eyelashes. She climbed up the embankment. A full moon bounced off the snow, illuminating the road.

Her feet lost feeling within twenty minutes. How long would it take to reach the convenience store? It would be more convenient a little closer, she thought, laughing at her own joke and then wondering if she were losing her mind already.

Another forty minutes trudged past. From time to time she heard a distant motor, but no cars ever came. Now she was falling down the road rather than walking. Eyes nearly closed, head forward. The wind and snow had cooled the burns on her face, but the cuts on her neck chafed under her coat. She welcomed the pain, knowing it kept her awake.

Then something bobbed in her peripheral vision. She slowed and raised her head. Was that a light in the woods? She blinked and rubbed gloved fingers against her eyes. The snow that had crusted her gloves melted against her face.

Yes! A light. But it could be small and close, or maybe large and miles away. Did she dare risk leaving the road to reach it? What if it went out before she got there? She'd be wandering in the woods.

The light blinked, as though someone had passed in front of it. She made her decision and stepped off the road into snow twenty inches deep.

Thirty minutes later she had picked her way across fallen trees and outcropping rocks, falling several times. The light had grown larger, encouraging her that it could not be too far away. But she was stumbling every few yards, lifting her feet as though they were encased in cement. Snow had found its way under all her layers.

She tripped once more and this time stayed on her hands and knees for a moment, letting the relief of stillness wash over her. A wave of dizziness forced her to sit. She leaned back against a tree and stared at the light, powdery snow half burying her already.

She was too tired to shiver. She should rest for a few minutes. Not long, just enough to regain some energy. Her eyes were heavy. Thoughts and images jumbled in her head the way they always did before she fell asleep. She would rest awhile and then head toward that light again. Just a few minutes of rest.

Words from a forgotten poem of Robert Frost's drifted across her mind as her chin dropped against her chest and her eyelids fluttered.

The woods are lovely, dark and deep,
But I have promises to keep,
And miles to go before I sleep,
And miles to go before I sleep.

CHAPTER 19

Nick exited Interstate 95 and turned the Expedition toward the Young-Meddleton Cancer Center. His phone was docked beside him, and he waited for the police station to pick up.

A female voice answered.

"I'd like to speak to Officer Tony Cabruzzi, please," Nick said. "My name is Dr. Nicholas Donovan."

"Just a moment."

Nick had lifted Cabruzzi's name from the newspaper as the officer in charge of investigating Brian Milburn's accident case. Nick had to find out what had really happened to Milburn.

The woman came back on the line. "Officer Cabruzzi is out on patrol right now. He'll be checking back in at the station before he goes off duty at seven o'clock. You could try back then."

Nick glanced at the dashboard clock. 6:01 P.M. "Okay, thanks."

Nick swerved the Expedition into the well-lit parking area of the cancer center. The snow had obscured the parking lines, but there were few cars in the lot, so he just pulled in beside another car.

He got out and looked up at the cancer center. Julia had told him he would find Stanford here. It made Nick's stomach tight just to think of it. *Stanford, what are you doing at this place? You can't be that sick. Not Stanford Carlton.*

He had an hour to visit with Stanford and find out what he could, no more if he wanted to catch Officer Cabruzzi before he went off duty.

The four-story, glass-enclosed atrium lobby of the cancer center surprised Nick. Warm colors of peach and pale yellow soothed the eye. Waterfalls tumbled over landscaped rocks on either side of the vast room, and each area teemed with plant life. The background sounds of trickling water and the smell of mossy dirt felt like a summer afternoon beside a stream in the woods. Nick felt his shoulders drop the moment he stepped inside.

Julia had said she'd have Stanford meet Nick in the lobby. Nick searched the area for Stanford's commanding figure.

"Nick, over here." A hand at the far end of the room fluttered.

Nick crossed the atrium, past a group of patients watching a small television. He forced his face to be still at the sight of his mentor. Stanford slumped in a wheelchair, his fingers tangled in the fringes of a plaid blanket thrown across his lap. His sunken eyes and cheeks testified to the medical onslaught of the past few months.

"How are you, Stanford?" Nick asked, grasping the man's outstretched hand.

"Not well, they tell me." His mouth curved into a smile. "But still fighting."

"I'm sorry I haven't caught up with you sooner." Nick sat on the edge of a plush, tan sofa, glancing at his watch.

Another man sat in a wing-backed chair nearby.

"Nick, this is Frank, a fellow victim."

Nick shook Frank's hand, mentally repeating his name several times, a little trick to overcome his name-recall problem. Frank looked about fifty, but Nick couldn't be certain. Unlike Stanford's pajamas and robe, Frank wore a button-up shirt and khaki pants. Stanford had said he was fighting, but to Nick, Frank looked a little more ready for battle.

"Frank's got liver cancer," Stanford said. "And he's in digital communications."

Frank smiled. "Stanford's been telling me about your genetic research. Fascinating stuff."

Nick nodded, turning back to Stanford. "I've left the university, though."

"I heard," Stanford said, his expression absolutely neutral. "SynTech Labs."

"Yeah. I wanted to talk to you before I took the job, but Julia said you were. . .not up to it."

Stanford smiled. Then he turned toward Frank. "Nick's working for my former partner."

"Oh, really?" Frank said. "Is that how you met Stanford, Nick, working for him?"

"Stanford was an instructor of mine in med school," Nick said. "He and Gregory Brulin—SynTech's chairman—both were. Stanford's let me tag along in his shadow all these years, trying to learn what it takes to be a great doctor and a great man."

Stanford smiled. "Actually, I just like having him around to entertain me. You should hear this guy play the piano, Frank."

Nick laughed. "So that's why I get invited to all your parties." He paused and leaned closer. "I did want to ask you, Stanford, about a few things at SynTech."

Stanford sobered. "How's it going there?"

Nick hesitated, glancing at Frank. "I'm still getting acclimated."

Frank stood. "I'll let you guys talk. I need to go see if anybody's thrown any more silver dollars in the waterfall."

Stanford watched him go. "Nick, you'll do well at SynTech. You have what it takes to succeed. I've always known that. Just don't get too involved with Gregory's ideas."

"I get the feeling that there are secrets floating around that place," Nick said.

Stanford's eyes bore into Nick's. Several times he seemed about to speak, but he never brought the words out. "Just be careful, Nick," he finally said. "And don't believe everything Gregory tells you."

Stanford raised his voice. "Frank, come back over here and tell us about the future of digital communications."

Frank headed toward them.

"Well," Nick said to Stanford, "how's your treatment coming?"

Stanford tilted his head back, taking in the room. "How could it be anything less than successful in such a life-affirming place as this?" A bitter smile tinged his lips. They talked at length about the effects of the disease and treatments on Stanford and his family.

"I finished the chemo and radiation two months ago," Stanford said in conclusion. "I guess my cancer doesn't like losing any more than I do. They say it's too far advanced for another surgery."

Nick's stomach churned. "What now?"

"I get a break for awhile. I'm staying here while they run tests for a few days. Then they try again. More drugs. More hormone therapies. More radiation." He shrugged. "I'll try to hang on until you can whip up a gene therapy for me, Nick, but you'd best get busy."

Nick studied the waterfall to his left, following the water's course down the rocks. He had an urge to step over there and let the cold water run over his fingertips.

"But I don't think any of those treatments will work," Stanford said. "Then I guess there's nothing left for me but the big sleep."

"Don't joke about that, Stanford," Nick said, surprised at how angry he sounded. "Death isn't funny."

Stanford chuckled. "I have to laugh at it, Nick. I have to. You'll understand one day. Anyway, Frank's trying to help me out, aren't you, Frank? Trying to get me some fire insurance before the end."

"Fire insurance?" Nick asked.

Stanford laughed at his own joke. "He wants to convert me, make sure I don't end up in hell."

"Oh."

Nick flicked a glance at Frank, hoping he wasn't offended by Stanford's flip remarks. To his surprise, Frank was chuckling.

"I haven't gotten to know you well enough down here on

earth, Stan," Frank said. "I want to have the rest of eternity with you. Beat you at a few games of chess. That sort of thing."

Nick checked Frank out more closely. Dressed well. Self-confident. It was clear the man had been successful before cancer had turned his life in a different direction. Not what Nick pictured when he thought of a Christian.

Frank returned Nick's gaze. "Stanford's been more successful in business than most men. He's built himself into something he can be—and is—proud of." He winked. "I've been trying to convince him that God's not all that impressed."

Nick winced. So, here were Frank's true colors. He was blunt and judgmental under the sophistication. "Now wait just a minute. Stanford's done more—"

"Don't be offended for me, Nick," Stanford said. "Frank's been at me like this for days. I'm used to it. Besides, he'd tell you that God's not impressed with you, either, or even with him, for that matter."

Frank nodded. "Believe it or not, I've gotten Stan to admit that he's not perfect. No matter how much he's accomplished in his life, how successful he's become, there's a more basic issue between him and God that has to be dealt with."

Nick eyed his watch: 6:40. "I'll let you guys talk about this in private," he said, shifting his weight forward on the couch. "Stanford, I'll catch you—"

"No, Nick," Stanford said. "Please stay. I want you to listen to this and give me your opinion."

Nick settled back again with a deep breath.

"Frank says that I've had my ladder up against the wrong wall all these years." Stanford stretched a leg away from the wheelchair as though it had grown stiff.

"Your ladder?"

"He says I've been climbing toward something, but now that I'm at the top, I can see that I had my ladder in the wrong place the whole time. He says none of it really meant anything."

Nick looked back and forth between the two men. "What do you think?" he asked Stanford.

"I think he's full of it. I've been a good husband, good father, good doctor. I've given to charities, helped my students. My foundation has helped push a cure for leukemia years ahead of where it would have been. I've done a thousand times more than the average man. What does a guy have to do to impress the Man Upstairs, anyway? What more could I have done with my life?"

Nick smiled. "You're one of the best men I know, Stanford. And your life has been an example to me. You know that." Nick frowned at Frank. "I can't imagine anyone saying otherwise."

Frank nodded, as though he did not disagree with Nick. "I'm just asking: When Stanford stands before God, will it be enough? When you stand before God, Nick, will you have done enough to convince Him that you're worthy of heaven?"

Stanford argued with Frank again, and for several minutes Nick went back to his position of onlooker, waiting for a chance to escape. The time rushed forward, the hand on his watch clicking toward 7:00 at double time.

Finally, Nick stood. "I've got to get going."

Frank stopped in midsentence. The two men looked at him.

"I'm sorry." Nick felt his face redden. "I have an appointment. I need to go. Stanford, I'll come back to visit you soon. Keep fighting." He gave the older man his hand again. "Frank, it was nice to meet you." Nick hoped the annoyance couldn't be traced in his voice.

He jogged through the snow from the front door of the cancer center to the parking lot. His watch read 6:58. If he was lucky, he might catch Cabruzzi before he called it a night.

CHAPTER 20

Stanford Carlton watched Nick flee through the automatic doors of the cancer center as though death pursued him. The corners of Stanford's mouth twitched in sad amusement. Why was it that men who had so much time in front of them were always running to their next appointment, while men who had death breathing down their necks did nothing but idle their time away?

The visit had tired him more than he ever would have admitted to Nick. He slumped in his wheelchair as Nick disappeared, closing his eyes and dropping his head forward.

"I'll take you back to your room," Frank said.

Stanford shook his head. "Thanks, but not yet. I like it here." Despite his flip remark to Nick, the lobby's plants and water did have a positive effect on his spirit, more so than his sterile room did. "Do you really believe all that stuff, Frank?"

"I believe God has a purpose for your life."

Stanford raised his head. "It looks like He waited too long to let me in on the secret."

"Maybe you haven't been listening."

Stanford smiled. "You're lucky I've decided that your bluntness can't offend me."

"I'm probably the first person you've met who hasn't told you whatever you wanted to hear."

Stanford laughed. "You're probably right. I guess neither of us has anything to lose. And," he said, staring at the waterfall, "I suppose I'm ready for a dose of reality."

"That's all I ask. Look around, think about what you believe."

"I believe in myself, Frank. That's all I've ever needed."

"And now?"

Stanford sighed. "Now I don't know what to think. I've always thought nothing could stop me if I believed enough in myself and what I wanted. But I'm not beating this thing. It's beating me." He dropped his chin to his chest again.

Frank moved to a closer chair, leaning toward Stanford before he spoke. "You've put your trust in an unflawed universe, designed to give you what you want, as though you were at its center."

Stanford lifted his head. "It's not that way, is it?"

Frank smiled. "It's not that way."

Stanford looked toward the wall of windows. "I don't think I've done enough to make the world a better place. There are things I could have done, should do. Things that would make my life mean something."

"Mean something to whom?"

"I think I'm ready to go back to my room, Frank. Will you get a nurse for me?"

"I'll take you." Frank held up a hand at Stanford's protest. "I'm feeling good today. I need the exercise." He maneuvered the wheelchair around the lobby furniture toward the elevators.

"What am I going to do, Frank?" Stanford said.

"I don't know."

Stanford swallowed. "I'm confused. Confused and tired."

"It's not hard, Stan. Just give it up." Frank pulled him into an elevator so that he faced the door with Frank behind him. "Give up all the trying to make something out of yourself. God's the only One who can make anything out of you."

"Even now? This late?"

"Even now, and for eternity."

Back in his room, Stanford lay awake for hours staring at the hospital ceiling. It wasn't over yet. He still had a chance to do something right. Sometime during his conversation with Nick, he had hit upon a way to stop Gregory Brulin without incriminating himself. Nick Donovan would be his stand-in.

However, he needed to be careful. If Gregory learned the truth, Stanford and Nick both might be facing eternity sooner than they'd planned.

CHAPTER 21

The clock on the dashboard read 7:00 as Nick's call to the police station went through.

"Officer Cabruzzi, please."

The person on the other end yelled for Cabruzzi.

A minute later, a new voice spoke into the phone. "Yeah?"

"Hello, Officer. My name is Dr. Nicholas Donovan. I work for SynTech Labs. I was hoping I could catch you there at the station to speak with you about Brian Milburn's death. Could I stop by, and—"

"Sorry, Donovan. I'm on my way out. Kid's got a school play tonight."

"Oh," Nick said, pounding the steering wheel.

"Besides, there's nothing I could tell you that wasn't in the newspaper. You need to talk to the family if you want more info."

"Could you tell me his wife's name, Officer?"

"Uh, yeah. Hold on. Here it is: Andrea Milburn."

"And you didn't find anything suspicious about this case."

"It was ruled an accident."

"Nothing strange about it at all, then?"

"Look, Dr.—whatever. Like I said, talk to the family if you want more."

Nick sighed. "Thanks."

Nick turned his car toward the highway, cursing under his breath. He would go back to the lab to search Milburn's files again, see if he could discover what tainted therapy his note was talking about. Though trying to find it would be like hunting for an aspirin in a truckload of gravel.

"Dial—" Nick stopped himself. The instinct to call Kate about his late-night trip to the lab had overcome his memory for a moment.

Kate. Bitterness soured in his chest as he thought of her final "no" at Melanie's house when he had begged her to come home. At times he felt angry, but tonight he just wanted her home. Every day they were apart felt wrong. He wanted to find a compromise.

But not just yet. Right now he needed to get that proposal going. To get it ready in three weeks he'd almost need to go without food and sleep. He couldn't afford to be wasting time worrying about Kate's crisis. They had years together—they'd get through this, too.

Somehow he had to find out why Milburn had nearly gone to the FDA. That was the thing that bothered him most. His predecessor, a man probably not unlike him, had discovered something rotten in the course of the very job that Nick was assigned to now. Then Milburn had died, apparently in a car accident that seemed a bit too convenient. It occurred to Nick that if Milburn had found something that would get SynTech in trouble with the feds, his death may not have troubled Gregory too much.

He found the SynTech building nearly empty, but when the elevator arrived to take him down to his lab, someone was inside. It was Frieda, the plant-watering lady, brooding in the corner of the elevator.

"Good evening, Frieda," Nick said, remembering his plan to melt her with kindness. He'd make an effort, despite his own sour mood. "You look lovely tonight." He smiled what he hoped was a charming, yet mischievous smile.

Frieda raised one eyebrow. "Same uniform I wear every night."

"And you wear it well."

"Hmph."

Nick pressed the button for Sublevel 2 and leaned back against the side of the elevator. "How's the arthritis tonight?"

"Killin' me by inches."

"Well, you must be almost finished, right? There can't be that many plants underground. Time to go home?"

She shook her head. "Show's what you know, Mr. Scientist. Got them fiber-optic thingies bringing sunlight down wherever you want it. There's plants everywhere in this building. And then I've got to do the third floor. Always save that till last."

"Your favorite floor?"

Another snort. "Brutal Brulin's got his plants hanging from the ceiling all over the place. I gotta drag a chair around and climb on it like some kind of blasted monkey just to get them plants watered."

Nick nodded. "I see." He watched Frieda's eyes travel to the numbers above the door. "You don't like him much, do you?"

She fiddled with the watering can. "Like him, don't like him. Makes no difference. I just don't trust him, is all."

Nick tilted his head, remembering Stanford's similar words. "Frieda, I think you're the first person I've met at SynTech who doesn't think Gregory hung the moon. Why don't you trust him?"

Frieda's face puckered into a frown, and she stared at Nick, as if deciding whether he was worthy to hear her opinion. "He's not right. In the head. That's what I'd say if they asked me. Which they don't. But I'm telling you, that man thinks he's one of his god statues come alive to save us."

The elevator doors opened to Sublevel 1, and Frieda got her cart going.

"You know what I think, Frieda?" Nick asked, holding the doors open for her.

"What's that?"

"I think you're one smart woman."

As she passed, he impulsively wrapped an arm around her frail shoulders and leaned down to kiss her tree-bark cheek.

She followed the cart through the doors, but she turned to stare at Nick with saucer eyes. Just before the doors closed, she reached a bony hand to touch her face.

Nick found Sublevel 2 unoccupied. He slid his keycard to

open his lab and headed to the computer. He already had a plan. He would do a search on all Milburn's files, looking for keywords that might be more personal entries, like the one about his concerns on tainted therapies.

A scraping sound at the door to the lab startled him before he had a chance to begin. He leaned back in his office chair as the lab door swung open.

A dark-coated figure pushed into the lab. Bernice.

She jumped when she saw Nick. "Oh! Dr. Donovan! I didn't expect you to be here." One hand fluttered at her neck. "I was, I mean, I needed to, I wanted to finish some work I was doing earlier, since I had been out sick. I hope it's okay." She bit her lower lip.

"Come in, Bernice." Nick stood and came out into the lab. "I admire your dedication."

"What are you doing here, Dr. Donovan?" She stepped closer and Nick could smell her candy-apple perfume.

"I thought I told you to call me Nick."

Bernice giggled. "Okay, Nick."

"Oh, just working on some things." Nick dropped to a stool, facing Bernice. "Say, since you're here, maybe you can help me out with something."

"Well, I'll try."

"What can you tell me about Brian Milburn?"

Bernice smiled. "He was brilliant. One of the best investigators here, always coming up with something new to try. I loved working with him. And he was so nice. He and his wife."

"You knew his wife?"

"Oh, yes. Andrea. They had me to their home several times for dinner."

Nick checked the time: 8:00 P.M. "Bernice, would you mind calling Mrs. Milburn and asking if I could meet her? I have a few questions. You could come along, too." He added that last part because he guessed that Milburn's wife probably wouldn't see him otherwise.

"You mean tonight?"

"Do you think it's too late?"

"I don't know," Bernice said. "But I'd be glad to call her."

Bernice put Nick on the phone after speaking with Milburn's widow for a few minutes.

"Mrs. Milburn, I'd like to talk with you about what your husband was working on before he died. I'm sorry to have to ask you about this now, but I've found some notes in his files that I don't understand. They have me. . .concerned. I'd like to see if you can shed some light on them."

A prolonged silence on the other end made him wonder if she'd hung up.

"You can come over, Dr. Donovan, I guess. But you may not like what you hear."

With that dire warning, Nick and Bernice left the lab and walked down the hallway.

"Bernice," Nick said as he pushed the elevator button, "I'd appreciate it if you didn't mention this visit to anyone else."

Bernice's eyes widened, and she covered a giggle with two fingers. "Okay, Dr.—Nick."

"How far are we driving tonight?"

"About a half hour," Bernice said. "You'll like Andrea. She's charming. At least she was before all of this happened."

As the doors slid open, Nick snapped his fingers. "My coat! Hold the elevator, Bernice."

He dashed the few feet to the corner, rounded it close to the wall, and slammed into someone's chest.

"Mr. Chernoff!"

Chernoff backed away, scowling. "Dr. Donovan."

Nick waited for an explanation as to the man's presence in this corridor at this hour, but none came. Instead, Chernoff continued to stare at him.

Nick edged around him and retrieved his coat from the lab. When he entered the hall again, Chernoff was gone.

CHAPTER 22

A warm voice called to Kate from somewhere far off. She fought to find that voice, fought to reach out to it. Her mind seemed frozen.

"Hey, are you okay? Hello?"

Her eyes blinked once, twice, then stayed open. A man's face blurred into focus. Long, blond hair; small, gold-rimmed glasses.

She swallowed, then forced out an icy tongue and licked her frozen lips. "I'm okay." The words grated in her throat.

The man smiled, revealing perfect teeth. "I thought we'd lost you there for a minute."

Kate reached her arms to the side and felt upholstery. She was indoors. The man knelt beside her where she lay on a couch. "I—I needed to rest." Kate closed her eyes again, still groggy.

"Come on," the man said. "At least take off your wet coat."

Kate coughed and tried to sit up. The room spun and then righted itself. "Where am I?"

He smiled again. "You're in my cabin. I found you outside in the snow."

Kate forced herself up. She still wore her coat and gloves. Her clothes felt like they'd been soaked in ice water. "Did you carry me here?"

"You're not heavy."

Kate looked around. Was this cabin the source of the light she had seen outside? It was hardly a hunting cabin, as she'd thought. Cathedral ceiling, hardwood floors, stone fireplace. Kate felt like a princess rescued and taken to a fairy tale hideaway in the woods. A fire snapped and popped in the fireplace, and soft music surrounded them.

"Thank you," she remembered to say.

He laughed. "That's me, SuperWinston, your very own superhero."

She held out a wet glove. "I'm Kate."

A confused look crossed Winston's face. "Hmm?" Then he shook his head and stood. "I should have some dry clothes you could wear."

Kate eyed her rescuer. He was much taller than she, but she liked his taste in clothing. A black, long-sleeved T-shirt and jeans hugged his narrow body. He must have taken his boots off after hauling her in here. His feet were bare.

Kate swung her legs off the couch. "That's okay. I'm wearing about three changes of clothing. Some of it must be dry." She peeled off her wet gloves and coat, then her sweater. A chill tickled her spine.

Winston smiled again, a perfect smile. "Why don't you take a hot shower to warm yourself up?" He motioned to a door off the main room. "There are plenty of towels in there. I'll make you something to eat while you get warm."

"No, that's okay," Kate said. "If I could use your phone—"

"It will take awhile for anyone to get here," Winston said. "You might as well be warm while you're waiting."

Kate bit her lip and glanced toward the bathroom. A hot shower did sound wonderful. "I feel a little strange about this."

Winston nodded. "I understand. But go on. There's a lock on the door." His smile softened the suggestion. "Be careful. You got pretty cold out there. Start with cool water and ease into warm."

Kate nodded. "Thanks."

The water took the edge off her chill but burned the scrapes on her neck. She was glad she had agreed, odd as it was to be showering in a stranger's bathroom. As the room filled with steam, Kate felt the tension of the last few hours slip away. When she stepped from the shower into one of Winston's fluffy towels, she heard the music even louder than before.

She went to the door to listen. It was one of her favorite

operas, Puccini's *Turandot*. She leaned her head against the door for a moment, savoring the steamy room and the velvety music.

A knock on the outside of the door startled her. She jerked away, glad she had locked it.

"Hello in there." He hadn't tried the doorknob.

"Yes?"

"I have an extra sweater and some sweatpants you could wear. They're warm."

Kate slid toward the corner, unlocked the door, cracked it, and put her hand through the narrow opening. "Thanks, Winston. Turns out I didn't have any dry clothes left, after all."

She dressed quickly and fluffed out her hair, knowing her thick, red curls would take forever to air dry. The scrapes from the seat belt weren't that bad. She found some antibiotic cream in the cabinet and used a little on her neck.

She put her hand to the doorknob, but a tenor voice that sounded too close to be the stereo stopped her. In the background, she could still hear the recording. Another voice had joined the opening lines of "Nessun Dorma." Winston was singing.

Kate tilted her head back and let Puccini's beautiful aria wash over her. Winston's Italian was flawless, and his voice was drenched with emotion. When the final notes had faded, she leaned her head against the door.

Standing here made the past few weeks with Nick seem like a bad dream. *He didn't even try that hard to get me to come home.* Kate thought of Winston on the other side of the door. Perhaps an evening with him wouldn't be such a bad thing.

When she stepped outside the bathroom, Winston looked up from the counter dividing the kitchen from the living area. "Feel better?"

Kate nodded. "Your voice is—marvelous." The compliment fell flat after the performance she had heard.

Winston smiled again. "Relax by the fire. I'm just getting you a drink."

I should call someone to come get me. But she didn't.

Winston joined her beside the fire. Kate ignored her inner voice as they talked and laughed, their conversation carefully avoiding anything about their personal lives. It was as if they were the only two people in the woods.

CHAPTER 23

From his darkened corner office on the third floor of SynTech Labs, Gregory Brulin watched the snow cover the grounds. The artificial lake stood out like a defect on alabaster skin. Inside, a small table lamp next to a couch tried to conquer the darkness.

He turned at a knock on the door. "Come in."

Lenny entered, his spiked hair and nose ring still intact. Only the name of the rock group on the T-shirt ever seemed to change.

"Sit." Gregory pointed to the chair in front of his desk.

"Here's this week's thing," Lenny said, scattering the papers onto Gregory's desk. Gregory caught a whiff of garlic. Double-cheese pizza, maybe?

Gregory tapped the disorganized pile into a neat rectangle, then studied the top sheet. "What good news do you bring me tonight, Lenny?"

"We got tons this week, man," Lenny said. "Too bad it's not in time for the free thing on Saturday."

Gregory shook his head. "We have more appointments than we can handle for Genetic Awareness Day. We'll wait a few months, then offer it again. Some of these will have made appointments by then."

Lenny dropped into a chair and propped his feet on Gregory's desk. "Saw you on TV this morning."

Gregory scanned the lists. "Oh?"

"You toasted that guy, man."

"People like Justin Hardegan rarely make a logical case for their position. It's not difficult to point that out."

Gregory turned a few more pages. The kid had hacked into the GenWorld database and could regularly access its DNA data. Along the way Lenny had infiltrated several major nonprofit organizations, pulling out their mailing lists of faithful donors. From these mailing lists Lenny had created a "target" database, adding to it from various sources he selected whenever he had time. Simple cross-checking between their target database and the GenWorld files each week produced a new list of names, people who would soon be blitzed by the marketing department with irresistible advertising for the Gene Therapy Center.

Gregory smiled at the updated list. Many new names. However, there were so many more to be had. When they expanded the treatments available, nearly everyone in the target database would be eligible for some type of therapy. The key was to increase the number of treatments.

What Gregory really wanted was one grand-slam treatment that would bring them flocking in. Cancer: That was the great plague everyone either contracted or would pay handsomely to avoid. He hoped Nick Donovan's research would produce effective cancer treatments. Soon. If only Milburn hadn't had to be dealt with, Nick could be working on those treatments now, not finishing up Milburn's project first.

"You've come up with quite a list here, Lenny."

"Yeah. Cool, huh?"

The office door swung open. The light from the small lamp cast a shadow on the figure in the doorway.

"Chernoff," Gregory said, "what do you want?" He placed the pages in front of him, lining up their edges again.

Chernoff twitched an eye at Lenny.

"Lenny, you may go for tonight," Gregory said.

The kid shrugged his shoulders, then loped out of the office, giving wide berth to Chernoff as he passed.

Gregory sighed as Chernoff filled Lenny's chair.

"Just came from Sublevel 2." Chernoff pulled out a cigarette and lighter.

Gregory spun the SynTech ring on the fourth finger of his left hand. "Donovan?"

"He and the homely girl. Heard them near the elevator." Chernoff flicked the lighter and studied the flame for a moment before lighting up.

"And?"

"They were talking about Milburn. Talking about visiting Milburn's wife, asking her questions." He flicked the lighter again and moved it back and forth, watching the flame dance.

Gregory's stomach twisted. "Then go take care of it, idiot! I don't want him talking to her."

Chernoff blew out smoke and stood. "I'll expect extra payment."

"I'm sick of your demands for more money, Chernoff. I've paid you well."

"Fine," Chernoff said, turning. "Find someone else to do what I do."

Gregory lifted his hand. "No, just—wait."

Chernoff shrugged. "I did Milburn for you under the package price. Then I did Donovan's patient so he'd come work for you. But that's the end of it. No more—including this with the wife—until you pony up some more cash."

Gregory sighed. "How much?"

"The same as before."

"What, again? Double?"

Chernoff grinned. "I work on installments, Dr. Brulin, didn't you know? I'll do your jobs for you until this installment runs out. Then we'll talk again."

Gregory clenched his jaw but nodded. Chernoff disappeared. A faint stink lingered in the air when he was gone.

Gregory took out a cigar and lit it with shaky fingers.

↩ ↩ ↩

The evening was getting away from Kate. Her inner voice was yelling now, too insistent to be ignored.

Winston lay on his side in front of the fire, his head propped on his hand. Kate sat beside him.

"Are you okay?" he asked.

No. I don't know what I'm doing here. Once she'd opened the gate, memories of Nick had flooded in. Their wedding, vacations, the life they'd shared together. *This is stupid. I don't want anyone else. For all our problems, I want Nick.*

Winston reached up and traced a line across her neck, just below the scrape. "Does it hurt?"

Kate felt the blood pounding in her neck. She pulled back slightly. "I should really make a call. It'll take forever for someone to come get me. Could I use your phone?"

Winston stood. "I was just going to make dinner. I've got this new indoor grill to try out. It vents all the smoke out of the house. How do you like your steak cooked?"

"Um, medium, I guess."

Winston went to the kitchen and began pulling things out.

"Could I use your phone?" Kate asked. "I should probably call a tow truck, too."

"What kind of car is it?" Winston asked.

"A Volvo."

"Safe car. That's good. Probably why you walked away."

Kate sat by the fire, watching Winston attacking an onion on the cutting board. A minute later she asked the question again, this time with her eyes focused on his face. "Could I use your phone?"

He looked up and smiled. "Maybe tomorrow we could cook some burgers."

CHAPTER 24

Trees seemed to wrap the Milburns' estate house with bare arms, in sharp contrast against the whiteness of the snowfall and the columns in front of the house.

Nick dropped from the driver's side into the snow and closed the door. The sound was deadened by the shrouded air. What did he expect to learn here? All he knew thus far was that Milburn had doubts and suspicions which he might have taken to the FDA if his life had not been cut short in Silver Lake. *Was such a random occurrence truly cause to be tramping across a stranger's yard at this hour of the night?*

A lamp beside the door flicked to life, shining a path across the snow. Bernice rang the bell. The door cracked open, and a pair of dark eyes peered through. No light came from the room behind the eyes.

"Andrea?" Bernice said. "It's Bernice and Dr. Donovan."

"I think you should go," a voice whispered from behind the door.

Bernice turned to Nick, a puzzled expression playing across her face.

"Mrs. Milburn," Nick said. "I need to speak with you."

"Please," she said. "Go away."

"But, Mrs. Milburn." Bernice pushed against the door with hesitant hands. "You said over the phone that we should come."

"I decided it wasn't worth it. I changed my mind."

Bernice pushed harder. "Andrea, I'm concerned about you. You don't sound well. Please let me come in."

Her distress seemed to melt the woman inside the house. The door fell away. "Bernice, you don't need to worry."

Andrea Milburn was in her late thirties. Her dark hair was swept away from her face and held in a clip. There were dark circles under her eyes. Nick had expected someone older.

Bernice led Nick into the house. "This is Dr. Donovan, Andrea. Andrea Milburn, Nick Donovan."

"Andrea," she said, nodding.

"Nick."

They stood in awkward silence for a long moment. Finally Nick broke the tension. "Andrea, I'm so sorry about your loss. I didn't know your husband, but I understand he was a brilliant man."

Andrea twisted her hands together and glanced through the window. "Come in," she said. "Sit in here."

They followed her into a darkened formal sitting room. A heavy clock ticked loudly on the mantel above the fireplace, and the room smelled musty, unused. Andrea sat on the edge of an upholstered chair, and Nick and Bernice took a seat across from her on a straight-backed couch. Andrea reached for a small table lamp beside her and switched it on. The lamp threw the rest of the room into shadows.

"I don't know how I can help you," Andrea said. She picked a piece of lint off the couch and thrust it from her.

"Mrs. Milburn—Andrea." Nick leaned forward. "I have been searching through the research files your husband entered, trying to catch up on his project. As I was going through them, I came across an entry about some suspicions he had." He caught Bernice's surprise from the corner of his eye. "Apparently Dr. Milburn had some concerns about the project. He had considered contacting the FDA about these concerns. I haven't found anything more specific. I was hoping you could help me."

"No."

Nick swallowed. "Andrea, I'm sure your husband's death has been difficult for y—"

"Difficult?" She seemed to spring to life. "You have no idea what it has been like. I have four children asleep upstairs. Four children to raise by myself. And all the while, never knowing if. . ."

Nick didn't speak, didn't move. Total silence might encourage her to continue.

She didn't.

"Never knowing what?" Bernice said, leaning forward, too.

Andrea turned away, searching the window again as though she were afraid of monsters that might lurk outside. "You don't understand. You can't."

"Help us understand, Andrea," Bernice said.

Andrea sucked in air as though it were her last breath. She turned back to face them, decision in her eyes. "I don't think Brian's death was an accident. That's why I changed my mind about talking to you by the time you got here. I'm afraid."

Nick sat back. *I was right.*

Bernice's eyes were wide with surprise. "What makes you think it wasn't an accident, Andrea?"

"Brian's car ran off the road into Silver Lake. There was nothing suspicious about the car, no drugs or alcohol in his system. The police assume he fell asleep at the wheel. There was one unusual note in the autopsy file." Andrea paused and studied the twisted fingers in her lap. "A 'blunt-force trauma' to the back of the neck. It didn't kill him. He—he drowned. But the injury doesn't make sense in that kind of accident. There was nothing more, so it was ruled an accident and closed. I told them that Silver Lake wasn't even on his way home, but they didn't seem to think it was important."

Andrea paused but then spoke quickly, as if determined to push through now that she had begun. "Brian called me that night. He said he had found something strange. He'd been disturbed for several days before his death. Whenever I'd ask him about it, he'd just say that it was something going on at work. When I pressed, he mentioned that he'd found a problem with a therapy he had sequenced, and he was trying to figure out how it had happened."

Nick perched on the edge of the couch, catching every syllable. "What therapy was it, do you remember?"

"I don't know. He didn't tell me. But he did say it was similar to the Fabry's therapy he was working on."

Nick leaned back against the couch, his mind working over the puzzle. If he could determine which therapy Milburn had sequenced and repeat the procedure, maybe he'd find out what had upset him.

A muffled crack outside the window startled all of them. An eerie, orange light grew outside.

"Something's on fire!" Andrea said.

Nick jumped to his feet. "I'll check." He reached the door in a half-dozen strides and yanked it open.

A wall of fire greeted him, blocking the doorway. He slammed the door against the heat and ran into the kitchen.

Hungry flames beat against the windows.

CHAPTER 25

Kate hadn't spoken to Winston in ten minutes. He seemed to have forgotten she sat beside the fire while he cooked. At times he sang along with the opera still playing. At times he talked to himself in a voice too soft for Kate to hear.

She had scanned every inch of the cabin. There was no phone. Now she sat with her knees drawn up in front of her, arms wrapped around them, her eyes studying Winston's every move. Could she be in danger?

The steaks sizzled on the indoor grill. Winston had thrown greens into a large bowl and chopped a tomato into it. He went back to cutting onions. Kate watched his long fingers wrap around the knife as he sliced and slid the onions into a skillet.

A hundred times she had opened her mouth to say something and then bit it back. Finally, she worked up enough courage. "What do you do, Winston?"

He looked up from the onions. "You know I'm a musician. I play classical guitar." He waved the knife over her shoulder. A guitar case stood at attention in the corner beside her. "Would you like to hear the CD I just recorded?"

Kate swallowed. "Sure."

As he walked past her, the sharp smell of the onions trailed with him. He started the CD and then headed for the kitchen again. As he passed, he dropped his hand to let his fingers brush through her hair.

Kate shivered at his touch, suddenly wondering if he had touched her like that—or worse—when she'd been unconscious. The last ounce of her temptation to have a fling with him dripped out of her.

"You have incredible hair," he said from the kitchen.

The music burst out then, much too loud.

"May I turn this down?" Kate called.

Winston looked up, unsmiling. "Don't you like it?"

"It's wonderful. Just a little loud."

"Leave it." He flipped the steaks.

Kate chose to remain silent again, keeping her eyes on her hands as she played with the fringe of the oriental rug in front of the fireplace. Should she ask about the phone again? Or should she just wait for a chance to walk out the door, back into the freezing woods?

When the meal was on the table, Winston crossed in front of her again and turned off the music. "Come and get it," he sang out.

She took her seat at the table. Winston poured wine and then slid into the seat beside her, taking her hand.

"Isn't this nice?" he said. "Just like we always wanted, Amanda."

Kate wrinkled her forehead. "Um, my name's Kate."

Winston squeezed her fingers till they throbbed. "I don't know why you left me, Amanda, but I'm glad you've changed your mind. We belong together."

I'm in trouble.

"When I came up here," Winston said, "I thought it would be to clear my head, to try to forget you. But now you're here. It's better than I imagined." He smiled and leaned over, brushing her cheek with a light kiss.

Kate pulled away. She picked at her food for several minutes while Winston tore into his. Had she stumbled into *The Twilight Zone*?

"Don't you like the steak?" he asked.

"Yes."

He tilted his head to the side, eyeing her. "Then eat it."

Kate nodded, cutting off a bite and forcing it into her mouth. The steak tasted like tree bark.

They ate in silence for several minutes, until Winston slammed his fork onto his plate and sat back in his chair like a peevish child. Kate's heart skipped a few beats.

"You're not talking to me," he said.

Kate fought the urge to scream. "Um, what would you like to talk about?"

Winston picked up his fork. "You could start by telling me how wrong you were to leave me."

"You know, I can hardly remember the reasons anymore."

"I remember. You said I had problems."

Yeah, I wonder why. "Did I say that?" Kate took a sip of water.

"You said I needed help. But I guess you were the one who needed help, right, Amanda?" Winston smiled now, like an indulgent father.

Kate didn't answer. Winston didn't speak to her for the rest of the meal. She glanced at him a few times, but his eyes were unfocused.

She helped him clear the table, then wandered around the cabin as he loaded the dishwasher, pretending to admire the artwork and collectibles on the walls. Within a few minutes she had worked her way around to the front door.

She waited till she saw Winston bend toward the dishwasher. She twisted the doorknob and pulled.

"I always keep that locked at night."

She turned to see Winston leaning his elbows on the counter, watching her. "You can't be too careful in the woods alone."

Kate forced her lips into a smile. The door was dead bolted with a keyed lock.

"I wanted to watch the snow fall," she said. "Could we open the door? Where's the key?"

Winston stood, patting the pocket on the front of his T-shirt. "Safe and sound. We can watch the snow from the back windows. Come over here."

He guided her to the back picture window. A snow-covered deck ran the length of the cabin, and a small lamppost perched on the railing, spreading a circle of light into the dark woods.

Winston stood behind her, his hands on her shoulders and his chin resting on top of her head. "Gorgeous, isn't it?"

Kate blinked back tears.

"I'm so glad you've decided to come back to me, Amanda. I know we'll be happy together."

Kate watched the snow fall, watched it fill up the world around her frosty prison, and wondered if God ever heard the cries of those who only call to Him in crisis.

CHAPTER 26

Nick tore out of the kitchen and back into Andrea's sitting room. "We have to get out. The back door."

"What's going on?" Andrea's eyes bulged.

"The front of the house is on fire."

"The children are upstairs!" Andrea ran toward the stairwell rising from the entryway. Nick and Bernice followed her. She rushed to the first door in the long hallway upstairs and burst through it.

Nick watched her scoop a small child from a bed shaped like a race car. "Where else, Andrea?"

"The next two doors. Two in the next bedroom. One in the last!"

Bernice ran past Nick and turned the knob on the last door. "It's locked!"

Nick opened the middle door. "Get these, Bernice."

She traded places with him, disappearing into the room. Andrea followed her. The little boy in her arms rubbed his eyes in confusion.

Nick pounded on the last door. "Open up!"

No answer.

"Open the door!" He didn't want to yell that the house was on fire if he didn't have to. The younger ones would only grow more frightened.

Andrea appeared beside him. He glanced down the hall to see Bernice herding two young girls down the stairs.

Andrea pounded her fist against the door. "Brian, open this door!"

Brian Jr.'s room, Nick assumed. A sulky adolescent with a locked door.

Finally, a groggy "Whaddaya want?" filtered out.

163

"Open the door, Brian," Nick said. "Now."

The bed creaked as though someone had turned over and settled in again.

"Andrea, go," Nick said. "Take the little ones out the back. I'll get him." He jerked his head toward the closed door.

Andrea hesitated, but then nodded and ran.

Once the two were heading down the stairs, Nick pounded again. "Brian, the house is on fire! Get out here now!"

The bed creaked again. Nick wondered if Brian Jr. was looking out the window to confirm things before obliging Nick with an unlocked door. The door swung open. Fourteen or fifteen years old, Nick guessed. Not happy.

"Who are you?"

"A friend." Nick grabbed his arm, but the boy yanked it back. "The house is on fire, Brian. Let's go."

Nick yanked the boy's arm till he felt Brian follow him. He headed for the stairs. There was already smoke in the hallway. Brian would figure it out in a second and then probably pass him on his way down.

Heat poured up at them as they descended. Flames had burned through portions of the front wall, a few feet from the bottom of the stairs.

"We have to go out the back!" Brian yelled.

They turned at the bottom of the stairs. Nick hesitated in the dark, but Brian pushed past him.

"This way!" The boy had finally caught on. "Where are my mom and my sisters and—"

"They're outside already." Smoke burned Nick's throat, and the words rasped.

Brian fell against a back door, and it opened. They found Andrea, Bernice, and the children huddled on the snowy deck.

"You have to get away from the house," Nick yelled.

Andrea was crying. "The children have no shoes on!"

"They'll be fine!"

Nick jumped off the deck and ran to the side of the house. The fire fed its insatiable appetite, racing toward the back of the house. At the corner, Nick tried to squeeze through a solid hedge wall that scraped up against the brick wall. Branches snagged his clothes and his face. They couldn't reach his car that way. He ran back to the others. In the distance, a siren screamed.

"The other side of the house—is there room to run around it?" he asked Andrea.

"Not much. I don't know. Maybe." Her eyes fluttered up to her flaming home.

"Let's go!" Nick picked up one of the little girls, handed her to Brian Jr., and then picked up the other girl himself. Andrea still held the little boy. Bernice looked terrified.

"Come on!" Nick launched out into the snow again, leading the way.

"Mom!" Brian screamed.

Nick turned.

Bernice now held the boy, surprise in her eyes. Andrea was running toward the house.

"What is she doing?" Nick yelled.

Andrea called something over her shoulder, but it was lost in the noise of the blazing house.

"Here," Nick said to Brian, "can you hold them both?"

"I'll try."

Nick looked at Bernice. "Can you get them to my car? Just get them in and back away from the house, okay? The keys are in it." Bernice nodded, her lips tight. Brian shifted his sisters who clung to him, the falling snow soaking their nightgowns.

Nick left them and ran for the house.

Total darkness surrounded him as soon as he entered. How could something burning be so dark? "Andrea!" His lungs seized with smoke. He dropped to his hands and knees, trying to remember the route back to the stairs. "Andrea!"

There was no answer.

Nick crawled around the house, calling Andrea and getting as close to the front as he dared. No answer.

She must have gone up the stairs. Nick crawled toward them. He dragged himself up two steps, but the smoke grew too thick. "Andrea!"

A woman's voice called from behind him. Nick shimmied down to the floor again and reached with groping hands.

"Andrea, where are you?"

"No, it's me. Bernice."

"Bernice, what are you doing in here?"

"The kids are safe in the car, down the street a little. I came back to help you."

There was no time to argue. "I can't find her."

A thumping sounded on the stairs above them.

"Andrea?"

"I'm here!" Andrea said from the darkness. Fear tinged her voice.

"Stay here," Nick said to Bernice. He crawled up several steps again and reached upward.

The burning wood splintered above them. Something ripped away from the ceiling. Nick looked up and threw his arms over his head. A beam crashed to the floor several feet behind him.

A scream came from the other side.

"Bernice!" She didn't answer. He crawled in that direction. His hands thrashed at the fallen beam. "Bernice!" He felt a leg, an arm. She was facedown and not responding.

Nick heaved the beam away from Bernice with adrenaline-pumping strength. He got to his feet and moved around toward her head. He wrapped his hands around her arms and dragged her through the hall and out the back door.

Nick squinted against the sudden brightness of the snowy night. He laid Bernice on the deck and checked her over, seeing nothing broken. Then a dark stain spread away from her head in the snow. Nick rolled her slightly. She had been crawling when the beam fell. It must have struck the back of her head. He couldn't see well enough to tell how bad the injury was.

Nick pulled his knit shirt off and wadded it up, bracing himself against the cold. He rolled Bernice to her back again, placing the shirt under her head. Hopefully the pressure of her head against the deck and the cold of the snow would slow the bleeding. At least until he could get Andrea out.

The sirens were louder now. Help was approaching.

Inside the back door, Nick dropped again. The heat seemed to have doubled in intensity since he had pulled Bernice out. He pushed forward, screaming for Andrea again.

Gagging nearby alerted him. He scuttled forward until his head rammed against Andrea's. "Are you all right?" he yelled.

"Brian's letters. I had to get his letters. All I—have left." She collapsed into coughing again. Nick pulled her toward himself and the door.

The white night glowed through the back-door window only ten feet away. Nick dragged Andrea toward it, both of them choking on the smoke.

Before they reached the door, the stairs beside them shuddered. With an earth-shaking rumble, the supporting wall collapsed. Pieces of wall showered down, blocking their path to freedom.

CHAPTER 27

Gregory Brulin flattened his palm on the small metal platform protruding from the wall, dropping his fingers one by one between the cold pegs. The palm geography reader took an instant to scan his hand before the green light flicked on. Gregory punched his security code into the keypad below the reader. The double doors buzzed, and he pushed them open.

Sublevel 3 of SynTech Labs was home to a few hand-picked investigators whom Gregory could trust with the ultimate direction of his mission. While the Gene Therapy Center began the work of Phase 1, cleansing, the research and procedures performed down here were perfecting Phases 2 and 3.

The lab was larger than any others he'd given his investigators. He needed space, and he needed to be ready for whatever procedures might come next. Bottles, beakers, and microscopes littered the large lab bench in the center of the room, and several six-foot refrigeration units lined the back wall. One door at the back opened into a smaller examination room, and another was the door to a small cold room.

Gregory sat on a stool and pulled out his notebook. New research had finished with FDA approval and had come down to Sublevel 3. It remained for him to alter the therapy slightly, enough to have an additional effect on the patient. Then it would be replicated and go on to the center, where no one would ever suspect that one gene on the seventeenth chromosome contained a mutated version of the ATCG protein-building code.

Gregory hunched over his work, carefully splicing the new segment, according to his notes. When the process was complete, he capped the vial and labeled it Version 2.

Gregory glanced at his watch. He had about ten minutes before the woman would arrive. He could hear Dr. Yang in the back, the specialist he'd hired to oversee Phase 2, cloning, and Phase 3, creating.

"You ready, Yang?" he said.

"I am setting up the ultrasound," Dr. Yang said.

Gregory walked into the back room and drummed the fingers of one hand on the counter. The tiny, bow-tied investigator sat on a stool, adjusting the machine. Gregory stood a few inches away and watched until Yang looked up from his work, forced to crane his neck to meet Gregory's eyes.

Gregory despised this precise, little man, as antiseptic as the lab he worked in and with as much personality as the cryogenic freezers. But he had the skills Gregory needed—and the proven ability to keep his mouth shut.

"What may I do for you this evening, Dr. Brulin?" Yang asked.

"You may give me a report on Phase 3. Is the embryo ready?"

"We have run across a few snags, but nothing that cannot be worked out."

Gregory chafed at Yang's serenity but did not flinch. "We don't have much time. She's already started the hormones."

"I realize that, Doctor. I will be ready."

Snags? Gregory glanced around the vast lab, wondering what good any of it was if he couldn't get competent people to run it. Time was his enemy. Time and the hormonal cycle of one woman's body. The hum of equipment accompanied the drumming of his fingers, but the sound deadened in here as though it suffocated, too far below ground level to ever escape. "And Phase 2?"

A knock sounded on the entry doors out in the lab.

"Perhaps you should ask her," Yang answered.

Gregory crossed the lab and punched the blue square that opened the double doors. A young woman, dressed in an elegant, black maternity dress beneath a fur-lined leather coat, entered the room. Her six-months-pregnant figure still looked fit and healthy, and her dark hair was swept into an stylish twist on the top of her head and secured with a gold clasp.

Gregory walked around the lab bench to greet her. "Ms. Milano."

"I'm early," the woman said, her accent betraying her New York City upbringing, "but you'll have to deal with it. I'm meeting someone. Can we get this over with quickly?" She pulled leather gloves from her hands and shoved them into a purse.

"I'm so sorry to inconvenience you, Tina."

"Don't take that sarcastic tone with me, Brulin. I'll walk right out of here."

"Dr. Yang is waiting for us in the back."

She pushed past him, knocking her shoulder against his as she passed. Gregory followed her, clenching his fists.

Yang had already darkened the room in preparation for the ultrasound. "Good evening, Ms. Milano. I trust you are feeling well?"

Tina's eyes narrowed. "I feel like I'm carrying two tons of someone else's baggage on the front of my body, Yang. How do you think I feel?"

"Yes, Ms. Milano. If you would please change into a gown? You'll find one in the rest room there." He pointed to a door behind Tina.

Tina turned to Gregory and rolled her eyes. "He acts like we haven't already done this a dozen times. I think I know the procedure by now."

She emerged from the rest room a few minutes later in the baby blue gown and climbed onto the examining table.

Yang pulled up the gown. Gregory did not look away.

Tina tilted her head back. Yang stood beside her. "I know, I know," she mumbled. "This will be cold."

Yang smeared her abdomen with gel before beginning the ultrasound. The picture on the screen above Tina shifted, and Gregory studied it as though the secret of life unfolded there. In a way, it did. The secret of his son's life at least.

It took ten minutes for Yang to take the measurements and punch them into the computer. "Everything looks fine, Doctor," he said, pulling off his gloves. "Still progressing with normal development, right on track. This healthy boy should be born in three months, as expected." He turned toward Gregory and bumped Tina's arm.

Tina propped herself up on her elbows. "You get more clumsy every time you do this, Yang."

Gregory tossed a towel onto her belly. "You forget yourself, Ms. Milano. You're a body-for-hire. And you're right, the baggage you carry does belong to someone else. Let's not forget who's paying for your expensive clothes and new lifestyle."

Tina raised herself from the table by rolling to her side and pushing up on one hand first. When she was sitting with her legs hanging over the side, she leveled her eyes at Gregory's.

"And let's not forget that I'm the one carrying the little treasure," she said. "If I disappear, it disappears."

Gregory's fists were still clenched. "Good day, Ms. Milano."

≀ ≀ ≀

Gregory tried to focus on the site-directed mutagenesis he was working on in the lab. This therapy was the last he needed to alter before Saturday. Once the formula was perfect, he could send it out for others to duplicate.

Tina Milano's arrogance irritated him, but what really caused the distraction was a nagging fear that his master plan might unravel because of Nick Donovan asking questions he shouldn't be asking. Gregory had faced that fear once already, with Brian Milburn. Would he need to do it again? Could he? He stood, circling his stool to reach the phone.

He punched the switchboard operator's number and got Nick Donovan's home number. A few seconds later a recorded message played into his ear. Nick wasn't home. The message had been recorded by Kate. Gregory hadn't heard the cheerful voice in years, and it disturbed him. What had happened with Kate was one of his life's regrets.

He replaced the phone, annoyed. Chernoff should have ended Nick's appointment with Milburn's wife by now. Where was Donovan?

As if in answer, a hand slapped the window of the lab's double doors. Gregory buzzed him in.

"Where's Nick Donovan, Chernoff?" Gregory asked without preamble.

The man's eyes were razor sharp. "Taken care of."

Gregory's blood pounded. "What are you talking about?"

"I did what you asked." Chernoff slid onto a stool, pulling out the ever-present cigarette and gold lighter. "I took care of him."

Gregory yanked the cigarette from Chernoff's mouth, dropped it to the floor, and crushed it with a pivot of his shoe.

"I gave them a slight—diversion," Chernoff said, snapping the flame on the lighter as though nothing had happened.

"What diversion?"

He flicked the lighter on and stared at the flame. "A fire."

Gregory held his anger long enough to press his fingers against his closed eyelids. "Donovan was there?"

"You said to do whatever it took."

"He's dead?"

Chernoff shrugged. "I do things my way, Brulin."

Gregory turned away. "I need him, Chernoff."

Two slow steps brought Gregory to a refrigeration box. He slid the glass front open and wrapped his fingers around a syringe, turning back to Chernoff. The corpse-like man narrowed his eyes as Gregory approached him, his hands at his side.

Gregory placed a cold hand on Chernoff's shoulder and jerked the syringe to the man's neck with the other hand. "Do you know how many ways there are to kill a man, Chernoff?" he asked. "Not all of them are as primitive as yours. A tap of the finger can shoot contaminated cells into your bloodstream that would leave you on the floor in seconds."

Chernoff's eyes registered a rare concern.

"You'll do things my way, Chernoff."

Chernoff leaned away from Gregory's syringe, his face twitching as though a spider crawled over it. "I don't know if he's dead. He had plenty of time to walk out the back of that house. But I figured Milburn's wife would get the message loud and clear."

Gregory lowered the syringe. "But she had time to talk to him before your 'diversion,' " he said, more to himself than to Chernoff.

How many of Nick's questions did Andrea Milburn answer? Perhaps Chernoff's approach was more effective, after all.

CHAPTER 28

"Andrea!"

Nick dug through the hot rubble, his fingers scrabbling for Brian Milburn's wife.

The pieces of wood and drywall shifted to the right of his hands. Nick plunged an arm into the mess and felt flesh.

"I'm okay," came the muffled response from under the rubble.

The smoke saturated even the air near the floor. Nick held his breath and dove over the pieces of stairwell, turning to find Andrea when he kneeled before the back door. Complete darkness made it impossible until he heard her scratching out of the pile. His fingers wrapped around a wrist, and he yanked.

Andrea gave a little scream as she broke free.

Nick pulled the door open, and the two stumbled into the night. The wail of sirens and men shouting orders pierced the snow-laden air as the two stumbled around the house. Firemen hurried to their aid. Andrea broke away when she saw her children leaning out of the car windows in the street.

Nick spent the next two hours answering police and fire department questions and shuttling the Milburns to a relative's home. As soon as he was free, he drove to the suburban hospital where Bernice had been taken. She had been admitted, listed in fair condition. Nick stopped in for a moment but found her sleeping. He drove home.

When he emerged from his hot shower, still feeling sooty, he fell into bed, too exhausted to contemplate the information he had gained from Andrea.

Tomorrow he would sequence the DNA of Milburn's suspicious therapy. If he could find it.

        ر   ر   ر

In Winston's cabin, Kate stood before the fire, fighting the chill that threatened to numb her senses. She needed to stay alert, to watch for her chance.

Winston stood behind her. His hands skimmed her shoulders. He wrapped his arms around her and buried his face in her hair. Kate swallowed, her back stiff.

"You must be tired, Amanda," he said. "Come to bed."

Kate stomach churned. "I'm not tired."

Winston pulled her against himself and laughed. "Come to bed anyway, then."

It was time to give the performance of a lifetime. Kate tilted her head to look into his face. "Please, Winston. This wasn't how I expected our reunion to be. The car accident, the freezing walk in the woods." She engineered a note of pleading into her voice. "My whole body aches, and I just can't seem to get warm. Couldn't I sleep out here by the fire tonight?"

Winston pulled away, a frown puckering his mouth. "But I've missed you, Amanda."

"I know." Kate swallowed. "I've missed you, too. That's why I wanted it to be perfect when we. . .you know."

A smile softened Winston's frown. "You always were a romantic. All right. If waiting makes you happy, Amanda, we'll wait. You see? I want to do whatever it takes to make you happy."

"Thank you," Kate said, relief flooding through her.

"I'll get some blankets," Winston said. "We'll get comfortable on the couch."

"Oh—I don't want you to suffer out here with me."

"I'm not leaving you alone, Amanda." He flashed his perfect smile. "You never have to worry about being alone again."

He returned a minute later with a stack of blankets. He took his glasses off and pulled her onto the couch. "Lay next to me. We'll just watch the fire." He pulled her toward him, both of them facing outward on the couch.

Kate cringed as he dragged his long fingers through the back of her hair.

"Comfortable?" Winston said.

Kate nodded, her eyes squeezed shut. *God, help me.*

CHAPTER 29

Wednesday, February 23

Nick sniffed as he entered the lab. The air still reeked of the sharp antiseptic the night cleaning crew used. The floor gleamed in sterile white, and the metallic shelves and equipment had been polished to a shine. Nick pulled a peppermint from his pocket. He had grabbed a handful from a glass candy dish that Kate kept filled at home. Even after a good night's sleep, another shower, a fast food breakfast, and three cups of coffee, nothing seemed able to counteract the acrid taste of smoke in the back of his throat.

He dropped his briefcase and coat into his private office and went right for the computer, taking a moment to check his E-mail. His Success Quote that day came from Ralph Waldo Emerson: "Once you make a decision, the universe conspires to make it happen."

Was that really true? So many success books talked about tapping into a "Higher Power." Was there something out there, Someone out there, who cared about what Nick Donovan did with his life? How could he connect with that Power? Wasn't it presumptuous to assume It would be listening?

Nick scanned the rest of his E-mail, all unimportant. His thoughts returned to what Andrea had told him last night about her husband's work.

Andrea believed her husband was murdered. And murdered because of his suspicions of a SynTech gene therapy with some kind of problem.

Was the whole thing better left untouched? His three-week deadline loomed large. If he didn't focus on the protocol descriptions, he'd never make it. However, if there was some kind of problem with the therapy Milburn had been using for Fabry's, then Nick would run into it, too. Which therapy would Milburn have used as a comparison with Fabry's?

Nick checked his watch: 8:30. He needed to get busy on the proposal. The Preclinical Studies section of the proposal was largely unfinished, and he needed to scour Milburn's notes for details, reporting what cells were the intended target cells of the recombinant DNA and tracking the percentage of target cells containing the added DNA in the animal studies. He couldn't waste the day searching for Andrea's mysterious other therapy. Even if he found which therapy Milburn had used, the DNA sequencing would take almost three hours.

Nick rubbed the muscles in the back of his neck, shook his head at his own foolishness, and started pulling up research files.

Thirty minutes later, he struck gold. "Gaucher's disease," he said, leaning back in his chair. Milburn's notes said he intended to study Gaucher's as an aid to developing the Fabry's therapy. It made sense. They were both lysosomal storage disorders. Nick continued to stare at the monitor as the outer lab door swung open.

"Morning, Jeremy," Nick said, not looking up.

A grunt was the only reply.

Nick swung his chair toward to the door and called Jeremy in. "Did Milburn ever talk to you about studying Gaucher's disease?"

Jeremy flicked his head to fling the hair out of his eyes. "Yeah, he looked at it at one point, I think. To compare."

"We're going to sequence it today."

"Why? We're past that phase, Nick. The Fabry's therapy is already done. We're just doing the paperwork, remember? Why do you need to compare it to anything anymore?"

"I still have some follow-up I want to do."

Jeremy shook his head. "Whatever."

Nick went down the hall to the cold storage room where therapies were kept. He was searching for a Gaucher sample when the door buzzed and opened behind him. A white-coated man Nick hadn't met pushed a hand truck through the door. He nodded to Nick.

"Hi." Nick extended a hand. "Nick Donovan."

"Louis Ward."

Nick saw that the crates were full of vials. He pointed at them. "You bring that many in every day?"

Louis adjusted his glasses. "Our output is significantly increased this week in preparation for Genetic Awareness Day on Saturday."

Nick found the sample Gaucher vector and stepped past Louis, who was unloading his delivery onto the room's metal shelving.

He returned to the lab, and he and Jeremy started the sequencing process. The state-of-the-art genetic analyzer was better than anything Nick had used at the university. Once they installed the plate of prepared samples on the instrument's autosampler and started the run, the machine could work for hours unattended.

The process was simple. The two strands of DNA would be separated and a primer added. The bits of DNA would filter down through the electrophoresis gel, and the fragments would migrate according to size. When the sequencing was complete, the raw data would output to the connected computer, resulting in an electropherogram he could analyze.

"Bernice should be here soon," Jeremy said. "She and I can finish this."

Nick mentally smacked himself. In his zeal to find answers to the Milburn problem, he'd completely forgotten to tell Jeremy what had happened to Bernice. "She won't be in today, Jeremy."

"Why?" Jeremy swung hair away from his face and studied Nick. "She call in sick again?"

"She's had a little—accident."

Jeremy jumped to his feet. "What! What kind of accident?"

"She's going to be okay, Jeremy. I called the hospital this morning. She's in stable condition." Nick explained the fire.

"What were you doing at Milburn's house?" Jeremy backed off, arms crossed.

"I needed to check out a few details for our project. Nothing important. It was a good thing we were there, though. Andrea might not have been able to get all the kids out by herself."

Jeremy paced the lab, muttering. "She never should have gone over there." He turned to Nick. "I'm going to go see her."

"You might want to wait until lunch," Nick said. "The nurse said she'd be sleeping all morning."

"Oh. Yeah, I guess."

Nick went back to the DNA sequencer. It was almost nine-thirty already. This search would take a few hours, and they might not find anything. "Jeremy, why don't you finish with the sequencing, and then let me know what you find? After that, go see Bernice. She's at St. Catherine's Hospital. I'm going to sit at my desk and try to get a little work done on the Fabry's proposal."

Jeremy scowled. "I don't even know what I'm looking for with this thing."

Nick debated. How much should he tell Jeremy? "I think there's something wrong with the Gaucher vector, Jeremy. I want to find the anomaly if there is one. Anything."

"Shouldn't we be concentrating on Fabry's?" Jeremy said.

"I will be," Nick said. "But for you this takes precedence for now, okay?"

Jeremy shrugged. "I'll tell you when it's done."

Nick slapped him on the shoulder, grateful for the second mind working on the problem. In just a few hours, he would have the answer to the Brian Milburn mystery.

CHAPTER 30

Morning sun filtered through the skylight in the cabin's cathedral ceiling, moving across the floor until it fell across Kate's eyes where she slept on Winston's couch.

She stirred, enjoying the warmth. Then she remembered. She snapped her eyes open but did not move.

Winston still slept beside her, his back braced against the back of the couch, one arm extended around the top of Kate's head. She lay on her back, her shoulder braced against his chest. She turned her head toward him, a careful eye on his face. Again she was struck by the perfect features hiding the impaired mind.

She had to get that key.

She studied the front pocket of his T-shirt, just above her shoulder. She could see the sharp edges of the key against the black fabric. Would it be possible to pull the key out without waking him? She had to try.

She lifted the top seam of the pocket with the tip of her fingernail. Winston still breathed a slow rhythm, his head above her. Her forehead nearly touched his chin. She slid her forefinger into the pocket, followed by her thumb.

She froze as Winston's breathing caught, hung, and then released again. She continued her easy slide into the pocket. Her forefinger felt the edge of something sharp.

She paused again, watching Winston's eyes. Her fingers pinched the key. She inched it toward the top of the pocket.

Winston sniffed and rolled toward her, taking her hand with him. Her hand bent under him, the loose fingers twisted together. She pulled the key out another fraction of an inch. She was so close.

Then Winston filled his lungs with air, rotated his body, and opened his eyes.

Kate kept a firm grasp on the key as he turned. It broke free of the pocket and was in her hand. She balled her fist over it and looked up at Winston. He hadn't seemed to notice.

He ran a hand through his hair. "Good morning."

She gave him a thin-lipped smile.

"Did you sleep well?" he asked.

"Yes, thank you." It was the truth. The strain of last night's journey through the storm, the accident, and her hike in the woods had left her exhausted. Once it had appeared that Winston was asleep for the night, she had slept without stirring.

Winston pulled himself up onto his elbows. "Tonight we'll sleep in the bed."

Kate stood.

"What would you like for breakfast this morning, Amanda?"

She shoved her hands into her pockets, letting the key drop inside. "Why don't you let me cook today?" She saw Winston's eyes narrow. "You could take a shower, if you like," she added.

He glanced at the door and then back at Kate, his expression dark.

"Do you like eggs?" Kate asked.

He stood beside her and brushed hair away from her face, letting his hand linger. She felt the heat of his hand against her cheek. "You know I do."

Kate strolled to the refrigerator, pulling out a carton of eggs. When she turned back, he was still watching her.

"This won't take long," she said. "You'd better hurry."

"There's some sausage in the freezer, too." He hesitated a moment, then walked into the bathroom, closing the door.

Kate set the egg carton on the counter and ran to her shoes. Her fingers trembled around the laces. She tried to tie them. They slipped from her grasp. With one hand she pulled the key out of her pocket. With the other she grabbed her coat.

The dead bolt resisted the shaking key's attempts to enter. The seconds ticked past. The key slid in. She clicked it clockwise, turned the knob, pulled. Cold air rushed in.

A hand shot over her head. The door slammed tight.

Kate whirled, her back against the door.

Winston glared down at her. He held his jeans in his hand, one of his fluffy white towels twisted around his waist.

"You can't keep me here!" Kate's voice cracked with the attempt at boldness.

"Amanda." He brought his hand down to her shoulder, then traced the contour of her jaw with a slow finger. "We've been through this before."

Tears streamed from her eyes. "Please, let me go," she said.

Winston closed his eyes, pulled her to him, pressing her face against his bare chest. His cologne smelled like the outdoors.

"Soon you'll understand," he said. "When you learn to trust me. Then we won't need locks anymore."

Kate spread her hands against his chest and shoved, surprising him into stumbling backward a step. "I will not trust you!" she shouted.

He stepped up close to her again, this time reaching around and yanking the key from the lock.

"Then I will keep this!" His eyes flashed like sparks.

Kate shrunk away from his anger. Since she had first opened her eyes on his couch last night, she had not seen him angry. His self-control was the only thing that gave her any hope. She could not risk cracking through whatever it was that kept him self-possessed.

"I'm sorry, Winston. I won't do it again."

He touched a soft finger to her lips. "I know."

Kate returned to the kitchen. She cracked eggs mechanically into a bowl and then searched for a whisk. Winston emerged from the bathroom minutes later.

Kate's hands were still shaking when she lifted her first forkful of scrambled eggs to her mouth. She wondered if Winston noticed.

"After breakfast, I'll play for you." He chewed his sausage as though it were a delicacy.

Kate swallowed the rubbery eggs. "That would be nice."

After they cleaned the breakfast dishes, Winston guided her to the living-room floor. He took her shoes off gently and laid them by the fireplace. Then he pulled his guitar from the corner and sat beside her.

Kate watched his hands as he played. He had real talent. The music tantalized her into losing her focus. If she was going to make it out of here, she'd have to stay alert and watch for opportunities. But Winston's fingers danced over the strings, melding selections from Bach and Vivaldi and Pachelbel into a hypnotic thread of silky sound.

Winston smiled at her after several minutes, as though waiting for a comment.

"That was beautiful," she said.

He laid the guitar aside. "Come here."

Kate waited. She was only a few feet from him already.

He patted the floor beside him. "Sit next to me."

She obeyed.

He turned his face toward hers, burying it in her hair. "You do everything beautifully."

Kate closed her eyes. Even though he was a nutcase, some part of her wished she could be Amanda, even just for awhile. When was the last time Nick had showered her with this much attention and affection? She felt his breath on her ear, her cheekbone.

"Amanda." He whispered the name, kissing her gently on the cheek.

She tilted away a fraction.

His fingers clenched around her wrist, though he did not move his head away. "Don't do that again," he said, his voice a rumbling in his chest.

His lips were on her face again. She felt them slide closer to her mouth.

"Stop!" She jumped to her feet and backed away from him toward the fireplace.

He stood. The eyes were like fire again, fire that wanted to consume her.

She took another step back, her hands behind her for support. Her hand felt cold metal. The poker. She clutched it.

Winston took a step toward her.

She brought the poker out like a sword. "Don't come any closer."

"Amanda." His voice sounded disappointed, like he scolded a child. "Put that down."

She didn't know what she intended to do with the poker. She held it at his chest level. Could she drive it into him? "Stay away from me."

"Amanda, I love you. I want to give every part of myself to you. To spend my life making you happy. I can give you anything you want."

"Oh, really? Then let me go."

"Now, Amanda, be reasonable." Winston held his hands out in front of him as he pleaded with her. She watched his handsome face as he begged. She should have watched his hands. In one quick motion he grabbed the shaft of the poker and twisted it from her grasp.

"You shouldn't have done that, Amanda." He pointed the poker toward her.

Kate ran for the bathroom. She heard his startled grunt and his feet behind her. She slammed the door and locked it before he reached it. In temporary relief, she leaned her head against it.

"Amanda!" Winston pounded the poker against the door. "I will break this door down!"

She backed up. "I need to be alone for a few minutes, Winston."

Silence.

"Can I please have a few minutes alone?"

More silence.

"Maybe I'll take another shower."

"You have ten minutes."

She heard him retreat. Ten minutes. What could she figure out in ten minutes? Her gaze bounced off the walls, around the room. For the first time she noticed the small window above the toilet.

There was no time to think. She hurried to the shower, turning the water on, lifting the knob to bring the water out the showerhead. She turned both faucet knobs on in the sink, running water full force. She flicked the switch beside the light. The exhaust fan buzzed.

She wore only a sweater, jeans, and socks. No coat. No shoes. No more time.

The window probably hadn't been opened in years. She tried to push with steady pressure that wouldn't cause a sudden noise. After about ten seconds, it gave way. She pressed against the screen. It popped out of the groove, slipped through the window, and fell to the ground.

She listened for a moment. Nothing but water running and the blood pounding in her own ears. She stepped onto the toilet and then swung one leg through the opening. She pulled the other up. It would be a tight squeeze.

She perched there for a second, her lower half out and upper half in. Her legs were instantly cold. The drop to the ground was not far, but the snow beneath her feet did not look inviting. She slid out, her back scraping against the window frame.

It took only a moment for the sharp, wet chill of the snow to shoot through her cotton socks. She ran.

The white woods with their stark prison bars of bare trees blinded her. She ran with no direction in mind. Away. That was all that mattered.

How many minutes passed as she ran? Five? Six? A cramp in her side forced her to slow to a walk. Her feet ached with the cold, and she missed her coat. Finally the running was beginning to warm her a little, though.

What was that? A rumble not too far away. Was she near the highway?

No, the rumble came from behind her, from the direction she had fled.

Did Winston have a snowmobile? A second later she could tell the sound was bounding toward her. He could follow her footprints like a hunter tracks a deer.

She ran again, ignoring the cramp that clutched at her side.

Could she hide? There were big trees, large rocks. No, he would see her footprints. She had to find help.

Her feet wouldn't obey her any longer. Unseen roots reached up to grab at her from under the snow. Twice she sprawled forward, like a child making face-down snow angels. The snow clung to her face, melting in tiny rivers down her neck and traveling under her sweater as she ran.

The snowmobile growled closer. Her breath burst out in tiny explosions, in rhythm with her pounding feet. She tried to look around for a cabin or a road and keep her eyes on her feet at the same time.

One glance over her shoulder. She could see red streaking through the woods behind her. She turned back to watch her path. What had been a brown spot in the distance leaped into focus. A cabin.

She sprinted like it was the final lap of an Olympic race. Closer, closer. Winston's engine roared behind her.

A rock under the snow caught her foot. She came down on the rock with the side of her foot. Her ankle turned outward, and pain shot through her leg, bringing her to her knees, only thirty yards from the cabin.

Then Winston was beside her. In front of her. He skidded sideways to a stop between her and the back of the cabin. Kate panted on her knees, holding her arms in front of her as if they could protect her.

Winston wore clear goggles and a bright red coat. He got off the idling snowmobile and walked toward her. "That was foolish, Amanda."

She looked up at him from the ground. "Please." She covered her face with her hands.

He grabbed her elbow. "Come home now."

A voice shot out from behind Winston. "What's going on out here?"

Winston swiveled to look. "No problem," he called, lifting Kate to her feet. "Just took a turn too sharply. My wife fell off the snowmobile. We're fine." He pulled Kate around as if to prove his words.

Kate saw the man standing on a small deck attached to the back of the cabin. Winston's fingers dug into the flesh around her elbow. Her ankle screamed in protest.

He pressed something cold into the small of her back and

brought his lips to her ears. "Don't say a word."

Kate pushed away. She stumbled toward the cabin. "Help me! He's—"

Winston pulled her back and wrapped an arm around her shoulder. He covered her mouth and turned her body away from the cabin. The balding man lifted a hand to shield his gaze from the sun-bright snow.

Just before Winston blocked her view, Kate recognized him. *Bert!*

"Okay, then," Bert yelled. "Be more careful next time." He turned and went inside.

Hot tears spilled down Kate's frozen cheeks.

Winston pulled her close, his gloved hand rough against her face. "I don't want this to ever happen again." His arms encircled her like chains of steel. "If you don't stop, you will force me to do things I don't like to do. I don't like to do them, sweetheart. But I will."

She nodded.

"Let's go," he said, dragging her to the snowmobile. "You'll have to hold on to me from behind."

Kate swung a leg over the snowmobile, her chest heaving with silent sobs. Winston mounted in front of her and reached for the key.

A gunshot pierced the silent winter woods. Birds flew out of the trees over their heads and flapped away from the intrusion. Kate looked over at the cabin.

"Get off the snowmobile, young man." Bert stood with a hunting rifle braced against his shoulder.

"There's no problem here, sir," Winston said.

Bert fired another thunderous shot into a nearby tree. "I said, get off."

Winston raised his hands a little and stepped aside.

Bert flicked his eyes at Kate. "You okay, miss?"

Kate burst into tears and limped toward the cabin.

Bert motioned Winston away from the snowmobile with the end of the rifle. "Inez!"

A dark-skinned woman trotted through the back door. "Oh, my goodness, what is going on?"

"Is Rudy still in the store?"

"Yes, he's having another cup of coffee."

"Tell him to get out here, quick."

Kate trudged up the rickety wooden steps leading to Bert's deck, dragging her injured foot behind and wincing with each step. She stood behind Bert, who kept his rifle trained on Winston.

"Next time you decide to take your 'wife' for a joyride, better give her a coat and some shoes."

Kate managed a grateful smile.

A police officer swung open the back door. "What's going on, Bert?"

"I'm not so sure," Bert said. "Ask the lady."

"He's crazy!" Kate said. "He's been holding me hostage."

Rudy's brow furrowed. He put down his coffee. "Okay, let's get rid of the rifle, Bert." He jogged down the steps and out to Winston. He pulled Winston toward the cabin and then glanced at Kate. "Let's have the whole story, ma'am."

Kate took a deep breath, unsure if she had the energy to explain. "My car ran off the road last night. I got lost in the woods." She pointed at Winston. "He found me and took me to his house. But then he wouldn't let me go. He kept calling me by someone else's name. I escaped through the bathroom window."

The last few words were nearly bitten off by Kate's chattering teeth. Both men seemed to come to themselves and realize her condition.

"Bert, why don't you take the lady inside and let her get warm," the officer said. "I'll have more questions for both of them so we can get to the bottom of—"

Kate's legs buckled under her.

"Whoa, let's get you inside," Bert said. He pulled her through the doorway. "Inez!"

Half an hour later Kate was wrapped in Inez's oversized bathrobe and had fuzzy pink slippers hugging her feet. She sat sipping hot coffee at the tiny kitchen table in the back of Bert's Bait and Tackle. A quick visit to Winston's cabin had produced Kate's ID, verifying her story. A few bizarre comments from Winston had convinced Rudy to place him under professional care.

Inez set the phone in front of Kate.

"I don't think I'll ever leave home without a phone again," Kate said. "What time is it?"

"About nine."

Nick would be at work already. Kate didn't know the number at SynTech Labs. Besides, this wasn't the way she imagined their first contact after her departure. She dialed Melanie's number. Scott picked up.

Kate poured out the story, sobbing by the end.

"I'll be there as soon as I can, Kate," he promised when she finished. "As soon as Melanie gets home to stay with the kids, I'll drive right up there."

"Where's Melanie?" Kate asked.

"She had that appointment at SynTech's Gene Therapy Center."

Brian Milburn Journal Entry #3
January 28

If Sam Spade were here, would he find a way to hack into restricted areas of computer networks? I daresay he would, and my hobby has paid off today.

"Particular patients" get the Version 2s, Louis had said. So, I thought, which particular patients?

I navigated around the network for awhile like a rat lost in a maze. When I found the patient files for the Gene Therapy Center, I started analyzing them carefully.

The folks down at the center do a thorough medical workup and history on every person who sets up treatment, so I had to wade through a bog of useless information before I hit on something. But I finally found it.

Attached to some patients' records, not all, there's a note that says "T-type 2." That can only mean "Therapy-type 2." Those are the patients getting the second version. So far, I don't know why these "particular" patients are slated to get the second version. But one thing I do know: Every one of them has an appointment scheduled for that Genetic Awareness Day next month.

I'm going to track down the other Version 2 therapies. The patient files listed T-type 2 treatments for all kinds of diseases, not just the Gaucher's sample I pulled. What's different about those other versions? Will I find the same alteration?

But time is something I have in limited supply. Besides the Fabry's proposal, I'm working against Genetic Awareness Day, too. I won't let those messed-up therapies get injected into anyone that day. But blowing the whistle now might not be the best thing. How is the FDA going to find out who's done this?

So I'm appointing myself their man on the inside. It's the only way to put a stop to the wacko responsible.

CHAPTER 31

Nick sat at his computer working on the Fabry's proposal. Jeremy was out in the lab waiting for the Gaucher's sequencing to finish. Nick's phone rang. "Hello?"

"Nick? This is Stanford Carlton."

"Hey, Stanford. Is everything okay?" Nick leaned back in his chair.

"Just checking up on you. You seemed a bit hesitant last night about things at SynTech. I didn't want to get into it with Frank there, but I wanted to make sure you're doing all right."

"Yeah, I'm fine, Stanford."

"Good."

Nick waited, wondering if he should mention the fire to Stanford.

"So I've seen the ads for the big Genetic Awareness Day," Stanford said. "You involved with that?"

"Not really. Gregory wants me to understand the project, be aware of marketing strategy, that sort of thing. But I'm not directly involved."

"Seems like a good project, don't you think?"

Nick reviewed a paragraph from the proposal on his screen. "I hope so."

"You have doubts?"

"Not doubts. No. It's just an interesting strategy. Targeting people and all."

"What do you mean, targeting?" Stanford's voice seemed to change pitch.

"I mean running their DNA profiles, notifying them if something comes up. It's interesting, that's all."

"Hmm." Stanford cleared his throat. "So, can I do anything to help you get acclimated over there? It's been awhile, but I still know a few people."

Nick considered asking Stanford about Milburn but decided against it. The man had enough to worry about. He sat behind his desk. "No, I'm getting on okay."

"Gregory's not putting too much pressure on you right away? I know how he can be."

"Well, the deadline's basically impossible, but we'll make it."

"It's just that he can be obsessive at times, you know?"

Nick pulled another peppermint from his pocket but set it aside. He swiveled his chair toward the back of his office. "Obsessive?"

"He's got big plans, that's all I'm saying. Sometimes he gets carried away with his grand ideas. Very passionate, you could say."

"I've noticed that."

"Just. . .keep your eye on him."

Nick leaned forward. "Why do you say that? Is there something I ought to know about Gregory?"

"No! No, nothing. I just meant, keep your eyes open. Don't let him. . .pull you into anything you can't handle."

Nick nodded. "We'll get the proposal done on time, I'm sure. I can handle it."

"Yes, well. . .good."

"Don't worry about me, Stanford. You just take care of yourself right now, okay? I'll stop in again to see you soon."

"Good, Nick. Thanks. Nick, I. . ."

Nick waited. "What is it, Stanford?"

"Oh, you'll be fine. Just. . .take care of yourself, okay?"

"Sure, Stanford, sure."

Nick hung up. He stared at the phone for several minutes, rolling the peppermint around in his hand without unwrapping it. What was that all about? He kept sounding like he wanted to say something else. Nick replayed the conversation. Stanford had especially emphasized two things: Genetic Awareness Day and Gregory's ambitious plans.

Nick shook his head and stood up. Whatever. He needed more coffee, though it was nearly lunchtime. He pocketed the candy and walked out of the lab where Jeremy was still working.

Even before he reached the cafeteria, he could smell the gourmet coffee. He took a minute to pour himself a cup, enjoying the steadying effect it had on his nerves.

On his way back into his lab, Nick bumped into Frieda—literally. She was backing her cart toward his door, and he barely managed to avoid sloshing hot coffee on her. He reached a hand out to steady her, but she pulled away.

"Coming to pay me a visit, Frieda?" he asked. "You'll never get those plants watered if you spend all your time with me!"

She lifted her watering can as though it were a weapon. "I just water the plants. That's all."

Back at his desk, Nick began working on the Patient Selection portion of the Fabry's proposal. However, his thoughts strayed.

What would the DNA sequencing turn up? It could only be something harmful if Milburn had been upset enough to go to the FDA. If his knowledge had really gotten him killed, who could have done such a terrible thing? Who would have given that order? Only one person made sense.

Was SynTech causing more harm than good? Increasing suffering, rather than relieving it?

In his mind, Nick saw Leon Weinman's blue-veined hand reaching out to him again. When Leon had died, Nick hadn't let himself think about Natalie. But now the memory flooded over him like a dam burst.

The summer that Natalie had gotten the diagnosis from the specialist was the summer Nick decided to become a doctor. Nick had never been close to his older sister, Lizzy, but he and Natalie had spent all ten years of their lives together, understanding each other's thoughts and feelings in a way only twins can.

Nick could still see the doctor explaining "meningitis" to his parents in the hospital corridor. The words meant nothing to him, but his mother's collapse spoke volumes. While his father helped his mother into the nearest chair, Nick sneaked into Natalie's room.

"Hi," he whispered.

Natalie tried to smile. Nick pulled a chair up to her bedside and leaned on the bed.

"What's happening?" she asked.

Nick shook his head. "I don't know. The doctor's talking to Mom and Dad."

Natalie groped for Nick's hand. He took hers in his own.

"I'm afraid, Nick."

Nick bit his lip. "It's going to be okay, Natalie."

She tightened her hold on his hand. "Are you sure?" Her eyes searched his.

"You bet. Doctors can do anything. They'll fix you up."

She smiled then, a trusting smile, and he squeezed her hand.

But the doctors hadn't fixed her. Within days she was gone.

Nick raged at his inability to stop the tragedy and then didn't speak for a week. When he finally emerged from his silence, he had vowed to spend his life finding cures for all the sick people in the world. His commitment had never wavered.

He'd thought of Natalie again the day he'd graduated from medical school. As he raised his hand with hundreds of others to recite his oath, the time-honored maxim of physicians burned into his mind and merged with the memory of Natalie's trusting eyes: "First, do no harm." His oath took on an almost spiritual depth at that moment. He would do something to put an end to suffering in the world.

Today Leon Weinman's eyes stared at him from his memory, too. Do no harm.

Could Nick believe that Gregory had altered the therapy with the specific purpose of harming people? If so, what could, would, or should he do about it? If he just marched up to the third floor and accused Gregory now, the only thing he'd accomplish would be getting himself fired. He could kiss senior VP—and all the trappings that went with it—good-bye.

He leaned back in his chair, his eyes focusing on the framed picture of himself and Stanford, his symbol of what he hoped to achieve in life. He couldn't allow himself to be lured by the money. It wasn't about that. But this job at SynTech had opened up the opportunity to help so many people. Could he throw that away on a hunch? There was no going back to the institute, not after the things he'd said to Rogan on his way out.

He sighed. Back to Fabry's.

*   *   *

Gregory Brulin tapped a yellow pencil against the corner of his office desk as he looked over the black-and-white landscape. Newly fallen snow drifted across the grassy, landscaped hills. Angry black gashes of parking lots staked their claim against nature. The muted charcoal grays of carpet and upholstery inside the office seemed to synthesize the black and white outdoors into an indefinable blend.

The office was as silent as a grave, except for the irritated tapping of Gregory's pencil. After several minutes the rhythmic sound became too much, and he balanced the pencil on top of two thumbs, his lips resting against it.

What should his next step be, now that Nick may have gotten from Andrea Milburn more information than he wanted him to have? He contemplated baring his soul to Nick, taking the chance that the younger man would join him in his mission. No, it was too risky. Maybe he should fire him now, before he got any closer. Or perhaps he should have Chernoff take care of him permanently?

He needed a cancer therapy to make his centers successful enough to fully execute his cleansing phase. The truth was he could get cancer therapies from someone else, if necessary. Nick Donovan might be at the head of the pack in cancer research, but he wasn't the only runner. Gregory's head told him he should get rid of Nick now.

His grip on the ends of the pencil tightened as his options narrowed. The yellow wood resisted the tension, then splintered apart, jagged ends shooting away from Gregory's face. He tossed it aside.

He would try a subtle threat. If that didn't work, Chernoff could take over.

Gregory pounded a button on his phone. "Sonya, get Nick Donovan in here."

∂ ∂ ∂

The ring of the telephone jolted Nick out of his newfound concentration on the proposal. He lunged for the phone. "Kate?"

"Dr. Donovan," a woman's voice said, "this is Sonya. Dr. Brulin would like to speak with you as soon as you're free."

"Oh. Hi, Sonya. Well, I'm free now." Not really. "I'll be right up."

∂ ∂ ∂

Nick arrived on the third floor, where the usual smell of cigar smoke mixed with gourmet coffee greeted him.

Sonya gestured to a chair across from her desk in the center of the reception area. "I'm sorry, Dr. Donovan, but Dr. Brulin is on the phone now. I'm sure he'll be right with you." She smiled. "Can I get you anything while you wait?"

Nick couldn't help smiling back. "Sometimes you seem more like a hostess than a secretary, Sonya."

She laughed. "Dr. Brulin needs a bit of cushioning around him at times, don't you think? I try to at least send visitors in to him smiling."

"How long have you been here, Sonya? It seems like Gregory couldn't run the place without you."

"I've been here for five years, off and on," she said, resting her forearms on her desk in a gesture that seemed to say she wanted to talk more.

"Off and on?" Nick asked.

She nodded. "I've needed to take some—personal time—on a few occasions."

Nick noted the wedding band on her left hand. "Do you have a family?"

"Just my husband, Dmitri. No children. Not yet, anyway."

Nick nodded. "My wife and I don't have any children yet, either."

Sonya's eyes filled with tears suddenly. "We've tried," she said.

Nick could have bitten his tongue. He had to lean forward to hear her.

"We've had some problems," she said.

"I'm so sorry, Sonya. Forgive me for bringing it up."

She shook her head and carefully wiped a finger beneath her eye. "Don't be sorry. Besides, Dr. Brulin has been so supportive and extremely helpful. Everything will be different soon."

The door to Gregory's office swung inward.

"Sonya, is Donovan—Oh, there you are, Nick. Come in."

⌐   ⌐   ⌐

Gregory held the door as Nick entered. He noticed that Nick's shoulders were broader than they had been in college, but still Gregory stood three or four inches taller. He took in the cut of Nick's department store suit as the younger man sat in the straight-backed chair in front of the desk. Nick rubbed his hands over his thighs, as though his hands sweated.

"Coffee?" Gregory asked, lifting his own company mug as he sat down.

"No, thanks. I've had my quota for the day."

Gregory sipped from his mug. Nick ran a hand through his graying hair. Much grayer than Gregory remembered.

＊

"I've been. . .doing some work in the lab this morning," Nick said.

Gregory nodded once. "Nick, I'm going to be up front with you. Something I probably should have done before I brought you on here."

Nick waited.

"I'm hoping you'll do some great things for us here at SynTech," Gregory said.

"I have high expectations for myself, as well."

"I'm hoping that you'll continue your research work alongside your administrative responsibilities."

"Research is my first love." Nick seemed to ease back into his chair a bit.

"We need a cancer therapy, Nick. Something broad based, effective for many types of cancer. Nothing else will build SynTech's capital as fast as I want it to grow."

Nick nodded. "I agree. Cancer research is like a calling to me. I admit I was surprised you put me on Fabry's. Don't you have someone else who can do that? I'd like to start up my cancer work again."

"That's my hope, too," Gregory said. "In fact, I'm hoping you can pick right up again here at SynTech where you left off at the institute."

Nick's face lost its interested expression, a mask of dispassion falling over it. "Continue? You mean begin again, right?"

"No. I'm hoping you've brought along some of the research you've already accomplished. That's what would really help us here at SynTech."

"Work that I did at the institute legally belongs to the institute, Dr. Brulin."

With the tip of his forefinger Gregory traced the gold double helix woven through "SynTech" on his coffee mug, letting the tension build with the silence. "Your work is your work, the way I see it. Your efforts have regressed at the institute. They cannot even do human trials at this time, did you know that? Why let all that work be wasted when you could continue the race for a cure right here at SynTech?"

Nick didn't seem eager to break the silence. When he finally spoke, his voice sounded husky, as though he was bringing the words out with difficulty. "It's not ethical, Gregory. Besides," he added, "my last patient in the trial died. Obviously the research was flawed."

Gregory set the mug down, stifling a small smile. If he only knew. "Actually, I'll bet your research was right on target, Nick. Either way, though, I feel confident that you could discover any problems that may be inherent in the treatment and move quickly toward developing successful therapies."

Gregory saw Nick still wrestling with the idea. He realized, with some dismay, that he might have to proceed with measures he had hoped to avoid. *Come on, Nick, play ball.*

"I'm thinking of accelerating my plans for you. As soon as you get Fabry's finished, how would you like to be in charge of the cancer-therapy teams? You could hit the ground running. What do you say?"

Nick tilted his head. "You mean I'd be senior VP of Cancer Research?"

"Soon, Nick, if you do what I ask. Besides, I need you in your lab doing research, not in some office doing administrative busy-work. Nick, think of all the people you'd be helping if SynTech brought a cancer therapy to market sooner rather than later."

Nick leaned an elbow on the chair's armrest and stroked his chin.

Gregory swiveled his chair to face the window, studying the snow. "You're much grayer than I remembered, Nick."

Nick remained silent.

Gregory faced Nick again. "A bit old to be starting over, aren't you? How many other offers have you gotten since leaving the institute? I'd think a man in your stage of life would jump at my offer." He picked up a figurine and studied it, waiting.

Nick dropped his arm. "I couldn't begin for a few weeks. Not unless you want me to drop Fabry's."

"No, no, a few weeks would be fine." He replaced the figurine. "So, you'll do it? You'll help SynTech help those dying people out there?"

Nick sighed heavily. "Yeah. I guess I will."

"Excellent." He stood and held Nick's eyes mercilessly. "So. . . keep your eye on the prize, Nick. Concentrate on the work at hand, not on unnecessary questions about the past. Clear?"

Nick frowned but nodded.

As Nick left, Gregory relaxed. He nodded to himself about how easy it was to overcome a man's supposed principles. Maybe Nick could eventually join him in this project, after all.

༶ ༶ ༶

Nick slammed the door to his office, not caring that Jeremy still worked a few feet away in the lab. One quick step took him to the corner of his metal desk, and he aimed a football-punting kick from his high school days at one of the four steel feet that supported it. The crack of his toes against the metal echoed through the empty office.

"Aahh!" Pain shot up his leg. He dropped to the chair beside his desk and attacked his foot in a vicious massage.

So this was why he had been invited to join SynTech Labs? He could be senior vice president only if he handed over institute research? He knew he had been near a breakthrough with his colon cancer research, but the realization that the only reason Gregory had wanted him was because of it angered him.

Gregory's subtle threat throbbed through his brain in rhythm with the blood pounding in his toes. There were others out there, with other cancer therapies nearing readiness. Gregory could find someone else, and Nick had no doubt that he would. Meanwhile, Nick had no other offers on the table.

He'd stalled Gregory, bargained for a few weeks. Of course he would never do what Gregory had asked, but he needed to stay on Gregory's good side long enough to find out what had happened to his predecessor. Forget Fabry's. Now Nick was certain that Gregory had gotten rid of Milburn. Wouldn't a man who didn't have a problem asking his employees to break the law find it a small leap to have a man removed who stood in his way?

The answer lay buried in Milburn's research. If he could find out what was wrong with that therapy, he would have something to work with. If nothing else, it was something to use as leverage against Gregory. Perhaps if he had answers Gregory didn't want made public, he could keep his job without betraying the institute. Then again, if he had answers, perhaps he would end up like Milburn.

The phone jangled, making him jump again.

"Nick?"

He recognized Scott's voice immediately. Why would his brother-in-law be calling him at work? "Is everything all right, Scott?"

Scott's voice lowered. "Listen, buddy. She didn't want me to call you, but I think she needs you."

Nick forgot his aching foot and bolted upright in the chair. "Kate? Is she okay?"

"Yeah, I think so. But she's had a pretty big scare."

"Where is she, Scott?" Nick stood, circling the desk toward the door.

"She's here, at our house."

"Be right there."

CHAPTER 32

Kate wriggled four fingers deeper into the water, watching the waves dance away, rippling over the polished-rock bottom of the pond in Melanie's solarium.

The solarium was the only modern addition to Melanie's historical property. It was her sister's favorite spot. Potted shrubs lined the perimeter, and she had planted flowers in the pattern of a charming English garden within them. Stone benches, small statues, and bubbling fountains dotted the solarium, and the humid warmth was kept constant even through the winter. Kate loved it almost as much as Melanie did.

The fear that had kept her shivering all the way back from Bert's store was finally ebbing away, but a tiny chill ran up her spine as she watched the water. Melanie had thrown a few ice blue stones into the pond with the other rocks, and the color reminded Kate of Winston's frozen eyes, watching her from every part of his cabin.

"Kate, come get some lunch." Melanie stood in the doorway of the solarium, peering through fern fronds to catch her sister's attention.

"I'm not hungry, Mel. Thanks."

Melanie opened her mouth as if to protest, but then nodded and disappeared.

Scott had reached her in record time at Bert's, and Kate had left Winston in the capable hands of law enforcement there. No doubt she would need to follow up the report she gave with ongoing testimony. She hoped that Rudy had been right and that Winston would be going to a hospital, not a prison. The local emergency room had released her with instructions to stay off her sprained ankle for several days. She was thankful it wasn't broken. A few days of rest and getting around on crutches wouldn't be too bad.

Melanie hadn't said a word to Kate about her returning to her own home, even though that had been Kate's part of the bargain. The idea was uppermost in Kate's mind now and had been for several hours. Could she abandon her ground so quickly? She had taken a stand, forced Nick to make a choice. And he had chosen his work. Why was she going back to that?

Winston's blue eyes flashed before her. No, if nothing else, that encounter in the forest had taught her that she wanted to be with Nick, whatever it took.

In graduate school, so many of their friends had been surprised that she and Nick had gotten together. He didn't have her fun-loving nature, always seemed so serious about his work and his education. No one understood that his single-mindedness was one of the things that drew her to him. While his peers were still out to have a good time, Nick was preparing himself to change the world. Her friends had joked about his graying hair, telling her that he was an old man in a young man's body. But he wasn't old; he was driven. And Kate loved that about him.

Melanie appeared in the solarium again, a yellow glazed mug steaming in her hands. "If you won't have lunch, at least drink this." She pushed it into Kate's hands. The warm aroma of minty tea tickled her nose. "I baked cinnamon bread. It's almost cool enough. You might have to fight me for it, though."

Melanie sat beside Kate on the stone bench, taking in her sanctuary with a trained eye. Kate wished she knew plants the way her sister did. Some of the blooms in here were breathtaking, especially in contrast with the drifting snow outside. The white glare beyond couldn't penetrate the steamy glass panels around the garden. The room felt like a tropical oasis in the center of a frozen wasteland.

Kate saved Melanie the trouble of bringing up the thing she obviously wanted to talk about. "I've decided to go back to Nick."

Melanie exhaled loudly. "I'm glad, Kate."

"You were right. My little temper tantrum wasn't the best way to work this out. Besides, the past day has shown me that forcing someone to do what you want isn't the best way to build a good relationship."

Melanie smiled and gave her a hug. "I'm so happy for you, Kate." She sat back. "I guess I should tell you this: Scott was still worried about you when you got back. He called Nick."

Kate sat upright, trying to hold the tea steady in her lap. "What?"

"I hope that was okay. Scott felt he should know."

"What did Nick say?" Kate tried to control the leaping in her heart.

"Not much. . ."

Kate swirled her tea, watching the liquid slosh around the edges of the mug. "Oh."

Melanie smiled. "Because he dropped the phone on his way out the door."

Kate searched Melanie's face. "He's coming here?"

"He should be here any minute."

Kate left her tea beside Melanie, grabbed her crutches, and hobbled out of the solarium toward the guest bedroom. The humidity in there had turned her curly hair to frizz, and she hadn't even looked in a mirror since fleeing Winston's bathroom. If Nick was coming to rescue her, she wanted to look better than an escaped prisoner!

$\sim$ $\sim$ $\sim$

A big scare, Scott had said. Nick jerked the Expedition around a corner, minutes from Melanie's house. What could that mean? Images of Brian Milburn's car in Silver Lake, of Andrea Milburn's flaming house, charged through his mind. He was convinced that neither had been accidents and had feared that he might be in danger next. But had the focus shifted to Kate instead? He punched the gas pedal.

The driveway was icy, and Nick slid to a delayed stop only

inches from the back fender of Scott's car. He left the keys in the ignition and kicked through the snow to the front door.

Melanie opened it, a smile creasing her face.

"That was quick." She stepped aside to let him in.

Nick searched the entrance to the kitchen, glanced up the stairs, and stepped into the family room. "Where is she?"

"She's in the guest room. Sit down. She'll be right out."

Nick grabbed Melanie's arm. "What happened? Is she okay?"

"Hey!" Melanie pulled away, laughing. "Relax. She'll be fine. She needs to tell you about it."

"Nick?"

He swung his head toward the voice he loved more than any other. "Kate!"

Crutches, her left foot lifted from the floor.

He was by her side in a heartbeat. He reached out anxious arms to wrap around her, but the crutches made it impossible. "What happened?"

"Can we sit down?" She took a few hesitant steps toward the family room, faltering with the crutches.

Nick caught up with her from behind. "Here, sweetheart." He took the crutches and propped them against the wall, then lifted Kate into his arms. She smiled, and he felt heat flood back into his heart which had been slowly turning to ice since she'd left home.

He stopped before he reached the love seat, lowering his head to give her a kiss that transcended petty disagreements and said that whatever had happened, he was glad she was safe. It was right and good to have her in his arms again. She responded as though she, too, wanted to forget the past.

He settled her on the love seat in front of the fireplace and sat beside her. Kate pulled one of Melanie's quilts toward her, covering herself in spite of the warmth from the fire.

Nick stroked her jawline with one finger. He could see the tension there and was almost afraid to ask. "What happened, Kate?"

Her story tumbled out amidst a few tears. She told him of Winston's hands in her hair, his touch on her. As she talked, Nick pulled her to his chest. Kate didn't look at him as she spoke. Her fingers traced the wedding ring pattern on the quilt. Several threads were loose, and she pulled at them absently, unraveling them further.

When the story was done, Nick admitted relief. The danger she had faced appeared to be unconnected to SynTech. But his fear for her safety was not so easily dismissed.

"I'm ready to come home, Nick," Kate said, wiping her face with the back of her hand and resting her head against him. "I realize that I can't expect you to do everything my way. I'm sorry I tried to make you do what I wanted. I want to work something out."

Nick pulled her hand away from the loose quilt threads, choosing his words carefully. "I'm so glad, Kate, that you want to come home. I know we can work together to find a solution." He swallowed hard, knowing he was taking a chance with what he was about to do. "But I'm not sure it's a good idea for you to come home. Not yet. I'm having some—problems—at work, and they're requiring a lot of late nights." He pointed to her ankle as he felt her body stiffen in his arms. "You're going to need help for awhile, and I think Melanie might be better for that job than I could be."

She yanked her hand away, her face unreadable. "I want to come home, Nick," she said, lifting her eyes to his.

"I know, and I want you to, I promise. Listen, after I get things resolved at work, we'll go away for awhile. Just the two of us, okay? But for now, I think it might be better for you to stay here for a few days."

"Because you don't want to be distracted by me. You want to be able to focus completely on your job."

The words were so familiar. But this time it was different, wasn't it? He was afraid for her safety. But he couldn't tell her that.

"No, honey. It's not about focusing this time." His mind scrambled for a suitable explanation. "Gregory Brulin is giving me some hassle about what happened in the past. He's putting unbelievable pressure on me to finish a proposal. Plus, there's this big Genetic Awareness Day at the center on Saturday. And I'm having some problems with the therapy I'm working on. I need to prove myself to him over the next few days; then things will ease up."

"What therapy?"

"It doesn't matter. I just want you to understand how overwhelmed I am right now. If you were home, I couldn't spend any time with you anyway. Not for a few days or so."

Kate went back to the loose threads. Nick watched the fire. The smell of cinnamon bread teased him from the kitchen, making him wish for a normal evening in this house full of people he loved. *I've got to stay away to keep them safe.*

Time ticked past, and it became clear that Kate was not going to speak again. "I need to go, Kate."

She didn't look up.

"I'm so glad you're safe." He clasped one of her hands again. It felt cold to his touch. He leaned over and kissed her cheek. "I'll call you tomorrow."

Kate shrugged her shoulders. "If you say so."

CHAPTER 33

Kate waited until she heard Nick drive away in the Expedition before she lifted the quilt from her lap and threw it onto the floor. Nothing had changed. Nick still put career over their marriage. He always would. How could she have thought about going back to that kind of life?

Still, what had she expected? She'd vowed to go back to Nick no matter what. Didn't no matter what include him never changing? She needed some ice cream.

What kind of trouble would Gregory be giving Nick about the past? She let her mind drift back to those days, before they were married, before they were even dating. Could she be the cause of this?

Kate hadn't seen Gregory Brulin since before she married Nick, but surely Nick had mentioned her to him. Could Gregory still be holding a grudge about the way she'd ended their relationship and be taking it out on Nick? Or what if Nick had learned about Gregory and her—could that be why he was being so cold to her? If she was the cause of this strain, should she approach Gregory about it to try to clear the air?

Melanie interrupted her thoughts with a plate of warm cinnamon bread and her generous smile. "Where's Nick?" She sat beside Kate and held out the bread. "Have you guys decided when you'll be going home?"

Kate smiled weakly. "Anxious to get rid of me?"

Melanie tilted her head and rolled her eyes in answer. "I want to know how well the big reunion went."

"Can I stay a little longer, Mel?" Kate reached for a piece of bread, keeping her voice casual.

Melanie took a piece herself and put the plate on the end table beside them. "What happened, Kate?"

"I told him I wanted to come home. But—he's not ready.

Some problems at work he needs to fix first. He says he won't have time to help me while my ankle heals."

"I see." It was clear from Melanie's voice that she didn't see. Neither did Kate.

"Give him a few days, Kate. He'll realize he's being an idiot." Kate laughed.

"Did you talk about children again?" Melanie's voice was soft, as though she was afraid to bring it up.

"No. We said we'd work out the situation." She sighed. "I guess my little manipulation didn't make him see how much I need a family to feel fulfilled."

Melanie was quiet for a moment. "Kate, you know I love my children. But I don't think even a family makes a person fulfilled."

"So what does? Oh, let me guess: God again?"

Melanie shrugged. "I'm just telling you how I feel."

Kate nodded. "So tell me."

Melanie bit into a piece of bread. "Being fulfilled is about finding your purpose and doing it. You can't look around at others to find where that purpose comes from. You have to look up. Neither your husband nor your children are ever going to make you feel completely fulfilled. You'll always feel like you're missing something until you find what it really takes."

Kate pulled the sugary crust from a second piece of bread and chewed it.

Melanie continued. "It's true you need a relationship to be fulfilled. But not a relationship with children. The only relationship that can truly fulfill you is the one that every person was meant to have—a relationship with the One who created you."

Kate thought about Melanie's words. The silenced lengthened. "I'm listening, Melanie," she finally said. "I'm just not sure I buy into it. I don't feel close to God, you know? I don't feel any relationship there. So how can that make me fulfilled?"

"We've talked about this before, Kate, and the answer is still the same. You're right. There is no relationship there, not yet. You haven't taken care of the thing that stands in the way."

Melanie's voice grew even softer. "You know I'm only saying this because I love you, right? Kate, we all begin with the things we've done wrong blocking our relationship with God. That's called sin. And Jesus died to deal with that barrier. All it takes is trusting in what Jesus did for you as the only way you can have that relationship with God."

"I'll think about it, Mel." A minute later, Kate broke the awkward silence. "How was your appointment at the Gene Therapy Center?"

"Good, I guess. They went over my DNA information. It looks like I'm likely to develop Acid Maltase Deficiency."

"Oh, Mel!"

"It doesn't seem like it's anything to get too crazy about, though. They've isolated the responsible genes and have a therapy to treat it."

"You'll do it, won't you?"

"My insurance won't pay for it, so I was going to say no. But then they told me that this weekend I could come in and have the procedure done free of charge. They're having some kind of promotion for people who can't afford treatment. I guess it's a PR thing."

Kate exhaled in relief, images of their mother's suffering fading away. "That's great, Melanie. Nick was telling me about that Awareness Day thing. Did you make the appointment?"

Melanie nodded. "By Saturday I'll be out of danger."

Kate smiled and hugged her. Then Melanie returned to the kitchen.

Kate's thoughts reverted back to Gregory Brulin. She pulled a phone book from the drawer in the end table and reached for the phone. With shaking fingers she dialed the main number for SynTech Labs, hurrying before she lost her resolve. "Gregory Brulin's office, please."

"Dr. Brulin's office, Sonya speaking," a pleasant voice said.

Kate swallowed. "I'd like to make an appointment to see Dr. Brulin."

"May I ask what this is regarding?"

Kate inhaled. "It's—um—personal, I guess."

"Oh, I see. What's your name?"

"Katherine Donovan."

"Donovan?"

"Yes, I'm Nick Donovan's wife."

"Just a moment, please." Sonya put her on hold.

Kate held her breath.

Sonya returned. "Ms. Donovan? Dr. Brulin would like me to set up a time to meet you."

Kate sat back against the plaid love seat. Perhaps this could work after all.

      *   *   *

Nick's drive back to SynTech was considerably slower than his race to Melanie's house had been. His arms ached with the memory of carrying Kate through the family room. She had wanted to come home, and he had refused her. Refused on the very basis she had left him for in the first place. How did he expect her to react? Was he a fool?

But he couldn't bear to think of her in danger. It was one thing to put himself at risk to investigate what Gregory was doing, but it was something else to take the chance of getting Kate caught in the crossfire. It was for the best, but it hurt like crazy.

It had been so good to hold her, to see her smile, even to see her tears as she told him about Winston. He gripped the steering wheel at the thought of her in that cabin with a madman. He wished he could have a few minutes with the guy. If anything had happened to her, if anything ever did. . .

The road in front of him blurred, and he brushed at his eyes to clear them. Tears wouldn't solve anything. It was time to get serious and find the answers at SynTech. Only then would he feel safe enough to bring Kate home.

Nick went straight to the lab when he got back to SynTech.

Jeremy looked up from the sequencer when Nick reentered. "I've been trying to call you."

"Sorry. Minor emergency. What have we got?"

Jeremy pointed to the electropherogram and frowned. "I don't think you're going to like it."

༄ ༄ ༄

Stanford fumbled for the television remote control in the sheets bunched up beside him. Nothing but talk shows and local news at noon. Stanford settled for the news, listening to the parade of fires, assaults, and burglaries. His eyelids were drooping when the name "Milburn" startled him.

"Fire officials won't comment on the cause of the fire. Mrs. Milburn and her four children and two guests escaped safely. This family has had a difficult time lately. Neighbors say that Mrs. Milburn's husband recently died in an automobile accident. Moving on to other news. . ."

Stanford pressed the "power" button at his side. The television hanging from the ceiling at the end of his bed went black. He stared past the vase of flowers on the windowsill at the noonday city skyline.

No first names had been given. Could it be the same Milburn? Stanford hadn't spoken to Brian Milburn in several years. He eyed the phone on the small nightstand beside his bed and cursed the ridiculous cancer that had weakened him beyond the point of sitting up and making a few phone calls.

"Lunchtime, Stan."

He turned toward the door. Frank was entering, a lunch tray in each hand. "Mind if I join you?"

Stanford waved a hand toward the plastic chair beside his bed. His room at the Young-Meddleton Cancer Center was like any other hospital room, with its white walls and white floors and white everything. The only thing that made it bearable was that Frank was stuck here, too.

Frank deposited one tray on a rolling table and swung it over Stanford's bed. "Looks like they've flown in a new chef from France," he said, pointing to the plate of noodles and unidentifiable meat.

"Do me a favor, Frank," Stanford said.

"Anything."

"I need to make some calls. Get a few questions answered. Will you help me make the calls?"

"Sure, Stan. If you'll promise to eat everything on your plate."

"Yes, Mother."

Twenty minutes later Stanford had his answers—and had eaten enough to satisfy Frank.

"Dial one more number for me, Frank. And then I'll need some privacy, if you wouldn't mind. . . ."

"No problem, Stan. Glad to help." Frank dialed the number Stanford dictated and left the room.

As the phone rang, Stanford's anger grew. He had thought he could stop all of this with a few subtle hints to Nick. Now it looked like it was going to take more than that.

His call, like the first one he'd made last month, went right through to Gregory. "What's this with the Milburns, Gregory?"

"Hello, Stanford."

"Maybe the police are buying the 'accident' theory, but if you think I'm going to sit here and be quiet while you're causing car accidents and house fires, you've got—"

"Stanford, I don't know what you're talking about."

"The Milburns! Don't think I don't remember Brian Milburn. He was one of the brightest investigators over there. If anyone would have caught on to you, it would have been him. Is that what happened? Did he catch on to you? Did you kill him?" Stanford collapsed onto his pillow, winded.

"It's not a good idea to get yourself so worked up, Stan—"

"Shut up, Gregory. Don't talk to me about my health. Answer my question."

"I have nothing to say."

"Gregory, I can almost understand your hatred for certain people. But are you now willing to kill completely innocent people just to accomplish your plan?"

"No one is innocent, Stanford. Not if they stand in the way of progress."

"So you admit it, then? Gregory, you have to stop!"

There was a pause, and Stanford imagined Gregory pressing his fingers against his eyelids, like he used to.

"Stanford, that is the second time you've dictated your will to me. You are becoming an obstacle to progress yourself."

Stanford snorted. "Is that a threat? Are you going to kill me now? I have news for you, Gregory: The cancer's beat you to it."

"There are many ways to convince a man, Stanford. One only has to find his Achilles' heel."

"You think you know me so well?"

"Stanford, if you speak of this to anyone, I will bring out the documents we spoke of earlier. There will be lawsuits. Many of them. Your estate will be tied up for years. Your wife and children will have nothing. Not even your good name to comfort them."

Stanford closed his eyes, forcing strength that wasn't there into his voice. "I have some proof of my own. Gregory, I didn't want to ever have to play this card, but I suppose it's come to that now."

"What are you talking about?"

He took a deep breath. "Did you think I would leave myself completely unprotected? If you don't stop, I'm seriously considering going to the FDA with what I have."

Gregory laughed. "What proof could you have? Besides, if you did, you would expose yourself as well, Stanford. And I wouldn't even need to bring you down with me." He disconnected.

Stanford closed his eyes again and swallowed, then reached a weary hand across the bed to set the phone on the table. He missed, and the phone slipped from his fingers and cracked onto the floor.

CHAPTER 34

Nick peered over Jeremy's shoulder at the Gaucher vector's sequencing data.

The printout wobbled in Jeremy's hand as he shook his head. "There's nothing out of the ordinary here. The therapy is exactly what it should be."

Nick pounded a fist on the bench. "That's impossible. Andrea said her husband found something disturbing when he sequenced this therapy."

"Andrea? That's what you went to talk to her about?"

Nick dropped to a lab chair. "Yeah."

Jeremy stood, shaking his head. He walked away from Nick and braced his hands against the counter at the back of the room. "Nick, I have to ask you something serious."

"Sure, Jeremy. What is it?"

"Don't think I'm crazy, but sometimes it crosses my mind that. . ." He stopped and turned to look anxiously at Nick.

"It's okay, Jeremy. You can tell me."

"Yeah, it's just that I don't know how you're going to take this."

Nick opened his hands. "Lay it on me, Jeremy."

"Okay. . ." He took a deep breath. "Ever since Dr. Milburn died, it's, I don't know, kind of occurred to me that maybe his death wasn't. . .an accident. Know what I mean?"

Nick nodded. "Yes, I totally agree with you. I think Milburn was murdered."

"You do?"

"Absolutely. I think it had something to do with what he discovered here. That's why I had you sequencing this therapy. I'm looking for whatever it was that got Milburn spooked."

"You are? Whoa." Jeremy rubbed his face. "Nick, man, I

should never have stayed quiet."

Nick blinked. "Quiet about what? What else do you know?"

Jeremy licked his lips. "I knew something was going on. I could tell Dr. Milburn was upset. Then when he died, I thought it would be better to just keep quiet. But if he did know something, and he was killed for it. . ." He turned away again.

"Jeremy, I don't think there was anything you could have done. In fact, you might not be alive now if you'd gotten more involved."

Jeremy whirled. "The fire! Was that part of all this, too?"

"I have a feeling it was, yes."

"And now Bernice is another victim?" Jeremy slapped the counter. "What are we going to do, Nick?"

"I don't know. Milburn's notes said he was using Gaucher's. Andrea said the therapy he sequenced—the one he got alarmed about, I think—was one he had studied for comparison with Fabry's. I'm going to check his notes again."

Jeremy looked at his watch. "Do we have the time for that? What about the proposal?"

"Jeremy, don't tell anybody, but as far as I'm concerned, Fabry's is history. I've got to find out what happened to Milburn, and I think you're with me in it, right?"

"Absolutely."

"Then the only time we'll work on the Fabry's proposal is when someone's looking over our shoulders, okay? The truth is we're officially on the Brian Milburn murder case."

"Outstanding," Jeremy said, showing Nick his first genuine smile. "Whoever hurt Bernice is going down, baby!"

They high-fived, and Nick ducked into his office, grinning in spite of himself.

He pulled up the file immediately and read again the note that had started it all: "I've just come from the speech tonight. The tainted samples are already arriving. This has gone on long enough. I am going to the FDA."

Nick sat back and ran a hand through his hair. What speech? Had Milburn given a speech at the center that night, maybe the same speech to prospective clients that Nick had given? Could he have seen something there at that facility, a different vector than the one Nick had pulled from the cold room here?

He headed out into the lab. "I'm going to the Gene Therapy Center to get another sample."

Jeremy's eyebrows rose. "What should I do?"

"Uh, I don't know. Maybe work on the Fabry's proposal?"

"Oh, man! I wanted to be a P. I. You said we only had to do Fabry's when someone was watching."

Nick opened the lab door. "Or when we're bored. See you later. I'll be back as soon as I can. Hey, why don't you go see Bernice?"

~ ~ ~

At the center, Nick found Rich Nowinski in his office. He explained what he needed. "I'm finishing up some work on a related therapy," he said, dropping into a chair.

"You want one of our Gaucher's samples?" Nowinski asked skeptically. "What's wrong with yours at the labs? I don't know, maybe I should check with Dr. Brulin on this."

Nick shrugged. "If you like. He's really pushing to get this proposal to trials, though. He's mentioned several times that he doesn't want any delays."

Nowinski nodded. "I know what he's like when he's driving for the goal. Tell you what," he said, standing, "I'll go get you the sample myself. Did you want a Version 1 or Version 2 sample?"

Nick tapped a finger on the arm of the chair, trying not to register surprise. "I'm sorry?"

"Version 1 or 2 of the Gaucher's therapy?"

Nick's mind raced. Two versions of the same therapy? Why? "Well. . .I mean, how do you determine which patients get which version?"

"We haven't actually started using both versions yet. But beginning this week, that information will all be on the profile we get from the main office. Each patient's genetic predisposition will dictate the therapy tailored for him or her."

"But there are just two versions?"

Nowinski nodded. "Right. Everyone falls into one or the other."

Which version had Milburn pulled from SynTech's storage? "Better give me a sample of each."

~ ~ ~

Nick stopped at the hospital on the way back to SynTech. Bernice brightened when he entered her room. This hospital had tried to make their rooms a little more homey, with floral wallpaper borders and a wooden rocking chair in the corner. Bernice lay on a bed, a blue blanket pulled over her hospital gown.

"Hi, Dr. Donovan!" She pressed a button that shut off the television.

"I thought I told you to call me Nick, Bernice."

"Oh, yeah." She put a self-conscious hand up to the bandage around her head.

"You look great," Nick said.

"No, I don't." She gave a crooked smile and pointed to a chair beside the bed. "Do you want to sit?"

"How are you feeling?" he asked, sitting.

"I'll be fine." She pulled the blanket around her waist. "Andrea Milburn just called me."

"How is she?"

"They're staying with relatives. She wanted to be sure I was okay. Wasn't that sweet?"

"Has she learned anything more about the fire?"

Bernice frowned. "The fire department says it was arson, but I just can't believe it. Who would do something like that? Her poor family's been through so much already."

A shuffle behind him made Nick turn toward the door. "Hi, Jeremy."

"Hey, Nick." Jeremy took a hesitant step into the room, holding out a bouquet of wildflowers like an offering. "Hey, Bernice."

Bernice's hand flitted up to her bandage again. "Hi."

Nick stood. "I'll let you two visit. Take my chair, Jeremy. Take care of yourself, Bernice. I need you back at SynTech."

Bernice smiled. "Okay. Thanks for coming by, Dr.—Nick."

"Sure." Nick hesitated for a moment. "Oh, Bernice, I wanted to ask you: Do you know anything about there being two different versions of the Gaucher's therapy that Brian Milburn might have been looking at?"

Bernice shook her head. "Sorry, Nick."

"Okay, no problem." Nick gave Jeremy a wink, waved at both of them, and left the room.

پ پ پ

Hours later, Nick leaned away from his computer and stretched his cramped muscles. He looked out into the lab. Jeremy was still at the lab counter, using a transfer pipet to fill the electrophoresis array. Nick wondered if the young man's narrow shoulders ever got tight.

It was nearly five o'clock. Jeremy had started the sequencer working on the two versions of the Gaucher's therapy Nick had gotten from the center. While the DNA ran through electrophoresis, they were working—halfheartedly—on the Fabry's proposal.

"Thanks for being willing to stay late, Jeremy," Nick said, stepping into the lab.

"You don't need to thank me. I'll do whatever it takes to find out who hurt Bernice."

Nick's eyelids felt weighted. He needed caffeine. "I'm going to get a soda."

"Okay." Jeremy turned from the lab counter to the computer.

The second set of samples had sent its data to be analyzed.

Nick estimated the amount of change in his pocket. "You want anything?"

"No, I'm cool." Jeremy didn't look up from his work.

Nick inserted coins into the soda machine at the end of the hall and made his selection, but the machine gave him nothing in return. Just like other parts of his life he could mention. His frustration found vent through his foot again, but this time the soda machine responded to a well-placed kick in the buttons. His Coke tumbled out. Maybe a little more caffeine today would give him the energy he needed to find some answers. If it didn't send him into orbit.

The Coke was half gone when he reached the lab door. He finished the rest before he yanked open the lab door and came face-to-face with Jeremy's sallow grin.

"I found something." He pointed to the computer.

Nick covered the distance in one stride. "What is it?"

"A misalignment in an open reading frame."

Nick compared the results from the two versions of the Gaucher's therapy. Everything was identical between the two columns displayed on the screen—except for the spot Jeremy had highlighted. There, in Version 1, the DNA code was AGGTC GCT. In Version 2, that same line read AGGCC GCT. Just one letter changed, but in genetics, that was like the difference between a hypodermic needle and a thumbtack.

Nick ran to the computer in his office and accessed GenBank, the National Library of Medicine's DNA sequence repository. Not all mapped genes had functions discovered yet. Was it known what this one coded for?

The answer popped up, and Nick felt his jaw drop.

Jeremy walked over. "What is it?"

Nick pointed to the screen. The gene that had been altered in the second version controlled the production of a crucial liver enzyme. Without its regulated production, the liver could not function properly. Whoever received this therapy would have his Gaucher's disease cured but would also be very likely to contract liver cancer.

"How did one version of the Gaucher's therapy get changed?" Jeremy asked.

"All I can think is that someone must've done it intentionally," Nick said. "We need to find out who else was involved in the Gaucher's research."

He couldn't ask Gregory Brulin for names of others involved in the project. He turned back to the computer and navigated through the company network until he had found the Gaucher files. He tracked down the names of five other investigators. He wrote these names on a yellow sticky note and stuck it on the edge of his desk.

Then he reached for the phone. "Could you connect me with Eleanor Dietrich, please?"

The switchboard operator's voice came back a moment later. "Eleanor Dietrich is no longer with the company, sir. Is there someone else I can direct you to?"

"Oh." Nick fumbled for the sticky note. "Okay, I'll speak to Anthony Bardi."

The operator paused. "Anthony Bardi is no longer with the company, sir. Is there someone else?"

Nick ran down the other three names, astonished that the switchboard operator seemed to find nothing strange in repeating her answer five times. He disconnected, leaning back in his swivel chair till it squeaked.

All five of them gone. Nick wondered fleetingly if they had all left the company in the same fashion as Brian Milburn.

He looked at Jeremy. "None of the people who worked on it are still here."

"Whoa. That's weird."

Nick paused, thinking. "How could these therapies have been altered without anyone knowing about it?"

Jeremy flipped his hair out of his eyes. "There's a lab below us. Sublevel 3. Hardly anybody has access, though. I think Dr. Brulin uses it."

ৎ   ৎ   ৎ

Sublevel 3. Nick looked at the palm geography reader outside the elevator, his heart pounding. Gregory could be right behind the double doors, could burst through them at any moment. But Nick had to find out if Jeremy was right. Was this where someone—either Gregory himself or someone in his employ—tampered with the therapies?

To open, this door required an access code, a SynTech ID, and a palm scan. Nick could only provide the ID, and he was pretty sure his wouldn't be coded to give him access to this lab, anyway. He punched the button beside the elevator again. The doors slid open with a hiss, and Nick jumped back in.

Now what? In his gut, Nick believed that Gregory had been the one to alter that therapy. It was the only answer that made sense, if Milburn really was murdered for his suspicions.

If Gregory wanted to alter liver enzymes to cause liver cancer, this was the perfect medical sabotage. It would take months or years for the effects to show up. When the cancer struck, it would appear to be random. There would be virtually no way to trace anything back to SynTech.

The question was why Gregory would do it. And what should Nick do about it?

If he wanted to find out why Gregory had altered the Gaucher's therapy, he was going to have to do it without arousing Gregory's suspicion. Everyone who had been connected to the project was gone. He didn't want to be gone, too.

Back in his lab, Nick sent Jeremy home and shut down the lab lights. Only the desk lamp in his tiny private office glowed. He sat at his desk, his head in his hands.

Stanford's emaciated face floated through his imagination.

Nick also thought of Stanford's friend, Frank. Cancer ate away at both of them. And Nick worked for a company that would dispense the disease hidden in the Trojan horse of a cure for Gaucher's disease, and maybe in other therapies, too.

Cancer had been Nick's focus at the institute. Gregory wanted Nick's cancer treatment. And yet, he had apparently built a cancer-causing factor into his therapies. Why was he curing one thing and causing something else? Was he only trying to make people sick so there would be more people to cure?

Nick grabbed his coat and stood. He needed to get some air.

Brian Milburn Journal Entry #4
January 31

This whole thing gets crazier every day. Now that I've sequenced more of the second versions and seen that they all make the recipient more susceptible to some form of cancer, I don't know what to think. Call me crazy, but it looks like somebody's trying to give people cancer. That only makes sense if SynTech offered a therapy for cancer, which we don't. Not yet.

And we certainly haven't developed therapies to patch people up after they've been injected with the other two vectors I sequenced today. Apparently my mystery villain is not content to give them only cancer. One of those two vectors changes dopamine levels so radically that it would drastically alter behavior, possibly contributing to violence. And the second vector codes for sterility! I ran the data twice just to be sure.

So the question of the day becomes WHY? And the answer must lie in who these particular patients are. Who are the poor saps targeted to get the altered versions? I searched the files I'd printed, but I couldn't find a common link.

Over the weekend I assumed a disguise and went door-to-door to some of the names on my list claiming to be taking a survey about their views on gene therapy.

Of the five patients whose doors I knocked on, four were quick to offer that they'd scheduled appointments for Genetic Awareness Day. Besides that, I still found nothing in common, unless one takes into account the somewhat less-than-enthusiastic response about genetic progress as a whole. One woman in her fifties made it clear she'd bought into the "gene therapy thing," but that I shouldn't expect her to start supporting "all that cloning garbage."

So tomorrow it's back into SynTech's computer network for Sam. I've got to find the common link between these Version 2 patients. I know it's the key to who's responsible.

CHAPTER 35

Kate approached the woman in the central reception area of the third floor of SynTech Labs, self-conscious of the crutches that she still could not maneuver with style.

The woman looked up and smiled sympathetically. "Can I help you?"

"I have an appointment to see Dr. Brulin. I'm Kate—"

"Yes, Mrs. Donovan. Dr. Brulin's expecting you. Go right in." She motioned toward a massive door with one hand, pressing a button on her phone with the other.

Kate heard her informing her employer that his five o'clock appointment had arrived. She leaned a crutch against her side and turned the doorknob, her purse strap sliding off her shoulder to hang from the bend at her elbow. Purse swinging, she pushed at the door. It was too heavy to swing open by itself, so she tried to force it open with her body. The receptionist rescued her, reaching in to hold it open as she bounced through it. Her interview hadn't even begun, and already she felt like a junior high student coming to see the principal.

Gregory looked up from his desk as she propelled herself forward. His face registered joy, then concern. "Kate!" He jumped up and jogged around his desk to assist her with the door. "What happened?"

"Just a sprain. I'm not supposed to walk on it for a few days." Her heart hammered with embarrassment.

The elegant decorating scheme of Gregory's office surprised Kate. She'd expected something more utilitarian from him, not the numerous hanging plants and the lovely grandfather clock in the corner.

Gregory helped her to a seat, his hand warm against her back, and then sat beside her in another chair placed in front of his desk.

It was a strange beginning after all this time. Kate's rehearsed speech disappeared, leaving her staring at Gregory's unchanged face. Same jet-black hair, same piercing eyes. He didn't seem any older, though he had to be in his late forties. She felt even more self-conscious.

"Kate, you're as beautiful as ever," he said, as if in answer to her thoughts. "Nick's a lucky man."

Kate felt the heat rise to her face. "You look wonderful, too. And you've made such a success of this company. You must be pleased."

Gregory nodded. "I believe passionately in the work here, Kate. The answers for humankind's future may reside inside this building."

Kate looked at the gray carpet, trying to bring back her practiced lines. "It's been a long time since. . .those days. How have you been?"

"Good. Life has not always been easy, but I am moving forward."

Kate nodded, unsure of how to bring up the one thing she knew she couldn't avoid mentioning. "I heard about your son. I'm sorry."

"Thank you, Kate. His death was devastating, as I'm sure you can imagine. But it has given me the motivation to do what I do here."

Kate smiled. "He lives on."

Gregory seemed suddenly alarmed. He spoke quickly. "What are you talking about? How would he live on? That's not possible. Science hasn't progressed that far."

Kate bit her lip. "I just meant, what you were saying—that he lives on in the millions of people whose cures you discover here."

"Yes. Oh. Yes, of course you're right." Gregory seemed to deflate. He stared into space for a moment. Finally he tilted his head toward Kate. "What about you? Are you still working in gene research?

Perhaps you could join our team, work alongside your husband."

Kate laughed. "I'm still at it, but I like the educational sector."

The conversation paused. Gregory folded his hands into a steeple, pressing the tips of his fingers against his lower lip. "Is there something I can do for you, Kate?"

Kate sighed with relief. Maybe her theory was wrong. It did not appear that Gregory still resented what had happened years ago. But she had to be sure. "I hope you can help me, Gregory."

"Anything, Kate. You know that."

Kate smiled. "I wanted to talk to you about Nick. I wanted to be certain that I'm not the cause of any problems between you two."

Gregory's face was unreadable. "Problems?"

"Yes. I know he is excited about his career change, and I wouldn't want to think that I—you know, you and me all those years ago was threatening that in any way."

Gregory's eyebrows knitted together in a thoughtful frown. Kate's heart beat faster. Had she said something wrong? The prolonged silence accented the ticking of the clock. Gregory crossed one leg over the other, bringing his foot within inches of her leg. She waited.

Gregory finally inhaled and spoke. "I'm sorry, Kate. I don't know what you're talking about."

She swallowed. "He mentioned that the two of you were having some problems over things that had occurred in the past. I—I thought it might be about me."

Gregory stood and went to the window, looking out. "Nick and I have never discussed you, Kate. I didn't think it—appropriate to bring up our past with him."

"Then—" Kate's throat closed, and she felt her face grow warm. "I guess your problems have nothing to do with me." She pushed herself out of the chair and reached for her purse and crutches. "I'm sorry I took up your time."

Gregory still watched the landscape. "Nick has never mentioned you, either."

Kate stopped. "He doesn't know about—about what happened with us."

Gregory turned. "Sit down, Kate."

She sat.

He returned to his seat, pulling it closer to hers this time. She felt his nearness, could pick out the faint gray pinstripe on his red silk tie. She avoided his eyes.

"You're right about Nick's having some problems here, but there are other causes. What has he told you?"

Kate studied her folded hands. "We—we're having some problems of our own right now. We aren't talking much these days. That's really why I'm here." She risked looking up. "I'm trying to understand what's going wrong so maybe I can fix it."

Gregory nodded and glanced at his watch. "I'm sorry I had to make our appointment so late in the day. And now I need to leave for a speaking engagement I have tonight, Kate. But I'd like to see you again." He touched her arm. "Have dinner with me tomorrow night. We can talk more about Nick's work here. Perhaps I can help."

Kate's mind tumbled. She admitted to herself that Gregory was still powerfully attractive to her. Did she dare go to dinner with him? She'd already made the mistake of flirting with one affair this week. But if she wasn't the cause of Nick's problem at SynTech, she wanted to find out what was.

She smiled up at him. "What time?"

˙ ˙ ˙

Nick zipped his jacket and walked out the main entrance of SynTech toward the artificial lake.

Groundskeepers had dutifully plowed the snow from the asphalt walking path around the perimeter, as if anyone would want to walk in this weather. Of course, here he was. A bench halfway around seemed a good place to stop. He sat.

If there had been sunshine today, it would be nearly sunset now. Instead, the gray slate ceiling above him looked angry.

Below, the black oval of the lake reflected the sky's emotion, churning in the wind.

Nick braced his hands against the cold stone seat, staring at the white stones that edged the lake.

The Gaucher therapy caused liver cancer. There was no getting around it. He had to report the problem—because in just three days people were going to start receiving that therapy. He envisioned himself telling Gregory what he'd found. Perhaps it was a mistake, and Gregory would be as surprised as him. Grateful, even, for Nick's dedication.

Or perhaps that conversation would end as Brian Milburn's had.

He could call the FDA, send samples of the injections and the DNA sequencing data for them to analyze. They would shut down the center. Probably with a call from him today they would shut it down before Saturday. But if the second version's errors were just a simple mistake, he would lose his job. Even if he was right and he called in the Feds, he would lose his job.

There it was, the choice before him. Risk his career by notifying the FDA or risk his life by telling Gregory what he thought he knew. It was a gamble. His decision had to be based on how convinced he was that Gregory knew about the alteration and intended to cause disease with that vector. His conviction would be a lot stronger if he could figure out what possible reason Gregory could have for doing such a thing.

A tall figure in a flapping black coat walked along the path toward Nick. As the man grew closer, Nick's stomach tightened with recognition. Chernoff.

The man drew all the way up beside Nick and sat on the bench beside him. Chernoff's gaze traveled over the surface of the water. "Deep thoughts, Dr. Donovan?"

"Can I help you, Mr. Chernoff?"

Chernoff's cheek twitched. "Nasty thing, drowning, don't you think?"

Nick watched Chernoff's drawn face until the man turned back to him.

"Icy water this time of year. Very nasty."

Nick turned to the water, scraping his hands against the stone edge of his seat. Chernoff rose from the bench like a vulture lifting away from its prey. He started back down the path toward the complex. "Have a good day, Dr. Donovan," he called, without turning his head.

Nick followed the ripples across the water. What was that but a threat? He looked up at the SynTech building. Had Gregory sent Chernoff out with that message? Was he watching even now? Nick shook his head. *You just made your first mistake, Dr. Brutal.* It was no longer a guess whether Gregory knew about the alteration or not. Chernoff's threat had made his involvement clear.

With that problem solved, Nick knew without doubt what his next step would be.

ᴄ ᴄ ᴄ

Stanford lay in his hospital bed, staring through the window at the city lights and the stars above them.

It had been a good bluff, telling Gregory that he had proof against him. Stanford wished it were true. Perhaps at the least he had bought Nick some time to stop Gregory.

Stanford raised a trembling hand to wipe away a tear. He wished he could avoid the questions that tormented him, but they marched in relentless succession across his mind. What good had his life been? What did any of it matter? Now that it was ending, had he fulfilled what he was meant to do? He'd achieved every goal he'd ever set, but now he couldn't remember any of them.

A sharp pain attacked. He reached for the PCA, the patient-controlled medication machine, and turned up the dosage.

His life was running out, and he still hadn't answered the most basic question a man can face: What makes life worth living? What should he leave behind? The legacy of a life well spent and respect well earned? Or the dying attempt to right a wrong he should never have allowed in the first place? Would either of them earn him a place of favor in whatever was to come? Was there anything to come?

He needed to hang on, if for no other reason than to stop Gregory. Though the "proof" Stanford had claimed to have was an illusion, it might be possible to make the illusion into reality, just as a backup plan if Nick failed.

Stanford needed to find a way to protect his family and to help Nick put an end to all of this. Before the cancer put an end to him.

He buzzed for the nurse. It was time to talk with Frank and make use of his digital communications expertise.

CHAPTER 36

The banquet at the Wyndham Plaza Hotel in Philadelphia was scheduled for six o'clock. Gregory's driver pulled his car up to the hotel at five-thirty. Gregory had spent the drive leaning back, eyes closed, trying to distance himself from the issues at SynTech and mentally prepare for the evening. His conquest of Justin Hardegan yesterday on *The Morning Show* had given him confidence that tonight would be another victory for genetic progress.

The car slowed at the hotel entrance. "Problem here," Gregory's driver said.

"What's going on?" Gregory eyed the crowd in front of the hotel.

"Looks like some sort of protest."

Wonderful.

A crowd of about fifty people milled in front of the doors. Placards and posters abounded. Gregory read "EMBRYO RESEARCH = MURDER" painted on one middle-aged woman's sign.

Gregory pulled out his phone and dialed the banquet coordinator. She answered on the first ring.

"This is Gregory Brulin. I'm outside your hotel. How am I supposed to get in there with a bunch of loons blocking the entrance?"

"I'm so sorry, Dr. Brulin. They've surprised us all by arriving out of the blue. The police are on their way. Please, pull around to the back of the hotel. Someone will meet you there and escort you inside."

Gregory pocketed the phone. "Go around back." A large object bounced off the windshield. Gregory ducked instinctively. The crowd rushed the car. Gregory felt for the door lock. "Get me out of here!"

People were next to the car now, their hands on the windows, yelling at him.

Gregory pushed himself farther into the seat cushion. "What are you waiting for? Move!"

"Sir, I can't move with all these people around us."

"Just start! They'll get out of the way." Gregory watched the angry faces, mouthing words he couldn't understand.

The placards were in his face now. "LEAVE GOD'S CREATION ALONE." "STOP DR. FRANKENSTEIN."

The car crawled forward, plowing a path through the crowd. The bodies parted reluctantly and flowed past him on either side. Finally, they were left behind. The car edged around the block and approached the hotel from the other side.

"Stop here," Gregory said. He collected his briefcase and coat. No one waited at the smaller entrance on this side of the hotel. Cursing, Gregory got out of the car and waved the driver off. It was too dark to see if the crazies had damaged the finish of his new car.

Inside, a tall security guard with bright red hair nodded to him. "This way, Dr. Brulin."

His escort led him across the hotel lobby where soft piano music provided the background for the conversation of the crowd lingering there. A large sign outside at the bottom of the central escalator welcomed the BioEthics Symposium to the hotel. Gregory took the escalator to the second floor and twisted his way through the crowd outside the Wyndham ballroom.

Inside the banquet room, dozens of round tables were set with bouquets of fresh wildflowers, blue-and-white china, and royal blue cloth napkins. Tuxedoed waitstaff moved among the tables with quiet efficiency, their only sound the soft tinkling of ice water flowing into glasses. Gregory surveyed the room, taking in the soft light shining in arcs on muted yellow walls and the potted trees in the corners.

A woman in an off-white suit stood near the podium, looking at papers in her hand. Gregory headed for her, passing a black-tie waiter filling water glasses.

"Ms.—"

His introduction was cut short by the waiter. "Excuse me, are you Gregory Brulin?"

Gregory took in the boy's clean-cut appearance. "Yes."

Gregory watched as if in slow motion as the boy set the water pitcher on the table, reached beneath his apron, pulled out a small pistol, and stepped around Gregory to circle an arm around his neck.

"Everybody out of here!"

Gregory glanced around the room. Every person seemed frozen in time.

"Out!" the boy screamed again. "I have a gun!"

The threat was enough to send employees running for the door, including the woman at the podium. Their exit was like a wave receding out to sea, sweeping the lobby guests with it.

Gregory stood still as the screams ebbed and the lobby emptied. Finally he found his voice and tried to pull away. "What are you doing?"

"Shut up."

He clawed at the boy's arm around his neck. "You're choking me."

The boy eased his grip and pushed Gregory toward a chair. "Sit down."

"What is this about?"

Two security guards appeared in the doorway.

His captor waved the gun toward them. "Get out!"

They backed out of sight. One of them brought his walkie-talkie to his mouth as he pulled back.

Gregory watched them go. "I don't understand—"

"I said, shut up!" the young man said. "I need to think!"

Gregory watched him pace across the carpet, following the geometric pattern woven in greens and golds. The kid was probably less than twenty years old and looked like a poster boy for an Ivy League school.

"Okay," the young man said. He swung another chair around and sat down backwards, facing Gregory with the gun braced on the back of the chair. "This is what you're going to do."

Gregory watched his face.

"You're going to call whoever you need to call, and you're going to cancel this free genetic thing on Saturday."

"Why would I do that?"

"Because I'm going to kill you if you don't."

The words were uttered with such lack of emotion that Gregory shuddered. "Are you with the group out front?"

"I'm my own group. But I understand their outrage."

Gregory shook his head, wondering how long it would take for the police to arrive. "Well, I don't understand it. Not one bit."

The boy laughed. "No, of course not. When there's money to be made, people like you don't think too much about the problems."

"I don't understand."

"Yeah, you said that already. You're not too bright for a doctor, are you? I saw you yesterday. On TV. Dr. Hardegan was trying to talk sense into you, but you wouldn't listen. You think no one knows that all your big talk about humans triumphing over disease is just a way to line your pockets with the money you make selling your cures?"

"This country was founded on—"

"Don't talk to me about history! You're perverting the future!"

"I am—" Gregory's phone rang. "May I answer that?"

The boy frowned.

"It's probably the police," Gregory said, "wondering about your demands. If I don't answer, they may come in shooting."

"Answer it."

Gregory pulled the phone out slowly. "Yes?"

"Dr. Brulin, this is Sheila Reynolds, symposium chairperson. The police were already on their way to deal with the mob outside, and they've been informed about your situation. They should be here any moment. Have you been injured in any way?"

"No, I'm fine."

The boy thrust a hand toward Gregory. "Give me the phone." Gregory handed it to him.

"Who is this?" He listened for a moment. "You'd better keep everyone out. We're going to stay in here until Brulin does what I've asked." He disconnected.

"Why do you want me to stop Genetic Awareness Day?" Gregory asked, leaning back in his chair as though chatting with a friend.

"Because you're sucking people in there for free just so you can turn them into mutants."

"Son, I don't think you fully understand what gene therapy is able to accomplish—"

"I don't understand? You're the one who doesn't understand, remember? Or if you do, you don't care! I heard you yesterday morning, mentioning the inevitable 'mistakes' that happen and how you learn from them. How nice for you to be able to dismiss your mistakes so easily. My sister doesn't have that luxury. She has to live with the 'mistake' for the rest of her life."

"What's wrong with your sister?"

"She was part of an experimental study for a rare kidney disease, but instead of curing her, it damaged her kidneys so bad she's on dialysis now."

"I'm sorry that your sister has suffered—"

"You're not sorry about anything. As long as you can keep making money, you don't care what happens."

"That's not true," Gregory said. "I have a deep concern for the betterment of society and would not want to see anyone harmed unnecessarily."

The boy shook his head. "We'd all be better off if all of you just stopped. Like Dr. Hardegan said, you're turning the world into a terrible place."

The phone rang again. The boy punched the "talk" button.

"What? No, I don't want anything from the police. Leave us alone!" He hung up.

He turned to Gregory. "This is what you're going to do. You're going to go on TV and announce that you're canceling the free day. You're going to say that you're reconsidering the wisdom of injecting so many people with these new therapies because now you think you may have made a mistake."

"I can't do that."

He stood and pointed the gun. "You will!"

A knock at the door on the far side of the room drew their attention. "Hello?" a voice called from outside the door.

"Go away!" the boy yelled.

"Samuel, it's me. It's Justin Hardegan."

The boy turned back to Gregory, but his eyes widened. "Dr. Hardegan? How do you know my name?"

"Some of your friends out here told me. May I come in, son?"

Samuel paused. "Yeah, come in. You're better at this than I am. Help me talk sense into this man."

Justin Hardegan's florid face appeared in the doorway. Gregory could see the sweat glistening on the man's balding head even from a distance.

"Samuel," he said, walking toward them, "are you sure this is a good idea?"

"Yes. We can't let him keep going. Just like you said on TV."

Hardegan nodded. "I agree." He stood a few feet from Samuel now, facing the boy. "But we are working hard to put a stop to all of it. In legal ways. Not like this."

Samuel bit his lip. "Your ways aren't working."

"We haven't been as successful as we'd hoped yet. That's true. But we are making progress. The word is getting out there."

"I don't know," Samuel said. "People are still going nuts over this genetic stuff, seems to me."

"I wish you could spend a day with me, Samuel," Hardegan said. "I wish you could read the letters I get, talk to the people I speak with in Washington. We are not alone, you and I. Plenty of people are working very hard alongside us."

"Really?"

"And they're counting on us, Samuel. They're counting on us not to jeopardize everything they're working for with actions that give our opponents a reason to call us fanatics."

Samuel's expression saddened. "I'm giving us a bad name, aren't I?"

"Not if you put an end to this now, Samuel. Give the gun to me. Don't let this turn into something we'll all regret."

Gregory felt Samuel's gaze on him, but he studied a gold diamond inside a green square in the carpeting. Out of the corner of his eye, he saw the gun change hands.

Hardegan took two steps backward from Samuel. An army of police officers swarmed the room. Samuel was handcuffed. An officer took the gun from Hardegan. Another checked on Gregory.

Minutes later the police were leading Samuel out.

A mustached officer approached Gregory. "In a minute I'm going to need to ask you a few questions, Dr. Brulin."

Gregory nodded, and the officer joined his colleagues, leaving Gregory alone with Hardegan.

"You didn't have to do that," Gregory said, straightening his dinner jacket.

Hardegan pulled out a handkerchief and wiped his forehead. "No, I think I did. But you're welcome." He held out a hand to Gregory. "I'm glad you're all right, Dr. Brulin."

Gregory lifted his chin. "Forgive me if I don't seem overly grateful. But it must be obvious that if it weren't for you and those like you spouting your ridiculous accusations, situations like this would not even occur." Gregory walked toward the vacated lobby, ignoring Hardegan's hand. "You seem to think you were the solution, Dr. Hardegan," Gregory said. "But I think you're the problem."

CHAPTER 37

Thursday, February 24

"Stella Ruhn, please." Nick paced the length of the lab three times before the FDA investigator came to the phone.

"Yes?"

"It's Nick Donovan at SynTech Labs, Ms. Ruhn." He gripped the edge of the lab counter. "Did you get the E-mail I sent last night?"

"Yes, Doctor, but I've only just arrived this morning. You'll need to give us time to process all of this information."

"Ms. Ruhn, perhaps I wasn't clear. This therapy is tainted. Everything's there in what I sent you: the DNA sequencing comparisons, the genes that are altered to stop production of the liver enzyme. On Saturday, SynTech will be—"

"Dr. Donovan, we understand. And you must understand that the FDA is not a SWAT team. We do not charge in, guns blazing. I'm certain you haven't forgotten our meticulous work last month on your own problem?"

Nick winced. "No, I haven't forgotten, Ms. Ruhn."

"So you know that we—"

"Ms. Ruhn, not only do I know that this therapy is tainted, I have reason to believe that Gregory Brulin may have killed someone—and attempted to kill others—to cover up that fact."

Stella Ruhn was silent. Nick rubbed his temples. He hadn't intended to drop that bomb yet.

"Dr. Donovan, do you have any proof to back up this accusation?"

"I believe that a researcher here may have learned—"

"Proof, Dr. Donovan? Because if you do, you should be calling the FBI, not the FDA. Do you have this proof?"

"No."

"Dr. Donovan, we'll be in touch."

"Ms. Ruhn—"

Click.

The lab door opened, and Jeremy came in.

Nick sighed deeply, then pocketed his phone. "Good morning, Jeremy."

Jeremy tossed his jacket onto a hook and grabbed a lab coat. "Hey."

Nick picked up a folder he'd shoved aside yesterday. "Ready to get to the proposal?"

Jeremy frowned. "No more detective work?"

"Not today."

"So what was up with that therapy yesterday? You gonna report it or anything?"

"It's taken care of."

Nick pulled out a stool and opened the folder. The words blurred, and he rubbed at his eyes, trying to focus.

"You okay?" Jeremy asked.

"Yeah, fine. Just tired."

Nick and Jeremy worked through the morning, but Nick couldn't concentrate. Would the FDA call Gregory? If they did, what would Gregory do? Nick half-expected Chernoff to creep into the lab at any moment.

It won't do you any good, Gregory. The truth's already out there. One more suspicious death will only make you look guilty.

He went into his office to check his E-mail, hoping to focus his thoughts. His Success Quote should have been comforting: "You can take yourself from rags to riches and from depression to joy, if you affirm your greatness, your genius, and the potential you have within you." Okay, so he needed to affirm his own greatness. He could solve any problem that came his way, couldn't he? Hadn't he until now?

By noon, Nick couldn't stand the waiting any longer. "I'm going to drive into town and get some lunch."

"What's wrong with the cafeteria?"

Nick shrugged. "I just need to get away from this place for awhile."

⁓ ⁓ ⁓

"Sonya, confirm my reservation for twelve-thirty at the Stafford Inn, please."

"Right away, Dr. Brulin."

Gregory snapped open his briefcase and deposited several pages into it. The tension from last night's disaster at the BioEthics Symposium Banquet had faded, but the anger it had fueled had not. The incident with young Samuel had made Gregory anxious for Phase 1, cleansing, to begin. The longer the fanatics were allowed to continue, the more damage they would cause.

Gregory closed his office door behind him as Sonya finished her call.

"Party of two expected at twelve-thirty," she said.

He ignored the look of amused curiosity on her face. "See you later, Sonya." He headed for the elevator.

Sonya smiled. "I hope you and Mrs. Donovan have a lovely lunch."

Gregory stopped and returned to her desk. "How did you. . ."

She laughed. "I guessed. But now I know."

"It's not for public announcement, Sonya."

She sobered. "I understand. I'm sorry, sir."

Gregory nodded. "You'll be ready later today?"

"Of course I'll be ready!"

"Good." He patted her shoulder and headed out.

The Stafford Inn boasted four intimate dining rooms in a historic setting. Gregory drove his own car and arrived first. He stood in the lobby, contemplating what he hoped to accomplish this afternoon.

The inn's roots as a farmhouse built in the 1700s were still evident in the lobby, where the dark wood flooring and walls were lightened only by gold leaf framed pictures on the walls. Heavy wooden beams overhead and antique wooden benches along the walls belied the four-star menu. This afternoon the lobby was empty, and only a few hushed voices and the faint clink of silver reached him from the dining room. The smell of a well-done steak made Gregory's mouth water.

Kate did not keep him waiting long. She had shed the crutches today, though it was clear she should still be using them. He took pleasure in the thought that she wanted to look her best for him. As she entered the lobby, he realized the petite woman was even more beautiful than she had been years ago. Maturity and poise had mellowed her lively spirit into a vibrant sophistication. Today she wore a dress the color of chocolate, and the sunlight in the lobby brought out the fiery highlights in her wavy hair.

Gregory held out his hands, and she took them. "Thank you for coming." Her fingers were icy, and he wrapped his hands around hers to warm them. "You look incredible."

She smiled and dropped her gaze. "I feel silly wearing this dress with these shoes, but I didn't want to risk high heels yet."

The maitre d' escorted them to the table Gregory had arranged in a corner of the smallest dining room. He held her chair, sliding her toward the table easily.

"No more crutches?" he asked as he sat down across from her.

"All better, I think."

After they had ordered, Gregory was the first to speak. "I have to admit to a bit of shock at seeing you after all these years."

Kate smiled. "Yes, it's a little strange, isn't it?"

"No. It's wonderful."

She blushed. "Could you tell me about Nick's work at SynTech?"

"Why don't you tell me about your work first? I'm interested to know what you've been doing all these years."

"Just the same project Nick was working on. I'm still at the Gene Therapy Institute. Nick is excited to have made the move, though. What kind of—"

"Cancer research, then? I've read all about the problems with your clinical trial, of course. What is your position at the institute?"

"I'm a lab assistant. Mostly tissue cultures. I help out with the animal testing. Nothing too close to the front line."

"I see." Too bad.

The waiter brought their salads, and the conversation waned as they chewed.

Gregory watched with amusement as Kate separated out the croutons from the rest of her Caesar salad. When their entrees arrived, Gregory took the time to savor the steak he'd been smelling since he arrived. The conversation continued in pleasant chit-chat as Kate slowly worked on her smoked salmon and Gregory finished every bite of his baked potato. Other guests arrived, ate, and left while the two caught up with their lives over the past few years and talked about the future of biotech.

Over dessert and coffee, Gregory moved on to his next goal. "You wanted to know about the problems Nick seems to be having at SynTech."

Kate looked relieved. "Yes. Please. I'd like to help in some way if I can."

"I'm glad to hear that, Kate. I know that Nick will be a valuable asset to the SynTech team, but he needs to focus on the bigger picture. He's spending too much time going down rabbit trails instead of finishing up the project he's been given. I have much bigger plans for him, but he doesn't seem to want to focus."

Kate nodded. "Nick's always been a very thorough researcher. But he gets the job done, Gregory. I know he could do great things at SynTech."

"I agree. But I have another, larger concern."

Kate raised her eyebrows, waiting.

"Nick realizes that there are some things I need from him, some things that will help everyone involved. But he's not been willing to be a team player, Kate. He's holding out on me, not giving everything he can for the effort."

"That doesn't sound like Nick."

"That's what I thought, too. Perhaps you can use your influence to persuade him to join us fully." Gregory swirled the coffee in the delicate china cup. "This has been such an enjoyable afternoon, Kate."

"It's a beautiful restaurant."

"Can we do this again? I'd like to spend more time reminiscing with you." He reached a hand across the table to where hers lay, covering it with his own.

"I—don't know." Kate studied the SynTech ring on his hand.

"I think it would be in Nick's best interest for us to keep talking about how to help him, don't you?"

"Well. . .I don't know if I can help."

"Nick's career is in my hands, Kate. You do realize that, don't you?"

Kate pulled her hand away slightly, though their fingers still overlapped. "I suppose I could see you again," she said, frowning, "if it's for Nick."

"Good." He smiled. "Very good."

Gregory walked Kate to the parking lot. "Is your car here?"

"My sister's car. I had a little—accident with mine."

"Ah, yes. The ankle."

Gregory said good-bye and watched Kate drive away. *I love vulnerable women.*

His phone rang as he reached the car. He leaned against it and punched the "talk" button, noticing a tiny dent in the roof, probably from last night's riot.

Three minutes later he disconnected and slammed a fist against the car. The FDA wanted a meeting. An "unnamed person" had told them one of SynTech's therapies was flawed, and they wanted a sample.

Gregory dialed a number. Forget getting Kate to bring Nick around. Donovan's career at SynTech was already over.

* * *

Kate stopped at a megabookstore on her way back to Melanie's house. She needed time to think.

As she wandered through the stacks of books, Gregory's seductive smile troubled her thoughts. Kate felt guiltily gratified that Gregory's reasons for wanting to see her again had been obvious. His intention to help Nick had been a transparent excuse, and his not-so-subtle manipulation—mentioning that he controlled Nick's job—had given her a good reason to agree to his suggestion.

What troubled her most was not that she'd been compelled to agree. The misgivings that needled her conscience as she absently browsed titles on the shelves came from the lingering effect of Gregory's hand on hers, his compliments, his smile. She'd agreed to see him again because she wanted to.

She had started this thing to save her marriage. Would she be the one to destroy it?

Brian Milburn Journal Entry #5
February 1

Sam Spade couldn't have been any more disappointed when his dame turned out to be the killer than I was tonight when I finally navigated my way into the direct mail advertising campaign files in the SynTech computer network. I'd thought SynTech held the answer for the future of disease treatment. Turns out it's a front for one man's twisted agenda of hate.

I'd seen some of the glossy brochures going out to prospective clients and knew that they mentioned specific predispositions to diseases. Why hasn't anyone questioned where they're getting their information? It's as if the whole world has thrown up its hands on the matter of genetic privacy and assumed that their DNA is public property. Meanwhile, somebody in SynTech's marketing department is hacking into GenWorld and downloading data.

That's not where it ends. Other organizations are having their mailing lists pilfered and cross-checked against GenWorld data. From that, SynTech gets a list of people who are connected with these organizations and who have predispositions to diseases we treat.

And who are these people who are going to receive these tainted therapies? What organizations are we going after? It looks to me like we're aiming for people who are opponents of embryonic research, cloning, and genetic enhancement.

The only thing scarier than all of that is the one fact I've been trying to avoid. This scheme does not involve a rogue researcher dropping alterations into therapies as a sick sort of game. It doesn't involve a lone hacker culling names from private mailing lists. It doesn't involve an isolated marketing exec sending brochures to only certain people.

This is a systematic, planned attack on a specific group of people, and it can only have been engineered by one person. Gregory Brulin.

CHAPTER 38

After his fast food lunch in the city, Nick swiped his keycard through the reader outside the revolving door near the SynTech building's lab wing. No green light. He tried a second time.

The reader didn't seem to be working. He checked the card. Had it gotten scratched?

He jogged across SynTech's lawn to the main entrance. Inside, the security guard stepped from behind his booth as Nick hurried forward. Nick held one side of his jacket open to reveal the ID pinned to his shirt pocket. The guard nodded.

Nick headed for the elevator. SynTech seemed to be humming at its usual pace. No SWAT teams charging in. Had Stella Ruhn even followed up on Nick's information?

He stepped into the elevator. His phone rang as the doors closed.

"Nick? It's Stanford."

"Yes, Stanford."

"Everything okay over there?"

"Well, since you asked, I'm having a few difficulties."

"Oh, yeah?" Nick noticed Stanford's voice seemed to gain energy at this news. A problem he could try to solve.

"What kind of difficulties?" Stanford asked.

"I think it's possible Gregory knows about a problem with a therapy, and he's covering it up. Do you think he's capable of that?"

The elevator opened into an empty corridor on Sublevel 2. The air was noticeably colder. Like a crypt.

There was a pause on the other end, and Nick's shoes clicked down the white tiled hallway, the sound bouncing back at him from the end of the hall. His lab was the second maroon door.

Stanford spoke, his voice low. "Nick, if you've found something, you have to go forward with it. You have to stop him."

Stanford took a labored breath. "I think Gregory's lost his mind."

"Really? Why do you say that, Stanford?"

Nick pulled his keycard from his pocket, slid it into the lock, and pushed against the door in one motion.

Nick looked at his keycard. The door hadn't yielded. Had he put it in the wrong way? He slid it in and tried the handle. Nothing. Glancing to the side, he checked the nameplate beside the door. Nicholas Donovan. He tried again.

His card wouldn't open the door.

I guess the FDA called after all.

He interrupted Stanford, whose conversation he'd been ignoring. "Stanford, I've got something I need to take care of. I'll check in with you later." He disconnected and pounded on the door. "Jeremy? You in there?"

No answer. He dialed SynTech's number. The operator put him through to his lab. He could hear the phone ringing on the other side of the door. Jeremy didn't pick up. Still out to lunch maybe?

Nick disconnected. There had to be a maintenance guy around somewhere. Or did they only work after hours?

At the end of the hall, Nick stopped at the supply room. Two large, glass-fronted refrigerators held plastic bottles of growth media—the reddish, nutrient-filled liquid they used to grow organisms. Across the hall, a door labeled "Maintenance" stood ajar.

"Hello?" Nick stuck his head in. The room was empty. He pushed the door open farther, stepping in. Maybe there was a master keycard around somewhere.

The room smelled of chlorine. A gray desk littered with piles of paper sat against the back wall beside a large metal cabinet. Mops, buckets, and industrial-size bottles of cleaning solution lined the other walls.

"You need something?"

Nick jumped at the gruff voice at his back. He turned to see a vaguely familiar face. It was the man who had changed his nameplate on his first day here. What was his name? The smudged stitching on the blue coveralls saved Nick from his usual memory lapse.

"Hi, Jimmy. Nick Donovan—we met on my first day here."

"Oh, yeah." Jimmy leaned a mop against the wall. "What can I do for ya, Doc?"

"I can't seem to get into my lab. Something wrong with the lock, maybe."

Jimmy sniffed and wiped a beefy hand across his nose. "Doubt that. All the locks in this area are on one system. When one goes down, they all go down, and I been getting into other rooms just fine." He pulled a ring of cards from his belt. "Let's give it a shot."

"Thanks," Nick said. He headed down the hall toward his lab, but heard Jimmy stop behind him.

"I'll just check this first one," Jimmy said. "If it's in good shape, then yours is good, too." Jimmy slid his master key into the lock and pushed against the door. It opened inward. He let it close again and turned to Nick.

"Looks good."

Nick pulled his card out again. "Maybe there's a problem with my card. Could you try yours in my door?"

"I don't know, Dr. Donovan."

"Is there a problem?"

"No problem. Just that sometimes they turn people's cards off. When they get fired or something, you know. So they can't get back in. I don't think I should open anything for you without word from higher up, you know?"

Nick turned his card around in his hands.

Jimmy shrugged. "Sorry, Doc. You could talk to the maintenance supervisor, Mr. Jankowski. He's on Sublevel 1. Or maybe you should talk to the system guy, the one who controls the locks."

"Yeah, I'll do that."

Nick watched Jimmy return to the maintenance room. As Nick turned toward the elevator, he slammed against a figure beside the door.

"Dr. Donovan?" Chernoff frowned as though he'd caught Nick stealing company secrets. "Dr. Brulin would like to see you."

I'll bet. Nick pocketed his keycard. "Is there some problem?"

"I'll take you there, Doctor."

Nick felt Chernoff's presence at his back as they walked toward the elevator. *I should get out of here now.* As they neared the elevator, Nick sped up. The stairs were only a few feet away.

Chernoff's fingers wrapped around his upper arm, pulling him toward the elevator. "This way, Doctor."

Up on the third floor, Chernoff escorted Nick from the elevator directly into Gregory's office. Nick felt like a criminal being led to sentencing.

Gregory looked up from his desk and replaced the phone. "Sit down, Nick."

Nick sat.

Gregory waved Chernoff out. He lit a cigar and leaned back in his chair. "Nick, I'm disappointed. I thought you had a promising future here."

Nick exhaled and squared his shoulders. "The Gaucher's therapy is tainted, Gregory. I had no choice."

Gregory puffed at his cigar. "No? You could have come to me. I would have pulled it immediately. We could have kept this in-house."

Yeah, with me at the bottom of a lake, right?

Gregory raised his eyebrows. "Is there something more you wanted to say, Nick?"

"What happened to that therapy?"

Gregory leaned forward and propped an elbow on his desk. "I have no idea. I'm sure the FDA will be wanting to know the same thing. You can be assured that I won't rest until I find out."

Nick watched Gregory's eyes. Nothing, not even a flicker, betrayed him. "Good." Nick stood and turned toward the door.

"Chernoff will retrieve any personal items from your office before you leave, Nick."

Nick paused, his back to Gregory. He clenched a fist, but there was nothing more to be done.

Gregory continued. "I had such high hopes for you, Nick. I thought you'd matured, that you were ready to play with the big boys."

Nick turned back to Gregory, scowling.

Gregory shook his head. "Together we were going to take on disease, ensure the human race's survival. I had hoped you would be an asset. Instead, you've become a liability."

Nick resisted the urge to say, "Like Brian Milburn?" He wasn't stupid.

Just before he left the office, Gregory said, "Perhaps your results were flawed, Nick. Did you ever consider that? I really don't think the FDA will find anything at all wrong with that therapy."

༄ ༄ ༄

Sonya Galasso stepped off the elevator on Sublevel 3. Gregory held the doors open until she entered the lab. Her eyes betrayed her nervousness.

"I take it Dmitri's not coming?" he asked.

Sonya shook her head. "He had to work. But you know how he is. Just wants the bottom line. Doesn't want to get involved in all the details."

Gregory ushered Sonya into a treatment room in the back and handed her a gown. He leaned against the wall outside her door while she changed.

This is it, he thought. The beginning of Phase 3, creating. By Saturday, Phase 1, cleansing, would be well underway. Despite all of Tina Milano's annoying qualities, Phase 2, cloning, was going perfectly. If today's procedure was successful, he'd have nine months before he knew if Phase 3 would really work. Six years of research came down to today.

Dr. Yang had perfected the strategy by experimenting with embryos gained from *in vitro* clinics around the world. Then this month he had begun the *in vitro* process with Sonya and Dmitri, working with the cells before fertilization until he had three viable, "enhanced" embryos. Three embryos that would be implanted in Sonya's uterus in just minutes and would go on to change the world.

Despite the Brian Milburns and Nick Donovans of the world, a new era was about to dawn. It would owe its immortal existence to Dr. Gregory Brulin.

CHAPTER 39

It was almost two in the afternoon when Nick dropped the cardboard box inside the front door of his townhouse. The framed picture of Stanford and him at the award ceremony bounced out of the box onto the entryway tile with a crack. Nick noticed a Y-shaped split in the glass. He left the frame on the floor and headed for the couch. The house felt like an empty shell without Kate in it.

An hour later, the phone woke him from an exhausted sleep. He rolled off the couch, staggering for the phone like a man twice his age.

"Dr. Donovan? Stella Ruhn."

Nick straightened.

"Doctor, I felt I should let you know. Due to your anxiety and insistence, we did send someone immediately to SynTech's Gene Therapy Center."

"Thank you, Ms. Ruhn. That's a huge relief to me."

"There does appear to be some slight variation in the therapy you told us about."

Nick exhaled and stretched the tension out of his shoulders.

"Dr. Donovan?"

"I'm here. Just relieved and gratified beyond belief."

"Yes, and I'm sure you'll also be relieved to hear there's no real danger here. The second version of the therapy does use a slightly different vector. We spoke to Dr. Brulin about filing the proper paperwork."

"What? A slightly different— Paperwork?"

"Yes, there has definitely been an oversight, and we will follow up. Thank you for bringing it to our attention. But neither therapy poses any threat to patients."

Nick's words left him.

"Dr. Donovan?"

"Ms. Ruhn, I personally tested the therapy and found serious problems with it. It causes liver cancer, Ms. Ruhn."

"Dr. Donovan," she said slowly, "I don't know how to say this. But. . .your attention to detail has not proven your strongest asset in the past, I'm sorry to say."

Blood pounded in Nick's temples. "Ms. Ruhn—"

"We'll contact you if anything further is needed, Dr. Donovan. Thank you."

Nick threw the phone onto the couch and slammed a fist against the wall.

He'd lost his job for no reason! He was on the outside now, and Gregory was still going to get away with his plan. Why hadn't he taken the Gaucher samples with him when he'd gone to get lunch? *Stupid!*

At least he'd forced Gregory to pull the Gaucher's therapy. He wouldn't dare keep using it now.

A thought occurred to him. He grabbed the phone and dialed SynTech. "Give me Jeremy—" What was his last name? Nick cursed his stupid recall problem. "Butler!"

The phone rang repeatedly. No answer.

It took several more minutes to track down Jeremy's home phone number.

Jeremy picked up on the first ring. "Yeah?"

"Jeremy, it's Nick Donovan."

"What's going on, Nick? You've already gotten me fired."

Nick ran his hand through his hair. "You, too? I'm so sorry about that, Jeremy. I didn't think things would happen this quickly. Listen, man, what did you do with the Gaucher data we were working on?"

"I left it right there. They didn't give me time to do anything but grab my coat."

"I need to get back into that lab," Nick said. "Maybe I could get Bernice's card. I'll call her at the hospital."

"Well," Jeremy said, "she's, uh, right here."

"Bernice is with you?"

"Yeah. She got out of the hospital this morning, and we are sort of seeing each other, you know. . ." Jeremy's voice trailed off.

"That's great, Jeremy. Ask her if I can use her card."

"That's not gonna work, either. They got rid of her, too."

"What? She wasn't any part of this!"

"No kidding. Lame, huh?"

Nick exhaled. "Okay, Jeremy. Listen, I'm really sorry for getting you both involved in all this. I'll let you know what happens."

Nick sprawled across the couch and stared at the ceiling. His mind drifted back to his conversation with Stanford this morning. *I think Gregory's lost his mind.* That's what Stanford had said. Nick had seen no evidence that Gregory was deranged. Why would Stanford say that? Maybe there was something there that Stanford wasn't telling him, something that might explain why he didn't seem to remember his time at SynTech too favorably.

Nick picked up his coat from the back of the couch, kicked the picture frame out of his way, and left the townhouse.

Gregory had some motive for using an altered version of that therapy, and Nick had a feeling that Stanford knew what it was.

↝ ↝ ↝

Nick found Frank sitting outside Stanford's room.

"Hello, Nick," he said.

"Hey, Frank. Stanford okay?"

"Yeah, I was in there with him, but the nurse kicked me out. She said she'd be finished with him in a few minutes.

Nick dropped to the chair beside Frank. "Mind if I wait with you?"

"No problem. How are things at SynTech?"

"Uh, up and down, I guess."

"I heard about the Genetic Awareness Day thing. Sounds big."

"Yeah, we're—that is, SynTech is hoping to boost public awareness and understanding of gene therapy. Many people are still uninformed about the benefits." The party line sounded false coming out of his mouth.

Frank nodded. "Did you know I've been treated at the Gene Therapy Center?"

"You? Not for the cancer?"

"No, before I got cancer. I was treated for Hemophilia B."

Frank uncrossed his legs and changed positions. "I don't know how much your public awareness needs boosting. It seems like everyone I know is talking about that place, even my more conservative friends."

"Conservative? You mean religious?"

Frank stared at a spot on the wall. "I'm not sure what you call 'religious,' but a lot of them do have a relationship with Jesus, yes."

Nick raised an eyebrow. "I see. Don't you find that a bit ironic?"

"Ironic?"

"Aren't all you religious types always lobbying the federal government to stop providing funds for embryonic stem cell research?"

Frank tilted his head, his brow furrowed. "Not all of us. But some. In fact, I was involved with a group like that for awhile."

Nick shrugged. "No offense, but it drives me crazy to see all these people picketing and protesting cutting-edge research, then turning around and taking advantage of the benefits of what was cutting-edge research five years ago."

He paused to check Frank's reaction, but the man seemed interested, not offended. "It's always been that way," Nick said. "The right-wing people screamed 'playing God' years ago when doctors first started doing heart transplants. Said it was unnatural, that no one should be allowed to change what God had given. Now, most of them wouldn't think twice about a heart transplant if that's what it took to keep them alive."

"That's true."

"So when you tell me that you and your friends are lobbying against embryonic research—but they're all excited about heading over to the Gene Therapy Center to have one disease or another eradicated from their bodies—it annoys me."

Frank nodded. "I can see why. And to set the record straight, I did say I'm no longer part of that group, right?" He smiled.

Nick smiled back. "So I guess you saw the light and decided that scientific research should go forward unhindered?"

Frank laughed, a rich, even laugh that sounded sincere. "I didn't say that."

"So what is your position?"

"You sure you have the time for this?"

Nick glanced at Stanford's room. "I need to talk to him, so I guess I've got nothing but time. Besides, I always enjoy a good bioethics debate, especially with a religious person."

Frank settled back in his chair. "All right. There was a day when I believed that Christians in the political realm represented the only hope this country had of retaining morality."

"And now even the Christians are immoral, right?" Nick chuckled.

"Some, yes. But beyond that, I realized something important: No amount of legislation will ever change people's hearts. If this country is to be saved, it won't be through the political process. It will only be through surrendering to Jesus Christ, one person at a time. I realized that people need Jesus, not better laws."

Nick scratched his jaw and looked out the hallway window. "So you've given up the protesting scene?"

"I've made a choice," Frank said. "A choice to dedicate my life to giving people the good news of the Bible instead of trying to get laws passed that try to force people to be good.

"When it comes to bioethics, Nick, I think some Christians forget the most important thing. They forget that all this fooling around with stem cells and embryos and cloning—it's all just messing around with the physical matter. No scientist ever created life, and none ever will. God and God alone causes life to begin and allows it to end. In fact, the Bible even says, 'Do not fear those who kill the body but are unable to kill the soul; but rather fear Him who is able to destroy both soul and body in hell.' Sometimes I think Christians get so wrapped up in trying to save the bodies, they forget about the souls."

Nick's eyebrows rose. "Whoa, this is a shock coming from you. So, you're saying that it doesn't matter if we create test-tube babies and do experiments that destroy human embryos—because it's all just physical matter? Frank, by that logic, Christians shouldn't be complaining about abortion or fetal-tissue harvesting or cloning or—"

"Nick, slow down. You misunderstand me. Will you let me use an analogy?"

Nick nodded. "Go ahead."

"I believe genetic-research progress is much like a prize Thoroughbred racehorse."

Nick frowned in confusion, and Frank smiled.

"Some Christians are trying to keep the racehorse locked up in the stable," Frank said. "On the other hand, some scientists want to let him loose, let him run wherever he'll take them. Now, who's right? Personally, I believe the horse definitely needs reins to keep him from running somewhere we don't want him to go. The problem is that no one knows who should be holding those reins, right? That argument is a very important one, and it's an issue I'm glad people are debating. But, Nick, all of that is a side issue, as I see it. My main concern is that the horse is on the wrong track."

Nick shook his head. "I don't get it."

"What is the ultimate goal of all genetic research, Nick? It's to erase every disease, to make us immortal, isn't it? That will never happen. Men hide behind the hope of eternal cures, refusing to look their own death in the eye." Frank nodded toward Stanford's room. "They hide all their lives, never giving thought to the soul that outlives the body—until death will not be denied."

Just then Julia and the nurse stepped from Stanford's room. In spite of her elegantly tailored suit and jewelry, Julia looked tired. Her usually straight shoulders sagged, and her eyes shone with unshed tears. "Hello, Nick."

Nick heard the tension in her voice, and his heart dropped at the thought that Stanford might have lost his battle with cancer already. "What's wrong, Julia?"

She wiped her eyes. "I'm glad you're here. He keeps mentioning you. I've called the children, but they haven't gotten into town yet. "

"How is he?"

"He'd never admit it, but I know he's scared. Talk some sense into him, Nick. He's all worked up about something he says he must do before—the end. He's wearing himself out."

Nick entered Stanford's dimly lit room. His mentor's face was white against the white sheets.

Julia came in behind him. "Nick's here, dear."

Stanford's eyes drifted in Nick's direction. "What are you doing here?" His voice was like sandpaper.

Julia poured him a cup of water out of a pink plastic pitcher on the bedside table.

He would never tell Julia to call me, Nick thought. She probably had to call their children without his knowledge, too. Stanford would fight to the end, certain he would win.

"Just passing by," he said aloud, willing his voice to sound cheerful. "Thought I'd stop in for a 'hello.' "

Julia held the cup of water to Stanford's lips and pushed the button beside the bed to raise his head. She stepped away to let Nick stand beside him.

Nick's hand shook as he laid it on the metal guardrail at the side of the bed. Stanford's eyes had sunk deeper into his face, creating lines Nick didn't recognize. Stanford's pain-medication unit blinked beside him, its control cord running down to Stanford's hand.

Julia saw Nick eyeing the machine. "He can self-administer more drugs whenever the pain gets too bad. But he refuses to do it until he's nearly unconscious."

Stanford managed a weak smile. "Dulls the senses." His eyes locked onto Nick's. "You understand."

Nick did understand. He would not want to go out groggy and disoriented. That might leave something undone. He would stay alert until the end, hoping to accomplish one more thing, help one more person.

Stanford cleared his throat. "So how are things at SynTech?" he asked, as though they sat in Stanford's living room, chatting over coffee.

"Little crazy right now." Nick glanced at Julia.

"Dear," Stanford said to her, "please get yourself some dinner. Nick will stay, won't you?"

"Of course."

Julia smiled and covered Nick's hand with her own. "I'll be back soon."

When she was gone, Nick turned back to the bed. "You're worrying me, Stanford."

Stanford closed his eyes. "They asked me if I wanted to put in a DNR order."

Nick nodded. Patients often filled out "Do Not Resuscitate" forms to instruct their doctors to let them go when death was inevitable.

"I couldn't do it," Stanford said. His words came in short spurts, with shallow breaths punctuating. "Julia didn't want me to. Since the kids aren't here yet. So it was easy to say no."

He rested, but Nick could sense there was more. Nick looked down, straightening his tie and wiping his sweaty palms on his pants.

Stanford began again. "It's too soon, you know? I'm not ready yet. I thought I'd have the chance to do more."

Nick placed a hand over his friend's. "It is too soon, Stanford. It's not fair."

"Lying here, though. Lots of time to think. I'm afraid I'd feel this way no matter how old I was. Life's so short, Nick."

Nick looked away, studying the skyline of the city, just beginning to light up in the darkening sky.

When Stanford's voice came again, it was a whisper. "I don't think anything I've done in my life has mattered, Nick."

"Don't say that! You're a good man; you've done so much good!"

Stanford chuckled softly. "You're kind to say it, Nick. But I don't think any of it mattered."

Nick stood and poured himself a cup of ice water.

"It's all the same at the end, Nick. Good or bad. Hardworking or lazy. Makes no difference. It's all worthless."

"No. That's not true."

"I've been pushing and pushing. All my life. Now I die." A tear pooled at the corner of Stanford's sunken eye, then ran down toward his ear. "What use was any of it? None of it makes a difference."

Nick shook his head. "You need to rest, Stanford. Let's not talk about that anymore. Besides, I have to ask you some questions, if you're up to it." He took a deep breath. There was no need to burden Stanford with his failed call to the FDA. "Stanford, this morning. . .you said that Gregory had lost his mind."

Stanford closed his eyes again.

"What did you mean, Stanford? Do you know why he's using a tainted therapy?"

Nick feared Stanford had gone to sleep. A few moments later his eyes opened.

"You don't know him, Nick. Things—happened."

"What happened?"

Stanford swallowed. His face twisted in pain.

Nick reached for the tumbler. "Do you want some water?"

Stanford shook his head.

"I'm sorry to push you, Stanford, but I have to know what happened."

"His son." Stanford breathed deeply.

"His little boy?" Nick said. "The one who died?"

Stanford nodded. "Never been right since then. Hates them all."

"Who does he hate?"

Stanford's eyelids drooped.

Nick heard a step behind him and turned.

A thickset, no-nonsense nurse bustled into the room. "He needs to rest now."

Nick looked at Stanford, who appeared to be sleeping. He laid a hand on his friend's shoulder then headed for the door. When he glanced back, he no longer saw the man he knew.

He saw an older version of himself.

↶   ↶   ↶

Stanford awoke and was disappointed that Nick hadn't stayed. But Frank came in again, and that was good. Things seemed blurry today. Tearful. Weary. The time for good-byes would soon be upon him.

He feared that Nick would fail in his efforts to stop Gregory. Stanford had nearly told him everything, but in the end he couldn't. There were still too many repercussions for admitting what he knew. Instead, he'd thought of a way to protect his family and stop Gregory himself.

"Nick's a good man," he said when Frank stood beside him. "Not good enough for God, though, right?" A hint of sarcasm cut through the pain.

Frank's lips tightened. "None of us are, Stan. We all want the blessings God can give, but without facing the barrier we've created between ourselves and Him."

"I don't believe in sin." Stanford panted. It had become an effort to speak, but conversation was all he had left. That and his doubt.

"I know you don't believe," Frank said. "You've lived as though you had no more purpose than to do what you wanted, and so whatever helped you achieve your goals was acceptable. That philosophy doesn't allow for good and evil, right and wrong. So many atrocities have been committed by evil people in the name of achieving their goals. But the standard is there, whether you believe it or not."

"It's too hard, Frank. Too hard to believe."

Frank shook his head. "Believing isn't hard, Stan. You've held beliefs every day of your life. Humility is what's hard. Admitting that you need Someone beyond yourself to reach down and do for you what you can't do for yourself. That's hard."

Stanford remained silent, thinking and trying not to think.

Frank sat beside him, wordless. Stanford turned off his pain medication. "I need your help, Frank."

Frank nodded. "I'm trying."

"No, more than this. I need your. . .professional. . .help."

Frank tilted his head.

"Your expertise in electronics."

Frank smiled. "Thinking of getting a new stereo, Stan?"

"I can't give you answers. You have to trust me. I need to record a conversation."

Frank leaned forward. "Now you've got me curious."

Stanford swallowed. Why did every conversation have to be such an effort? "I don't know where it will be. Here or on the phone. Hopefully here. I need to be ready for either. But I need to be able to record both sides of the conversation."

"What's this about, Stanford?"

Stanford shook his head. "Can't explain. It's very important. Will you help?"

"I'll help."

Brian Milburn Journal Entry #6
February 2

Why did I ever start down this path? When I look back at my earlier entries and see how such a short time ago I was so cavalier about the whole mess, I feel sick.

I've just come from the library. The public library, because I'm now afraid to access any information at SynTech's library. Who knows who might be watching?

The news wires are full of information on Gregory Brulin. I can still see the picture of five-year-old Michael Brulin. The most informative thing I found on him was a straightforward opinion piece about opponents of embryo research slowing down cures. Michael Brulin's case was used as an example of a needless death. There was an interview, and the quotes attributed to Gregory spewed hatred at all right-wing opponents of embryo research.

So now I have it all, don't I? I started out playing detective and ended up getting just what I wanted. Mystery solved: Gregory tainted the therapies in order to avenge himself on those who oppose embryonic research. So if I've done my job, why do I feel so sick?

I'm here at home now, but I have to run over to the center in a few minutes to give a speech. I've taken to locking this notebook in the fireproof safe box I keep at the back of my book-shelf in my study. Am I paranoid now, or what?

What will happen when I tell the FDA of Gregory's actions? I can't imagine. He'll go to prison. I may lose my job. Price you pay for being Sam Spade, I guess. I could always be a private detective.

I've put all my findings on the computer at my lab and here at home as a backup. I need to go by my lab after my speech tonight to pick up the Version 2 samples so I can have solid proof of Brulin's tampering. Then I'll head to the FDA with my findings and the samples. My one consolation in all of this is that I've stopped something truly awful from happening on Genetic Awareness Day.

I could barely contain my contempt for Gregory when I saw him at a meeting earlier today. He's a smug, self-righteous, nasty piece of work, and I know he thinks he's completely justified. I nearly threw the whole thing in his face, but in the end I managed to confine myself to a bland comment about his son's death. I do feel pity for him. But revenge against innocents is a sick response. Sam Spade would never let him get away with it.

And neither will I.

CHAPTER 40

Nick let the car idle in the twilight at the cancer center's parking lot exit. It was five o'clock. He didn't know where to go. He couldn't get anywhere at SynTech, and the townhouse felt like a dungeon without Kate. A car behind him beeped a protest at his wandering thoughts.

The ringing of his phone made him decide to swerve back into the cancer center's parking lot. He put the car in park and answered the phone.

"Dr. Donovan? It's Andrea Milburn."

"Hello, Andrea! I've been meaning to give you a call. How are you and the children doing?"

"We're okay, I guess. Staying with family while we figure out what to do. But I've been working through what's left of our house during the day."

"I'm so sorry. That must be difficult."

"I have something to show you. Something I found today."

Nick straightened. "What is it?"

"It must have been in Brian's study. A fireproof box. I couldn't find the key, but we pried it open."

"And?"

"Can you meet me? I want you to see this."

"Name the place, Andrea."

$\wp$ $\wp$ $\wp$

One hour later Nick found himself sitting in a garish diner that had called his name as he'd been driving past.

A yellow, spiral-bound notebook sat on the table in front of him. He stared at it and took a deep breath. When Andrea had asked him to meet her at her parents' house, he didn't dare hope that she had something he could really use. Was he ever wrong.

The moment Andrea had given him the notebook, he'd opened it and read it in disbelief. Now he wanted to read it again more carefully. His hands shook as he opened the cover.

Detective Sam Spade here, ready to take on the seamy underside of SynTech Labs and wrestle its secrets into the light.

The aging, ruby-lipsticked waitress who had seated him in the vinyl booth brought him a menu. The blue curtains wilting in the front window testified that the diner had also seen better days. "Here you go, hon," the waitress said. "You want some coffee?"

"Hmm? Oh, yeah, thanks. Black."

"You got it, sugar. Be right back."

Nick placed the journal on the chipped table in front of him and opened the menu. Its laminated pages resisted his effort, clinging to each other in gummy persistence. The only other patrons were a couple in the corner, arguing over something. Nick tried to concentrate on what to order, but his attention swerved back to the notebook. He continued reading.

When did any of our therapies get approved for different versions—much less all of them?

Nick shook his head. All of them?

"You ready to order?" The waitress was back, and Nick hadn't read a word from the menu.

"I'll have some pie."

"Apple, peach, cherry, key lime, or strawberry-cheese?"

Nick watched her earrings bob as she counted off the selections. He couldn't concentrate. "Um. . .apple."

"Apple pie." She plucked the menu from Nick's grasp and disappeared.

Nick went back to reading the journal.

I sequenced that Version 2 therapy today, and it is most definitely not the version approved by the FDA. . . . This is serious, nasty business. . . . Version 2 causes cancer.

His pie arrived. Nick sipped the coffee first, his gaze wandering over the walls beside his booth. The diner had made an effort to be trendy, adding old-fashioned signs and memorabilia to its garish, gold-framed watercolors. A little blue-and-white sign nearest Nick caught his attention. The Morton Salt girl stood with her umbrella, declaring "When It Rains, It Pours." No kidding.

Nick picked up a fork and took a bite of pie, but his stomach revolted at the oversweet apple filling. He pushed the plate aside and kept reading, finishing the second entry and continuing to the third.

So far, I don't know why these "particular" patients are slated to get the second version. But one thing I do know: Every one of them has an appointment scheduled for that Genetic Awareness Day next month.

The waitress returned. "You need anything else, hon?"

"No. Thanks." Nick watched her wind her way through the tables in the middle of the room, thinking of Brian Milburn, working his way through the SynTech network to track down clues, trying to find a reason for the unbelievable thing he'd discovered.

...opponents of embryonic research, cloning, and genetic enhancement. . . . This is a systematic, planned attack. . .and it can only have been engineered by one person. Gregory Brulin.

Nick pushed through the last entry, all the pieces falling into place as he read.

Michael Brulin. . .a needless death. . .the quotes attributed to Gregory spewed hatred at all right-wing opponents of embryo research.

The final words of the journal blurred in front of his eyes: *Sam Spade would never let him get away with it. And neither will I.*

Nick checked the date of last entry. February 2. The day Milburn died. Also the day of Nick's first interview at SynTech. The thought gave him a chill. What had happened that night? Milburn must have come back from his speech at the center where the tainted therapies were arriving and made the note in the computer file. Sometime after that his car ended up in Silver Lake.

He hates them all, Stanford had said. Now Nick knew who Stanford had meant. Gregory hated anybody who opposed the research that might've saved his son. Of course he hated them. It all made perfect sense now. If those people hadn't protested, little Michael Brulin might still be alive.

If Milburn was right, Gregory had designed a way to exact revenge on those people or people like them.

But if it was true. . . It was too terrible to contemplate. On Saturday, two days away, hundreds of expressly targeted people were going to flood the center to be treated during the free Genetic Awareness Day. Hundreds of people injected with a gene therapy specially designed to destroy their lives.

Nick checked the time and pulled out his phone. It was after six o'clock, but maybe he could still catch Stella Ruhn.

The FDA switchboard put him through.

"I've got proof, Ms. Ruhn."

"Dr. Donovan, we've been over this—"

Nick lowered his voice. "Remember I told you that someone had been killed to cover this up? I have his journal, detailing what he knew."

Stella cleared her throat. "All right, Dr. Donovan. I'd be interested in seeing that. If nothing else, you've piqued my curiosity. But I must be honest. With nothing more than the unsubstantiated diary of a dead man, I don't think there is much we can do."

Nick exhaled. "Come on, Stella! What's it going to take to make you believe me?"

"We need some sort of physical proof, Dr. Donovan."

"I gave you proof! The Gaucher's disease therapy."

"But, Dr. Donovan, there was nothing disease-causing in that therapy. Your sequencing charts didn't match the samples. You made another error, Dr. Donovan. If you want us to take action, you're going to have to give us something definitive. A sample of this cancer-causing therapy you keep claiming to have, a memo directing someone to alter the therapy. Without something like that, you just sound like one more vengeful ex-employee."

Nick pushed the notebook away. "I'll be in touch."

He put the phone on the table and pounded his head. Unbelievable. He tried to make himself think calmly. Proof was what it was going to take. Physical proof. If he could somehow get samples of the altered therapies, he could prove Gregory's wrongdoing to the FDA.

Kate, I need to talk to you. She would understand. She would know the right thing to do.

Was this ever going to be over? He wanted his wife back, wanted to explain everything. Nick looked down at the tight ball of crumpled napkin in his hand. From the kitchen he could hear the clatter of dishes being washed. He wanted to go home. He was ready to end all of this.

Nick pressed his fingers against his temples. If he was going to stop this thing from happening on Saturday, he had to get those tainted therapies, either from his lab or the center. But he couldn't exactly just waltz in there and get them. It wasn't going to be easy. He thought of Chernoff. It wouldn't even be safe.

Was he ready to die? Or should he just walk away from it and let hundreds of people be harmed?

First, do no harm.

Nick choked down half of the bitter coffee, threw some money on the chipped table, and stood.

He would find a way to get into the center tonight. He'd pick up where Brian Milburn had left off. He'd get the samples and prove his case to the FDA.

Or die trying.

Part Three

FEAR NO EVIL

Where, O death, is your victory?
Where, O death, is your sting?
1 Corinthians 15:55

Nick strolled through the front doors of the SynTech Gene Therapy Center, his eyes focused on the double doors that led to the main corridor.

Several dozen people crowded the lobby, reading magazines on couches, milling around the seating areas. A Vivaldi symphony played in the background. Nick ran his hand across the Greek statue of Aesculapius as he passed it. Ten steps from the double doors, he heard a female voice aimed in his direction.

"Can I help you, sir?"

Nick kept walking, his eyes on the doors.

The voice materialized into a young woman with a SynTech jacket and a pleasant smile.

"Do you have an appointment, sir?"

"Yes." He glanced at his watch. "At 7:00. I'm running a few minutes late. So if you'll excuse me. . ."

Instead, she stepped in front of him. "And your appointment is with—?"

Nick hesitated.

"What is your name, sir?"

Nick took a step backward. "Perhaps I have the time wrong?" He pulled out his phone. "I'd better make a call, just to check. Excuse me."

He turned away, pretending to dial, and headed out of the center.

Outside, he reevaluated. There was no way he was going to give his name. There had to be other ways into the building.

Nick walked around to the back of the building in the dark, searching for another door. A metal dumpster, overflowing with trash, stood under a buzzing light several feet from the building. Nick circled it and spotted a door on the other side. He tried the handle. It was locked.

Nick leaned against the dumpster in the shadows, watching the door. How long would it take for someone to come out?

He only had to wait ten minutes. He'd positioned himself to slip through the door behind anyone who came out to toss something in the trash. When the blue-jumpered man pushed through the door, empty boxes balanced in his arms, Nick waited for his moment and slid into the corridor.

It was empty, but the maintenance man would reenter any moment. Nick jogged up the hallway, trying every door. The first two were offices. Locked. The third was a supply closet, deep enough to step inside and close the door.

Nick held his breath, listening. He heard the back door open again. Heard the man's footsteps approaching on the tiled floor. Would he stop to get something from the closet?

The footsteps passed. Nick waited, but the hall remained silent.

He tried to reconstruct the layout of the center from his trip earlier in the week. The treatment and counseling rooms were all in one wing, the offices and conference rooms in another, and the medical facilities must be in the third—in the wing Rich Nowinski had gone to get the Gaucher vectors.

Nick nudged the door open several inches and studied the hallway. The white-tiled floor and antiseptic walls gleamed in the fluorescent light, but the hallway was empty.

As long as he could look official enough, maybe he'd get past any employees who saw him. There were little plaques on the walls pointing the direction to various rooms, including the cold storage room where therapies were kept.

Nick passed two nurses in the supply wing. His heart pounded, but he didn't make eye contact, and they ignored him. The signs finally led him to the storage lab. The double doors were locked.

The hall was empty now. Nick stood to the side of the doors and leaned toward the two five-inch square windows that were cut into the door at eye level.

He edged his head toward the tiny window until one eye had a clear shot of part of the room. He scanned it quickly.

Two white-coated technicians, a man and a woman, stood in the room talking. The woman seemed to be explaining something to the man. He nodded, looking around the room.

Nick leaned farther, till he could see into the room with both eyes. It appeared to be empty except for the two in the middle. Cold storage units stood against the side wall. The bright lighting would make him easy to spot, but the room was so cluttered with equipment Nick hoped he could remain hidden long enough to get into those refrigerators. He stepped aside and ran a hand over one of the doors.

Steel-reinforced, with no handles on the outside. The two doors met without so much as a hairline of overlap to get his fingers into.

Just past the storage room, a small door opened off the hallway. Nick slipped over to it and peeked in. A small maintenance supply closet, filled with shelves of cleaning supplies, several mops, and a trash can on wheels. The closet was large enough to squeeze into. Since the door opened away from the room he could leave it slightly ajar and have a perfect view of the doors.

It had worked once, why not again? He slipped inside and waited.

A loud buzz inside the room sent Nick pushing backward into the closet. A moment later the doors swung inward and both the man and woman left the room and turned away from him.

Nick counted to two, then took several catlike steps to the doors, squeezing through before they sealed again. He was inside!

He took in the layout at a glance. Cold storage units, cryogenic freezers, metal shelving along the back wall, equipment everywhere. A door in the back opened into another room.

Nick spotted a portable cold storage container on one of the metal shelves. It would hold more than enough vials for the proof he needed. He grabbed the unit and turned toward the cold storage.

He pulled on the cold-room door. It was locked. Before he could think of a plan, a footstep fell behind him. Nick whirled.

A thin, white-coated man stood there, his thick glasses magnifying insect eyes. "Can I help you?"

Nick lifted his chin, his offense all in his attitude. "Who are you?"

"Dr. Watson. Who are you?"

Nick resisted the urge to answer, "Sam Spade."

"You shouldn't be in here," Watson said. "I'm going to call security." He reached for a phone on a nearby lab bench and pushed a button.

Nick knew he could take this geek easily. In two steps, he knocked the phone from his hand, skittering it across the polished tile floor.

"What are you doing!"

"I can't let you call anyone," Nick said, measuring the distance to Watson's nose. One good punch ought to do the trick. He balled his fist and launched his punch.

Watson's forearm came out of nowhere and blocked it.

Nick's eyes got wide.

Watson smiled. He grabbed at his glasses, tossed them onto the bench, and faced Nick in one angry movement. "It's going to be that way, is it?"

Oh, great.

Nick was committed now. He launched another punch. This one connected. He felt a crack where fist met face. But the man came back from the hit, fury in his eyes.

Watson's first blow smashed into Nick's stomach. The air *whooshed* from his chest and ended in a choking cough. Watson brought a stiff arm down onto the side of his neck. Nick's knees buckled.

Wonderful. Millions of nerdy scientists in the world and I have to run into Dr. Jackie Chan.

"Thought you could mess with Watson, didn't you?" Watson said, looking about to go into Matrix mode. "Come to beat up on the smart kid again, huh? Well, guess what, punk? Fatsy Watsy's gone and learned tae kwon do."

From the floor, Nick groaned.

"Get up," Watson said.

Nick tried to disguise his next punch as part of his rise to his feet.

It didn't work. Watson leaned out of the way of the punch, grabbed Nick's arm as it went by, and punched Nick in the ear.

Nick tried to recover, but Watson held his wrist. The man lifted his right leg and kicked Nick in the gut three times in a row, then followed it with another blow to the side of the head. Nick went down in a heap.

Watson danced over him like the welterweight kickboxing champion of the world. "You done, punk? Or you want some more of Fatsy Watsy's home-cooked lovin'?"

Under an equipment cart, Nick spotted a multiplug power strip with a heavy cable. He pulled it out quietly and held on to the cable. He didn't have to fake the look of pain as he struggled to rise to his feet, not facing Watson. In the corner of his eye, he judged the distance.

Then he let fly with the power strip, flailing it like a cat-o'-nine-tails.

Watson blocked with his forearm, but the cord wrapped around and the metal multiplug box nailed him in the cranium. Watson crumpled to the linoleum.

"Ha!" Nick shouted. He charged to the cold storage unit and yanked on the door again. He turned back to Watson and knelt over to search him for a key.

A loud buzz brought him back to his feet.

The doors swung open. A sour-faced man who looked like an administrator trotted in, his lips tight in a disapproving frown. "What's going on here? What is all the shouting? And what on earth is Watson doing on the floor?"

Watson groaned.

"I'm going to call security," the man said.

Nick vaulted Watson and ran for the center's main entrance, leaving the cold storage room—and his plan—behind.

⌁ ⌁ ⌁

The quarter moon did little to lighten the midnight darkness above Nick's townhouse. Cold sparks pricked the ebony sky. Nick sat on a lawn chair outside his back door, a melted ice pack on his ear.

Apparently he'd escaped the center without anyone recognizing him. He had plenty of aches and bruises to show for his efforts, but nothing worse. And no Version 2s.

There were times when perspective was called for. This was one of them. Nick often tried to find that perspective in the night sky. He dropped his head back against the bench, letting his eyes adjust to the darkness, watching the stars come into focus.

So many stars. The universe was so big. A familiar twinge of panic made him lift his head from the bench and look at the trees instead. Sometimes he felt like he could fall into the unending blackness. Strangely, it was the same fear that sometimes plagued him when he looked into a microscope. The universe was also so small. Tiny units of life. Infinity in both directions. And him floating somewhere in between. Where did he fit into all of it?

Was this mission to find the answers at SynTech the purpose for his life? Would saving those people—if he could pull it off—be enough to impress God, as Frank had said? How could that man be so sure of things anyway?

Nick's eyes returned to the stars, back to the problem at hand. If he couldn't get into the center, how else could he get the proof he needed?

There was a chance that the Gaucher information was still in his lab. He could try to slip into SynTech when everyone was leaving work tomorrow. In the meantime, maybe Jeremy and Bernice would be willing to help him with an idea that was forming in his mind.

Was this his destiny? In spite of unemployment and professional disgrace, at the end of all this, would he find himself fulfilled? Or was there something more, something missing?

Stanford's face floated through his memory. *It's all worthless.*

Was it true? Would he battle to the end of his own life, only to whisper those same words? To achieve, succeed, gain respect. To give yourself to a dream and do all you can to make it a reality. These were his life goals. These were the things Stanford had achieved, which he now tossed aside as a waste of time.

Why do I want to do all those things? Do I believe they'll make me happy?

He had to admit that he did believe that. He had seen the public figures who had achieved outstanding success and yet led miserable lives, enslaved to addictions, a trail of broken relationships behind them. He had believed that he would be different, like Stanford. But what if, inside, Stanford was just as miserable as those others?

What if I achieve all my goals, and I'm still not happy?

CHAPTER 42

Friday, February 25

Kate rolled two lavender flower petals between her fingers. She crushed them to a deep purple and then dropped them beside the vase onto the white linen tablecloth.

Though it was 8 A.M. on a Friday morning, the restaurant Melanie had picked for breakfast was empty except for the two of them and an older man reading the newspaper at a table across the room. Two waitresses talked loudly in the back of the dining room, the morning rush apparently over. Kate could smell coffee and wondered when one of the servers would get around to offering some to them.

"You're quiet this morning, Kate," Melanie said. She laid her menu on the table in front of her.

Kate's thoughts had been battling in her mind like two prizefighters ever since her lunch with Gregory yesterday, leaving her tired and confused. Melanie had suggested they go out to breakfast as soon as Scott and the children were off to work and school. Kate agreed halfheartedly, thinking she was too troubled to eat. She wondered if Rocky Road ice cream was on the menu.

"Lot on my mind, I guess."

"Have you heard from Nick?"

"Not exactly." Kate plucked a few more petals and mashed them, studying the gray sky outside the restaurant window. "I found out Nick's been lying to me."

"In what way?" Melanie leaned forward, folding her hands on the table. A waitress arrived to take their orders and pour coffee, leaving the small silver pot on the table between them.

"Remember that he told me he didn't want me to come home because he was putting in extra hours to compensate for a problem he was having with Gregory Brulin? A problem stemming from the past?"

"Right, you told me," Melanie said, stirring cream into her coffee. "Well, you didn't expect the two of them to work together and not have a little bit of rivalry, did you?"

"Maybe not, Mel, but that's not it. I found out what Nick told me isn't true. I talked to Gregory, and he said there's no problem between them at all, except that Nick's putting in much more time than necessary and not being a 'team player.' Oh, Mel, I don't think Nick wants me to come back at all."

"When did you see Gregory Brulin?" Melanie asked evenly.

Kate sipped her coffee. It was too strong. She ripped a sugar packet and poured it in. "Oh, I had lunch with him yesterday."

Melanie raised her eyebrows. "Kate?"

"He wanted to talk about Nick." Kate heard the defensiveness in her voice. What did she have to be defensive about?

"Wasn't that a bit awkward," Melanie asked, "considering the past you two have?"

"We don't have a 'past,' Melanie. It's not like we were engaged or anything."

"Whatever you call it. Didn't you feel strange?"

"He was kind."

"Uh-oh." Melanie sat back against her chair.

"What's that mean?" Kate heard the edge in her voice again.

"I've seen that look before."

Kate rolled her eyes.

"You still feel something for him, don't you?" Melanie said.

Kate studied the silver coffeepot, catching her blurry reflection. Had she aged much in these past few years? Was she still the girl that he had once called 'angelic'?

"Kate, you're only hurting yourself." Melanie's voice had softened. She reached across the table to Kate's hand. "I've seen the way Nick looks at you. The way he's acted the last few times he's come to the house. I don't believe he doesn't want you."

Kate stirred her coffee.

"Don't trade one relationship for another because the one you have isn't meeting every need," Melanie said. "The next one won't, either."

Kate felt tears threaten to spill over. She closed her eyes and made her decision.

The waitress brought a plate of sliced cantaloupe and honeydew melon and a basket of crusty bread.

Kate tore into the bread. "Are you nervous about your gene therapy appointment tomorrow?"

"Oh, I forgot to tell you. They rescheduled. I guess they got such a good response to Genetic Awareness Day that they're starting the appointments tonight." She shrugged. "I'm not nervous about it. Everyone I've talked to tells me it's routine. I'm glad they're offering these treatments free of charge, though. I couldn't do it otherwise. Remind me to thank Nick when he comes to bring you home."

Kate smiled. What would she ever do without Melanie?

CHAPTER 43

Nick pulled into the parking lot of the SynTech Gene Therapy Center. "Have you got the form?"

Jeremy folded his arms. "You've asked me that twice, dude. I've got it."

"I don't know about this," Bernice said, shifting uneasily in the backseat of Nick's car. She wore a straw hat to cover her bandage. "I feel very—"

"You'll be fine, Bernice," Jeremy said.

Nick parked and turned to the backseat. "Bernice, maybe you shouldn't go in."

"No," she said, "I want to help. If what you told me about Dr. Brulin is true, then I have to try, don't I? Besides, if Jeremy's going in there, I'm going, too."

Nick nodded but hoped they weren't making a mistake. Inside that center was the proof he needed to show the FDA that Milburn's journal was true and that Gregory Brulin was false. He parked near the lot's exit. The dashboard clock read 11:30 A.M.

"Where are you going to be?" Jeremy asked.

"I'll hang out in the waiting room." He opened his door and stepped out.

"You sure?" Jeremy said. "What if someone recognizes you?"

Nick reached back into the car. "I brought a disguise." He donned the red Phillies cap he'd thrown in the car before he left the house.

Jeremy raised his eyebrows. "Great," he said. "I'd never know you."

Bernice closed her car door and stepped to Jeremy's side.

"Ready?" Nick asked.

She nodded.

Nick gave them a head start into the center, then sauntered

through the front doors and found a chair where he could watch them go to work.

The waiting room was not as crowded as it had been earlier in the week, but the atmosphere was the same—a Beethoven symphony accompanying the trickling fountain and hushed conversations all around.

Nick leaned over to the coffee table in front of his chair and picked up a magazine. He kept his head down, hoping that the receptionist who'd stopped him last night wasn't working today.

Nick wasn't sure his drafted coconspirators were up to the task, but they were all he had. If they could pull it off, they'd be walking back out with samples of at least two Version 2 vectors in just a few minutes. As long as no one looked too closely at the signature on that form.

Another man dropped into the chair beside Nick. "Hey, how ya doin'?" the man said, nodding and smiling.

"Fine, thanks."

"What are you in for?"

Nick cleared his throat and flipped through the magazine. "Just a consultation."

"Yeah, I came a few weeks ago for that. Getting the shot today."

Nick murmured appropriately.

"Just might do a write-up on this place, you know?"

"Write-up?" Nick tried not to sound overly interested.

"Yeah, I'm a reporter." He stuck out a hand, a business card in it. "Austin Chambers. Maybe you've read my column?"

Nick reached across to take the card. "I don't get much time to read the paper."

Austin's forehead puckered. "Too bad." He shrugged. "This place would be a great subject for an article."

"Why's that?"

"Oh, you know. Progress. Mankind's evolution. The triumph of technology. That sort of thing."

Nick watched the main doors out of the corner of his eye. "So did your paper send you here to get some background information?"

"My paper? No. My boss gave me the power plant assignment. Possible layoffs. But I don't really pay much attention to the assignments he gives me. I write whatever I think is best for my career."

Nick hid a smile. "How does your boss feel about that?"

Austin shrugged. "Never asked him."

"Doesn't he have certain stories he wants covered, the stories he assigns you?"

"Well, yeah, but I do my own thing, you know?"

"And you expect your boss to keep publishing your column?"

Austin folded his arms. "I've got to do what's best for me. That's why I'm here, you know?"

Nick nodded again, wondering how long it would take Jeremy and Bernice to get what they came for.

 ∼   ∼   ∼

Jeremy still found it hard to believe that Nick had trusted him with this job. He pulled at the lapels of his lab coat and led Bernice down the corridor where the supplies were kept. Nick had told him where to find the right storage lab.

He turned to Bernice. She looked cute but a little weird with a straw hat on over her lab coat. "You ready?"

She nodded and bit her lip.

Jeremy checked the signs on each of the doors they passed. When they found the right room, he knocked.

A slight man with large glasses and a large white bandage on his forehead answered the door. "Yes?"

Jeremy shoved the form at him. He forced a note of nonchalance into his voice. "Here to pick up some samples."

The man whose ID badge read "Henry Watson" studied the form. "Okay, come in, I guess." He was still studying it as Jeremy and Bernice followed him into the cluttered room. "Who sent you for this?"

Jeremy pointed at the paper in Watson's hand. "It's all right there." He sighed and let his eyes wander around the room. "This gonna take long?"

Watson pursed his lips. "I'll pull the samples for you." He went to the refrigerator beside the wall and pulled a key from his lab coat pocket.

The doors behind them swung inward. A slim man with a bad comb-over entered. Jeremy recognized him. He took Bernice's hand.

The man noticed Jeremy and changed course to come over to them. "Jeremy, right?"

"Yeah, right. How ya doin', Dr. Nowinski?"

"Fine, fine. Haven't seen you for awhile."

Jeremy nodded and turned back to Watson. He held several vials in his hand, and the refrigerator door was swinging shut behind him.

"Can I help you with something?" Nowinski asked.

"Ah, no. Just picking something up." Jeremy reached for the vials.

Nowinski stepped between him and Watson. "Weren't you working for Brian Milburn the last time I saw you?"

"Yeah, but not anymore," Jeremy said, his voice quivering. "I mean, of course not anymore, right?"

"Right." Nowinski crossed his arms. "But doesn't that mean you're working for Nick Donovan now?"

Jeremy tried to reach around Nowinski for the vials, but couldn't without looking desperate. "Well, I was, but then Nick got fired. So I guess I'll just have to see, huh?"

Nowinski put his fists on his hips. "Lock those samples up, Watson." He took a few steps to his right and reached for the phone on the lab bench. "Security. I need—"

Jeremy yanked Bernice toward the door.

"Hey!" Nowinski dropped the phone and charged toward them. He grabbed Bernice's arm. "Don't you go anywhere! Help me, Watson!"

Watson touched his bandage. "You don't pay me enough for this."

Jeremy cracked his arm across Nowinski's forearm. The man's hold on Bernice broke. "Let's go!" He tugged the door open, and the two dashed into the hall.

✴ ✴ ✴

The main corridor doors flew open, and Nick pulled himself away from his peculiar conversation with Austin Chambers.

Bernice and Jeremy darted out.

Nick jumped to his feet and met them in the center of the lobby. "Did you get them?"

Jeremy grabbed his elbow. "No. Let's go."

A center employee jogged through the double doors. "Hold it!"

Nick turned away and moved quickly toward the front door.

"Dr. Donovan?"

Nick recognized Rich Nowinski's voice. He could hear the center director's footsteps behind him. He followed Jeremy and Bernice through the front doors and onto the sidewalk. "Come on!"

The three broke into a run. A minute later, Nick was driving out of the lot with Jeremy and Bernice in the backseat.

"Well?"

Jeremy shook his head. "Everything was fine at first. The guy didn't even look at the signature. He just went to get us the samples. I think it was the guy you kung fu'd, Nick. Anyway, while we were waiting, Nowinski came in. He recognized me, knew I used to work with Milburn. Then he figured out that I was working with you."

Nick pulled the Phillies cap from his head and smacked the

dashboard. "So Brulin's already spread the word that I'm persona non grata, it seems."

"Looks that way."

"Well, that's it for now." He crossed into another lane. "Thanks anyway, you guys."

Bernice leaned her head on Jeremy's shoulder. "You totally saved me, Jeremy."

Jeremy took her hand. "Nah, you coulda gotten loose yourself."

Bernice seemed to remember they weren't alone. "We're sorry we couldn't be more help, Nick."

"No," Nick said, "I'm sorry I got you involved in any of this. How's your head with all that running?"

"It's fine."

Nick dropped Jeremy and Bernice at Jeremy's house, where they'd met, and offered more apologies and promises to call. The two stood in the driveway and waved as he pulled away.

Nick fought depression as he drove home. It was already two o'clock on Friday afternoon. Everything he had tried had failed. What next?

Nick pulled into his driveway and jumped out of the Expedition. The door of the townhouse adjoining his own jerked open. His neighbor, Mrs. Perkins, stood inside, pulling a bathrobe around her withered body. Her gray hair was rolled tightly in pink curlers. She motioned him over to her door.

"Hi, Mrs. Perkins. How are you?"

"Nick, are you in trouble?"

Nick looked around as if expecting SynTech security cars to converge on him at any moment. "Why do you ask?"

"Because if you are," she said, "I don't want any part of it. I don't want any trouble."

Nick frowned. "Mrs. Perkins, have I ever been any trouble to you?"

Her shoulders dropped. "I'm sorry, Nick. It just unnerved me, those police asking about you."

"Police?" Again Nick turned to check the road. "What did the police want?"

"They didn't say, really. Just wanted to know when you usually get home, that sort of thing."

"They didn't say why they needed to find me?"

"You're in trouble, aren't you, Nick? Did you rob a convenience store?"

"No, Mrs. Perkins," Nick said, laughing in spite of himself. "Everything's fine. I'm sorry you were bothered."

Nick headed toward his own front door. He pulled out his keys and stuck one into the lock. When Mrs. Perkins's door closed, he removed the key and ran back to his SUV.

Nowinski would've called Gregory about Nick's little subterfuge. And now Gregory must've sent the police after him for trespassing and for beating up Fatsy Watsy. Nick couldn't stay at home.

There was only one place he could think to go, one person who might still be able to shed light on what was happening at SynTech Labs.

But first he needed to get to the nearest car rental place and switch to something more anonymous.

CHAPTER 44

Nick parked the rented Toyota Camry in the slushy parking lot of the Young-Meddleton Cancer Center and went inside.

On the way over he'd stopped at a convenience store, still laughing at Mrs. Perkins's comment, to pick up a huge cup of coffee, which he'd now consumed. He was worried that his half-night of sleep would sabotage his alertness for what he needed to do here.

He had tried to call Kate when he'd left the car rental agency. She didn't even know he'd been fired, let alone become a wanted man. But he'd had to leave a message. He'd catch her later. It was two-thirty, and time was passing too quickly. Nick needed to get some answers and figure out a plan.

He entered Stanford's room quietly, watching the man's chest rise and fall in shallow breaths. His eyes were closed.

It was so frustrating knowing Gregory's plan but failing at every attempt to stop it. As much as he hated to bully a dying man, Nick knew his only hope lay in getting Stanford's help. Nick glanced around for a chair and noticed Frank sitting in the corner.

"Good afternoon, Nick," Frank said.

"Hey. I didn't see you there. But then, it seems you're always here."

Frank put down a small electronic device and smiled at Nick. "There may not be many chances left to talk." He motioned to another chair. "Have a seat. He tends to doze off and on all day. It's the meds."

Nick pulled a chair up next to Frank's and sat, noting again how at ease Frank always seemed to be. He wore a white dress shirt and khaki pants that looked like they'd just arrived from the dry cleaner's.

Nick looked at Stanford. "I really need to talk to him, Frank. Do you think I could wake him up?"

"I'm hoping he wakes up in a few minutes." Frank crossed one leg over the other. "Let's talk awhile. If Stan doesn't wake up in a minute, you can try to wake him."

Nick sighed heavily. "Want to get in one more sermon about death?" He hoped his smile offset the sarcasm.

Frank smiled and shrugged. "I told you that's my agenda now. To give people the good news."

Nick snorted. "If I remember right, it sounded like a whole lot of bad news to me."

"It starts out bad, I'll admit. But you already knew the bad news, deep down, right?" His eyes locked onto Nick's. "You're going to die, Dr. Donovan. Have you thought about that?"

Nick paused and eyed Stanford breathing shallowly in his sleep. He didn't look well at all this morning.

"Nick?" Frank leaned forward. "Have you thought about your own death?"

Nick stood and went to the window. Dirty snow in plowed-up piles lined the parking lot below him. The afternoon sun shone behind an icy cloud filter.

In his mind's eye, Nick saw his sister Natalie's face, so full of trust. He turned away from the image, but he couldn't avoid the fact that what Frank said was true: Death was unbeatable. Nick had gone into medicine to make it false. How had he never seen that he was doomed to fail? Even if he could somehow cure every kind of cancer known to man, other things would take its place.

He watched Stanford's reflection in the window.

Nick was going to die. What difference did it make if it was soon, like it would be for Stanford, or at an old age? Every elderly person he knew said, "Time goes so fast." Tomorrow or in fifty years, he was going to die.

And then what? That was the part that always freaked him out, the part he distracted himself from focusing on.

Frank spoke quietly. "I knew a man once who was so afraid of dying that he made his life into a frantic race to achieve all he could before time ran out. Nick, my friend, are you anything like that man?"

Nick leaned his head against the glass. "I think I might be."

"Good, Nick, good. Admitting it is half the battle. Remember, there is good news for you if you're willing to receive it."

Nick turned back to Frank, waiting.

"I think you resist the idea of death so strongly because it goes against your basic nature. You were made for eternity, Nick." Frank pointed to Stanford. "The body wears out. But the soul goes on."

"I understand that belief," Nick said. "I think it's probably true. In some way we don't understand, we go on to another place."

"But wouldn't you rather understand it?"

Nick smiled. "Yeah, me and a lot of other people."

"Nick, I know you're a busy man, so I'm going to give it to you as succinctly as I can. You're spending your life trying to build toward peace and purpose, instead of building on it."

Nick looked out the window again. "This is the 'You've got your ladder leaning up against the wrong wall' speech, isn't it?"

Frank chuckled. "That it is. Nick, you can't earn eternal life or forgiveness or peace and purpose. It's a gift. But there's something in the way of your taking that gift for yourself. If you were to die today, you'd fall before a holy God with every less-than-perfect thing you've ever done standing in accusation against you. All that must be dealt with. It can't be ignored, can't be reasoned away by man's logic, and can't be bought off by hard work and sincere effort. Either you must pay the consequences or someone else must do it on your behalf."

Nick sat down.

"That's the good news, though, Nick: The debt's been paid for you. The obstacle has been removed. Jesus Christ, God's perfect Son, died in your place and suffered the agony you deserve. Then He rose from the dead Himself to prove that resurrection is the destiny of every person whose sins are paid for. Now God calls you, inviting you to accept the gift He's offering. That's the life designed for you. The only one that will bring you a sense of purpose and fulfillment."

"So what's the catch?" Nick asked, folding his arms. "What do I have to do?"

"Nothing. Believe that it's been done for you. Accept it as a free gift."

Nick shook his head. "Too easy."

Frank smiled. "Let me put it another way. If I remember the gene therapy lecture I got at your center, you use retroviruses as little delivery vehicles to get the perfect DNA into a person with messed-up DNA, right?"

Nick nodded, a puzzled smile forming.

"Well, Nick, we're all infected with the one disease you'll never find a cure for—death."

Nick nodded again. For some reason, today he was willing to face that truth.

"No analogy is perfect, but think of Jesus as the delivery vehicle, Nick. What do you call that?"

"A vector?"

"Right, think of Jesus as a vector. He was both human and God. His perfection can be delivered to all of us who have this disease of death, healing our souls and giving us the cure. God has made a way. Just like your retrovirus goes to work inside the body to provide the cure. The only difference is that when Jesus became the cure, He took the disease onto Himself."

Frank leaned into Nick's field of vision. "Did you know that God's Word says that 'the punishment that brought us peace was upon him, and by his wounds we are healed'?"

"No, I've never heard that."

"Jesus also said, 'I am the resurrection and the life.' "

Nick looked at his feet.

"Nick, what do your patients need to do to be cured by your vectors?"

"Nothing. They just get the injection."

"Exactly. And have you ever injected a vector into an unwilling patient?"

"Of course not. Every patient signs a consent form."

Frank nodded. "It's the same with sin and death. There is nothing you can do to rid yourself of the sin in your life. You just have to accept the cure. But Jesus never comes into a life and transforms it without consent."

Nick sighed. Frank made too much sense.

A rustling across the room drew their attention.

Stanford's eyes opened. Nick and Frank stepped to his bedside.

"And I thought I was your only target," Stanford whispered to Frank.

Nick laughed. "He's an equal opportunity preacher." He held the bedrail. "Stanford, I really need to talk to you."

Frank slipped out of the room.

Nick told Stanford about his findings, his calls to the FDA, Milburn's journal, everything. He watched Stanford's eyes carefully as he spoke. Was the older man too tired to register surprise, or was none of this news to him?

"I've tried twice to get into the center to get samples for the FDA. I can't get in there. I'm desperate, Stanford. I'm hoping you can help me somehow. Maybe a paper trail, something you've saved for years. . . ?"

Stanford shook his head. "I don't have anything like that. What about the sample you sequenced?"

"It's still in the lab. Since they fired me, they turned off my keycard code. I can't get back into my lab to get anything. Besides, they've probably cleared it out by now."

"There must be samples somewhere other than your lab and the center, though," Stanford said.

Nick straightened. "Wait, that's it, Stanford! The day I pulled the Gaucher sample from the cold storage room at SynTech I met a researcher who was there unloading crates. He said they were cranking out big batches for Saturday. I'll bet there are Version 2 therapies in that room now. Stanford, I have to get back into the SynTech building. Somehow I'll find a way."

"Be careful, Nick. I know you'll do your best. I'm proud of you."

      *   *   *

Nick fiddled with his car-radio buttons, trying to find a station that didn't grate on his nerves. He gave up and mashed the "power" button with his thumb. He wouldn't try to get into SynTech until after 5 P.M. It was only three-fifteen. There was nowhere to go, not even home. He just drove through the gray slush of the Philadelphia streets, following one-way signs around blocks of businesses and restaurants.

You are going to die, Dr. Donovan.

Frank had gotten to him. Somehow the well-dressed, well-spoken businessman had earned his respect and then zapped him with his religious message. It was in his brain, playing and replaying till he wanted to rip it out himself.

That's the life designed for you. The only one that will bring you a sense of purpose and fulfillment.

Frank made sense, Nick would give him that. But it was all so odd, so. . .spiritual. Maybe Nick really had been focusing on the physical far too long. He trusted what he could see under a microscope.

Of course—he let himself admit it for a moment—everything he'd ever seen under a microscope screamed that life had a Designer.

He thought back to his lecture at the Gene Therapy Center, to his joke about a bioengineered retrovirus being a perfect combination of the human and the divine. Just like Jesus. And according to Frank, all he needed to do was admit that he couldn't cure himself and then give his consent, trusting that Jesus was the cure for the sin that kept him from God and for the death that would be the outcome.

But what then? What would God expect from him?

Oddly, Nick's thoughts jumped to Austin Chambers, the reporter he'd met at the center that morning who didn't care what his boss wanted and yet expected his boss to continue supporting his career. "I've got to do what's best for me," he had said.

Am I doing the same thing? Living my life with only my own purposes in mind and expecting a Higher Power to support my efforts? Could that Higher Power have a different plan for me, one that I'm ignoring?

Nick shook off the introspection and glanced at the time. Three-thirty. Would Kate be back at work today or still at Melanie's?

His phone rang before he had a chance to dial Melanie's number.

"Hello, sweetheart." His mother's voice sounded tense. "Just checking in on you."

"How's that new job, Son?" Dad was on the line, too.

"Challenging," Nick said, hoping Dad wouldn't push.

"Everything okay with Kate?" his mom asked.

"Why do you ask?"

"Just wondering."

"Quit beating around the bush, Leona. Tell the boy."

"Oh, honey, I'm sure it's nothing. But you know how people talk."

"Who's talking?" Nick asked.

"Just the Cavanaughs, that's all. I was talking to Nancy this morning. She and Jim were at the Stafford Inn yesterday. She mentioned that she saw Kate there."

Dad broke in. "With another man, Son. Some rich-looking guy, she said."

Nick hesitated. Nancy Cavanaugh loved nothing better than a juicy bit of gossip, but he'd never known her to fabricate one.

"I'm sure there's an explanation."

"You see, Patrick? There's an explanation. I told you."

"Well, good, Leona. Now Nick will tell us what that explanation is. What is the explanation, Nick?"

"Um, Mom, Dad, I've got to go. Thanks for calling."

Nick gave the "disconnect" command before they could talk again.

~ ~ ~

Gregory listened with only half his attention as Tina Milano rattled on about her "needs." She sat in his office, in the same chair Kate had occupied yesterday, tossing her black hair and tapping bloodred nails on the armrest.

In the end, Gregory agreed to everything Tina demanded, even though he knew it would only encourage her to ask for more the next time. What else could he do? His entire cloning phase depended on her. His precious Michael depended on her.

On her way out, Chernoff appeared in the doorway. She leaned away from him as she left.

"What do you want, Chernoff?" Gregory asked.

Chernoff closed the door behind him and took out his cigarette and lighter.

"I want my money."

"I'm not paying for that fire you set. I never said to burn the woman's house down. That was your twisted entertainment for the evening."

Chernoff approached the desk and blew smoke toward Gregory. "You said, 'Take care of it,' remember? I took care of it. The woman got the message, and Donovan didn't die. You owe me an installment."

"Get out."

Chernoff flicked the flame of his lighter and picked up the Osiris figurine from Gregory's desk. He tilted his head to the side as he idly waved the flame back and forth under the statue.

Gregory stood and snatched the statue. "Fine. I'll pay you. Into your account, like usual. Just get out!"

"Don't make me collect in person again." Chernoff slammed the door behind him.

Gregory slumped in his desk chair, studying the figurine. Now that Nick was gone and the FDA had come up empty-handed, the need for Chernoff's services would be greatly diminished. Especially after tonight and tomorrow. It was time to "take care of" Mr. Chernoff.

Sonya buzzed. "Kate Donovan on the phone for you, Dr. Brulin."

Gregory snatched the phone. "Kate?"

"Hi, Gregory. You asked me to call to set up a time when we could talk about Nick."

Gregory paused. "You still want to get together?" Why didn't she know about Nick being fired?

"If you think there's a way I can help—"

"Yes, fine. I have some meetings for the rest of the afternoon, but could you come by the office at about six this evening?"

"I'll be there."

Gregory disconnected and turned toward the windows. Their relationship must be worse off than Gregory had imagined if Nick hadn't even told his wife he'd been fired. He'd take her to dinner tonight. If she and Nick really were headed in separate directions, who knew what else she might be open to? The phone buzzed again, and Gregory sighed.

"Stanford Carlton calling, Dr. Brulin."

Gregory groaned and picked up the phone. "Stanford, this is becoming tiresome."

"Gregory—" Stanford's voice cracked. Finally he found his breath again. "Gregory, I want to see you."

"We've said everything there is to say, Stanford."

"No. Not everything. Proof I'll give the FDA. We have to talk about it. But the telephone—too hard for me. Come here.

Young-Meddleton Cancer Center."

Gregory pressed his fingers against his eyes. Stanford sounded inches from death. He could put him off a few days, and the problem might take care of itself. But he couldn't take that chance. If Stanford really did have proof. . .

"You owe me this, Gregory. After everything."

Gregory exhaled. "When?"

"Come now."

CHAPTER 45

Stanford clenched his jaw. No matter how bad it got, until Gregory left, he would not give himself any pain medicine. He intended to be fully alert for this meeting.

"I think that should do it," Frank said, placing a tiny disc recorder at Stanford's bedside. "It's voice activated. When you're ready, push this button, put it under your blanket, and have your conversation."

"You're sure it's sensitive enough to record clearly through the blanket?"

"That thing will record the nurses' gossip in the hallway. Don't worry." Frank's forehead creased. "Are you ever going to tell me what this is about? I'm worried about you."

"Don't be worried about this, Frank. As you keep pointing out, I've got bigger things to be concerned about. Like eternity."

Frank gave him a half smile. "I'm not laughing anymore, Stanford. I'm afraid you're going to procrastinate until it's too late. Where's the guy I've heard so much about from Nick and your family? The one who always gets the job done—under budget and ahead of schedule?"

Stanford fiddled with the recorder. "That's what I'm doing."

"I mean the job of figuring out answers for your life. When does that goal get accomplished?"

"Not tonight." Stanford waved him away. "You'd better get out of here."

Frank shrugged. "I hope you get what you're after."

Stanford waited. Hours seemed to pass. Julia came and went, fussing around his bedside until he sent her home again.

Finally, Stanford heard a step in the hall. He pushed a button on the recorder in his hand and slid it under the blanket.

He'd forgotten how commanding Gregory was when he

walked into a room. His oiled black hair, the full lips, and heavy jewelry. Gregory wore a black suit with a royal purple tie. He strode in as though in charge of the world. Stanford watched a flicker of something pass over Gregory's face as he entered. Compassion? Fear? Disgust?

"I came, Stanford."

"Thank you. Sit, please."

Gregory sat in the chair beside the bed, his back erect and arms folded.

Stanford's heart hammered. Where to begin? "Are you still going through with it?"

"Yes." Gregory inclined his head. "Unless you've got a very good reason why I shouldn't."

"I do, Gregory. I want to talk about our past."

"I try not to dwell on the past, Stanford."

"I can imagine. How old would Michael be now? Nine, ten?"

"What is this about, Stanford?"

Stanford turned his head farther toward Gregory. "I just need to know why, Greg. Why do you feel you must do this?"

"We've been over this before, Stanford. You know my reasons. You knew them when you left SynTech. Nothing has changed. I don't know why you thought I would never follow through."

Stanford swallowed. He needed Gregory to be specific. "I was foolish. I see that now. I wish I would have stopped you then."

"You could no more stop me years ago than you can now."

"Ah, that's where you're wrong, Greg. Tell me," Stanford said, looking up at his IV bag, "how are you going to do it?"

Gregory's eyes narrowed, and then his gaze flicked around the room. "What difference does it make?"

"I want to know. I have a right to know everything."

"You walked out on the project, Stanford. You have no rights." He stood up. "You said you wanted to talk about this alleged proof of yours. We're not here to talk about me. Show me your proof, or I'll call you a liar and leave you for the last time."

"Tell me about the project. Is it just Saturday? Does it end there?"

Gregory laughed. "You have no idea."

"No, I don't. Tell me."

Gregory shook his head. "I don't have time for this, Stanford. And it doesn't look to me like you do, either. Shouldn't your family be with you? Saying good-bye and all that?"

The pain Stanford had been trying to ignore made a furious attack. He closed his eyes. He was botching the whole thing. He had to break through Gregory's composure.

"Michael would not have wanted this," Stanford said, playing his ace. "He was a sweet boy. Compassionate. Remember how he loved that junior lab coat you bought him? How he said he would grow up to be a doctor, to help people, just like his daddy? Michael would not have wanted you to be consumed by revenge."

Gregory scowled down at him. "Don't you dare tell me what my son would have wanted. I have told you already: This is not about revenge. It is about cleansing."

"You used that word before. You plan to cleanse the world of Christians?"

"It's not really about Christians, Stanford. Most of them aren't intelligent enough to be of consequence. I've targeted any fools who are vocal enough to hold back progress and too blind to see they're killing people in the process."

"So you'll kill them?"

"Not all of the therapies I've altered have a fatal effect, Stanford."

"Then what? Chronic disease?"

"Some, yes. Ongoing health problems will keep some of them too busy to worry about politics, but I don't see why you should bother yourself about it."

"So that's it, then? You'll wipe out the enemies of genetic research—especially those who oppose embryonic research, right?"

Gregory grinned slyly. "And I hope to see the birthrate decrease among them, as well."

"You're sterilizing them?"

"You still don't see it, do you, Stanford?" Gregory said, frowning. "Not even after all these years fighting them yourself, trying to move forward with your research." He left Stanford's bedside to pace the room. "All our lives we've fought disease, both of us, because disease is the enemy of the human race. But I realized something somewhere along the way: Those who hold us back, they are the disease, too. We're no different, you and I. We've both dedicated ourselves to eradicating it."

"We're nothing alike."

Gregory stopped pacing and faced him. "We are both destroying pathogens!"

"People aren't pathogens, Greg."

"There are so many cures out there, Stan, waiting to be found. If we could only be free of those who are corrupting the human race and destroying us in the process!"

"You're talking eugenics, Greg. Trying to create a pure, perfect race makes you no better than Mengele and Hitler."

"No, Stan. They were misguided. I am on the right path."

Stanford turned away. He had gotten almost all he needed. There was one thing left on the list.

"If I had known four years ago that this is what it would come to, I would never have remained silent. I never believed you would do it."

"I know you didn't. You walked away because you didn't have the stomach to do what needed to be done. I was glad to see you go. I could never have accomplished any of this if you had remained at SynTech."

Stanford took a deep breath. Relief and pain blurred his focus. He reached for the patient-controlled analgesia.

"You're a sick man, Gregory," he said. "Sicker than I am. I had hoped to reason with you. I see now that's impossible."

"So what is this proof you held over my head?"

Stanford shook his head, fatigue overwhelming him. "You were right. I have nothing. It was a bluff. I was only hoping to convince you to stop. But I see now it's useless."

Gregory came to his side and gripped the bedrail. "They killed my son, Stanford. They had his life in their hands, and they chose to snuff it out. Every day they ignore the suffering of millions to push their outdated agenda onto the government and into the scientific community."

He turned to leave but stopped in the doorway. "It can't go on, Stanford. Some sacrifices are always necessary in order for a new era to begin."

When Gregory was gone, Stanford turned off the recorder and lay back against the bed. He had gotten what he needed, but the conversation had left him nearly unconscious. He nudged the pain-med dosage up again and tested the recording.

The conversation had been recorded onto the tiny audio disc with perfect clarity. Stanford closed his eyes. He didn't have much longer. Hard as it was for him to delegate anything, he needed help with the final task of this project. He reached for the phone to call Nick.

Afterward he needed to have one last talk with Frank—about what he'd had his ladder up against all these years.

CHAPTER 46

Nick checked his watch for the hundredth time as his car snaked around the artificial lake beside SynTech Labs. Five o'clock. The late afternoon air had grown heavy with the possibility of snow again, and Nick blasted the heat in the car. More than anything, it was the thought of what he was about to do that chilled him.

Since this whole thing began, he had felt the cold fingers of death wrapped around it. He had no idea what Gregory hoped to accomplish by intentionally giving people cancer and other disorders, but the man seemed capable of going to any lengths to do it. Even arranging Brian Milburn's "accident" and having Milburn's house torched. Nick's visit with Stanford had left him all the more convinced that death was something he was not ready to face.

Nick was hoping to use his old plan of slipping into SynTech when someone was coming out at five o'clock. But what if it didn't work? His idea to find a master keycard in the maintenance rooms was a long shot. What if he couldn't get into his lab for the Gaucher data? Or into the storage room for the other vectors?

Breathe, Donovan, breathe.

He parked the rental car at the edge of a cluster of cars. There were others in the building somewhere. But were they others that Nick needed to avoid? Chernoff's gray face replayed in his memory. He did not want to meet that guy on a deserted sublevel again.

He walked toward the side entrance, his eyes on the lighted windows above him. Was that Gregory's office? Was he up there watching Nick?

He slowed as he approached the revolving door. He had to time this right. Just as he reached the door, a researcher he'd never met pushed through on his way out. Nick gave him a friendly nod and slipped into the door as it continued its spin.

Other employees filtered through the main corridor, heading out. Nick turned toward the steps.

He tried to walk softly down the two flights of concrete steps to Sublevel 2, but his footsteps still spiraled their hollow echo all the way up the stairwell above him. He pulled out his phone and turned the ringer off, just in case.

The door to the hallway groaned as he pulled it open. More footsteps clattered down the hall outside the door. He waited until he heard the elevator doors *whoosh* open, then poked his head into the blinding-white corridor. Every maroon door was closed. The hall was empty.

The fluorescent lights in the hallway illuminated every inch of space. Fifteen steps brought him to the outside of Jimmy the maintenance guy's door. He pushed his back flat against the wall, holding his breath. There was no sound coming from Jimmy's room, but the door stood ajar. Nick reached a finger across and urged it open, waiting for someone inside to speak.

Half a minute passed. He edged into the empty room and slid the door almost closed behind him.

The chlorine smell still hung in the air, and it didn't look like Jimmy had organized his mops, buckets, and rags any better than when Nick had been there last. The gray desk occupying half the back wall was his best bet to find keycards. He flung drawers open, wincing as the top drawer clanged as if it were full of metal chains. He studied the contents. Mostly assorted wrenches and screwdrivers. He searched through more drawers.

Jimmy had left the door open, which probably meant he was still in the building. If Nick didn't hurry, he might be caught with his hand in the cookie jar. Gregory would hear about it.

Don't panic. Search everywhere. His heart vibrated against his chest. There was nothing here.

Footsteps in the corridor. Nick twisted, his glance leaping around the room, searching for a spot to squeeze into unseen. He spotted a small door to his left. He jogged to it, turned the knob, and pulled. It gave an inch, but no more. He yanked again, harder this time. Sweat greased his palms, and he wiped them on his pants.

One more yank. The door popped loose with a crack. Nick jumped into the tiny closet and quietly closed the door behind him, praying that he'd be able to get it open again later.

He heard someone's heavy steps cross the room. The metallic squeak of the chair on wheels being pulled out. A moan as someone—Jimmy, he presumed—sank into the chair and its springs cried out.

The dizzying smell of ammonia in Nick's closet sickened him. Several minutes passed. He longed to change positions. A shelf jabbed at his lower back. The air grew stale.

The chair squealed and groaned again. Nick heard metallic sounds, maybe that large cabinet opening. More footsteps, a door closing.

He let out his breath forcefully. Maybe Jimmy had left. Maybe not. But it was as good a chance as he was going to get.

He turned the knob and pushed, not surprised that the door stuck. He tightened his grip on the knob, pulled back the few inches he could and threw his shoulder against the door.

It broke free. He staggered into the empty room, grateful for the oxygen rush, even if it did smell of chlorine. The air in the room was noticeably cooler than the closet. Nick wiped sweat from his forehead with the back of his arm. He had to get out before Jimmy came back.

Where to? He scanned the hallway in both directions. Did he dare try the maintenance supervisor's office on Sublevel 1?

He trotted toward the stairwell, unwilling to take a chance on meeting someone while trapped in the elevator. Twenty yards from the stairwell door, he heard a lab door opening behind him. He sprinted, flinging himself against the metal bar on the door and falling into the stairwell. He sat on the bottom step, catching his breath, waiting to see if anyone followed him.

Thirty seconds passed. No one came.

Nick hauled himself up the stairs to Sublevel 1.

He opened the stairwell door and leaned out. In the hall, a white-coated employee was stopped in front of a lab. Nick yanked his head back, counted to twenty, and looked again. Clear.

He raced down the length of the empty hallway, sliding to a stop in front of the maintenance supervisor's door. One turn of the knob confirmed his fear. The office was locked. The supervisor had left for the night.

Nick felt exposed in the hallway. He ran back toward the stairwell.

Now what?

Just before he pushed through the metal door to the stairs, Nick's gaze landed on the large potted tree at the end of the hallway, positioned under its fiber-optic sun.

Frieda.

∼ ∼ ∼

Stanford opened his eyes. Julia was prying the phone from his fingers. He hadn't been able to reach Nick. He'd been forced to leave voice mail for him instead, urging him to come to the cancer center immediately.

He couldn't check that off the list yet. He sensed that time was running out.

"Stanford, the children are here to see you."

"Need to do one thing more first, Julia."

Julia's voice became stern. "No, Stanford. Not this time. On your deathbed you will put your family before work."

Stanford smiled. "Oh, sweet Julia. Now I've gone too far even for you. Yes, send them in."

Matthew, Jonathan, and Melissa crowded around his bedside. Julia only let them stay for a few minutes, but they promised to remain close. When they left, Stanford gave Julia's hand a weak squeeze. "I'm sorry, my love."

She kissed his hand. "You're a stubborn fool, Stanford Carlton. But I love you."

Tears formed and leapt from Stanford's eyes. How long had it been since he'd well-and-truly wept? He held his wife in as tight an embrace as he could muster. They didn't talk for a long time.

Finally, he lifted his face to hers. "My love, please. I need you to do something for me."

"There's nothing more you need to do, sweetheart. Just rest."

"No. Need you to write a letter for me."

Julia pursed her lips but nodded.

When they had finished, Julia left for a few moments. Melissa sneaked back into the room. She tried to say good-bye, but Stanford wouldn't let her. Not yet. There was something else still on his list.

Julia returned.

"Julia," he said, barely able to swivel his head. The letter had taken nearly all the strength he had left. "Get Frank."

His friend entered immediately. "Hello, Stan. You wanted to see me?"

"Tell me again," Stanford said. "Convince me."

"There's nothing more I need to say, Stanford. You know the truth. You just need to let go. Don't let your pride stand between you and the God who's been calling you all your life."

Pain knifed him again, this time leaving him short of breath and tired. He clutched at Frank's arm. Julia stood behind Frank, tears flowing unchecked. She called the children in. It was all winding down.

"Can't come to Him now, Frank. Haven't done anything for Him."

Frank smiled and patted Stanford's hand. "That's just the point, Stan. There was nothing you could have done to reach His standard, anyway. You have to trust that He did it for you."

"Doesn't seem fair. Not right."

"It wasn't fair. But He did it, anyway. Because He wanted a

relationship with you. All you need to do is accept the gift."

"I. . .usually return gifts."

Frank laughed. They all did.

"I'll bet you do," Frank said. "You've never taken a handout in your life, I'm sure. You're a proud man, Stanford. But pride won't buy you eternity with God. Only humility will. You've got to admit your own inability to please God. Trust that Jesus did it for you."

Stanford shook his head. "Deathbed conversion. Never thought it would be me."

Frank smiled and leaned forward. "Tell it to Him, Stan."

Stanford fought to stay conscious, searching for the words.

"God, help me," he finally said. "How many foolish years have I studied the design and ignored the Designer? Forgive me, God. I think I knew all along that You were there. And I want to accept the gift You've offered."

Stanford looked at Frank who nodded, tears streaming down his face.

"O Father," Frank prayed, "You are an awesome God, calling all men to Yourself. Thank You for hearing this man's plea, for welcoming him into Your family, for making him Your son. Even today, in a way we can barely understand, he has crossed from death to life. Thank You, Father."

Stanford let his tears go, smiling through them. Frank released his hand and smiled back. Stanford looked at his precious wife and children. They'd seen him admit his limits. They'd seen him reach out to God. Would they follow his example? Would they join him in eternity?

Maybe he'd done one thing that mattered, after all.

                 ~   ~   ~

"Hi, Frieda."

The elderly woman jumped. "You trying to give me a heart attack, Dr. Donovan?"

It was the first time she'd called him by name. The realization made Nick feel even guiltier for what he was about to do. "Just checking on my favorite plant lady," he said. "Feeling okay tonight?"

"These bones won't rest easy till they're resting six feet under, I'm afraid." She pushed the cart out of the third-floor office and into the hallway. Nick eased her hands from the handle and pushed the cart for her.

"You finish Dr. Brulin's office yet?" he asked. "All those hanging plants?"

"No." She sighed. "That's last. But I guess I can't put it off no longer."

"Let me do it tonight, Frieda."

"What?"

"I'll do it. I won't need to climb on anything to reach the plants. It'll only take me a minute." Nick waited.

"Dr. Brutal would skin me alive if he found you watering his plants."

"He won't find me. If I see him, I'll tell him I'm there for some other reason." They reached a small sitting area outside some larger offices, and Nick paused. "You sit here for a few minutes. I'll be right back."

Frieda looked at Nick, at her cart, down the hall toward Gregory's office.

"Go ahead," Nick said. "You deserve a break."

"You're not fooling me, Dr. Donovan?"

Nick's heart twisted. He'd find a way to get into his lab and still water Gregory's plants if it killed him. "I'm not fooling."

"Okay. Just this once. If it weren't for this arthritis. . ." She dropped into an upholstered chair.

"I know." Nick pushed the cart a few feet away from her, then stopped as if he had remembered something. "I guess I'll need your keycard, Frieda. Mine won't open his office."

Frieda's eyes narrowed. "My keycard?"

"For the door," Nick said, feeling like a kid caught stealing candy. He looked away from her stare.

"What's this about, Dr. Donovan?" she said.

"It's about watering plants."

She shook her head. "You look me in the eye, young man."

Nick looked up.

"I don't think so," she said. "I've been around too long to be fooled by the likes of you. What are you up to? What do you want with my keycard?"

Nick exhaled. He lowered himself into a chair beside Frieda and laid his head against the wall.

"You're right, Frieda. I'm sorry. The truth is, Brulin's locked me out of my lab, and I need to get something out of there."

Frieda massaged one hand with the other. "Why did he lock you out?"

"It's a long story. Let's just say that we're not seeing eye to eye right now."

"He fired you, didn't he?"

"Uh, yeah, I'm afraid he did."

"He's up to no good, ain't he?"

"I think you might be right, Frieda."

She shook her head. "This place is more S-I-N-Tech than S-Y-N-Tech." She eyed Nick critically. "Can you stop him?"

He sat forward, watching her. "Maybe. If you help."

"Well, why didn't you say so in the first place? Come on." Frieda pulled herself to her feet and grabbed the cart handle. "Let's go unlock your lab."

"What about Dr. Brulin's plants?" Nick asked.

"Let 'em croak."

Frieda left her water cart in the elevator. She followed Nick down the hall to his door on Sublevel 2. She grinned at him. "Feels like I'm doing something worthwhile for a change." At his lab's door she pulled the keycard ring from her apron, slid a card into the reader, and pushed the door open.

"Thank you, Frieda!" He kissed her on the forehead.

"Cut that out, you rascal," she said, smiling roguishly. "Now you get in there and make me proud."

"You're an angel, Frieda." He slipped into the room and held the door open. "Will you wait for me, for just a minute or two?"

She nodded.

Inside, it took only a few seconds to see that everything had been cleaned out. The lab bench was clear; the DNA sequencer held no data.

He went to his office and checked the computer. All the files he needed had been deleted.

He took a last look around the lab and went back into the hallway where Frieda waited, her arms crossed.

"The thing I need isn't there anymore, Frieda. But if you could let me into one more room, I think I'll find some answers."

Frieda shrugged. "In for a penny, in for a pound."

Nick led her to the cold storage room where she unlocked the door, and Nick went in.

The room was mainly comprised of metal shelving, attached to all four walls and running in three rows down the center. Nick pulled his jacket tighter across his chest. A gentle whirring insulated him from any sounds outside the room. He studied the layout, his gaze traveling over the storage containers stacked three high on the metal shelving.

"Pay dirt!"

He opened the first container he came to and started pulling out vials.

Footsteps echoed outside the room. Nick paused, his hands in midair above the vials. A rolling squeak traveled past. Another mop and bucket on wheels. Perhaps it was Frieda, but it could also be Jimmy or someone else. How long did he have before someone entered the room?

He slipped vials in and out of the container. One vial of every therapy coded with a "2" went into his coat pocket.

He moved through the containers, pulling therapies. *Good*

grief. There's got to be a Version 2 for every therapy SynTech offers.

The minutes slipped past. Nick could feel the mop and bucket closing in on him.

Hold on, here's something. A therapy for Acid Maltase Deficiency. AMD was the disease that had killed Kate's mom. He pocketed the sample marked with a "2."

Doubts nudged at the edge of his mind as he closed the last container. Would a handful of Version 2 vectors be enough to convince the FDA that Gregory had some evil plot? Mistakes were made all the time. Nick wished he knew how these therapies had been altered.

He glanced at the closed door. Did he dare get Frieda to let him into his lab again so he could sequence them?

He decided against it when the sound of whistling traveled down the hall outside the lab.

He checked the time. Five-thirty. He'd been here for thirty minutes. Felt like a week. Now if he could just get out of the building without being seen. Nick glanced around the room at the way he'd left the containers. He took a minute to shove containers back onto the shelves where he'd found them, then turned out the lights and put his hand on the door handle.

A shuffling sound on the other side of the door stopped him. He heard a keycard slide in and out, felt the handle turn under his hand.

A quick look behind him told him what he already knew. There was nowhere to hide in here. He stepped away from the door and watched it open.

Jimmy's sharp intake of breath quickly turned to an officially stern look.

"I thought you were locked out, Dr. Donovan?"

"Yes." Nick fumbled over an excuse. "I was. But I—uh—it must have been my card. Something wrong with it. But it's okay now. Thanks."

Nick slid past Jimmy, certain his odd behavior, as well as his presence in the storage lab, would find its way to Gregory's ear.

He took the stairs to the main floor. He'd have to go out the main door, since the revolving door needed a keycard to exit after five o'clock. He strode to the main entrance, his head down, and out the front door.

His car was all the way out in Parking Lot #6. He followed the shoveled and plowed paths out to the lot, the cold biting his face. Off to his left, the black lake slashed a hole in the snow, its dark waters rippling.

Footsteps behind him quickened his pace. He was halfway there. He started jogging now. Was he imagining that the footsteps behind him were keeping up?

He risked a glance over his shoulder.

Chernoff!

Nick ran for his car, one hand holding his coat against his body to protect the vials, the other hand searching for his car keys.

He was still ten cars from the Camry when he felt himself jerked backward and nearly knocked off his feet.

"Dr. Donovan," Chernoff said, hissing into his ear from behind him, "I was told you were no longer employed here."

"You're right. That's why I'm leaving."

Chernoff stepped around him and patted him down. His eyebrows went up when his hand tapped against Nick's coat pocket. He reached in and pulled out a few of the dozens of vials Nick had stashed there.

"I can't believe these are your property, Doctor."

"Would you believe they're my favorite test tubes?"

Chernoff pointed toward the building. "Let's go."

"Actually, I'm leaving, Mr. Chernoff. You can keep those."

A gun suddenly appeared in Chernoff's hand. "I said, let's go."

CHAPTER 47

Chernoff made a call to Gregory on their way back to the building. "All right, I'll bring him to you."

Nick's heart thudded as he realized the elevator was going down instead of up. There was something sinister about Sublevel 3. He'd rather meet Gregory in his upstairs office.

When they reached the hallway of Sublevel 3, Chernoff shoved him toward the door of Gregory's lab and slapped at the glass window. Nick was surprised he didn't have access to the lab using the palm geography reader. *Even Brulin doesn't trust this guy.*

Nick could see the lab through the window and again noticed how much larger it was than his. This one even had its own cold room. Gregory was seated at the lab bench in the center of the room, working on something. He stood and approached them, still wearing his latex gloves. The door swung inward, and Chernoff pushed him through it.

Gregory's expression revealed nothing. Nick watched for a flicker of any emotion. The man was immobile.

"Why are you doing this, Gregory?"

"You have no idea what you've found, Donovan."

Chernoff reached his hand out from behind Nick, several vials in his palm. "He had these on him. More in his coat pocket."

Gregory took a step toward Chernoff and wrapped his gloved hand around Chernoff's wrist. He examined the vials, then took them from Chernoff, and placed them on the lab bench. "I'm impressed, Nick. Perhaps you do have some idea of what you've found."

"I know you're going to inject people with therapies that will cause disease. People who oppose research that could have saved your son."

Gregory's face darkened. "You've gotten further than I'd

imagined. I don't know how. But still, you've only scratched the surface. Chernoff, take the rest of those vials from his pocket."

He crossed the lab to a refrigeration box and pulled out a syringe. "I can't allow you to jeopardize everything I've worked for, Nick. Milburn was the first intrusion into my plan. I hope you will be the last." He handed the syringe to Chernoff. "Take him to his own lab."

Gregory smiled at Nick. "Dr. Donovan was a dedicated investigator," he said. "He was committed to learning all he could about the diseases that kill us. This devotion led to the ultimate sacrifice when he accidentally injected himself with some deadly cells. Let his life be an inspiration to those of us who continue his work."

Chernoff moved toward Nick and nudged him with the barrel of his gun. "Let's go."

Gregory stopped them. "One more thing, Nick."

Nick turned.

"I'll be certain to tell your wife how often you mentioned her when I have dinner with her this evening. Oh, but wait, you've never mentioned her, have you? Tsk tsk, Nick. You really ought to be more attentive to a beautiful woman."

Nick scowled. "What are you talking about?"

"Kate, of course. We had such an enjoyable lunch together yesterday, we decided to see each other again today. It was her idea, actually. She called me today to set it all up. Perhaps I can be of some comfort to her as she mourns your passing." He smiled. "I would even dare to hope that we could be more than friends."

Gregory finished his speech by punching the blue square that opened the doors.

Chernoff turned to Gregory on his way out. "Fatal accidents cost more."

Gregory closed his eyes and nodded.

Chernoff yanked Nick through the doors and dragged him to the elevator.

In the ride from Sublevel 3 to Sublevel 2, Nick had enough

time to realize he'd lost his career, his future, and his wife. In a few minutes, he'd face the greatest loss of all, the one he'd worked so hard to avoid.

↙ ↙ ↙

The corridor was deserted when Nick and Chernoff stepped off the elevator. Nick had been praying that a researcher, an assistant, a maintenance man—anyone—would be there. Someone who would see the gun jammed into Nick's lower back and remember later.

Gregory's plan depended on Nick's death looking accidental, like Brian Milburn's. If it looked suspicious, perhaps Gregory's research would be investigated. If Nick was going to die anyway, he needed to make sure it was the gun that killed him, not the needle, just to raise questions for those who would come after.

Chernoff slipped a keycard in and out of the lock and pushed Nick into the lab. No one had seen them.

Chernoff shoved Nick farther into the lab and switched on the lights. He lifted the syringe he carried, studying it closely. "It looks like you're not going to feel that icy water, after all, Doctor."

Nick's mind raced ahead. Chernoff would need to put down the gun and switch the syringe to his right hand, or he would have to inject Nick with his left. The first option would leave Chernoff unarmed except for the syringe, the second would make it awkward for Chernoff to get the needle in. But with a deadly weapon in each hand, Nick doubted that he could overpower Chernoff. His options were dwindling.

"Let's make this easy, Doctor." Chernoff took a step closer.

Nick backed away. Chernoff was forced to follow him, gun in one hand and syringe in the other. In a surreal game of tag, Chernoff's pace quickened till he was chasing Nick around the island in the center of the lab.

Nick stopped without warning at the door. He whirled to face Chernoff. With a kick his high school football coach would have been proud of, he slammed his foot against Chernoff's syringe-holding arm. The deadly injection flew across the lab. It bounced off the large centrifuge unit beside the wall and slid to a stop on the counter at the opposite end of the lab.

Chernoff shook his arm, anger flashing out of his eyes. "Very foolish, Dr. Donovan. You're forgetting that I'm the one with the gun."

"But it won't look like an accident if you shoot me," Nick said. He lunged at Chernoff's right hand. Cold steel met his grasp. He pushed upward with every bit of strength he had. Chernoff grunted, using his other hand to pry Nick's fingers from the gun.

Chernoff's arm twisted down and collapsed into his chest. Nick's arms followed it and were pulled into Chernoff's embrace. They struggled head-to-head for five seconds. Nick smelled Chernoff's cigarette breath. Finally, the gun slipped from Nick's grasp.

Nick heard the gunshot, like a freight train roaring through his head, before he felt the pain. When the pain came, it was hot and bloody.

CHAPTER 48

Gregory slammed his office door behind him. Nothing had gone according to plan. Nick's cancer research was lost to him, and he had been forced to do something he disliked. All because Nick would not stop prying.

He took a deep breath and sat at his desk, where he allowed himself a small sense of relief. Though what he'd had to order was unpleasant in the extreme, it was probably over by now. Chernoff was nothing if not efficient. No more worrying about what Nick might do with the information he dug up. Now that Stanford's proof had vanished in smoke, Gregory was home free.

The timing of Chernoff's call had been perfect. Gregory had needed only minutes to prepare the gauze pad in his lab. Chernoff had not even reacted as Gregory pressed his gloved hand against Chernoff's forearm when he took the vials from him.

He glanced at the gold clock on his desk. Six o'clock. Nick was dead by now—and in less than four hours, Chernoff would be dead, too. On top of it all, Kate should be arriving any moment. Life was good.

Should he tell Kate of her husband's tragic accident? No, better to wait until the police were involved. Gregory knew Chernoff would arrange to have Nick's body discovered soon. Until then, it would be best for Gregory to stay away from the situation.

Perhaps he would be with Kate when she got the call tonight. Perfect, he thought. She'll need someone to lean on, someone she can trust in the coming days of grief. He pulled a cigar from a drawer and rolled it between his fingers. Perhaps Nick's death would be a good thing, after all.

He struck a match and watched it blaze up between his fingers before he lit the cigar. He took a generous puff on the cigar, shaking out the match. He blew smoke at the ceiling, nodding in satisfaction.

In spite of losing Nick, his plan would proceed. In only an hour, Genetic Awareness Day would begin purifying the human race. Phase 3, creating, had made a huge leap forward this morning when Sonya's embryos had been successfully transferred into her womb. He had sent her home to rest for a few days. Hopefully, they'd soon hear the good news that the embryos had implanted.

Poor Nick. He'd learned a surprising amount about Gregory's Phase 1, but he'd never had any idea about either the cloning or creating phases. In a strange way, Gregory wished he could have shared it all with Nick. It would've been good to talk to someone about the son he was going to have back and the near-divine race he was going to create. Sometimes the loneliness of his mission depressed him.

And so his thoughts circled back to Kate. He leaned back in his chair, savoring the cigar and letting the smoke hang above him. Perhaps loneliness would not be an issue much longer.

A knock on the door several minutes later brought a smile. Kate had arrived.

↶ ↶ ↶

Kate entered the cigar haze of Gregory's office at his invitation. *Why did I agree to this?* She hobbled forward into the room. *What would Dr. Rogan think if he knew I was running all over town flirting with other men instead of keeping my ankle propped up during my "sick days"?*

Gregory snubbed out the cigar and smiled. "Good to see you again, Kate."

"You, too." She advanced to a chair.

Gregory stood. "Don't bother to sit. I'm taking you out to dinner. Do you like Italian food?"

"I like all food."

He laughed. "The second of what I hope will be many enjoyable times together."

Several minutes later, seated in the back of Gregory's Town Car, the driver heading who-knew-where, it occurred to Kate that she hadn't even stopped to see Nick while she'd been inside SynTech.

Kate, what are you doing?

CHAPTER 49

The gunshot threw Nick backward, away from the door. He looked down, expecting to see the life pouring out of him. A jagged hole in the side of his shirt below his ribcage proved the bullet had been there. He pressed his hand against the pain. Blood soaked his shirt.

The bullet had grazed him, taken off a serious bit of skin, but he was still breathing.

Chernoff would soon put a stop to that. Now he had no reason to search for the syringe. With a gunshot wound in Nick's side, the accident ruse wasn't going to work: He might as well shoot him again. He looked up at Chernoff, standing with his back to the door. As the man leveled the gun at Nick's chest, Nick closed his eyes and cursed the arrogance that had fooled him into thinking this moment would never come.

The familiar sound of a suction being released made him snap his eyes open. He watched as the lab door was shoved open from the hallway, knocking Chernoff aside.

Seeing his chance, Nick lowered his head and drove into Chernoff's chest like a charging bull. The force of the blow knocked the man into the corner of the room. The gun flew over the center lab bench and skittered across the floor on the other side. Chernoff leaned over the counter, panting.

Jimmy stepped into the lab, his mouth standing open. "What's going on here?"

"Thanks, Jimmy," Nick said, standing.

Chernoff groaned in the corner.

Out of the corner of his eye, Nick saw Chernoff's fist close over the syringe lying on the counter beside him. He jerked his arm upward, ready to inject.

Nick couldn't reach the gun before Chernoff reached him.

He picked up a microscope from the lab bench. Chernoff slammed his arm down toward Nick's shoulder, but Nick dodged the blow. Chernoff's arm met empty air, and he staggered forward. Nick smashed the microscope down onto the back of Chernoff's head.

The man crumpled like a lab skeleton dropped from its metal pole. He fell to the floor and didn't move. The syringe rolled out of his hand and across the white linoleum floor. Nick tossed it into the biohazard trash can and scooped up the gun.

Nick jerked the door open with a quick backward glance at Chernoff. Dead or unconscious, he couldn't tell and at this point didn't care.

Jimmy stepped away from Nick, fear in his eyes. "Don't hurt me!"

"I'm not going to hurt you, Jimmy. I'm the good guy!"

Jimmy shook his head. "How do I know that?"

"Look, I'm trying to—ah, forget it." Nick ran down the hall and pressed the elevator button, the pain in his side dismissing the possibility of the stairs. He pressed a hand against his side, under his coat. Blood soaked through his shirt and wetted his palm. He closed his eyes as he willed the doors to open immediately.

With a *ching* the doors opened, and Nick jumped in.

Jimmy watched him from the doorway. "I'm going to call security, Dr. Donovan!"

Nick punched the "door close" button and looked up. "Jimmy, that was security."

Nick watched the numbers above him as the elevator climbed upward. If Chernoff was still alive, how long would he have before the man called out reinforcements? He had to make it to his car and off the SynTech property before that.

The doors opened onto a quiet main corridor.

Nick jogged to the main entrance. He pulled his coat closed, hoping the blood hadn't soaked down to his pant leg yet.

Outside, he slowed to a fast walk. If he tried to run, he'd pass out before he ever reached his car. He looked over his shoulder, expecting security guards to flood from the building.

Still quiet.

Lot #1. Lot #2. Could he make it to Lot #6?

The blood pounded in his temples, but at least that meant blood was still getting there, not pouring out his side.

His rented Camry felt like a haven. He needed something to press against his side. He grabbed a handful of fast-food napkins he'd thrown on the passenger seat, wadded them against him, and threw the car into gear. He wasn't out yet.

As he rounded the lake, his phone vibrated against his waist. Incredulous that the world could still go on during all of this, he let go of the napkins long enough to pull the phone out, turn the ringer back on, and click it into the docking station.

"Yeah?"

"Is this Nick Donovan?"

Nick breathed heavily, swerved onto the highway. "Yeah."

"It's Frank, Nick. I'm calling about Stanford."

Nick cleared the SynTech complex. He was safe—beside the fact that he had a bullet wound in his side and a genocidal madman gunning for him.

Not now, Frank. "What's happening?"

"I think you'd better come. . .right now."

"Yeah, thanks, Frank. I'll try."

Nick disconnected, then heard the tone that signaled he had messages. He ignored it for now.

Stanford. Could he let his friend and mentor pass away without saying good-bye to him? The reality of death slammed against him again.

This is no way to live a life. There's got to be more to it than the way everyone defines success.

Everyone except Frank.

Nick took the next turn, wincing at the pain in his side, and punched a button to play his messages. His heart missed a beat at the sound of the voice.

"Nick? It's Stanford. Get here as soon as you can. I have the proof you're looking for."

Nick dug his hand through his hair. He could be at Young-Meddleton Cancer Center in thirty minutes. He hoped it wasn't too late. For Stanford or for him.

↶ ↶ ↶

Gregory twirled his crystal water glass by the stem, forcing himself to concentrate on what Kate was saying. The two sat in Café con Leche, a tiny, family-run Italian restaurant overlooking the Schuylkill River. Gregory had picked the restaurant because of its intimate dining room, accommodating only a dozen tables. Perfect for collapsing after terrible news.

How long would it take for the police to contact Kate about Nick's unfortunate demise? He had already planned to whisk her from the restaurant to an even more private place when she heard. Perhaps she'd need to go identify the body. He'd go with her.

"Do you have your phone with you?" he asked abruptly.

"Yes. Why?"

"I wondered if Nick would be able to contact you, since you're not at home."

"Oh." Kate looked embarrassed. "Actually, I'm staying with my sister and her family for a little while. Nick was concerned that I'd need more help with my ankle than he was able to give, since he's been so busy at SynTech."

"Ah," Gregory said. "With your sister and her family? Small children?"

"Yes," Kate said, her smile erasing years from her face. "Two."

Gregory nodded. "I'm surprised you don't have a family yet yourself."

Kate looked away. "That's another thing Nick and I can't

seem to agree on. He says he's not ready."

The quiet Italian music grated against Gregory's impatience this evening. He studied the low-hanging doorway to the kitchen, wondering when the food would arrive. Minutes later, the waiter brought their large plates of pasta with scallops and roasted vegetables, but the garlicky aroma barely tempted him.

Kate picked at her food, too.

"Not hungry?" he asked.

"I'm sorry. It seems like I've done nothing but eat in restaurants lately!"

Gregory smiled, patting his lips with the bone-white napkin.

A phone rang.

They looked at each other. Kate raised her eyebrows, as if wondering why he didn't answer. *It's mine,* he realized.

Gregory pulled it out and answered with a grunt. He cringed at the sound of Tina Milano's voice.

"Listen, Gregory, Yang tells me that I can't leave town during this whole thing. Is that true? I never agreed to that. You don't own me, you know."

Gregory exhaled through clenched teeth. *Not now.* "Now we both know that isn't true, don't we?" he said. "You'll never walk away from the money, so why don't you stop harassing me?" He punched the "disconnect" button and looked up at Kate. She was studying him, frowning. "Uh, sorry about that."

She sighed and looked away, but Gregory sensed he'd made a serious mistake in letting her see that side of him.

"You mentioned that I might be able to help Nick in some way," Kate said.

Gregory shrugged and concentrated on his pasta. "You know, I think we may have our problems worked out now."

She straightened. "You do? I'm so glad to hear that. I really want Nick and me to work out our differences. I know we're meant to be together."

Gregory didn't miss the not-so-subtle message. He looked at

his water glass as a bead of moisture swelled on the outside of the lip. *Why don't the police call?* He watched tiny rivulets of water join the droplet on his glass until it grew heavy and dripped to the tablecloth.

"Do you remember Stanford Carlton from the university?" Kate asked, sipping her water.

Gregory studied her face. "What about him?"

"He and Nick are still pretty close. Nick found out a few weeks ago that Stanford has terminal cancer."

Gregory frowned. "They still see each other after all these years?"

"Not too often. I think Nick was going to visit him this week. I don't know if he's had the time or not."

His phone rang again a moment later.

"It's me." Chernoff's voice seemed fuzzy, indistinct.

"Yes?" Gregory glanced at Kate, but she was chewing on a scallop and watching the dark river. A small boat drifted past the restaurant, a single light on its prow.

"He got away," Chernoff said.

"What?"

Kate turned her head toward him.

"Will you excuse me for a moment?" he said, smiling. He strode out of the dining room to the tiny hallway that led into the restaurant.

"You'd better be joking, Chernoff," he said.

"He's got a kick you wouldn't believe. I winged him. But I don't know where he went."

Gregory paced the hallway, out to the steps that led up and out of the restaurant. "Winged him with what? The syringe?"

"The gun."

Gregory cursed. He should have waited until Nick was dead before giving Chernoff the poison. *Will the man live long enough to take care of Nick?*

"Any ideas where he'd go?" Chernoff asked.

Gregory clenched a fist. "Try the Young-Meddleton Cancer Center. Stanford Carlton's room. If he's not there, try his house. And, Chernoff?" Gregory stopped pacing. "Don't mess up this time."

∂ ∂ ∂

The cancer's beaten me. I know it has. They're all here. If I can keep my eyes open long enough, I can see each one. Oh, please, let me see a little longer.

Julia. Don't cry, Julia. Is this the end? Is that why the children are here?

Matthew. Tall and strong. A man now. Be a good man. I know you will. Are those tears for me? A good son. No father ever had better.

The darkness for a little while. My eyes open again.

Jonathan. Laughter and good times. Sunday football. Graduation.

And Melissa. Oh, Melissa, and more tears. Holding sweet baby Courtney. First granddaughter. Tiny baby fingers. Soft baby hair. How I wanted to see you grow up. Watch your mother, Courtney. Be a woman like her.

A little more darkness.

Frank! Where are you, Frank?

There. Good. Say something more. Something to make me unafraid.

Darkness again. Waiting.

Eyes open. Are you still here? All of you? Those I've loved. Those who've loved me. Good.

Hands on my arms. All of them close now. Julia's hand on my face. Every line in her face so beautiful. Don't cry, my beautiful Julia. Are those tears mine?

Good-bye, my dear family. I must say good-bye. You are fading.

Darkness again. And then. . .Light.

ҩ   ҩ   ҩ

Frank was standing outside Stanford's door when Nick trotted up. His expression told Nick all he needed to know. "I'm so sorry, Nick, I know how much he meant to you."

Nick's mind spun, and he put a hand on his side.

Frank took in the bloody shirt and gasped. "What happened?"

"Accident."

Frank led him to a short, stern-faced nurse, whose firm hands guided him to an empty room where she pulled off his shirt and examined the laceration. Nick watched her, seeing nothing.

"What did you do to yourself?" she asked. "You could probably use a couple of stitches. I'll dress it, but get yourself to an ER." Her eyes narrowed. "It almost looks like a bullet grazed you."

Nick stared at her. His brain wasn't sending messages.

Frank patted Nick's shoulder. "I'll take care of him, Darlene. Thanks."

Darlene glanced at Frank, her expression softening. "Okay. Just make sure he gets that looked at."

When she left, Frank pulled up another chair and sat facing Nick, their knees almost touching.

The pain etched into Frank's face finally broke through Nick's haze. "He's gone, Frank?"

The older man nodded.

Nick's breath caught in his throat. He tried to breathe normally, but a choking sob overwhelmed him. "I don't think I really believed it would happen. Stanford always wins at everything. I just can't believe something beat him."

Frank nodded but said nothing.

Nick thought of Stanford's voice mail message. Now he would never know what Stanford wanted to tell him. One more chance to stop Gregory—maybe his last—gone. But it wasn't the loss of

Stanford's proof or even the loss of Stanford, if he were honest, that really bothered him most.

"It's so—so real, isn't it?" he asked Frank, swiping at the tears that coursed down his face, feeling like a fool.

"What is?"

"Death."

"Death is very real, Nick. Are you ready to face it?" Frank's comforting hand on Nick's shoulder belied the brutality of his words.

"Stanford didn't need your answers." Nick knew he sounded like a defensive child. "I don't, either."

"Nick, Stanford found peace with God just before the end."

Nick looked at him sharply, gauging the truth in his eyes. Then he shrugged. "People will say anything when they're about to die."

"Even Stanford? Does that sound like the man you knew? You can't keep running from it forever, Nick. I must ask you again. Are you ready to face death?"

Nick's heart was hammering inside his chest. He wasn't ready. Five minutes with Chernoff had proven to him what a lifetime of self-delusion he'd led. What had Stanford said the first time Nick met Frank? *I've had my ladder up against the wrong wall all these years. Oh, God, what was the point of any of it?*

"I have to go," Nick said. There had to be something more he could do to stop Gregory, even though Stanford's proof had died with him.

Frank nodded. "I understand. Take care of that injury."

Nick stepped into the hall and saw Julia crying. Stanford's children and granddaughter clustered around her, heads down. Nick walked over and embraced her. "I'm so sorry, Julia."

"Thank you, Nick. He loved you, you know."

His tears came again. "I know."

"Stay here a minute, Nick. I have something for you." Julia disappeared into Stanford's room and emerged a moment later with a white, business-size envelope. "He left this for you." She looked him in the eye. "I know you'll do the right thing with it."

Nick took the envelope from her hand. It felt as though it contained only a single sheet, but one end was rigid with something circular. He ripped the envelope open and slid out a small disc. He looked up, but Julia had returned to her children.

Nick's heart rate sped up. Could this be Stanford's proof? It almost was too much to hope for.

CHAPTER 50

Nick left Stanford's wing and all but sprinted into the lobby of the cancer center, ignoring the pain in his side. He headed for a couch near the waterfall, Stanford's envelope clutched in his hand.

The small disc was the new standard size used for computer archiving, video and audio recording, and a hundred other things. Nick pulled a handwritten letter from the envelope. A yellow sticky note attached at the top read, "Nick, Stanford dictated this to me and asked me to give it to you. Julia." The letter itself bore Stanford's shaky signature at the bottom. Nick took a deep breath and began reading.

> *Dear Nick,*
>
> *I have many regrets looking back over my life, but none so great as those that remind me of my failures as a human being. I fear my atonement may come too late, but it is all I have left.*
>
> *I am not the man you thought me, Nick. I have known of Gregory's plan from the beginning. He was a good man once, but he let grief poison him until he could think of nothing but revenge. We were more idealistic then, he and I. We thought we could change the world. For awhile, I allowed myself to be pulled into his twisted reasoning.*
>
> *I should have gone to the FDA years ago, but I was afraid. Gregory threatened that he had manufactured proof of my involvement—but I never had anything to do with his awful scheme. Still, if anyone can make people believe what he wants, it's Gregory. I was afraid people would believe him, and everything I'd worked for would be lost.*
>
> *Even now, this week, I have been unable to come forward, unable to risk the only thing I leave my family—a*

legacy of success. And I hoped that you would find the proof
you needed to stop him on your own.

    But it does not appear that you will. And so I have
finally done what I should have done years ago. This disc
contains the proof you need. It is an audio recording.

    Use it so that Gregory will not be allowed to continue.
That is the only legacy I have to leave to you.

    You have been like a son to me, Nick. I love you.

Stanford

P.S. Listen to Frank. I think he knows what he's talking
about.

Nick swiped at the corners of his eyes and carefully refolded
the letter. He slid it back into the envelope and pulled out his
phone. Finally, there was something he could do.

"Stella Ruhn, please," he said to the FDA's switchboard
operator.

The number rang twice, and then voice mail answered. What
did he expect at 7 P.M. on a Friday? Nick punched "0" to return
to the operator.

"This is an emergency, " he said. "I need to contact someone
immediately."

"Whom do you need to contact?"

"Stella Ruhn is the only person I know there, but she's not in."

"Sir, the offices are closed for the weekend."

"You don't understand: This is an emergency. It's about—
about—drug tampering." Sort of. "Don't you have some kind of
emergency number or something?"

"I'll put you through to the hot line, sir."

She transferred Nick, and he tried to explain the situation to
the person on the other end.

"I'll pass this information on to the appropriate person,
Doctor," the man said.

"When will they follow up?"

"I'm sure it will be immediately, sir."

Nick ground his teeth. "Fine. Pass the information on. And transfer me back to the operator." Nick left a message for Stella Ruhn, promising that this time he had the physical proof she needed. He disconnected and sat back in his chair.

It wasn't enough yet. Maybe Stella or someone else would follow up before appointments started tomorrow morning. Maybe not. Nick rotated the disc between his fingers. He had what he needed to stop Gregory, but had he gotten it too late?

He pulled out his phone again and fished in his pocket for the business card he'd shoved there at the center this morning. He pulled out the crumpled card, smoothed it, and dialed the number.

"Is this Austin Chambers?"

"Who's this?"

"My name is Nick Donovan. We met this morning at the SynTech Gene Therapy Center. In the lobby."

"Oh, yeah, Nick. What can I do for you?"

"I think I may have that story you were looking for."

Five minutes later he had told Austin enough to get him to promise to call up his buddies at the ABC affiliate TV station, but not enough to send him running to SynTech yet. Nick promised him the exclusive insider's story in exchange for his help and silence until he could meet him at the Gene Therapy Center in one hour. Nick pocketed his phone, the disc, and the letter and walked out of the cancer center into the darkened parking lot. He'd get home, make certain the disc contained the explosive truth he thought it did, and make a few copies. After that, he'd meet Austin and the TV news he'd promised and give them a big enough story to generate some publicity to keep people away tomorrow. Then he'd track down Stella Ruhn at the FDA and make her listen to the disc.

Nick's rental car was parked at the outer edge of the parking lot. His fingers were numb by the time he pulled his keys from his pocket. He activated the remote door lock just before he reached for the driver's side handle.

A heavy blow to the back of his neck dropped a veil of black over his eyes.

↝　↝　↝

Gregory didn't know how much longer he could stall Kate without it becoming obvious. They had moved slowly through dinner. He'd ordered an apple crisp for dessert, chewed slowly, and asked for a third cup of coffee. Kate was tapping her fingers on the table.

"Nick mentioned he was having problems with a therapy he was working on," she said. "Do you know if he got that straightened out?"

Gregory sipped his coffee. "What therapy was that?"

"I don't think he told me."

Gregory sighed. In one evening, Kate had gone from asset to liability. His phone rang again. The blood pounded in his head.

"I've got him."

Gregory exhaled.

"Do you want me to bring him to your lab again?"

"I'll see you there."

Gregory snapped his phone shut, pulled out a money clip, and stood. "Let's go, Kate."

She stood, smiling in apparent gratitude that their evening together had ended.

She was dead wrong.

CHAPTER 51

Gregory's breath clouded the February night air outside the restaurant. He helped Kate into the back of his car, then circled to get in beside her.

"Back to SynTech," he told the driver.

"Thank you for dinner," she said as the car lurched away from the curb.

"I'm afraid it wasn't the evening I wanted it to be."

Kate sighed. "I think I need to see Nick. As soon as we get back to SynTech, I'll check his lab and see if he's still there." She looked out the window. "I haven't even seen it yet."

Gregory smiled in the darkness and leaned back against the cold leather of the seat. He loved the smell of this car.

A dismal rain began, puddling down into the dirty piles of slush that lined the road. The wipers squeaked against the front windshield.

As the car slid up to the main entrance, Kate put a hand on her door.

He would have to do this quickly if he didn't want to arouse suspicion. Before Kate had closed her car door behind her, Gregory was around the car, his hand on her elbow. "May I show you to Nick's lab?"

She frowned. "I think I can find it myself."

"Actually," he said, pulling out his keycard, "you can't even get in without me or one of these. It's no trouble, really."

Gregory guided her into the building and down the steps inside the main entrance, giving the security guard a friendly nod. Kate jogged beside him to keep up with his rapid pace. He pulled her past the elevators to the stairwell. "Why don't we take the stairs? These elevators can take forever."

At the entrance to his lab on Sublevel 3, Gregory punched in his code, scanned his keycard, and laid his palm on the reader.

Kate lifted her eyebrows. "I didn't realize Nick's lab had such high security."

"You can't be too careful."

Once inside, Kate immediately searched the room. "I don't think he's here." Her eyes traveled back to Gregory's face, concern still not registering on her face.

Gregory smiled. "He will be."

↶ ↶ ↶

Kate wandered around the lab, appreciating the expensive equipment that SynTech had provided.

Gregory was making a phone call, so Kate drifted into the back room. She came out when Gregory disconnected a moment later.

"Why does Nick have an ultrasound machine in his lab?" she asked.

Gregory crossed the room and put his hands on her shoulders. "Let's not talk about Nick, hmm?"

Kate took a step backward, sliding out of his grasp. "Why not? Where is he?"

"Kate, why have you suddenly turned so cold toward me? I thought we were enjoying getting reacquainted."

Kate watched Gregory's eyes, wondering about the intensity she saw there. "I don't mean to be cold, Gregory. It's just that I'm married to Nick. Even though we're having problems, I know we belong together."

Gregory closed the gap between them and put his hands on her shoulders again, this time weaving his fingers into her hair.

She pulled away, but his hands held her hair. "Ow! Gregory—" She saw him lower his face toward hers. "Gregory, no!"

She tried to untangle her hair from his grasp, but he pulled her closer. His lips found hers.

She pried his fingers open and yanked her head back. "Stop!"

She took three steps backward, till her body made contact with the wall. "What are you doing?"

Gregory came closer. "Kate, don't be a fool. I can give you so much."

Kate glanced toward the doors. Was Nick coming or had that been a lie? Was this really happening for the second time this week?

"I think I'd better leave."

Gregory's face was inches from hers again. She slapped him, hard. "Get away from me."

Gregory took a step back and lifted a hand to his face. Kate noted with satisfaction that her hand had left an imprint.

"That was stupid, Kate."

"I don't want to have anything to do with you, Gregory. Is that clear?"

He frowned. "I'm sorry to hear that."

∼   ∼   ∼

Kate's gaze went from Gregory, as he tore a blue-and-white hospital gown into three-inch-wide strips, to the blue square panel that opened the electronically activated doors, her only means of exit. She waited until Gregory's eyes were on the fabric.

Now.

She threw herself against the panel on the wall.

The doors hissed open. She leaped toward them.

Gregory grabbed her from behind.

"Help!" she screamed, knowing even as she did that there wasn't anyone there to rescue her.

Gregory pulled her back inside the lab and shoved her toward a chair. "Sit."

She tried to push past him, but he grabbed her arms and pushed her onto the chair.

"Why are you doing this?" The question squeaked out of her as the lab doors closed behind them. Kate felt like her insides had frozen solid.

Gregory smiled, tearing another strip. "It's involved." He rolled her chair to an empty space in the lab, far from the blue panel.

She straightened her back against the seat back, holding her body tense and her feet propped on the foot ring.

Gregory spun her so that she faced away from him. He laid a hand on her shoulder and slid his fingertips down her arm, till he grasped her wrist. She pulled, but his fingers dug into her skin. He caressed her other arm the same way before tightening her wrists against one another.

"What are you doing?"

She felt the torn strips of the gown tighten around her wrists. When his hands released their pressure, she realized her arms were tied to the back of the chair.

Cold fingers brushed against the back of her neck, under her hair. Gregory's voice whispered into her ear. "You have no idea how I wish things could be different, Kate. . . ."

She shuddered, realizing he could do whatever he wanted to her now. "Stop it! Where is Nick?"

Gregory pulled up a stool and sat facing her. "He's coming."

"Why are you doing this?"

"Kate, it would take a lifetime to explain everything that Nick has tried to ruin."

Kate pulled at her bands, testing their hold on her. "It looks like we have some time." *Besides, if you're talking to me, you're not doing other things.*

"Your husband has discovered a few secrets that I did not intend to come to light. And he's trying to use his discoveries to destroy what I consider the highest calling of my life."

"And what is that?"

"To perpetuate the existence of the human race by defeating its greatest enemy."

Kate took a deep breath at the faraway look that had come into Gregory's eyes.

"Disease, Kate. It's all about disease."

"Why would Nick want to stop you from curing disease?"

"Because he's a fool. He believes that the only diseases that exist are the ones that can only be seen with his microscope. But some diseases are walking, talking, breathing ones. They must be destroyed as well."

"Are you talking about people?"

Gregory's gaze leveled to hers. He casually crossed one leg over the other. "Some people, yes."

"You're sick. Nick won't let you get away with this. He can't stand to see people harmed."

Gregory nodded, his smile widening. "That's what I'm counting on."

᠀   ᠀   ᠀

Nick opened and closed his eyes several times, but there was no difference in light when he did. He shifted positions and groaned. The back of his head throbbed like he'd been kicked by a horse.

The ground he was lying on was vibrating. Nick put his hands out to steady himself. The walls were tight around him. He sat up. His head banged against the ceiling. Pain shot through his temples, and he fell onto his back again.

I'm in the trunk of a moving car.

Panicked, he thrust his knees upward. The metal above him didn't budge.

Nick grabbed at his coat pocket, then breathed in relief. *The disc is still there.* Whoever clobbered him must not have searched him. *As if I don't know who it was.* He felt for his watch and pressed the tiny button on the side till the face lit up. Seven-fifteen. Friday night. Time was running out.

Was Chernoff taking him somewhere to dump his body? Silver Lake, maybe? Was it time to start thinking about God again? Nick thought of Stanford, changing his mind at the end. Was that okay with God? Didn't a person need to do something to prove himself?

The car stopped. Nick held his breath. Could he surprise Chernoff and overpower him?

The trunk lid beeped and clicked.

"Donovan, if you're conscious in there, don't try anything. I'm armed." The lid opened slowly to reveal Chernoff with his gun trained on Nick's head.

A pole lamp above him pierced the darkness. Cold air *whooshed* into the staleness of the trunk. Nick blinked his eyes and tried to focus. Where was he? He sat up slowly and noted with surprise that they were in the parking lot outside SynTech Labs. "What are you going to do with me?"

Chernoff's face twitched furiously. "Just get out."

Nick climbed out of the trunk. His knees cracked as he stretched them out after their cramped position in the trunk. "We going back to my lab for an injection?"

Chernoff motioned him toward the building with the gun. Did Nick imagine it, or was the man swaying on his feet? Chernoff nudged him with the gun barrel. "Walk."

Ten minutes later Chernoff pushed him off the elevator on Sublevel 3. They walked toward the doors to Gregory's lab.

Nick peered through the tiny window to the two figures inside. Kate! She and Gregory sat facing each other as though they were old friends visiting. They were both dressed up.

Chernoff pounded his hand against the glass.

Gregory jerked his head up, then approached the doors. The doors swung open with a release of air pressure. Chernoff pushed Nick forward.

Nick had noticed during the walk from the parking lot that Chernoff really was having some kind of trouble, and it was getting worse. He was stumbling now more than walking.

Gregory came near with a smile. "Welcome, Nick."

Nick pushed past him to Kate, leaving Chernoff behind him at the door. "Kate, what are you doing here?"

Her arms were bent at an awkward angle, tied behind her, but it was her terrified face that tore at his heart. Nick reached for the bindings.

"Leave her there, Nick."

"She's tied up? What is this, some kind of bad movie? Let her go, Gregory. She doesn't have anything to do with this."

Gregory waggled his finger back and forth as though he were scolding a naughty child. "I don't think so. Back away." He turned toward Chernoff, who was bent at the waist, sucking in air like he couldn't get enough. "Everything all right?"

"Feel sick," Chernoff said.

Gregory leaned over and wrapped his hand around Chernoff's gun. "Let me take this for you." He took the gun and pointed to a chair. "You'd better sit down, too."

Nick put his hands on Kate's shoulders and searched her face. "Are you okay?"

She nodded. "I'm so sorry, Nick."

He shook his head. "Sorry for what?"

"She means she's sorry for spending so much time alone with me," Gregory said, motioning Nick away from her with the gun. "We've been renewing our relationship, you know."

"Relationship? What are you talking about?" Nick's question was for Gregory, but he watched Kate's face.

Gregory circled the island lab bench and stood beside Kate, his left hand on her shoulder.

"Haven't you told him, darling?" Gregory laughed.

"Told me what?"

"Why, Kate and I were quite intimate back in the old days. Weren't we, Kate? Oh, yes, quite intimate. I'm sorry, Nick. Didn't you know?"

Nick glanced back and forth between the two.

"Of course, we kept it quiet," Gregory said. "My divorce wasn't final yet. And she was a student, after all. Would have been scandalous, I'm sure." He squeezed her shoulder. "I don't think she's ever quite gotten over me, have you, Kate? When you ended up here, Nick, it was obvious that she and I were meant to be together."

"Nick—" Kate said but stopped with a wince.

Nick could see Gregory's fingers gripping Kate's shoulder. He took a step closer. "I don't believe you."

Gregory lowered Chernoff's gun toward Nick's chest. Nick looked into Kate's eyes, wanting to see that none of it was true. But he could read only an apology there.

His eyes went back to Gregory's. "You won't get away with this. I've already notified the FDA and the press. They'll be on the front walk of the Gene Therapy Center tomorrow morning, way before the first appointment."

"What are you two talking about?" Kate asked. "Nick, why do you want reporters at the center?"

Gregory shook his head. "My, my, you two must never talk. Not healthy for a marriage, you know. Kate, we're doing the public a service, offering our therapies free of charge."

"I know that," she said. Then she turned to Nick. "But why are you trying to stop it?"

"Gregory's altered the gene therapies he's giving away for free," Nick said. "He's designed them to cause disease, not cure it."

Kate's brow furrowed. "What?"

"And did you know about the sterilization?" Gregory asked. "No? That's an added bonus. We're bringing them all in for free, though, so they should be grateful."

"Wait a minute," Kate said, her eyes wide. "Your free therapies. . .make people sick? Gregory? And. . .you're sterilizing people, too?"

"He's trying to eliminate people who oppose embryo research, Kate."

Kate's face whitened. "No. That can't be. You wouldn't do that, Gregory. Would you?"

Gregory sighed. "Oh, Kate. I told you, it's involved."

She began to kick her legs backward, trying to make contact with Gregory.

"Hold on now," Gregory said, swiveling her feet away. "My, Kate, I didn't know you were such a friend of the religious right. We're going to have to solve that little problem in our relationship." He wrapped an arm around her throat and squeezed gently until she stopped thrashing.

Kate raised tearful eyes to Nick. "Melanie," she said, her voice barely a whisper.

"What?" Nick asked.

"Melanie has an eight forty-five appointment at the center."

Nick's eyes widened. "Why is she on your targeted list?" Nick stood, his fists clenched. "She's not part of any activist group!"

Gregory shrugged. "What difference does it make, really? Maybe she sent for some antigenetics newsletter once or something. That's where we get the names, you know. We cross-check these right-wing organizations' mailing lists with the GenWorld Database and—" He snapped his fingers. "There's our list of targets and their disease predispositions. Very simple."

"You'll never get away with it," Nick said. "The FDA will catch on when people start getting sick."

Gregory snorted. "Doubtful. How would they trace any genetic defects back to us? And even if they did, I'd just dump the mutated versions and give them the originals to study. I have you to thank for that little ruse, Nick."

Kate twisted away from Gregory's arm. "Nick, we have to do something. We can't let him do this to Melanie!"

Behind them, a retching sound drew their attention. Chernoff was leaning over a biohazardous waste container, vomiting.

Nick thrust his chin toward Chernoff. "Doesn't look like your assassin is up to the job of killing us, Gregory."

Gregory shrugged. "No matter. I'll see to your 'accident' myself." He looked at Chernoff. "You can go for the night, Mr. Chernoff. I can see you're not well."

Chernoff stumbled toward Gregory. "Did you—do this—to me?" He dropped to his knees.

Gregory stepped back until he had both Nick and Chernoff in front of the gun. "You've outlived your usefulness here, I'm afraid, Mr. Chernoff. It was time for me to end your employment."

Chernoff raised dark eyes to Gregory's face. "What have you done?"

"There will be some pain." Gregory shrugged. "But it won't last long. You'll suffer respiratory or heart failure within an hour or two."

"Don't understand."

Gregory smiled. "Nicotine poisoning," he said. "Isn't that ironic? You'll appreciate this, Nick. Mixed it with a little dimethyl sulfoxide and applied it to his skin a couple of hours ago, just before he was supposed to have killed you the first time. Didn't know if he'd hold up long enough to get you here. But everything worked out, didn't it?" He looked at Nick and Kate. "Now, what to do with you two. . ."

"No one's going to believe that both Kate and I had a fatal accident here, Gregory," Nick said. He rolled Kate's stool to his side.

"No?" He changed his voice slightly. "Yes, Officer, I was just having dinner with Kate Donovan this evening, and she expressed how much she wanted to reconcile with her husband. I offered to bring her back to SynTech, where I knew Nick was working late in his lab." Gregory shook his head. "So terrible about that faulty rotor in the centrifuge unit that caused the explosion. I was just reading about the same thing happening at Cornell. We'll have to check all our units, won't we?"

Out of the corner of his eye, Nick saw Chernoff lunge upward and grab at both of Gregory's wrists. Gregory turned to fight him off.

Nick took his chance. He snatched a lab stool by the legs,

took three steps forward, and slammed it against Gregory's back. Nick felt a searing pain across his side and knew his gunshot wound had reopened.

Gregory staggered forward but drove a knee into Chernoff's chest as he fell. Chernoff crumpled under him. Gregory regained his balance and stepped away from the two men, the gun still in his hand. "Get out, Chernoff."

Chernoff dragged himself to his feet and pressed the blue square. "This isn't—over," he said, stumbling toward the open doors. "You're going down with me."

"There's nothing more you can do!"

Chernoff's facial muscles convulsed, and his breathing was ragged. "All those—chemicals in your—precious Gene Therapy Center," he said. "They'll burn—like the Fourth of July." He stepped through the doors just before they began to close.

"You'll never make it!" Gregory shouted to the closing doors. Chernoff spit at the glass and headed toward the elevators.

Gregory turned back to Nick and Kate, scowling.

Nick raised his eyebrows. "Now what, Gregory? You don't have time to set up our little accident if you're going to stop your friend the pyromaniac."

Gregory reached his free hand up and gripped the back of his neck. He looked at the door, then back to Nick and Kate. "I could just shoot you."

"That wouldn't look very accidental," Nick said. "You're already being investigated."

Kate leaned forward. "Chernoff's probably already gone by now."

Gregory grunted. He scanned the lab. His eyes came to rest on the door to the cold room. "Untie her," he said to Nick.

Nick circled to Kate's back and tore at the fabric strips with shaking fingers.

"Get over there," Gregory said, pointing with the gun. He prodded them across the room, until he reached the keypad outside the cold room door.

Oh, great. Nick's eyes snapped to Gregory's hand on the keypad.

"Turn around," Gregory said.

"Gregory, you don't want to kill us," Nick said.

"You're right. I actually wanted you to join me. But you're still the same fool you always were, Donovan. You never could see the big picture." Gregory shielded the panel with his gun hand while he punched in five numbers.

Nick focused every nerve of his body on listening to the sequence of numbers Gregory punched into the keypad. He knew he could duplicate it. He sang the little tune they made in his mind several times. Five numbers. He put words to them to help him remember. "God-has-made-a-way." They were the first words that popped into his mind, something Frank had said earlier this morning.

The door swung open, and Gregory shoved them forward. "Get in. I'll be back for you later."

The code was still playing in Nick's mind. It was a better chance than going for the gun and getting shot. Besides, getting out with the code after Gregory had left would be a better outcome than the other one he'd come up with—the one in which police used the bullet holes in their corpses to start getting suspicious. Much better.

Nick gripped Kate's hand and led her toward the cold room.

She gave him an odd look, and he realized he was humming the security code out loud. He forced himself to be silent before Gregory caught on.

Gregory looked into his eyes, then slammed the door.

CHAPTER 52

Gregory left the lab behind and dashed up the three flights of steps to the main corridor. Chernoff had a few minutes on him. Gregory couldn't let him destroy the center.

He ran through the darkness to his reserved parking spot in the patterned-brick parking lot. The light rain of an hour ago had ended, but now the car was encrusted with a thin layer of ice. His driver had gone home for the night, but Gregory always kept a set of keys himself. He scraped a hole in the ice on the windshield, just enough for him to see through, then revved the engine and charged around the artificial lake.

How had it come to this? Such a short time ago, his plan had seemed perfect. Now he was fighting to hold the whole thing together, right up until the last moment. Would Chernoff live long enough to torch the center? If he did, it would set Gregory's plan back months, if not years.

Forty minutes later, Gregory's car squealed into the jammed parking lot of the Gene Therapy Center. The center was already busy with the Friday evening start of Genetic Awareness Day. He left the car at the curb and bolted into the lobby. The private sitting areas teemed with patients waiting for appointments.

The receptionist standing behind the counter smiled at his abrupt entrance. "Good evening, Dr. Brulin."

"I'm looking for Chernoff," Gregory said, breathing heavily. "Is he here?"

The girl looked down at a sheet in front of her. "I'm sorry, sir. Does he have an appointment this evening?"

"Forget it," Gregory said. *Where would he go to set a fire? Aha!* Gregory ran for the stairs.

The lower level of the Gene Therapy Center contained mainly supply rooms and storage areas, as well as the HVAC systems room. Gregory slid along the dirty concrete floor, listening for anything. But there was no unusual sound. At the edge of the first doorway, he paused. He leaned into the room and swept his gaze around. Nothing.

At the next doorway he repeated his search. Empty.

The HVAC systems room was next. Gregory knew instinctively that Chernoff would be in there. He faced the wall, took a deep breath, and pulled Chernoff's gun out of the waistband of his pants. In one decisive leap, he jumped into the equipment room.

It was empty.

Behind him, he heard a pop. He ran back into the corridor. Chernoff was slumped against the wall.

"What have you done?" Gregory asked.

Chernoff raised his eyes to Gregory. His pupils were completely dilated, making his eyes look like black holes. He dragged in a ragged breath. "Help—me—Gregory," he said. "Do—something."

Gregory looked through the doorway beside Chernoff. In the back of the storage room, a tiny flame was spreading over a pile of rags.

Gregory cursed at Chernoff and sprinted to the small fire, not much bigger yet than four or five candles' worth. He stomped it out quickly. Still cursing, he waved at the smoke frantically, trying to disperse it enough to prevent the smoke detectors from going off and ruining everything.

He came back out to the hallway and kicked Chernoff in the leg. "You idiot!" He kicked him again.

Chernoff grabbed his leg. "How—could you—do this to me? Make it—stop!"

Gregory looked at the smoke detectors on the ceiling. So far they were keeping their peace. Maybe he had averted disaster, after all. He looked down at Chernoff, head tilted. "It's nicotine poisoning, Chernoff. There's no stopping it. But you know what they say: Cigarettes will kill you." Then he raised the pistol and fired once into Chernoff's chest.

He took a deep breath, regaining his focus. His plan was still intact.

He dragged Chernoff's body into the room, shoving it behind some equipment. He'd come back to take care of it later. Right now he needed to tie off the last two loose ends—Nick and Kate Donovan.

Gregory jumped out of the stairwell on the main level of the center. Four employees stood in the hallway. They looked at him oddly. He raised a hand to straighten his jacket and hair, and walked past, head down.

Outside, the February air swirled around him, chilling him instantly. Or maybe it was the news van parked at the curb that gave him the shivers.

What have you done, Donovan?

A light glared from its position on a pole. A woman with long, black hair stood in front of a camera, a microphone in her hand. Gregory watched as she sprang to life, a look of intensity on her face.

"Thanks, Lucy. I'm here at SynTech Gene Therapy Center, where people are flooding in to receive what some are calling 'injections from the Fountain of Youth.' SynTech Labs has generated patents on over thirty new gene therapies in the past two years, and all that research is kicking into high gear here tonight. SynTech's Genetic Awareness Day was scheduled to begin tomorrow, but the promotion generated such a good response, center executives decided to begin early. Gene therapy, as you probably know. . ."

Gregory smiled and walked toward his car.

CHAPTER 53

When the cold room door slammed shut behind them, Nick spun to face Kate. "Sing this song with me." He sang the tune: "God has made a way."

"What are you talking about, Nick? We've got to get out of here."

"Sing it, Kate. God has made a way."

"No. I don't understand."

"It's the code, Kate. It's the tune of the five numbers of the door code."

Kate's eyes widened. "God has made a way."

Nick smiled. "Let's hope He has."

He turned back to the keypad, punching in his best guess at the tones and pressing "enter." Nothing.

The cold seeped into him in spite of his coat, setting his teeth chattering. His side ached. A ten-digit keypad wasn't the same as an eighty-eight-key piano, but he was certain his sense of pitch wouldn't fail him.

A dozen tries later, his confidence was faltering.

His hand shook. It shouldn't be this cold. Gregory must have lowered the thermostat down to freezing—or lower. The room was capable of reaching absolute zero. Kate still sang behind him, her arms wrapped around herself, but he could hear the wavering in her voice as she fought to stay confident.

A moment later she stopped singing. "Nick."

He turned.

"I love you."

Nick's vision blurred. She was preparing for the worst. He pulled her into an embrace, still humming the tune. "I love you, too."

"What Gregory said, about our past relationship—"

Nick shook his head, pulling her head onto his chest. "Shh. I don't care."

The tune was fading as they clutched each other, their breath clouding around them, but there were other things he needed to say. "Kate, I don't know what will happen here. But I want you to know that I've been rethinking my life this week. I know there's something missing."

He felt her head nod against his chest. "I've felt it, too."

"I'm thinking that it might be God that we've been missing, you know?"

She squeezed him. "Oh, Nick, you're really scared, aren't you?"

Nick smiled into her hair. "Yeah, I'm scared, and I hate to be one of those people who only talks to God when he's in trouble."

She nodded again, remembering her cries to God in Winston's cabin. "I know what you mean. Maybe we should have gotten all our questions about God answered before now."

"I know, sweetheart. I know." Nick knew Kate's smaller frame would succumb to the cold more quickly. Her coat wasn't very heavy. He searched the lab for anything that could help them stay warm. There was only metal shelving with growth media and other assorted bottles. "Take my coat, Kate."

"No! I'm okay. You need to stay warm to get us out of here."

"Keep singing."

Nick pulled Kate over to the keypad, trying to keep her warm as he punched in numbers. He repeated his tune and tried another combination. And another. 9-3-6-2-1-Enter. The keypad lit up and buzzed.

Nick released his hold on Kate. He pushed against the door. It opened!

Heat washed over them in waves. Nick pulled Kate from the cold room and closed the door behind them, embracing her and wondering if he'd ever let go. "We've got to get out of here."

Kate tightened her hold on him.

He wiped her tears with his thumbs, then bent to kiss her

mouth. "Come on," he said, stroking her cheek, "let's go."

Kate grabbed her purse from the lab bench. "Nick, we have to get to Melanie before she gets her shot!"

He glanced at his watch as they ran into the hall. Eight o'clock. "Her appointment's not for another twelve hours, hon. We'll have plenty of time to call her, and then notify—"

"Her appointment's at eight forty-five, Nick!"

"I know—"

"Eight forty-five tonight!"

Nick grabbed Kate's arms. "What are you talking about?"

"They rescheduled it for tonight, since they had so many appointments for tomorrow."

"What? Then—we've got to hurry. Come on." He pulled her toward the lab doors.

She stumbled. "Nick, my ankle!"

He supported her waist and handed her his phone. "Try to call her."

Kate dialed as they took the elevator to the main floor.

"Scott?" she said. "Where's Melanie? I thought I called her number?" She paused, listening, and then her voice rose an octave. "Why didn't she take her phone with her? No, forget it. I'll talk to you later."

Kate disconnected. "She's left already, and she didn't take her phone. I didn't tell Scott. He can't get there any quicker than we can."

Nick took the phone from her and dialed the center. "We'll catch her there." But a moment later he punched the "disconnect" button. "Lines are busy."

The elevator doors opened.

"What if we don't get through, Nick?" Kate asked.

"We will."

They bounded off the elevator into the main corridor and raced for the main entrance, Nick holding Kate's arm to support her.

Nick pulled up short when they pushed open the doors.

"What is it?" Kate asked.

"I don't have a car."

"Where is it?"

"I, uh, kind of got here in Chernoff's trunk." Nick's thoughts spun ahead to a vision of Melanie holding out her arm to a SynTech employee. His heart broke for her and for Kate.

"We can take mine—I mean, Melanie's!" Kate said. She was already limping toward the parking lot.

Nick followed, his mind feeling muddled. "Kate, why is the car here? Why are you even here?"

"I. . .came to meet Gregory for dinner."

Nick gave her his arm as they hurried toward the lot.

Kate looked up at him. "I'm sorry about all that, Nick. What Gregory said—I was trying to clear things up between—"

"Don't worry about it, honey. We can talk about it later." They reached Lot #4. "I'll drive," he said. "You keep trying to call the center."

⁓   ⁓   ⁓

Nick and Kate raced through the city to reach the center. They pulled up to the massive parking lot as the dashboard clock in Melanie's car read 8:42. Kate hadn't been able to get through the jammed phone lines. They had to find Melanie in person.

A black-and-white arm blocked the entrance to the lot. A teenage attendant strolled out to meet them. Nick lowered the window.

He leaned in, resting his forearms on the window frame. "Sorry, guys. No parking left."

"This is an emergency," Kate said. "We'll pull up to the curb."

He shrugged. "Sorry. Can't let anybody in till somebody comes out."

Nick had his hand on the door handle, ready to make the trip across the huge lot on foot, when headlights swung around from inside the lot. The attendant stood.

"Here comes somebody," he said. "I can let you in now."

They roared the last hundred yards to the curb and hurtled from the car. Nick half-dragged Kate past the crowd that had gathered near the news reporter outside. Inside, the center hummed with its usual serenity, the classical music and fountain blending with dozens of quiet voices.

"Melanie!" Kate's scream was like a shot fired into the tranquility of the center's lobby. Nick thought at first she must have seen her sister but then realized she was yelling for her out of desperation. He left her to join him as quickly as she could and ran past the statue to the front desk.

"Dr. Donovan," the receptionist said, looking anxious. "You're not supposed to be here anymore. I'm going to have to call security."

"Where's Melanie Lange?" Nick said, slamming a palm onto the counter.

"Sir—"

"Melanie Lange!" he said, hearing Kate arrive behind him. "She's got an appointment at eight forty-five. It's an emergency! Find her!"

The girl was shaking when she typed into her computer. "She's already been checked in."

Kate's hand flew to her mouth.

"Room 117," the girl said.

Nick bolted for the hall, sensing Kate limping at his heels.

Just inside the double doors leading to the hall, Nick spotted a fire alarm on the wall. He paused just long enough to pull it. The shrieking alarm sounded immediately.

Room 117 was halfway down the hall. Nick threw his body against the door and burst inside.

Melanie screamed. She sat alone in a metal chair.

"Are you okay?" Nick asked, grabbing her arm.

Kate followed him in, rushing past him to smother her sister in a hug.

"Of course I'm okay!" Melanie said, pulling away from Kate. "What's going on? Is there a fire?"

"Have you been treated yet, Mel?" Kate asked. She placed a hand on Melanie's cheek.

"No." She smiled at Nick. "Could somebody call the management? I've been waiting for over twenty minutes!"

Kate collapsed beside her sister, laughing.

Melanie looked down at her, a frown creasing her face. "What's going on? What's with that awful alarm?"

Kate began shouting her explanation to Melanie. Nick led them back to the lobby. The crowd there was making a semi-orderly retreat from the building, most of them holding their ears. Center employees ushered patients out the door. The fire alarm's wail added to the chaos.

Nick, Kate, and Melanie twisted their way through the lobby toward the front doors. Outside, cars and people mobbed the parking lot. A fire truck's horn blew somewhere beyond the parking lot.

The moment they stepped from the door, lights on poles surged to life, people yelled, and camera crews zoomed in with reporters in front. Austin Chambers had done what he'd promised.

"Dr. Donovan! Is there a fire inside?"

Nick clutched Kate, keeping his head down as they plowed through the crowd.

"Dr. Donovan, is it true you've discovered fatal side effects to SynTech's gene therapies?"

"Dr. Donovan, what can you tell the people who've already been treated here?"

Reporters closed in like ants swarming over a sandwich. One reporter got too close, and her microphone tapped against Kate's teeth.

Nick held up a hand. "Everyone, please step back. I will make statement." Nick felt his coat pocket once more. The disc was still there. It would stay there.

The crowd quieted. Nick spoke into the bunch of microphones aimed at him.

"There is no fire. I pulled the alarm myself in an effort to evacuate the building as quickly as I could. I know that's kind of against the law, but in my mind this was an emergency worse than a fire. The building had to be cleared, and this was the best way I could think of to do it in a hurry."

He took a deep breath, seeing himself reflected in ten zoom lenses. "It has come to my attention that SynTech Labs was planning to use tainted gene therapies on these people, these patients who have come for free treatment this weekend. I believe it is an intentional attempt to cause harm to targeted patients, harm that includes giving them therapies that, far from healing them, would give them cancer."

The crowd gasped.

"The cancer and other diseases these people would have received tonight wouldn't show up for months, thus preventing anyone from making a connection between SynTech and the onset of disease."

Questions shot at him from twenty directions. He heard one: "You say these people were targeted. Why them?"

Nick raised his voice over the other questions. "I believe that those targeted share one common trait: SynTech believes they are opponents of embryonic stem cell research."

More questions came, but Nick had said enough. He spotted Austin nearby. "I'll call you," he mouthed to the writer.

Nick sighed deeply. He was satisfied. The news coverage wouldn't let up tonight, and if the FDA didn't respond tonight, Nick would come back in the morning and make sure the center didn't reopen.

He held up a hand again and turned to the cameras. "That's all I have to say tonight. Thank you."

He grabbed Kate's hand and led her and Melanie away.

Genetic Awareness Day was over.

e   e   e

Nick turned on the television in the living room as soon as he walked in the door of the townhouse. A quick stop at the emergency room had confirmed that the gash in Nick's side would heal on its own, and he was relieved to finally be back in the house. With Kate back in it, the house felt right again, like home.

Kate hung her coat in the closet and came to stand beside him. She leaned her head against his shoulder as he punched the remote control, cycling through the prime-time shows.

Kate yawned. "I don't know if I can stay awake until the eleven o'clock news."

Nick circled her shoulders with his arm. "They'll break in."

She snuggled closer. "Can we at least watch it from the bedroom?"

"Yeah. Okay." Nick was about to press the "power" button when the Action News logo and theme music interrupted the program.

The anchor's voice, cheerful yet dutifully concerned, broke in.

"Good evening, I'm Cynthia Hollister. We bring you a breaking news story tonight from the city's SynTech Gene Therapy Center, where allegations of intentional misconduct have sent patients running back to their homes, with many unanswered questions. Lucy Espanoza is downtown at the SynTech Center. What can you tell us, Lucy?"

Kate tugged on Nick's arm, pulling him toward the couch. He squeezed her hand as they sat. He hadn't even removed his coat.

The picture switched to a young woman standing outside the center. "Thanks, Cynthia. This has been an evening of chaos here at the Gene Therapy Center. Earlier tonight a former SynTech employee, Dr. Nicholas Donovan, admitted to pulling the fire alarm, an action which evacuated the building. He then exited the center and made a statement to news stations that can only be described as a wild accusation."

Nick leaned against the back of the couch and exhaled. "What?"

Kate fell against him.

The shot switched to Nick making his statement in the parking lot. The caption under his picture read, "Says free therapies give people cancer."

The reporter's face reappeared. "Cynthia, you may remember just hours ago we reported that SynTech's highly publicized Genetic Awareness Day began tonight, a program intended to offer free gene therapy to people unable to afford it. Well, Dr. Donovan alleges the company was offering more than free therapy. That, in fact, they were using what seemed to be a benevolent gesture as a means to infect hundreds of people with tainted DNA, thus giving them cancer or other debilitating diseases."

The camera zoomed out to reveal Gregory Brulin standing beside the reporter.

Nick leaned forward on the couch. "Oh, great."

"I have with me here Dr. Gregory Brulin, Chairman and CEO of SynTech Labs. Dr. Brulin, thank you for joining us. What can you tell us about these serious allegations?"

Gregory nodded into the camera. "Lucy, we're all shocked, of course, by the accusations of Dr. Donovan. Early this morning I received an anonymous E-mail from a right-wing political organization claiming they would not allow Genetic Awareness Day to go on. As you may know, Lucy, just last night I was held hostage at gunpoint by a member of such a group, making demands about stopping Genetic Awareness Day.

"These people insist that we're meddling with God's creation, and God will not allow it. I believe this same organization is behind the rumors tonight. I also have to conclude that Dr. Donovan has joined them in their campaign."

Nick stood and paced, restraining himself from kicking the television.

"But isn't Dr. Donovan a geneticist—working for you?" Lucy

asked. "What could he possibly have against what you're doing here?"

"He is a geneticist, Lucy, and a good one. But I am afraid he has been acting erratically the past few days. In fact, I was forced to let him go just this week. I fear there may be some revenge motivating his actions here tonight."

"So you maintain the allegations are false?"

"Of course they're false. SynTech Labs has developed the foremost gene therapies in the world. We have some of the best and the brightest in genetic research working for us. But I've come to accept that genetic research will always be opposed by those who don't understand it. Just as people opposed airplanes and telephones, Lucy."

"So you believe all of this is the result of one disgruntled employee?"

"I'm afraid so, Lucy." Gregory turned to look imploringly at the camera. "Nick, wherever you are, know that I forgive you."

Lucy Espanoza turned back to the camera. "So there you have it. A former employee with a grudge? A right-wing, anti-bioengineering faction? The questions are far from answered. For tonight, it's one man's word against another's. Nicholas Donovan's accusations have been enough to shut down SynTech Labs for the evening. But the doors will open again tomorrow unless Donovan's proof is forthcoming. Lucy Espanoza, Action News."

Nick stared at the screen.

Kate pulled the remote control from his hand and turned the TV off. "That, um, could've gone better."

Nick groaned. "Gregory, what a performance!"

"How will you prove any of this, Nick?" she asked.

He reached into his coat pocket and pulled Stanford's letter and disc from inside. "Let's go upstairs."

Minutes later, she sat on the edge of the bed, holding the envelope in her hands. Nick sat beside her and pushed the button on his disc player.

They sat in silence and listened to the recording. As they heard Gregory condemn himself with his own words, something inside Nick that had been clenched for a very long time began to relax.

When it was over, he made a few copies. "One for the FDA, one for the police, one for Austin Chambers, one for the safety-deposit box, and one for me. I'll have to make sure the FDA gets a list of anyone already given a Version 2 therapy tonight."

He laid the disc player aside and ran a hand through his hair. "Wow, Stanford has done it. With a couple of sound bites, Gregory was able to throw my statement into doubt. If I know him, by this time tomorrow he'd have me looking like a laughingstock. I'd never work in genetics again. But even from his deathbed, Stanford has done what I couldn't do." He pulled his wife close. "He was a good man, Kate."

"I know, honey."

"I hope he knew it."

Kate laid her head on Nick's shoulder. He wiped his eyes and turned toward her. She was crying, too.

"It's over, Kate," he said, stroking her cheek. "All of it. Finally."

~ ~ ~

Gregory Brulin unlocked his office door at SynTech Lab's corporate building and stepped into the darkness. Had it been only five hours ago that he had left to have dinner with Kate? It seemed more like a year.

He had given interviews to every local news team that descended on the center, repeating his assurances that the rumors were nothing more than the product of Nick's desire for revenge. In the morning, he would need to find a way to put a better spin on the disaster. Right now, he wanted a cigar.

Gregory crossed to his desk and pulled open a drawer. Before he reached in for the cigar, he saw the cardboard envelope on his desk.

He picked it up. It must've been delivered by messenger sometime while he'd been out of the office. There was no return address.

Gregory sat behind his desk and ripped open the envelope. He slid out the single page, laid it on his desk, and tilted the envelope. A small disc slid out. He lifted the letter again and checked the signature. The name he saw made his hand tremble slightly.

> Gregory,
> It is a time for endings. Your threats carry no weight where I am going, and I can only hope my actions today will improve my chances in the place to come. This disc is a copy. By now the FDA will have the original.
> I can no longer allow your madness to continue.
>
> Stanford

Gregory laid the letter on top of the envelope and aligned their corners. He pulled a small disc player from his drawer. As the disc began to play, Gregory took out a cigar and lit it.

He heard himself speaking, giving everything away.

After the recording ended, he continued to puff at the cigar for some time, thinking about the past and the future.

Phase 1, cleansing, had been thwarted. He'd told everyone on TV that the center would be open for business tomorrow, but now the FDA would never allow that. He shut his eyes. He was still committed to the cause of cleansing the idiots. He would make sure the center's Version 2 therapies would still be put to good use.

But it was time to move on. Phase 2, cloning, would have its true beginning in three months. Gregory was sure that no matter where he went, Tina Milano would follow the money. And Phase 3, creating? That would be more difficult. He'd have to find a way to bring Sonya to him later.

Gregory placed a call to Lenny, the kid genius who'd hacked his way into countless right-wing organizations. "Get over here to SynTech. We've got some backing up to do."

While he waited, he jotted a few notes. The fire would need to begin toward the back of the Gene Therapy Center, far enough from the computers to give firefighters time to save them. The security system would record that Gregory had swiped his key-card to enter that night, but that he had never left. That was important.

Gregory twisted the custom-made ring on his left hand, studying the SynTech logo. A few pieces of jewelry on Chernoff's body, and the identification shouldn't be a problem. He'd drive out of the city in Chernoff's car, with all the Version 2 therapies he needed in the trunk.

By morning, there would be no visible traces of what he'd been attempting to do at SynTech. Unless one took into account the two women who carried the future. His destiny remained intact.

Nicholas Donovan had stopped Genetic Awareness Day, but nothing could stop genetic progress.

CHAPTER 54

Saturday, February 26

The morning sparkled with sunlight. The last of the snow trickled away, exposing the pale green grass beneath.

It was nine o'clock, and Nick and Kate sat with Frank beside the waterfall in the spacious lobby of the Young-Meddleton Cancer Center. Nearby, another patient watched the morning news on television.

"So, Frank," Nick said, "you're saying that God has a purpose for my life, beyond what I've come up with?"

Frank chuckled warmly. "Nick, I think you'll find that God understands you very well. Remember, it was His idea first to save the world." Frank smiled. "He wants you to be part of that, in a better way than you'd ever imagined."

The background noise of the television broke through to Nick's consciousness. He turned toward it, hearing the words "SynTech Labs."

Kate moaned. "I don't know if I can stand to hear this again."

The reporter's voice was hard to ignore, so they watched the report together.

"As if last night's shocking allegations were not enough, sometime in the night, while the city slept, SynTech Gene Therapy Center erupted in flames."

The shot switched to smoking embers. Nick's jaw dropped.

"Fire officials have yet to confirm that arson is to blame, but investigators have been on the scene since late last night, searching for the cause of the fire, which burned out of control for more than hour."

"Nick!" Kate's eyes were wide. They both scooted closer to the TV.

"We go live now to Graham Paxton, who's standing at the scene. Graham?"

The image switched to a middle-aged reporter standing in front of the remains of a building Nick could vaguely recognize as the center. Firemen could be seen behind him, sifting through the smoldering ruins.

"There's not much left of the back half of the SynTech Gene Therapy Center this morning, after claims last night that a right-wing group opposed to genetic research promised to stop the work being done here and a former employee claimed that the center's therapies were tainted. It may take days, even weeks, to sort out what happened here in the past twenty-four hours, but I can say this: Police and fire officials suspect that SynTech's chairman, Gregory Brulin, may have been inside this building when the fire erupted."

Nick watched in amazement as the reporter detailed that a body had been found inside the center. The camera panned around to the parking lot. There was Gregory's black Town Car.

"You can see right there," the reporter said, "that Dr. Brulin's car is still in the parking lot." The camera panned back to the reporter. "Sources tell us that the center's security system shows Dr. Brulin's entrance into the building last night, but the system did not record his exit. The body was found in a conference room toward the back of the building, burned beyond recognition, but fire officials say jewelry found on the body may help with identification."

The story wrapped up with footage, without audio, of Nick making his statement last night and the reporter's speculation about Nick's "wild accusations."

The program passed on to other news. Nick pounded the arm of the chair. He looked up tentatively at Frank.

Frank smiled. "I don't need to know the details, Nick."

Nick nodded. "Thanks."

Nick's phone rang.

"Dr. Donovan? This is Stella Ruhn with the FDA. Dr. Donovan, we'd like you to meet with us at SynTech Labs as soon as possible."

"I understand. I'll be right there." Nick disconnected and stood. "The FDA," he said to Kate. "One way or another, Gregory will not get away with this." He turned to Frank. "I'm sorry to cut our visit short."

Frank smiled. "Just come again, all right?"

Kate took Frank's hand. "We will. Frank, Nick has told me everything you've done for Stanford and for him. I can't wait to get to know you better." She leaned over to kiss him on the cheek.

Frank grinned up at Nick.

Nick shook his hand. "We'll be back, Frank. There are more questions we need answered."

ℓ   ℓ   ℓ

Some sacrifices are always necessary in order for a new era to begin.

Stanford's recording ended with those sickening words from Gregory's mouth. Nick studied his hands, folded in front of him on the conference-room table.

Stella Ruhn clicked her pen, closed her notebook, and stood. The two other FDA team members who sat at the table in the small SynTech room stood as well. Stella popped the disc out of the player, slid it into her briefcase, and looked down at Nick, who was still seated.

"I—I don't know what to say, Dr. Donovan. I wish we had gotten involved sooner. There was so little to go on, you understand. . . ."

Nick waited.

"But still, I apologize for not taking you more seriously," she said. "And I thank you for your help and for not just giving up. I think a lot of other people would've. So. . . Oh, and please extend our thanks to your two assistants, also." She stepped toward the door. "I'm certain we'll be calling you again."

Nick pushed back from the conference table. "You'll have to reach me at home, I suppose. It would appear I don't have a job."

Ruhn's face softened into a genuine smile. "Go home, Dr. Donovan. You've had a rough couple of months. Don't let losing a job get to you. Who knows, maybe there's a career for you in the FDA—investigative department, maybe?" She allowed a half smile to lift the corner of her mouth.

Nick laughed. "I just might take you up on that."

Stella pulled a business card from her briefcase. "My direct number's on there. Why don't you call me on Monday?"

Nick pocketed the card and stood. "Thanks, but it might be a Monday a few months from now. I think I'm going to take some time off to spend with my wife." He smiled broadly. "You know, Ms. Ruhn, there really is more to life than just a career."

T. L. Higley is the author of *Marduk's Tablet* and a playwright with more than fifty drama productions for church ministry to her credit. She lives near Philadelphia, Pennsylvania, with her family.